Miniatures

Miniatures

A novel by

NORAH LABINER

COFFEE HOUSE PRESS :: 2002

COFFEE HOUSE PRESS is an independent nonprofit literary publisher supported in part by a grant provided by the Minnesota State Arts Board, through an appropriation by the Minnesota State Legislature, and in part by a grant from the National Endowment for the Arts. Significant support was received for this project through a grant from the Jerome Foundation. Support has also been provided by Athwin Foundation; Beim Foundation; the Bush Foundation; Buuck Family Foundation; Elmer L. & Eleanor J. Andersen Foundation; Lerner Family Foundation; McKnight Foundation; Patrick and Aimee Butler Family Foundation; The St. Paul Companies Foundation, Inc.; the law firm of Schwegman, Lundberg, Woessner & Kluth, P.A.; Star Tribune Foundation; Target, Marshall Field's, and Mervyn's with support from the Target Foundation; James R. Thorpe; Wells Fargo Foundation Minnesota; West Group; Archie & Bertha Walker Foundation; Woessner-Freeman Family Foundation; and many individual donors. To you and our many readers across the country, we send our thanks for your continuing support.

COFFEE HOUSE PRESS books are available to the trade through our primary distributor, Consortium Book Sales & Distribution, 1045 Westgate Drive, Saint Paul, MN 55114. For personal orders, catalogs, or other information, write to: Coffee House Press, 27 North Fourth Street, Suite 400, Minneapolis, MN 55401.

A portion of this book was previously published under the title "Decade" in *Columbia: a Journal of Literature and Art*.

LIBRARY OF CONGRESS CATALOGING-IN-PUBLICATION DATA

Labiner, Norah, 1967–
Miniatures : a novel / by Norah Labiner
p. cm.
ISBN 1-56689-189-136-1 (alk. paper)
1. Americans—Ireland—Fiction. 2. Remarried people—Fiction. 3. Suicide victims—Fiction. 4. Housekeepers—Fiction. 5. Young women—Fiction. 6. Authors—Fiction. 7. Letters—Fiction. 8. Ireland—Fiction. I. Title

PS3562.A2328 M56 2002
813'.54—DC21   2002071283

FIRST EDITION
1   3   5   7   9   10   8   6   4   2

PRINTED IN THE UNITED STATES

*Give orange me give eat orange me eat
orange give me eat orange give me you.*

—Nim Chimpsky

Appomattox

Proust died in November. Into his unheated room the doctors came and went administering syringes of camphor and adrenaline. Outside the rain began to fall and the afternoon grew dark. Scattered about his bed, its sheets lace-edged, and on the bare wooden floor were revisions of *La Prisonnière,* handkerchiefs, teacups overturned, empty. He asked for peaches, apricots, and sugar. There were inkpots and pens. The walls of the room were cork-lined. The fire remained unlighted. *Now expect nothing more from me but silence,* he wrote in his last letter, *and follow my example.*

Franz Kafka lived to forty. When he succumbed to tuberculosis he was six feet tall and weighed 120 pounds.

Freud, eighty-three years old, asked his doctor to administer a lethal injection of morphine.

De Quincey, he died with his arms full of holes.

Percy Shelley drowned.

Balzac, caffeine poisoning.

Babel, disappeared.

Bruno Schulz, shot.

Emily, the tallest of the Brontë sisters, died of typhus. Her coffin was twenty-two inches wide.

When Zora Neal Hurston died in 1960 in a Florida welfare home after having spent her last years as a maid, her books were long out of print. She was buried in an unmarked grave in a segregated cemetery.

F. Scott Fitzgerald was eating a Hershey's chocolate bar and reading his Princeton alumni newsletter when he suffered a massive coronary attack.

When the door was opened to his bunker Adolf Hitler was found lying on a sofa soaked in blood. He had shot himself through the mouth. At his right-hand side lay Eva Braun, who had taken poison. The time was half past three. It was the afternoon of Monday April 30, 1945, ten days after Hitler's fifty-sixth birthday. One biographer wrote of Hitler: *Dostoevsky might well have invented him.*

On May 19, 1864, while on tour of New England with President Franklin Pierce, Nathaniel Hawthorne died quietly in his sleep in Plymouth, Massachusetts.

Albert Camus, who did not trust the mail, died in a head-on automobile collision with a tree while driving from Lyons to Paris to deliver a newly completed manuscript to his publisher. He was sitting on the passenger side. The driver lived.

In his final interview a month before his death, William Faulkner spoke of animals and farms; the intelligence of dogs, horses, and rats; growing cotton and wheat; how he did not like cars or buses and wished he could ride everywhere on horseback, even to the movies.

Anne Sexton removed her rings and placed them in her pocketbook. She put on her mother's coat, fur with a satin lining, carried her glass of vodka to the garage, turned the ignition of her red Cougar, switched on the radio, and waited.

Branwell Brontë, the bad painter, died at the age of thirty-one.

Anne caught a cold at Emily's funeral. It progressed to pneumonia. Anne, the youngest, the most forgettable, and all agreed, the prettiest of the Brontë sisters, died five months later.

Edgar Allan Poe was discovered raving and delirious outside a pub in Baltimore. Soon after being admitted to the hospital he slipped into a coma. Two days later he spoke lucidly to visitors. He died the next day. In a brief obituary the *Baltimore Clipper* reported that Poe had died of "congestion of the brain."

On the morning of March 28, 1941, Virginia Woolf rose early and wrote notes to her husband and sister. She made her way to the river Ouse, left her walking stick on the banks, weighted down her coat pockets with rocks and threw herself into the water.

On the evening of July 2, 1904, while suffering from consumption in a German spa, Anton Chekhov announced he was dying. He drank a flute of champagne, lay on his left side, and stopped breathing. In the silence of the room a moth fluttered against a lightbulb. The cork exploded from the champagne bottle. His body was returned to Russia in a refrigerated railroad car with *For Oysters* painted on its side.

Dylan Thomas spent his thirty-ninth birthday, October 27, 1954, in New York City staying at the Chelsea Hotel. In poor health, complaining of hallucinations, promising the world he would never live to see forty, he went on a drinking binge, fell into a coma on November 4, and died November 9 having never regained consciousness.

Charlotte Brontë, who buried Maria and Elizabeth in childhood, who in succession grieved for Branwell, beloved Emily, and rival Anne, was married June 29, 1854. She was thirty-eight years old. She wore a white dress of embroidered muslin and a bonnet trimmed with green leaves. She and Arthur Bell Nicholls honeymooned in Wales and went on to spend six weeks in Ireland. In December of that year she complained of headaches and nausea. By January illness left her bedridden and weak. She did not believe she was dying. She wrote out a will leaving everything to her husband and on February 17, 1855, she told him, *God will not separate us. We have been so happy.* She died in March. Arthur Bell Nicholls moved to Ireland and later married his pretty young cousin Mary Anne. He took her to the same Welsh inn where he and Charlotte had honeymooned. He burned Charlotte's letters and sold her manuscripts. The second Mrs. Bell Nicholls, by all accounts a sweet and even-tempered girl, allowed her husband to hang a portrait of Charlotte over their mantel.

Byzantium

I, Fern Alice Jacobi, being of sound mind and body, being neither a
borrower nor lender, being of upright stature with opposable
thumbs, born under the sign of the crab with an ascendant in fire,
borne from the past into certain and unredeemable failure; shy,
aloof, defensive, intolerant, bitter, once innocent, twice denied;
being prone to excess but free from addiction; I, being all these
things and less, swear to tell the truth, the whole truth, and nothing
but the truth, so help me God. Truth #1: I am sitting before a Smith-
Corona typewriter and have allotted myself exactly three days to
compile this memoir. At midnight on January third in the year of
our Lord, 1999, I promise I will remove my fingers from the keys and
commit this document to the ashes of apples and earth where it
belongs. My typewriter will be transformed into a pumpkin, and I,
glass slippers and party dress restored to rags, will suffer to fall off the
page and disappear forever. My time choice is arbitrary. My mode is
ink. My method is confession. These truths are situational. Others
are relative, suspect, or ugly. Watch out for them; they may leave
scars or stain the carpet. Truth #2: I am not a biographer. I admit this
readily and offer it as both apology and explanation. I find myself in
the awkward position of having to tell the story of a woman whom
I never met and who died several years before I was born. Did she,
does she need me to defend her? Of course not. But let's say history
needs a slap in the face to wake it from its own nightmare. Let's say
that she, Frances Warren Lieb, the first wife of Owen and predecessor to Brigid needs me far less than I need her. Things in life have
roots in death. There's a rarefied pearl of wisdom for you, a new
catchphrase for the dress-in-black crowd, a painful anodyne for what

ails us all. We can't escape ourselves so let's join the party! Don't you
ever feel that the age-old homilies are all lies? That whatever does not
kill you, does not, in fact, make you stronger? Stopped clocks may
be right more than twice a day? All roads lead to roam? Don't you
ever feel outraged by the grand conspiracy that is life in general and
your own life in particular? Whatever you have thought or dreamed
or run from, believe that. Believe this: they are out to get you. And
if they could get to her, to Franny, the first Mrs. Lieb, they can get
to anyone. So please, I implore you, read on with skepticism. I hope
that you cannot find it in yourself to believe me. You like books that
promise either facts or the revelation of mysteries. You don't like to
sit on the fence. I know, I know, I feel the same way myself. It is only
that in attempting to tell this story, to tell the *truth,* I find I don't
even know what that word means and really, honestly, I cringe every
time I strike those keys. I feel like a beleaguered cheerleader: T is for
the time we spent together; R is for—; well, you get the idea. Read
the biographies. Run your own set of tests. Hire professionals. I wish
none of my story were true and that ultimately your disbelief will
offer me some respite, hope that perhaps I am merely delusional,
wrong, untrustworthy, that not only did these events not transpire,
but that these people, myself included, do not exist. Having undertaken the idea, having recalled and recollected and become perhaps
vengeful, perhaps authoritative, but more than anything else, having
become—I know too what I have so long denied and feared. I
remember everything.

   These are the facts as I recall them. During the months of
September and October of 1990 I found myself employed by a married couple of modest fame, ill repute, and certainly, more than anything else, beauty. And while I had heard of them, or more
specifically of him, of Owen Lieb, I had never encountered or con-
tacted them before that autumn. I was initially hired for a single project, perhaps two or three days, but we all seemed so happy together;

we were strangers in a strange land. It was so naturally unnatural, that they asked me to stay on with them. Or rather, he asked me to live with them as a companion to his young wife who was fragile and lonely. He worried that she would not last through the oncoming winter in such a desolate location. I did not think about ghosts or history, about the ridiculousness of my own guilt and innocence, my susceptibility, no, no, my inability to understand the game being played around me. It begins now, my story, no more digressions, no further preambles. It begins and began in September on a day all of sun, but it will end on the night of Halloween with a rainstorm that turned first into hail and then unexpectedly into snow which fell and did not stop until twelve inches had accumulated and blanketed the tiny fishing villages and farms all along Galway Bay to our house near the western seacoast. The three of us were trapped, yes, I suppose that is the word for it, trapped, together and perhaps we thought it was the end of the world, because for some reason we were all impelled to tell the truth, to reveal our secrets and scars and tattoos. The whole truth and nothing but the. So help me.

At the time of the events in question I was twenty-one years old. Frances Warren Lieb was thirty years dead. Owen Lieb was a thousand and barely looked fifty, while his young wife, Brigid Lieb née Pearce of Indianola, Iowa was twenty-nine. We are the major characters in this strange little drama. I regret that the ending of this story will be less than happy. Although I have not yet written it, I can tell you that as I foresee it, as the events play out again and again in my memory, exactly, so that the most minute details do not change from year to year or dream to dream, I can see the white nightdress Brigid wore as she came down the staircase on the night of the storm and how she held the banister and the sharp perfect angle of her elbow awkwardly turned out as she misstepped and almost fell, but then caught herself and smiled down at us and said

in her familiar tone, gone now, lost now: *How's that for an entrance?*
And often too I see Lieb take his wife by her thin delicate arm and
lead her to the sofa, and it seemed that he loved her, and no one in
the world could doubt that. It was only for the sake of Brigid that I
came back.

There have been any number of books about Frances Warren Lieb.
This is not one of those books, not in the strict sense. She, in her
lifetime, wrote two and published only one novel. You probably own
it. You may have certain passages memorized. Owen Lieb has, to
date, eighteen books, no, there was a new one only last month, so
make that nineteen books to his credit. Three are psychological novels; there is a play or two, screen adaptations, a translation of the
complete works of an unpopular French Symbolist poet, a strangely
obfuscating memoir about his boyhood, two volumes of poetry, and
the rest, however many that adds up to, are short prose. When she
was twenty-five Brigid Lieb published a slim and pretty collection of
stories, *Julia's Room,* about an unhappy Midwestern girl out of place
at an Eastern college, a girl who begins to drink overly much and in
the final award-winning title story meets a dark and mysterious character not unlike Owen Lieb himself. On the cover of the paperback
edition there is a soft-focused photograph of a vanity table strewn to
look carefully careless with girlish collectibles: lipsticks, a romance
novel, matchbooks, a painted china kitten, diaphragm case, wrist
corsage of pink roses, a string of pearls. They are, all in all, the Liebs,
mister and his various missuses, a bookish and prolific lot.

   Brigid, during those brief months of our acquaintance, was at
work on her second book, a biography. It took perhaps nine, maybe
more than ten years to finally complete—but it was for her a new
homeland, the one place in the world where she felt truly safe. She
set up house in that book. She arranged the words like furniture,
reupholstered, stripped down, polished up, decorated with clever

throw pillows, dreamed, restored, replaced. Nonfiction offered her all of the amenities and little pain of the past. So it is no wonder, you see, that she had no real incentive to finish. She wasn't tearing across the keys at my frantic and fevered pace trying to sweat the sickness of a story out of her system. There is no nostalgia or fondness here; there is nothing pretty. I'm in the mood to smash the remaining evidence; anything left, anything delicate, I'll shatter. Anything flammable, I'll set aflame. I want nothing more than what you see around me. This room: imagine it. This is the place where stories are told without regard to continuity or consequence. Every bodice-ripper and tale of international espionage, each penny-ante mystery novel that you read into ragged submission—cover torn, pages thumbed, fingerprints of strawberry jam like the trail left by the reckless killer himself—it was, they were written in this room on a black typewriter that sits on a desk beside a window outside of which snow has either just stopped falling or is falling fast on all the foreign cities and towns and forgotten avenues of the past. This place is nothing more than a shell of necessity. There may be a bed; there must be a bath? And enough paper to last through the next ice age. I've set the dial on the time machine to return me home in exactly three days. Why three? Why not three thousand? Or seven days, after the mode of the Lord's creation? Perhaps because I don't want to dwell on the events. I want to rid myself of them. With this limited time frame, you have my assurance; I'll stick to the facts. I won't wander off course. I'll tell my story and then get out before I can do any more damage. I've seen how it happens in the movies; the longer one spends reliving the past the less chance there is to get out unscathed. I could alter atoms and events by mistake. I could change outcomes with a keystroke. Could it happen like that? Could I become trapped back there, the ghost of autumns past? Cloaked in a cape, with broomstick and scythe, condemned to an eternity of bobbing for apples? The headless horseman lobbing rotten eggs at sweet-faced kids in Superman suits? A waterlogged witch sinking in a bathtub? I am and have been certain of so few things in my life, but I know that I will finish this story, not necessarily in a stylish or pretty way, perhaps in a manner that will best be described as brutal, traitorous, or self-destructive, but I will finish *because*. Well, because I have a mean streak or believe in what I can only call, no matter how idiotic it sounds, cosmic justice; because I am vengeful; because. I'll leave it at that. While I will finish for the sake of being done with the entire sordid mess, Brigid never wanted to leave the pages of the epic biography that she felt held within its monumental reach and grasp the ghost of her own beginnings. Of course, I admit I have not seen her since the night of the storm. Do you want again to see her coming down the stairs that night to make her grand entrance? I do. I wish I could more than recollect the pale nightdress, her unloosened hair, bare feet missing footing a step to slip to fall to catch herself by and for and with the grace of her thin bare arms to catch the banister. And the rain had, I think, already begun. Owen Lieb stood by the window and parted the curtains.

I was at this time, among other things, painfully shy, nervous, lost, and full of an aimless and unrequited self-loathing. And if I was not happy, I cannot say that I was, in fact, unhappy. I was incendiary, wayward, and moody. Or was I sleepy, docile, and undemanding? I admit that my personality changed, fluctuated according to the independent axis of my life: whatever I was reading at the time. For a long time I favored biographies. It's funny, no, strange to temper the past and announce with polite authority and discriminating taste, *I favored biographies*—when the truth is, I used to crave them, biographies. As a child I took a morbid and yet educational pleasure in reading the deathbed scenes and breakfast menus of historical figures. Why? Did it make them more real, or me more heroic because much like Nathaniel Hawthorne I too tended to run the other way when walking down a street at dusk I recognized in the half-light the face of someone I knew but to whom I could not bear to speak? Hawthorne took to wearing a black veil and ran into the woods to avoid conversation. Sweet young Mary Shelley learned to read tracing the inscription on her mother's tombstone. Heidegger ate seasoned pork sausage fried with onions every morning. Flaubert died a raving syphilitic. Ida McKinley, the President's wife, knitted slippers to make the hours pass. In one year she knit 3,500 pairs of booties. The Marquis de Sade spent thirteen years in prison for poisoning prostitutes with the aphrodisiac cantharides. The extracted heart of ten-year-old Louis XVII, the lost dauphin, was wrapped in a handkerchief and kept by an attending physician as a souvenir. Need I go on? And while I knew on some level that biography as a genre, as a subset of the truth, was morally wrong in its subjective re-creations of lives better left for dead and dust—I could not stop myself from wandering the aisles of the library or buying thick paperbacks whose midsections shined with the promise of glossy photo inserts picturing how the world was once, when everyone was younger, when we were all civilized. I know it is and was all a lie, the first lie, the only lie—that any given life can be detailed, inventoried with some semblance of truth or connection to reality—but still I read about Jackie-O, Benjamin Franklin, Elvis Presley, Florence Nightingale, Dostoevsky facing the firing squad, Tina Turner and her rocky years with Ike, Lizzy Borden took an axe, Edie Sedgewick, Ingmar Bergman's youthful embrace of Nazi ideology; there were pop idols, inventors, film stars, brave doctors who fought disease, saints who suffered, presidents, pornographers, authors, royalty, comedians, athletes, models, and murderers. I never truly gave up on biographies, but gradually I began, no, I forced myself to look to other genres, to explore mysteries and romance novels. And while for a brief time they made me happy and brought a slightly pink-cheeked delusional pleasure to my uncertain young life, they did not offer the guilty and morally bankrupt thrill of opening a new biography for the first time and allowing yourself, myself, to become entirely from breakfast scraps to deathbed rigors, someone else. A girl can dream, I suppose, although most of the time she shouldn't. Most of the time she should run into the woods and never look back. I regret that my running has left me wary of strangers and tourists with cameras strapped around their necks, and yes, yes, familiar faces who approach me in the twilight but then as they near me, I know, I am relieved to find they are always strangers, and I drift back into anonymity as I become to them, to myself, to anyone on the darkening avenue, a passerby.

It was on a bright morning that I set out by bicycle for my journey. I was hired by the Liebs to clean their house. They did not hire me specifically; they happened to contract the cleaning service for which I was working, illegally, yes, paid out under the table in lodging and incomprehensible foreign bills, in morning tea and cream biscuits. Was it an anonymous choice, a strange vagary of fate that caused me to be sent to the Lieb house instead of the other cleaning girl (what was her name? Ellen? Eileen? Or, no Aileen, who wasn't feeling well that day—the flu? A cold? Perhaps an allergic reaction to shellfish? Something that required a week of bed-rest and broth.), and thus, inadvertently my story was set in motion? Or did it start when my parents packed me overseas less out of desire for me to see the world and have madcap adventures than to separate me from the boy I was seeing, for whom they did not, cough, cough, in particular care? Maybe it began years before when I was a child and haunted the library stacks like a store detective in search of shoplifters. When does anything start? Not at the beginning, but only at the moment of re-creation, the lie. It begins only now when I see how it was then but tempered with the knowledge of how it will all undo itself. I packed a knapsack with an apple, Jackie Collins's *Hollywood Wives*, orange soda, and a sweater. I had been told that a box of cleaning supplies, gloves, solvents, and the like would be waiting inside the house for me, and a key would be under a flowerpot near the front door. Was it a mythic journey on which I set out that morning? Was this the beginning or had it begun years before? I hated myself; did I mention that part? Because I was self-centered and lived in a proverbial dreamworld, because each journey was mythic, each boy was *the one*, all memories brought me to tears, and every story had to revolve, if only by virtue of first person narration, around me.

There I was. Fern. Can you see me? Pedaling my bicycle on that warm autumn morning into a wind that promised the underside of the cold months ahead. There I go, riding, aimless, idiotic, unsuspecting, all twenty-one years and three months of me, the kind, the sort of girl who falls through the cracks willingly, and if not cheerfully then waving up at the onlookers as she careens downward. While I'm on the subject of confessions, I'll tell you something else: she, that girl, doesn't seem very much like me. I don't think she even looks like, you know, resembles me. She is a little taller. Her eyes seem suspiciously blue. She is after a fact another Fern entirely, a fiction, but a truthful one; we are less ourselves in the past because we didn't know, we couldn't know what would happen and how innocent we would seem when finally forced to put that version of ourselves into words. But let's get back to that girl. She is almost there, almost winding her way up the ruined drive speckled and spattered with windfall apples. It is impossible; there is still time for her to turn back.

Unlike the Liebs I was neither by nature nor trade a writer. I was then simply another girl who graduated from college without plans or hopes and allowed herself to be pulled along, twisted into one of those last-minute knots of fate. And for a while, I admit again, there was a young man and we shared a terribly happy unhappiness against the scenic backdrop of a Midwestern college town, but then,

as you can imagine, it fell apart as those sorts of things always do.
My overly cautious parents, worried that out of their five children, it
was their only daughter who showed precocious and intemperate
wildness, exiled me off to Europe as a graduation present. And I
found myself alone in Dublin, pretending to be foreign while studying DART train maps with a duffel bag slung over my shoulder. In my
accumulated possession: glossy picture postcards in the shape of beer
bottles, a Bram Stoker key ring purchased at the Irish Writers
Museum right down the street from the James Joyce Museum on
Parnell Square where on a sunny weekday afternoon I was overrun
by twenty-six French schoolchildren on holiday clamoring *Oolissee*
as they clattered down the staircase (note: no curios bought then in
the crowded gift shop; I told myself I would go back, but of course
I never did), a tourist's cheap camera, coins, buttercream scones
wrapped in bakery paper, and an ever-dimming memory of the boy
at home who suffered painlessly, I was certain, from the absolute lack
of me. I headed by train up to the north, but once there, after spending three rainy August days in the ravages of the British Empire, after
innumerable cups of tea in shops where the reproving face of Queen
Elizabeth the Second stared down from framed portraits, after a
young man took my arm on an empty street whose large parking lots
were fenced in and twisted with razor-wire and I was briefly thrilled
only to realize that I had wandered into an IRA control zone and he
was helping, not soliciting me, after the girl at the concession
counter at the Virgin Cineplex in Belfast asked when I ordered pop-
corn: *sweet or salty?* I left the north and found myself on a bus
packed with cheerful Swiss tourists en route to an oyster festival in
Galway, where Nora Joyce had grown up. It was as likely a destination as any. I was that aimless. It was in June of that year that I
began to keep a notebook into which I scrawled the intimate details
of my travails. Note: my three favorite books that summer were *The
Myth of Sisyphus,* Danielle Steele's *Daddy,* and a tattered collection

of Victorian erotica entitled, *The Pearl,* found, strangely enough, abandoned in a women's restroom in the airport in Amsterdam. Quoting myself, August 30, 1990: *My life is going to change. I can feel it. And if it does not, what difference will it make?* Minus my French existentialist bitter twist of lime at the end, was I right? Did I foresee the future and how the next two months, how September which was bright and burning, and October, a month all of rain, would change the course, the past and future both, of my life? In September the Liebs returned. And by October the days became dark and we were forced too much, too long to spend our hours together in the living room with Brigid curled up on the sofa wearing her reading glasses, her book fallen to the floor, the gray cat sleeping precariously on her hip; Lieb in the armchair reading aloud with contempt a film review from the newspaper; while I with a bucket of oil soap and sponge scrubbed clean the grime, the years, the dust from the mouldings and baseboards. *Oh please, stop, please,* Brigid used to say. *Let's all pretend we're civilized. Oh please, Fern, come here and sit with us.* And the dog, John Paul Jones, slept on through the rains, patiently, long-suffering, the most faithful one of the bunch, at Owen Lieb's slippered feet.

And I, not to confuse you, that is, the girl on the blue bicycle who does not and cannot anticipate October even in September, arrives, arrived at the house on that day of sun and suspiciously promising wind. And it was not without a certain amount of trepidation that I approached, because I knew about the first Mrs. Lieb, the young novelist who died an ocean away from her home in that house during the coldest winter any biographer could dream up, left alone with only her young son, she died, and they taught us this in school: no one could save her because she was unwilling to save herself. As rumors, obituaries, and legends told it, she died at the age of thirty in the second-story bathroom down at the end of a long hallway, electrocuted in the bath while a storm raged outside. And yes, some people said the place was haunted; and many speculated that her death was less than accidental, and that Owen Lieb never returned out of fear of the worst sort of revenge—*poetic justice*. For almost thirty years with only the benefit of a caretaker visiting to clear away the refuse of the seasons, the house had been abandoned; the windows boarded over, the garden grown wild and then dying off into bitter weeds and beehives, the drive ruined, the orchard wracked. When I arrived for the first time that morning, I felt if not a genuine foreboding, then a sort of secondhand fear. My instincts (and on what else could I rely?) told me that I should turn back, head home, and forget I had ever seen the Lieb place.

In my defense, ladies and gentlemen, you sometime skeptics, you who are prone to disbelief until the exact thrilling moment that suspension is warranted, to you I will confess all that is left of the truth. Something drew me in. I could not turn back. Now in the course of remembering that girl with her ragged fingernails, unruly curls, legs speckled with mosquito bites, her inability to drive a car or perform simple mathematics, her morbid obsession with deathbed drama, her love of chocolate bars, coffee too light with cream, pop songs on the radio, her hyperopia, her flannel shirt with sleeves rolled, charm bracelet jangling; in the course of re-creating the image of that girl I am tempted to swing the pendulum toward fiction and away from truth. Say instead she does not get off her blue bicycle, but rather, seeing the day has suddenly gone gray and threatens rain, she takes it as an omen, a portent of ill favor, and turns back in the direction from which she has just arrived. And so she goes anti and against the sun and into a future impossible to predict; but no, this will not happen, *because?* Because today we are not in the business of fiction. Today and forever in this story, suffice it to say that this Fern, our Fern, the one who comes always between us, approached, left her bicycle in the high grasses of the ruined drive and proceeded on toward the house.

I could not stop myself. Perhaps it was years of mystery novels about proper old ladies sleuthing crimes and uncovering bloody butter knives buried in the garden among the zinnias. Perhaps it was the strange similarity between the words *mother* and *murder*. I left my bicycle in front of the house and then, to prolong my indecision and fear and uncertainty, I walked around back to the orchard. On the trees already were small hard apples, row after row of trees having grown wild and sweet from years of decadence, of sun and season. I turned back to the house and went as I had been directed to the front entrance only to find absence of both flowerpot and hidden key. I was about to leave when as an afterthought I tried the door. It did not resist me any more than I can resist confessing to you. We will have to go carefully. There are nails, shards of glass, and splinters on the floor. I turned the handle and the door opened.

Before we go in, there is one more thing that I should tell you. Do you know that maddening riddle about the man who announces that he either always lies or else speaks only the unadulterated truth? And the impossible convolutions of logic that you go through to figure it out: is he lying when he says he lies? And thus telling the truth? Or is it the other way about? Does he lie when he says he speaks the truth? How can anyone ever trust a storyteller? Let me tell you, from here on trust neither the truth-teller nor the liar; choose heads nor tails, rely on your own intuition and cast the odds aside. Stop reading now before we go into the house or promise me that you will read this confession in its entirety and reserve judgment on me and my story until our three days are concluded; then you may announce: *She lies! She speaks only truth.* God help us all.

I found myself in an unlighted vestibule and so moved forward impelled by darkness, dust, shadow, by memory and mothball, the musty odor of lives prematurely shut-up and closed-down, by something read in a book and long since willed away, a story dreamed and soon dismissed. I ran my fingers over the velveteen wallpaper. And as I walked down that dismal hallway I became less and less myself until I was more and more the unlikely heroine of a romance novel: an orphan, heiress, or innocent aviatrix. At that moment, passing through the entryway of the house as though some grand transforming mirror, I could have been anyone at all. I stood in the kitchen taking in the ruin of that once monumental room— its marble counters and boarded-over hearth. I saw through the darkness the work ahead of me, the generation of neglect, haste in which the previous occupants had left, an old calendar hanging on the wall, pots and pans still years later drying on the drainboard. A door leading from the kitchen outward into the rest of the house was closed, but I knew as though I had been in those rooms a hundred thousand times before that it would lead to the living room and beyond that to the staircase up to the second story where the bed-rooms were, and at the end of the hallway, the bath looking out, as the books promised, onto a grove of lilacs. I pushed through the doorway from the darkness of the kitchen with the inexplicable awareness that there was no going back. I opened the door.

It was just briefly impossibly bright, first, and then second, I was certain I heard whispering, so I feared that it was true, ghosts— everywhere—and in the light which disoriented me I turned by sound and then shape and then saw the shrouded sofas and chairs, rolled rugs, boxes, no one there, no one; I was alone. And then I heard it again and so turned toward the western window, or was it the east? There was sunlight where the slated wood had been torn away—a crowbar on the floor, nails, sheets, sawdust, her, a girl, yes, I saw her then on the floor with her pale hair unloosened and her back to the sun and her face toward me and her white shoulders white, breasts bare. I should, of course, have seen her immediately, but sometimes it is difficult to see real people when you are in search of ghosts, and she was real enough, the girl, naked in the sun, her eyes closed. There was a man with her—at first I didn't see him, or maybe I didn't want to see the two of them naked amidst the dust and decay. He was obscured from me by a shrouded heap of sheets. But then her eyes opened, and I stood for a moment watching them before running from the room with all the embarrassment that they themselves did not feel. I ran from the house, and I recalled only moments later as though it had happened years before—the girl in the sun with her back to the window and her eyes opening suddenly, sleepily without shame or remorse or more specifically surprise that this tryst, that she and her lover had been uncovered, found, Eve, the two of them, and Adam, hiding, hidden from the world in a place that should have been but was not abandoned. And as I ran from the house into the brown golden brightness of the morning, it occurred to me: I have only just met the Liebs.

Canary Islands

The second Mrs. Lieb, Brigid, sat across from me at the kitchen table. She held her hands one palm flat resting under the bone-white saucer while two fingers of the other held delicately the handle of her teacup in which I could see her coffee, black, causing in me embarrassment for all my weaknesses. It was September. The afternoon was bright; I remember this much about it. I remember that the windows were open and the air was cold, northerly, it blew a racked course through the house, swirled around us, blew the ghost sheets still draped over the furniture, passed through the fine chignon at Mrs. Lieb's nape, all golden, upset a stack of mail, mostly, she laughed, bills and subscriptions, change-of-address forms, love letters and suicide notes, as she reached down to collect the scattered envelopes. A large dog lay near her feet, opened one eye at the shower of papers, closed the eye, slept on. The second Mrs. Lieb heaped the papers back on the table, asked me, did I want, would I like more coffee? Pausing, she rubbed the dog's back with a bare white foot, and even though I had answered, no thank you, she poured me another cup from the press and proceeded to add cream. I did not fear Mrs. Lieb. It was only that she was not at all what I had expected.

"I knew you would come back," she said.

She picked up her cup, two fingers and palm. She waited.

Some days are themselves ghost stories. We sat in the kitchen papered floral, ivy and bluebells, down to the wainscoting, knotty and light, perhaps pine, and after saying that they would be happy here, she and her husband, Mrs. Lieb leaned over and knocked her fist to the wall, for luck, she said. And it was with a certain pale charm that she added, why tempt fate? And because she urged me on, because I wanted at that moment to be her accomplice, I too reached over to the wall on which from a series of unevenly spaced nails hung metal spoons, measuring cups, strainers, red calico pot holders, and an old calendar from which I averted my eyes and in so doing turned to face Mrs. Lieb across the table. She knocked on wood. The wind was growing colder as though for the select and sentimental purpose of ripening the apples. You see how it is, don't you? Some days cannot help themselves; they are good for nothing but ghost stories. Blackbirds hovered, circled, landed and picked among the ruins of the garden, all weeds now. There was no doubt about the present tense. This, the promise and the threat of the past lay on the table between us, shining like our spoons, worthy as the china patterned with small blue flowers, capable as Mrs. Lieb's hands, long-fingered and ringless. The fact that I returned the next day after stumbling upon the married couple—this return should have meant nothing to her except a token of my own poor judgment, and that it did, I ascribed to her politeness or even loneliness, nothing more.

I hated myself for any number of reasons that afternoon: for the pale of cream in my own cup, for the way that I could not look at her face but instead kept my eyes on the table, the dog, the legs of the second Mrs. Lieb which were bare beneath her plain brown skirt, for the lives we had led which had taken us through strange courses, routed from avenue to lane, houses, rooms, beds, places gone now, through fears which lingered endlessly in dreams to find ourselves for no apparent reason, together. It was improbable, you see, that was it, the sheer improbability, the toss of the coin that caused me to find myself on that day, on that afternoon bright, windy, and ripe for ghost stories with the second Mrs. Lieb sitting at the kitchen table drinking coffee relieved by cream, sweetened by sugar, as the dog slept, the letters went unanswered, the light loose hair at the back of her neck unkempt, disturbed by wind; she raised a hand to

push it back, tuck it under, and I could not look at her face. It was
because I could not face her that I went to the doorway and looked
at the living room beyond, where the crates and boxes were heaped.
I saw the shrouded sofas and the staircase. You see, she said, we've
got so much work to do, don't we? And I sat back across from her.
But it was then as though we rose together from our chairs, she and
I. It was as though we were little girls running from the room, skip-
ping up the stairs, holding the wooden banister, smooth and cool;
hand in hand we walked, pigtailed, singing nursery songs up those
stairs, our rhythms almost military, our feet bare leaving imprints in
the dust. We did not stir. Only our spoons turned endlessly. It was
without moving that she and I made our way together up the stairs;
tourists, gawkers, detectives, girl scouts, we seemed to change shape
with each step. She held my hand in hers. It was without disturbing
the placement of the cups and saucers, without waking the dog
asleep on the kitchen floor; perhaps it was the wind itself that blew
us up the stairs to the room at the end of the long hallway. And it
was without surprise that the door opened before me, before us, as
doors can only in dreams, silently and of their own volition, and I
saw then what should have remained hidden, the grand white marble bathtub in which the first Mrs. Lieb succumbed a hundred times
in Calgon and soapy water, pills and razor blades until finally, fatefully, a current of electricity brought an end to her suffering.

Brigid, the second wife, wore that afternoon a plaid flannel shirt
with the sleeves rolled, the aforementioned shapeless brown skirt,
bare legs and feet, no jewelry, and the faint stinging scent of lavender,
more likely from soap than perfume. She was dressed for unpacking,
moving in, uncrating, dousing the floorboards with oil soap, pouring
bleach down the drains, exorcising the ghosts and untarnishing the
demons. She had wanted to get an early start but she had let, she
apologized, the morning slip away. When I suggested that we should
get started, she waved her hand and said, no, no, drink your coffee,

we have so much time, too much——. She had a habit of letting her sentences trail off, and turned with unfinished words but completed idea still wavering, and smiled expectantly at me as though to say, you know what I mean, don't you? And I smiled back as best I could because I didn't know what she meant, not then, and I sat as the afternoon grew more and more bright causing her at some point to raise a hand to her eyes against the light, and say something ridiculous about the weather, but when I turned as if to confirm her forecast I realized she was not talking to me. Her husband stood behind me in the small vestibule, the garden entryway into the kitchen. He momentarily blocked the brightness.

He extended his hand to me without speaking.

"Don't be so damned menacing," said Brigid. "You'll scare her away."

He shook my hand with gracious but mock formality.

"Are we scaring you?" he asked. "Because we wouldn't," he stood behind his wife, lifted the teacup from her hand and drinking from it, set it back upon the table, "want that."

He placed his hands on her shoulders.

"Just half a cup?" said Brigid. "I thought you liked my coffee."

"I do," he said.

"I remember," Brigid said and she leaned back and tilted her face upward to look at him, "hearing that somewhere, someplace else——"

"She's clever," he said and paused to meet her, to kiss the top of her head. "What a hostess you are, Bee. Aren't you even going to introduce our guest?"

She smiled and set down her teacup. "We the people," she began, "in order to form a more perfect union——"

He shook my hand again, held it for a moment, seemed to be on the verge of making a statement of great importance, and then turned to his wife to ask, "Did we bring coffee? Was it here? For God's sake, you didn't use something you found in the cupboard did you?"

"You interrupted my lovely introduction," said Brigid. "I was going to say something about how pretty her name is—*Fern,* although, I've never been able to get them to thrive, ferns, I mean, as they need so much attention, but I think I will lavish all my attentions on her." She turned to me. "On *you.* I hope I can make up for in coffee brewing what I so lack in botanical acumen. *Fern Jacobi,* I like it very much, but what exactly is it? Is it Jewish? It sounds fake. It sounds like Swedish-Jewish, if there is such a thing, although you don't really look Swedish, but then I don't really look Jewish, do I? And I am certifiably one-eighth Jewish, although it may be one-sixteenth. Also I was going to say something about how we should be very nice to her because there is so much work to be done and we are intolerably lazy. Don't you agree, O?"

"Entirely," he said. He coughed. "In fact if it wasn't for that coffee I would be nodding off even now in the midst of your interrogation of our prisoner."

Brigid smiled, pointed at herself, and said, "bad cop," pointed to her husband and announced "good cop," and said didn't he remember when they stopped at that little market and bought the coffee there? He said, yes, it was all coming back to him. He asked her to be kind and not subject me further to too many non sequiturs. She laughed and he asked of us: will you ladies excuse me? He removed his hands from her shoulders, offered a mock salute, and passed through the room, out of the room, and I heard, although I did not look, I heard his footsteps on the stairs.

In school the second Mrs. Lieb had been called sometimes *Birdy* both after her height and as the result of one of those unfortunate childhood language transpositions—maybe a misspelled Valentine's card, *O Birdig, I LUV Y. BEE MINE?* She rose and studied her kitchen, touching, unpacking, cataloging objects, attempting to project and protect a semblance of order in her life. She was nicknamed *Birdy* or

Bee, and found it funny, she admitted while unfolding dishtowels, that she was called by the name of a creature of flight when she felt so damned earthbound. As the poets say, that's irony, she said, and turning her attention back to me she asked if I was lonely traveling by myself so far from home? Was it terrifying or a thrilling adventure? Had I left behind someone unforgettable? Was I running to or from the specter of this *someone?* Did I believe it was possible to fall out of the world?

The second Mrs. Lieb did not tend to wait for the answers to her questions. She spoke first slowly, waveringly, and as though moving downhill, treading the slippery slope, her words began to gain speed and momentum. She did not wait. She did not need to. It could have been the coffee. It could have been some modicum of politeness and reserve that caused her to ease into conversations before taking them over and reshaping them into soliloquies, repeating details of feelings, memories, things she had forgotten only to have awoken and remembered this morning, and why today? Why, she asked and did not wait, did she remember her name misspelled on a Valentine's Day card in the third grade and did I think that sort of thing was intentional? Do children do things like that on purpose? Did I find her hopelessly out of date, out of, ahem, the loop that loops its way around the real world? Were there children in the world who were strange and wonderful enough to think that misspelling a name was some grand cosmic insult? Think about that, she laughed. She might as well have lowered her head, rested a cheek on the cool wooden surface of the table, and said, are they still out there? Do children still exist? Are they still tiny? Do they like licorice? But she did not, and instead she asked me in a way that was both straightforward and conspiratorial: have you read my book?

The Liebs had returned to Ireland after twenty years of exile. But for Brigid the displacement was psychological. The grand Georgian house existed for her as an absence; a place to which she had never been but from which she was nonetheless outcast by virtue of her marriage vows. A home in which she had never been housed. She had heard the ghost stories just as I had. She knew that she and her husband were barred from this house through no fault of their own, mind you, no one was at fault. And while there was no mandate to leave, no threats, no reason to stay away for so long, similarly, there was no sign that it was time to return. One day Owen had said to Brigid: *I want to go back to the old house.* Or, Brigid smiled her thin, graceful smile, had he said he *needed* to return? She couldn't quite recall although she understood the vague nuance of difference between Lieb's wants and his needs. She looked around the room as though no time had passed from the moment of her husband's suggestion until now, to the fact of her sitting in this kitchen. She asked me if I thought there would be apples enough yet in the orchard to bake a pie. She held her face in both hands. Tell me about yourself, she said. Tell me everything.

Brigid went to the window and stared out at the garden. So much to do, she said. And then she turned toward me and continued in her intimate way saying, I am going to be lonely when you leave. It was more than the distance from town that made this house remote. Past farms with washlines fluttering, past lone houses of stately despair, roads lined with high stone walls; the Lieb place stood, this haunted house, the last refuge in the world. Owen and the caretaker worked to remove the boards from the windows and open up the fireplaces. The trees had grown weepy, too heavy with fruit, so thick in autumn the boughs snapped. The rain wracked, the sun bleached, the ice wore down, but still the house stood. For the most adventurous of summer tourists who knew about the house, it was enough to drive past and point, to shiver or remark upon, perhaps to stop the car and get out and gaze from a distance at its haunted face, to daringly hurl a rotten apple for good luck before moving on to the next attraction. I can't say how I found myself there that morning slipping away into afternoon with Brigid Lieb. It seemed that perhaps every instant in my life had led to it, and all the rest would lead away from it. Some days are like that, all sweet and no salt. The house had stood vacant for a quarter of a century until on a day without warning, on a day without rain, on a day of diffuse sunlight and apple ripening wind, on a day in September the Liebs returned home.

Brigid, called Birdy or Bee, did not tell stories. She left the blanks unfilled, associated where a different sort of person would have narrated. She remembered ends before beginnings and certain objects glittered in her memory waiting to be addressed. Several things about that day are still improbable to me; one—that I am there; two—that I have found myself in the company of the Liebs; three— that the dog has not awoken; four—that the French coffee press seems inexhaustible, impossible to empty and we drink cup after cup like princesses in a fairy tale only to find we cannot reach the bottom, as though to spoon up the grounds would not mean simply the end of this moment but entry into a new place, a world from which neither, or at least one of us might never return.

Have you ever found yourself in a situation that while it was improbably surreal was also so narcotic, so desperately at a remove from the rest of your life that you had no choice but to give yourself over to it from the inception? To without coercion, pretense, or exertion become immediately someone else? I tell you, I swear to you that I could not recognize my own reflection in the coffee spoon, that my voice, my very presence seemed foreign the moment I passed through the kitchen doorway, the moment Brigid turned her wrist on the handle of the door which stuck for a moment, and then the sudden swing of the door as it gave way to Brigid, as we all would have in a similar situation.

The second Mrs. Lieb, Brigid, in her plaid shirt and house-cleaning skirt, with her hair pulled back off her face and knotted loosely at her neck, sat at the kitchen table which was now her own and tilted her head at the afternoon. She had a fine beautiful face. It was impossible not to look at her. The girl who sat across from her, the girl who has thus far kept her back to you, the girl, I admit, who was me on that September afternoon was not so much younger than Mrs. Lieb herself. It would be only later when I was no longer the girl I used to be that I would wonder why it was that Brigid Lieb showed if not shame then at least a requisite embarrassment. It would be later still when I would realize why this was, and I would hate myself more for not knowing, not understanding than I would ever hate the Liebs for their recklessness, for what they had or had not done. There were spoons and knives, sugar cubes, cream in a little blue pitcher, the local newspaper folded discreetly on a chair. There sat Mrs. Lieb, the second, and her guest, holding both of them, teacups and speaking of certain solvents and soaps that would wash away the mystery. In the presence of the second Mrs. Lieb, the girl sitting across the table had a tendency to hunch her shoulders forward, but checked herself, caught the slouch, and sat up straight, found herself again slipping and tried, fought against it. If you stood behind Mrs. Lieb very much the way her husband had only moments before, you would have a view of her slim shoulders and hair worn without barrette or pin, wound only around itself to form a knot. Standing behind Mrs. Lieb you face the other girl, the one whose hair darkens as the afternoon grows more impossibly bright so that time seems to move in the space of moments counterclock-wise so that the date on the forgotten calendar might eventually, gradually move back year by year becoming more perfect, correcting itself, holding us accountable not for our own actions but for the sins of the generation in which we were born. She, like Brigid, wore a flannel shirt, and if I admit that with this she wore denim shorts rolled at the knee and brown work boots, know that this is because the other, the one who was me, was not there to make a social visit, to have coffee and tiny shortbread cookies which Brigid produced from a tin in the refrigerator or when I said again, no thank you, the iced lime wafers she offered, brilliantly green and dusted with powdered sugar. How could I refuse her? She left the tin open between us on the table. A cat appeared. The dog's ears rose slightly, fell. The cat jumped on the table, sniffed at the cookies, licked a paw distractedly. I was not there to idle, as pleasant as it was, as pleasant as it would always be to know that I had sat at that table with Brigid Lieb as though the world were civilized, as though women could do things like that, like this, to finger tiny lime flower cookies and drink pressed coffee like refugees of the Great War, talking, gambling, gossiping in the serene quiet of revolutionary places.

Danzig

When Owen Lieb walked through the door of the kitchen from the bright morning turned surreptitiously into afternoon to pause and sip from his wife's flowered teacup, I did not happen to mention: his height, weight, hair, his eyes, the sort of shoes on his well-shod feet, his hand on the china cup, his mouth on the kiss of his wife's slightly but sweetly disheveled blonde hair unfastened by the wind, or how many fingers formed his nautical salute good-bye—*good-bye sweet ladies*, he called to us as he sailed from the kitchen through the open doorway. I did not do justice to either his entry into this story or my life. And if I hadn't told you maybe you wouldn't have noticed at all. But that's me. That's the kind of girl I am. I feel the need to confess; I'm like one of those nonsensical characters in a movie who throws off the police, the private investigators, and the plot by admitting to murders I didn't commit because I have a guilty conscience. Because someone has to take the blame and it might as well be me. It is only that by the time Owen Lieb walked into the scene I was recounting, I was utterly lost in the memory of Brigid. When I tried to pin her character down into words I was caught in contradictions. She was young and old, sharp and oblivious, spy and accomplice, trustworthy and unreliable. The best I could do was admit Owen's entry into that sunny kitchen and relay the dialogue as I remember it happening. I was uncomfortable. I knew that I didn't belong there with them. But I admit (again, the confessions—the ravings—the ramblings—and I have only just begun my story. This can't be a good sign.) that I feel the onset of a rare bout of fairness; we are all equal partners become characters in this strange little drama, so Owen deserves upon his return to the house that he and his first wife purchased thirty years before, if not

a hero's welcome, then at least a proper introduction. I am not here to
judge him. That is your job. I am only the material witness. You will
have time to ask questions later. Submit them to me on folded scraps
of paper. Disguise your handwriting to ensure my impartiality. The
best that I can do now is wind up the doll that is Owen Lieb and walk
him into the room again. He came through the door. He paused. He
spoke briefly. Something about coffee. *I do*s exchanged like the rings
neither husband nor wife wore. He offered us a mock salute that at the
time was charming in a witty and irreverent way.

So how could you have known that Owen and Brigid Lieb had
been living for the past three years, since their nuptials, in Paris? Or
that Owen was revered in France for his poetic parables with their
dark undertone of mystery after the style of another authentic
American, Mr. E.A. Poe? Both Lieb's prose and verse had a brooding
melodrama that lent itself to comparisons and strange new genre
formulations; he was called a Moral Romantic Authoritarian,
Pseudo-Fabulist, Shtetl-Erotic, and my personal favorite, Franco-
American Gothic. Really, I know it's juvenile of me but when I first
heard Brigid invoke the latter term, I thought it was funny. I
thought it was hilarious. I hold this laughter up as proof to you:
Exhibit C. See how young and innocent I was? How easily I giggled,
hopped trains with no destination in mind, went thoughtlessly from
one word to the next not caring if my subjects agreed with my verbs
in number and gender? Oh, I find I have in no way expressed or
detailed, flatteringly or un-, Owen Gamliel Lieb, whose curious
presence was in itself best described as Crypto-Byronic.

By way of explaining my explanation of cher Monsieur Lieb, let me
tell you, doctor, about my lousy childhood. I am the fourth of five
children, the only girl in a house of boys, born into a wealthy but cau-
tiously severe Jewish family. I see myself then as an undersized zombie, and school photographs bear this out. They seem to varying

degrees overexposed so that my face is a white moon framed by lank dark hair while terrified unblinking eyes (blue which in the garish Technicolor of the day translated into flat black) stare out, dark-ringed, lemur-like, showing no sign of sentience or anything beyond abject fear. In my second-grade picture I am missing teeth; it only adds to the morbid, feral effect. Once, I recall, on photo day a sympathetic teacher tried to take me into the girls' restroom and comb out my tangled hair. I bit her hand. I have never been good with thanks. So I was left alone, a strange child who coveted the cool lonely darkness of the library stacks and lived, as it has often been said, in a dreamworld. Yes, yes, it was not all silence; there were the occasional violent outbursts, semihabitual thumbsucking, eczema, dark moods, and carsickness. I was, as you can see, a normal American girl who spent her days in front of the television watching soap operas and drawing ladies in stylish dresses like those in my mother's fashion magazines. I was not, I feel it is important to stress, one of those girls who evinced a childhood love of ponies and with tracing paper copied in detail from adventure books pictures of horses, the manes woven with roses, tails braided fancy into knots, a rainbow blazing in the distance. At the time those girls terrified me. They hoarded the good crayons in art class. They skipped jacks in the shade during recess already worrying about their delicate complexions. I played kick-the-can with broken bottles found in the school parking lot. The green glass shined, shone in the forever autumn of those afternoons. I was a mass of bruises, cuts, and abrasions. I was always in a state of coming out of my own skin. I imagined I was a lost Romanov daughter whose premature death was foretold in every skinned knee or the rope burn of the tire swing's noose. Once I drank lemon Joy dish-soap because the television commercials made it look so delicious; it burned my throat. It made me sick. I eyed with thirst the sturdy drum of bleach in the laundry room. I was searching for a clean right down to the shine. The seasons went from sun to snow, and we sat in art class instead of going outside. The teacher read aloud wholesome stories from *Jack and Jill* magazine. The girls drew horses with sheets of tracing paper overlaid on the pages of library books. Our class pet was a reclusive hermit crab who never came out of his shell. Boys wrote dirty words on the desks in poster paint. I wiped my runny nose on my sleeve. I was always sick, miserable, the days seemed endless and what could I do but try to create, replicate this misery if only in sketches of the world as a planet spinning toward collapse? I devoted myself to drawing free-hand, no template, no copying. I was a biter, a kicker, an exiled princess, a conscientious objector in the playground wars, a child who regularly threw up in neighbors' cars coming from or going to school; but I was, I believed earnestly, never a cheater. I hoarded my faults the way the other girls stockpiled the butter-yellow, citrus-orange, and sunshine-colored Crayolas. My failings were all I had to call my own. Other children were bedwetters, fistfighters, finger-snappers, nose-pickers, scab-peelers, treat-hoggers, cup-wavers, flashers, thieves, bul-lies, tattletales, girls who kissed indiscriminately and lifted their skirts in response to the undone show-and-tell trousers of little boys. I was banished to speech class because I would not speak. They gave us ice cream. I spent hours in the remedial workshop because I refused to hold a pencil in my hand and instead insisted on clamping it between my sharp little incisors. I was a tiny self-imposed Helen Keller. I know, I know, I read an illustrated biography (infuriatingly misshelved in the school library under *Fiction*) three times, each time driven anew to tears. I was sent to the principal's office where she speculated with Jungian archetypes and finger puppets on why I wasn't more like my reliable older brothers, Ira, Simon, and Ezra (called EZ, so easygoing!) who had all passed through these halls before me with no blemish on their permanent records; or my studious younger brother, Walt, on his way to academic excellence in kindergarten. So week after week, from snow to thaw, from boots to raincoats, in art class or the gymnasium, those petite equine enthusiasts with their hair ribbons, their Friday nights at Roller World mooning to the tunes of Olivia Newton John as they skated arm in arm, with their Jordache jeans and Dr. Pepper lipgloss, with their beleaguered and probably stoned Dexatrim-popping mothers who picked them up in station wagons and herded them to tap class, heel, toe, heal tow, left tow, right, those girls with their crisp tracing paper visions of the world, their impossible futures, date rapes on the frat house stairs, cellulite, temp jobs, their turquoise-ringed fingers typing 120 words a minute, collagen injections, self-improvement tapes, smoker's coughs, diet sodas, cruise ship vacations, faith in Jesus, padded bras, abortions, the Arabian ponies they would never own but about whom they would never cease nightly dreaming across the lush green pastures of the unconscious mind; those girls shunned me. And if it hurt, it did not matter. What did I care? What possible difference could it make? I thrived on rejection; it tasted of peppermint. How did Dostoevsky put it? *My liver hurts? Well let it hurt more!* I studied the shapes around objects. I used Scotch tape to fasten my eyes shut. I drew both what I had never seen and what I did not remember remembering: flowers, trees, apples, women walking avenues of the past in winter coats and cloche hats from which might spring a single perfect iris. Here is what I did not draw: men. Why? Oh, doctor, if only I knew. I became as adept as I was friendless at landscapes, perspective drawings in which Western ghost towns disappeared into the ominous and forever unreachable V of the horizon line, mournful seasides, still life with peaches, vermilion goldfish, the limbs of women reclining, the lovelorn faces of strangers. I became certain that others suspected about me what I had only just come to fear. My inability to draw men came from my failings, my perverse fledgling amorality that showed itself in the shape of every apple, pear, pumpkin, and banana innocent enough on the table until I came along and inked another version, one dark and bitter with desire. Say that it should have been easy for me: a matter of squaring off the jaw and shoulders—*I know, I know.* Teachers gave me books to study. My

promise was spoken of in hushed tones; at last I would be of use to the
world. But how could I admit that this one flaw, my inability to draw
the Renaissance form of man, was not an obstacle to be overcome; it
was the opposite. It was the obstacle that would overcome me. My
world was complete. It was only that I would have to learn to accept
its dim lighting, seedy back alleys, its jealousies, temptations, whispered innuendoes, the infidelities of characters I had yet to meet, and
worst of all, my own complicity, my own refusal to acknowledge that
this was my fate. I would never be free from it. And still I was only a
child. My youthful gift became spoken of less and less, until one day
it was forgotten about entirely, and I crept off unnoticed to my seat in
the back row. And so I feel years later, using a typewriter rather than
magic markers (sadly), that I am in a similar situation. I am afraid I
will not be able to convey, to create a true portrait of Owen Lieb, that
instead as I begin to sketch the lines of his face you will find only my
unsteady hand, grubby fingers smearing ink, and my suspect cross-
hatching disguised as shading upon which to comment.

Owen Lieb was tall, over six feet, but under seven. He was, I would
say, rakish, but not foppish; his hair unruly but not overtly curly, more
silver than gray (one biographer mythologized Owen Lieb's transformation at his first wife's death to Moses at the burning bush; his black
hair turned silver overnight). He was dark-complexioned, more brown
than olive, a descendant, he claimed, of Turkish Jews, a twisted and
tangled bloodline back to the mythic Khazars themselves. His eyes
were blue and although I have since heard them described as hazel, I
never saw them stray to either or any of the varying greens of jealousy,
the ocean, pine needles bedding a forest, dewy meadow at dusk, para-
trooper's fatigues, or the Emerald Isle herself. They were simply blue.
He wore that afternoon, if I recall correctly, workaday chinos (Brigid
shared with me in one of our infinite, limitless girl-to-girl digressions:
Owen hates pleated trousers. He finds something very unsavory about

pleats), a dark shirt (he favored grays and blacks, sometimes deep maroons, shades that girls at the cosmetic counters call complimentary to "winters"; and if he was not wearing gray on that first occasion, I saw him any number of times afterward wearing a smoky shade of mourning as he wrestled a sock away from his dog, who although French in origin, was called by the full grand title, Admiral John Paul Jones), and as the morning was still damp and chill, he wore also a black cardigan sweater, a bit shapeless with time-frayed elbows unraveled away. He had spent the morning mucking about in the garden where he used both shovel and trowel to dig out, to root and excavate the skeletal remains of carrots, tubers, wildflowers, burnt offerings, and buried treasure. He wore work boots, battered admirably. Once I saw him in suede loafers. And on a dismal afternoon when he was driving to meet a friend all the way back in Dublin, I recall him finely attired in black wing tips and charcoal trousers, a herringbone jacket, white shirt with French cuffs, and a tie that I recall because I complimented him on it, because it was not the sort of thing you often see; gray silk with a winding pattern of apples. It was utterly elegant to the point of being satanic. Which is not to imply or ask you to draw parallels between Owen Lieb and any or all incarnations of Lucifer. He was not the devil; even I have to admit that. He only happened to possess a tie whose subtle style was undiminished by the fact that it commended itself to certain myths and metaphors of the Judeo-Christian tradition. The only other tie of his that I recall was equally interesting if not as seductive; it featured in shades of umber, slate and muted russet, Grecian urns after a trompe l'oeil style. His wardrobe contained also: pajamas, bathrobes, wool socks, slippers, flannel shirts for working outside or translating rugged sonnets into or out of dead languages, dungarees (we call them *blue jeans)*, as well as one of those trademarked "barn jackets" that can be ordered from a catalog, but on the morning that I saw him, on the morning that I returned to have coffee with Brigid and re-begin our awkward beginning, on the morning

turning to afternoon when he walked into the kitchen he wore chinos,
a cardigan sweater, boots, and a dark gray shirt. He paused to kiss his
wife, who I have already suggested in the previous chapter was rather
pale, pretty, and remarkable in her own right, and oh, yes, he greeted
the girl sitting with his wife (or failed to greet? We made acquaintance,
he and I, through the absence of introduction. *Faire la connaissance de,*
is how the French say it. To know. To meet. To meet the unknown.).
This girl was five-foot seven inches tall, which made her the shortest
person in the room. She was, like the other two parties, unequivo-
cally American and a little at odds with her landscape, so she allowed
herself to feel less discomfort with this regal married couple than she
might have if they were enjoying caramel rolls and Sanka under similar circumstances in say, Ashland, Wisconsin or Great Falls, Montana;
there is something about being abroad that makes all fellow expatriate
countrymen dear old acquaintances if not relatives, connected by a
slutty first cousin called Homeland. Okay. The guest, Fern, was a real
find for the Liebs for this very reason. It was unique for an American
girl to be working, especially cleaning houses out here in this seaside
town past the tourist season. The Liebs would have admitted that they
wouldn't have minded if an Irish girl had been sent to help them with
the house; it would have been educational. They could have asked her
cultural questions and directions and where to find the best fruit markets, as Owen was very particular about his diet. He was not at all fond
of the Irish proclivity for boiling or pureeing vegetables down to a buttered paste; he was, by his own admission and with apologies to Mr.
Lévi-Strauss, more a devotee of the raw than the cooked. And while
our Fern had been hired only to clean, Brigid and Owen, accustomed
to their Parisian flat in the Fourth Arrondissement, to their lazy mornings of brioche and dark coffee, were hoping that the girl might be
able to do the cooking and laundry. Fern was after all a *find,* a curiosity, the third leg of their American triangle, if you will, and they could
talk, the three of them if it came down to it, about the difference

between here and there, home and away, the now and the then, about place and displacement. Fern, who was five-foot six inches tall but rounded her way up to seven and didn't mind the creeping height of her lie, had already had two cups of coffee to her hostess's four and was distractedly kicking her leg against the side of the table without realizing it when Brigid looked at her and asked, *Does too much caffeine make you nervous?* Brigid had inadvertently begun to speak in lines from television commercials and advertisements. It had started the moment she alighted from the plane, Aer Lingus from Roissy-Charles de Gaulle to Dublin, and had turned to her traveling partner slash husband and announced dismally: *It's the only way to fly.* He had no idea what she was talking about and rested his palm briefly against her forehead testing for fever. *Did you take your pills?* he asked. She nodded and they headed toward customs, lost and briefly separated from each other in a crowd of Canadians wearing plaid tam-o'-shanters emblazoned with maple leaf decals. *They don't want to be mistaken for Americans,* said Owen to Brigid when they were reunited. *They're scaring me,* said Brigid. And they walked, this time arm-in-arm, impossible to disentangle, to the baggage claim. He passed for French, and she was mistaken for German. If they did not speak, no one suspected that they were American, and that was how they liked it. He was not a murderer but a well-loved poet, and she was not on her way to the chopping block, willingly, exquisitely, in a simple black sleeveless dress and chunky shoes that the girl in the shop on the rue de Rivoli had said were all the rage with the young ladies in London. The Liebs were elegant, tall, voiceless, polite, and anonymous as they picked up their rental car and began the drive westward.

I can't draw a picture of Owen Lieb. And perhaps I have not achieved even a playground's shovelful of depth toward his character. But he did have two memorable neckties and made sure his pretty young wife took her Dramamine with food before boarding either trains or airplanes, and I have succeeded in dressing him up like a paper doll. Fit him in a poet's blouse for translating Rimbaud. Dungarees and straw hat for whitewashing the past. I am lousy at this typing business. Safety glasses for forging in the smithy of his soul! The misspellings are so thick that I take a pen to page as soon as I pull it from the carriage. If I don't check it immediately I won't remember what word it was, in fact, that I was trying to spell. As though it matters. They all end up saying the same thing. I will fail you. With this story. Because it will not match those days and how they unfolded. I was going to insert a metaphor about the days unfolding like Brigid Lieb's legs from under the table. But I don't like metaphors. I find them precious and distracting. It is difficult to recall so many things, those days themselves each from the next. For the sake of my everdiminishing authority and the importance of primary sources in historical documentation, I now submit two journal entries from my notebook:

9/14/90: Marie left a note on my door that she had a house to be done. Americans, it said. She must think we seek out rather than hide from each other. Took my coffee and bread down to the seawall. Dip your finger in and it is salty. Found Marie who said it was "the Lieb place" that needs working on. Marie's face is perfectly round. Bumble Bea on the steps trying to undo her tiny sneakers. She peeks at her baby brother in the bassinet. He's done up in blue. Marie and I have discovered that she is exactly twelve days older than I am. I ask, you mean the Liebs, the writers? And Marie says, yes, the very house and now he's coming back with his new wife. Buzz, buzz, says Bea imitating her namesakes in and around the garden. I biked out to the place, about a half-hour's ride and in my supreme idiocy walked right in on a couple fucking on the living room floor. Girl on top. Was embarrassed (me, not them) and left immediately. When I got back and told Marie about it, she laughed (oh Jesus & co: give up the Puritan ghost already) and said that I should go back tomorrow. And maybe only then did it occur to me that they were, the couple on the floor, the Liebs. It was only that she, the girl, was so young. I thought she would have been older, that's all. So Marie says go back tomorrow and make a fresh start. Then she asks me if I can watch Bea and the baby for a while and I say, okay. Am doing this now as I write. Bea is throwing stick for fetch to Prince, who would rather be herding sheep (new bumpersticker?) but who relentlessly brings back whatever the little girl tosses his way, rotty apples, clothes pins, her doll, baby's bottle, etc.

9/15/90: Brigid, the wife, is pretty and so young. Head hurts. Weighed myself this morning on Marie's scale. How many stones in a pound? Going to sleep now.

So it would seem that I documented the things that were either the most obvious (Brigid is pretty) or impossible to understand out of temporal context (Marie made me weigh myself that day because she thought that I looked awful and might be coming down with the perpetual flu from which Aileen suffered; really, sadly, I looked the same as I ever did, slightly green, foreign in any setting, nightmarish) or details utterly nonessential (Prince had an endless capacity for fetching sticks) to the reconstruction of the story at a later date. It is difficult enough for those of us who were there to describe the events—so how, I wonder, how do biographers do it? To years later write about people whom they never met, let alone never loved, never saw removing a shoe, scratching a spider bite, drawing lipstick without mirror on a mouth already swollen with kisses, falling down a flight of stairs, digging a grave in the soggy dirt of the garden for burial of a dead bird, struggling to shut a jammed window during a rainstorm, or fumbling with a metal ice-cube tray after two or three vodka tonics? How do the biographers, they who were never there at all, know where to begin, when I who was witness find that each moment

I spent with the Liebs is now multiplied by itself and what I thought
was the space of days has grown into a collection of lifetimes?

Please pencil in your answer at the bottom of the page.

We will return to it later.

Please draw a picture of yourself and mail it to me, c/o: Dead
letters.

As Mr. Herman Melville asked: *Are they not like dead men?*

His biographers say he was gay. That he never stopped dreaming of the South Seas. That his wife was miserable. That his son
killed himself.

Please say that biographers have some insight, unseemly as it
may be, that they are doing more than tracing horses with fancy
braided tales. We fed them, Brigid and I, that afternoon, apples
and carrots from our outstretched hands, dray horses in the fields.
You think, I know, that I am awful because I have shown neither
sym- nor empathy to the fair-haired ghosts of my girlhood who
could not stop themselves from growing up and being loved or hated
or raped or abandoned or hopeful or humorless or prematurely
adult, who did not have the advantages I have been so repeatedly
told that I had. Brigid fed with her ringless fingers a sugar cube to a
speckled gray workhorse. In the end advantages, like sympathies, are
relative, I suppose. The wind blew her hair. She said to me, *I was one
of those girls—who loved, no, no, who lived only for horses. But then I'm
sure you know what I'm talking about. I'm sure you were just the same
way when you were little, weren't you?* I looked out across the fields.
At that moment I pretended to be someone else and she was happy
enough, that girl, happier than I had ever been. Everything in the
world was a deep damp shade of green. There was no history or past,
only the endless afternoon awaiting us. Marie's dog Prince was chasing sheep. Poor John Paul Jones looked on frantically and strained
his leash. And Brigid, taking pity and laughing, allowed him to
search her jacket pockets for sweets.

El Dorado

"Where do we begin?" asked Brigid.

She looked around the kitchen, surveyed the disorder of cups and plates, ran a finger over the dusty wooden table to form a letter L, and smiled expectantly at me.

I didn't know how to answer her.

I still don't.

Owen Lieb began by returning to his dusty abandoned house with his second wife, Brigid. They returned to write books, think unfathomable thoughts, do daring domestic couplings on the drawing room floor, wallow in the bliss of their wedding bed, and eat the wanton wild apples weeded from the orchard. But they also returned, and perhaps I have not mentioned this yet? Because Brigid had grown nervous, anxious, voluble to the point of absurdity, and Owen worried for her. Or it could have been that her thoughts had achieved such a rare degree of individuality that she begged for isolation from the endless connotations of even the most banal of everyday speech? Her husband began to note a sort of astonished perplexity when his wife spoke or listened to conversation. He watched her in her seat on the airplane tilting her head to hear the discussion of two matronly ladies nearby. Brigid tugged his sleeve and whispered, *Oh do you hear? It's utterly wonderful! First they were talking about birdwatching, but now they are swapping recipes—remind me not to forget to buy some Dutch cocoa—for chocolate birdsday cake, how delicious.* She seemed astonished that she could understand the language those around her were speaking, and this went beyond the distinctions of French or English, but into the realm of the skittering and associative circumlocutions which turn memory into symbol into speech into the written word. So they packed up their things, shipped boxes and carried suitcases; Owen returned with this fragile wife to the very house where his first wife had lost her struggle and will to continue. It would seem to those of us on the outside that this was not a singularly good idea.

I don't have the authority to speak for them, only *about* them.

I can only tell you what I know.

Frances Warren Lieb was electrocuted in the bath. It was an ending strange, sad, and enigmatic enough to begin an industry of biographical speculation. The first Mrs. Lieb was either a suicide or a murdered young wife. The novel on which she was working at the time of her death disappeared, as did notebooks and letters. Owen Lieb is credited with editing (some well-intentioned cynics say redacting) *The Collected Letters of Frances Warren Lieb,* published in 1972. The myth of the "lost Lieb letters" grew out of a comment her younger sister, Elisabeth Warren, made in an interview with a biographer after the epistolary collection appeared in print. She said, "I don't know how it can be that Franny's letters sound so little like her. I can barely recognize notes addressed to me that I once read and eagerly awaited. I can't find anything familiar here. It is nothing more than a collection of absences, a cut and paste-up version of my sister." And after making this statement, she refused to speak further on the subject of her sister or brother-in-law. Whatever Elisabeth Warren's intentions may have been—did she imply that she didn't know the unhappy person her sister had become in the end—or was she announcing that there were crucial letters suspiciously missing from the collection? Whatever she meant is shrouded now in her silence. Ms. Warren, reclusive and reticent, teaches English Literature at a private girls' school. Years after Frances Lieb was scattered into ashes the mystery of her death continues to perpetuate itself, grow and gain momentum, not with the increase of information on her short life, but with the continuing lack, the diminishment of document.

It does not help the case of the missing letters that Franny Lieb's first biographer, Susan Rhys, wrote with romantic aplomb of events that occurred in the days soon after the author's death. She wrote in her authorized biography that Owen built up a bonfire in the orchard and burnt *"—photos and clothing; each heap of papers that he threw upon the symbolic funeral pyre sent another spark of flames heavenward against the frozen winter sky."* But there is reason to believe that the letters in question, having been sent from Franny to her younger sister, were still at the time of Owen's makeshift memorial ceremony in Elisabeth's possession. And it was only later that Elisabeth with the best of intentions returned them to him for publication in the collection. Ms. Rhys's explanation for Owen's brief flirtation with pyromania was his devotion to his wife and desire for the protection of his young son. Later biographers of the unauthorized variety suspected less noble motivations, not the least of which being that at the time of his estranged wife's death he was living in Dublin with another woman.

I've written a few regrettable letters.

The papers of Frances Warren Lieb (what is left of them, that is) are housed in the archival collection at the Rosewood College Library.

I keep my regrettable letters in a shoebox.

Owen Lieb did not have in his possession the lost letters of his first wife. We can clear this up immediately. He obfuscated the whereabouts of the manuscript of her second novel, and he burned photographs and boxes of belongings, but he did not burn that ribbon-tied bundle of letters for the simple reason that he could not find it. Someone, some ghost or specter lost in the cobwebs of the past, had managed to steal the papers from him. Blessed is the match. And the hand that lights it. He left the house years before without them; still he knew that one day his wife's letters would reappear. And when he returned to the old house he could not stop searching for them. He went through the rooms. There were no dresses in the closets, no rings on the bedside table. The curtains remained. The floorboards remained nailed into place. Dishes and pots, cups and saucers, glasses and teapots, these things remained. As did the forgotten calendar and its companion, a stopped kitchen clock. And if this searching was for the purpose of finally putting to rest the memory of his first wife, who can say? Perhaps he wanted to locate the last missing fragment of Franny, to protect their past from the probing pens of the sentence dissectors, the mad syntax-vivisectionists who laid her body of work out on the coroner's slab? What of the grave-robbers? He knew they were waiting to etch his epitaph. He knew they were lurking out there in the darkness, fondling phrases, pining, pausing to pen the last chapter in the life of the Liebs. When he could not find the letters in the house, when he could not bear to open another empty drawer, he began to dig in the garden.

I returned to America, November 3, 1990. Contents of my duffel bag included: unwashed whites and damp woolens, notebook, paperback novels, camera, bundled papers, picture postcards, and an address book filled with the names of friends to whom letters were never sent. This is, was, will be my inauspicious return home, and the advance ending of this memoir.

And now I begin my story proper, which really begins with Brigid wanting to know how one begins cleaning a long-abandoned house, with Brigid wanting to begin so that she could tell me her story and we could scrounge and scavenge for endings. There will be, I'm afraid, no middle. No sooner will things begin than they will abruptly sputter to a close. I used to have photographs, but most of them are gone now. I lost the few snapshots taken of Owen and Brigid, and one I recall in particular that Owen took of Brigid and me with the ridiculous scarecrow he fashioned out of a broomstick to keep blackbirds out of the garden. There were also shots of Beatrice, the bumblebee, playing fetch with her sheepdog. And Marie holding up blue-blanketed Tommy for the camera. And unremarkable landscapes, shops, streets, and avenues; pictures which would have been useful beyond their sentimental scrapbook value as illustration of my story. But no. I will rely on nothing so pretty, nothing in bright colors, nothing that would reveal too readily the easy charm of the Liebs and so influence your understanding of the story. I submit to you only clumsy words and my furiously dusty attempts to begin. Paper, red pen, black ink, no photographs, a new calendar pinned to the wall: Happy New Year 1999.

The beginning of me is the history of failure. This is the opening line of Franny Lieb's only published novel, *The Bright Corner.* Or perhaps you are more familiar with the disastrous 1983 film version which begins with a famous young actress reciting this line in the voice-over. She adds a certain lilt of Hollywood incredulity, a trace of suspenseful irony as if she does not quite believe what she is saying because she has read the script and knows the ending is destined to be happy. Throughout the film and the indignities suffered by her character, the radiant young actress whose name escapes me remains ethereal and luminous, a celluloid creation of box-office bravado. A paperback edition of the novel was reissued with a picture of the actress on the cover.

A is for Apple, J is for Jacks, sang Brigid as she ran water over the dishes in the sink. *Cinnamon toasty Apple Jacks! You need a good breakfast; that's a fact! Start it out with Apple Jacks!*

What did I learn from the study of biography? Did I learn anything at all about history? Do I remember dates and dialectical materialism? Do I recall decapitated regents and whiskey-soaked insurrectionists? I know that Princess Anna Comnena had a face that was said to be a "perfectly chiseled circle." She, the daughter and promised heir of the eleventh-century Byzantine Emperor Alexios I, was so enraged when the crown passed at her father's death to her younger brother that she conspired to kill him. The plot failed and she spent the rest of her life locked up in a convent writing the *Alexiad,* a fifteen-volume biography of her father. And in the Swiss Canton of Vaud 3,371 women were executed, burned at the stake as witches, between the years 1591 and 1680. I was delighted by useless details, giddy to read that a state dinner for President George Washington in 1789 included: *soup, fish, roasted and boiled meats, gammon, fowl, apple pie and pudding, then ice creams and jellies, then watermelon, muskmelon, apples, peaches, and nuts.* Or what of Stonewall Jackson who was convinced that his arms and legs were mismatched pairs? To stimulate his system, he took a bath every morning in cold water, even during winter. He was often seen sucking on a lemon to the cure the pain of chronic indigestion. General Grant weighed only one hundred thirty-five pounds during the war. He was a sparse eater. He abhorred red meat of any kind, and the sight of blood made him ill. Consequently, he insisted on meat being cooked to the verge of being charred. He would not eat any kind of fowl, but was fond of pork and beans, fruit, and buckwheat cakes. More than one medical specialist hypothesized that Hitler's mental condition was caused by the tertiary stage of syphilis. And what of his young cousin, Geli, for whom he showed an obsessive fondness? A year after Geli's death, Eva Braun, then twenty-one, tried to take her own life, and thus cemented the sympathy of Adolf, still smitten with the memory of his dead cousin. Eva Braun, a pretty blonde girl, worked in a photography shop. She was an excellent skier and swimmer; she enjoyed sports, cinema, animals, and no doubt, long walks on the beach. I sought shadowy figures who fell into the bindings of books, those whose stories were condensed into a footnote—Cora Pearl, a courtesan of second-empire Paris, called Prince Napoleon her *Plon-Plon* and was rumored to dance naked on a carpet of orchids and bathe before her dinner guests in a silver tub full of champagne. And I have one more confession: I read two biographies of Frances Lieb long before I read *The Bright Corner*.

Me, me, me was the pathetic refrain of my life. That's how Camus said it years before his car hit a tree and forced a summarily pat answer to his ontological questions. After two months spent wandering in Europe, I devised a plan in which I would never return home. I found a job with Marie by sheer happenstance. She was waiting at the station to pick up a cousin who was coming to town to work for her— but the girl never showed up—and I did. When Marie arrived I was there at the station. I was already in the process of disappearing. How easy it would be to be forgotten. Good-bye to all that! The great plains, the Great Lakes, bleached wheat prairies, the elephant eyes of corn, Manifest Destiny, Betty Crocker and her secret trysts with Chef Boyardee, Yankee Doodle Drive and the Fargo Walk of Fame, the newest binge-and-purge diet and shopping fads, any and everything prefaced or prefixed with the word *mega*. Was I elite, revolutionary, or simply small-minded? I once knew a girl who won a regional thimble-collecting contest. It was, she insisted, an obsession like any other. She longed for a tiny world. I admit that even now I am sometimes homesick for the things of the past that have brought me the most pain.

Marie offered me a place to stay. Her children were sweet and her husband was good-natured. And there was nothing at home for me. There was, yes, a romance and betrayal of either the literal or figurative variety. I was doing self-imposed penance for crimes yet untold. I was not cleaning houses as an impracticality, one of those novelties dreamed up by newly graduated college girls who want to see the world from the gritty side up and so suffer a summer to slum and then in the autumn return to slip their prettily blistered feet into size seven leather pumps and work dutifully in an office at typing or filing all the while being a solid team player and reminiscing at the water cooler with girls ever younger, steadily older, more beautiful, bearable, or believable than oneself about the plight of the common man, the clear beer of Vienna, the way things used to be before they were this way, which is always, in fact, no way to be, no way at all. You may choose to see me less as an individual than a cultural marker, a product of my generation. Say maybe that I never knew what I wanted, only what I did not want. That I came by cleaning not from love, drive, or avocation, but from the random draw of the card. What if I say that my failure was not from lack of trying? That I tried and, as the saying goes, tried again, only to admit that from lack of skill, ambition, and impetus, I found myself that summer struck down to the root, scrubbing blindly. Say that I was a failure, a bad liar, a future thief from the very house that took me in, a not-so-gifted storyteller, a secondhand suicide, a two-time loser, a puritanical libertine, a monkey-see monkey-do kind of girl who followed Brigid Lieb from room to room as the Angel of Death went from house to house in Egypt searching for the marked doors which promised exemption from the final plague, death of the first-born.

I think it is useful to have reference materials nearby when reading: a Bible and dictionary at the very least. What if I used the word *shibboleth*? You would need both, wouldn't you? I don't know what it means; there's no shame in admitting it. *Shibboleth,* let's call it the password for a new generation of bashful semioticians. Do you have everything you need? Compass? Treasure map? Are you thirsty? Should I wait? Are you still out there or have you left me rambling to myself alone here in the wilderness? I don't mind. I'll wait. I can wait. So cheer up! We'll get there together, clasping our Bibles like out-of-work pilgrims, checking cross-references, chanting *shibboleth, shibboleth, shibboleth* more times than Mr. Faulkner at a football game, synchronizing our watches, recalling the place-names, using maps, carbon dating a cache of purloined letters for authenticity; we'll crash and smash it all down and maybe afterward we'll get together, you and I, for a drink some evening on the veranda of a monumentally ramshackle hotel with striped awnings. We will be almost but not quite civilized. We will nibble fruit as the sky darkens and sip coffee light with cream and talk about everything but. What we did. And what we have undone. And pretend that we never spent these days together. Maybe we won't have coffee at all; perhaps it will be mint juleps? Or a drink so bright it will blot out the ironies of the past with a single sip. So push the little paper umbrella out of the way and bring the Bible with you when you return. It is going to come in handy—especially the story of Genesis, of Abraham and his two wives. Or Exodus in which collective guilt becomes a commodity valuable enough to gild the golden calf. A Hebrew edition is preferable, but I'm not going to stand on ceremony and demand it. Edgar Allan Poe loved Hebrew, did you know? He saw the language as a code to be cracked with its curious subsentence vowel system. History cheated Poe, betrayed his memory, led us to believe he died drunk in a gutter wearing an ill-fitting suit that was not his own. And so they say he died young for no reason, no reason at all, for all of his dreams of Paris, ruing the Rue Morgue, of extracted molars and monkeys committing murders in rooms more locked than Freud's own office with the blinds drawn, ghosts still whispering: *Ah little Hans, tell me again?* E.A.P. was found slumped on the sidewalk, his own impending death the greatest mystery of his cryptograms. I'm sorry. I strayed off track, but I admit, as I have undertaken this story, the lives and especially the sordid deaths of writers have become increasingly fascinating to me. I worry for myself. I check my temperature; it rises by a tenth of a degree every hour. I see the signs. I have known anorexic girls who return to the living only to find themselves longing for just a moment of starvation. Or alcoholics who begin the ritual descent back to drink before ever unscrewing a lid. Too frequently I stop by the bookstore under the pretense of buying a newspaper or magazine only to find myself lingering over the glossy pages of the latest tell-all biography, the ghostwritten saga of a child film star's drug-addled early years, or the heartwarming tale of a five-star general's triumph over poverty and a fatherless upbringing to command the troops on to victory. I long to read their stories, but I leave the book on the rack for the next shopper. I leave my little hovel less and less. I crave the world on the other side of the mirror, the place where all stories have endings. I know that I am haunted most by the fear that my life began and ended both on an autumn day long-gone. To quote someone or other who knew, who had the exquisite sense and grace and bitterness to understand that Nero never stops fiddling and Rome never stops burning: *Everything undoes itself. Everything undoes the next thing.*

My failure consists not only of my inability, but unwillingness to commit to the present tense. I have never fully enjoyed those inspirational biographies of individuals left to tell the tale. I read (and that's the past tense, honestly, pronounced *red*) biographies for the strange natural plot that defines both life and sentences: the birth of the noun, the frantic action of the young verb, simpering seductions of adjectives and adverbs, death with the shuddering instance of terminal punctuation. Oh Freudy-Freud, if only your mother Amalie had been less beautiful and your father Jacob more forgiving, would I now see the world differently? Oh Absalom, Absalom, how the mighty are fallen! I am thinking of Charlotte Corday killing Marat in the bath; Snow White in her glass coffin; Odysseus spying on Nausikaa in the reeds; Franny Lieb unwinding the extension cord down the winter-darkened hallway as the spigots in the tub jet hot water. I am thinking of Alice with her golden curls going through the looking glass that separates the wheat from the chaff, the water from the wine, the boys from the men, so that drinking from a bottle marked *XXX DRINK ME*, she becomes at once a miniature of herself in an oversized world, or was it the other way around? *EM KNIRD XXX,* Alice? Did the world serve to shrink while she outshined it? I saw once in a museum an oil painting depicting the incarnation of the sin of vanity as a girl standing naked before a handheld mirror. Before I return to the moment that I cannot again bear to see, and yet cannot avoid, to the afternoon when Brigid and I began the exhumation of our exquisite corpse, our piecemeal replacement of fable with fact— before we do this—see yourself in the gallery as I was, gazing at that portrait of the naked girl and judging her for her vanity and corruption, her fallen state of grace; note too the expressive rich red hues the artist uses to highlight her just-round breasts, the golden light playing on the mock halo of her curls, and understand what this means. Her sin is not her nakedness, but in holding the mirror up to herself. Un cagnolino, a tiny dog rests on a velvet cushion, crimson-tasseled, at her feet, unslippered, gazing upward mute with adoration.

Don't think that I wasn't a little star-struck by Owen and Brigid Lieb.

I admit that I was.

Yes, yes, yes, how the past becomes the present and we become the past, and we, us, Brigid and myself, Fern, having finished our coffee, having discussed the first moon-walk, the Russian Tarot pack, the inhumanity of declawing cats, the curious beauty of hybrid roses, topiary sculpture, aromatherapy, and a home remedy of boiled licorice root and crushed elderberries for the relief of migraine headaches, having recalled with flushed cheeks the names of boys not-so-long-forgotten, the height of heels and length of hemlines, the mysteries of the combustion engine, the physics of desire, we paused on the subject of favorite literary titles until she, having chosen *Children on Their Birthdays,* and I, having confessed to *Raise High the Roof Beam, Carpenters,* we ceased speaking only to break our silence moments later with the spontaneous and jinx-like ejaculation of the title we had both secretly loved but dared not admit. We announced as one, *The Bright Corner.* We were quiet then. It seemed blasphemous to speak of it in that kitchen, at that table. It was Brigid who rose from the table, a plate in one hand, a cup in the other. "Do you remember," she said, "how it went? I always come back to it—" She broke off. "—*The bright corner, the place that I went to, where I found myself that fateful summer has never existed. One went through the mirror while applying lipstick, while studying the familiar blue of one's own eyes to find the world on the other side reversed. It felt thrilling to be so desperate. All corners were bright, safe places where you could curl up, take your medicine and die for an hour or two without making a scene.*" And she, my host, Brigid, placed the cups in the sink and turned to ask me, blushing and earnest, how one begins to clean a house which really for the sake of art and history, furniture and fate and failure, belongs to the ghost of another woman?

Fairbanks

Frances Warren was born October 27, 1933 in the seaside town of Egdon, Massachusetts. She had a younger brother, William, born April 27, 1935 and a sister, Elisabeth, born June 27, 1937. Frances, also called Franny as a child, brother Billy, and Lizzy, nicknamed Lizard by her doting older sister, devoted their early years to water. Summers they spent picking wild raspberries, trooping to the library to borrow biographies of American heroes, nurses, and aviators; running relays, playing statues, running farther, faster until exhausted they ran home and to the ocean and rushed in unafraid of the undertow, with sun hats tied by strings around their necks the girls ran into the water calling *Marco, Marco,* and each awaiting the other's distant half-submerged response, *Polo,* while Billy on the shoreline built and squashed, heaped up and collapsed innumerable sandcastles; he was crowned with a seaweed diadem by his sisters, *Mr. Sandcastle King, 1945.*

Were we all so sweet as children? Even those among us who were in youth neither dreamy nor undomesticated, who lived through childhood for the sake and purpose of becoming sensible and sincere adults, even they may sometimes care to think back on it, to long for the past and stop to recall with something akin to nausea how it was then and how the world seemed to stop each day for some momentous event. All three Warren children would remember years later the birth of their youngest brother. They would remember counting the days on the calendar, mystified, old enough to understand the improbability and yet young enough to believe it could happen again; Frederick, called Freddy, Ricky, or sometimes the terse, abbreviated Fee, was born February 27, 1941. It snowed that day, all day.

Frances wrote a poem entitled "Four Little Fishes and the Deep Blue Sea." Billy, in a cape fashioned of a bath towel and a pirate hat from the previous Halloween, recited it to the family. Lizzy drew a fish in pink chalk at the bottom of the page. This paper, a torn scrap from a notebook, was found twenty-one years later in one of Mrs. Lieb's journals along with the notation: *It was the only happy time in my life and even then I was not happy.* Stories of the atrocities of war made their way home, crept even into the lives and imaginations of three small children by the sea. Daily deprivations caused the children to see themselves as soldiers; the girls rationing invisible cups of tea to their dolls lined up in rows like a tiny makeshift hospital. Franny had nightmares. Liddy, scared more by Franny than the threat of an unseen army, took to hiding under tables. William was growing tall and skinny; he could not catch up with himself. The girls called him Bones. The baby was round-faced, cooing and oblivious. He had been born bright yellow with jaundice. Lizzy said that he looked like the man in the moon. Frances Warren Lieb wrote in a letter to her sister in 1960: *I long for the tiny world, when we were miniatures of ourselves, when the fishes were pink and I can still—please don't make me, no stop—recall the screams of delight in the summer that we cried among the garden at the sight of ants, big and sturdy, crawling deliriously over the peonies. How sweet.*

The autumn of 1963 had been difficult, and the winter that followed was worse. The seasons did not live up to their promise. Rain turned to ice. Franny woke at four in the morning while the sky was black or was it bleak? Either—it was always in a state of one converging into the other. The baby barely slept, and oh—he had colic or he was teething—his cries were miserable, unrequited. While and when Jonathan called Johnny was finally and fitfully put down to sleep, his mother sat at the kitchen table and wrote longhand on unlined paper. She preferred the typewriter but worried about waking the baby. And by this time her husband was gone. He had packed his things and left her there alone with the solemn baby who tolled the hours in tears. There was the dark of morning and the gray of afternoon and the black of evening. All shades that varied only by the substance of shadow or the absence of light. She was working on the draft of a novel entitled *Ten-Twenty-Seven*. In 1962 in a letter to her sister Elisabeth she pronounced it: *a torrid locked-room mystery of the worst sort. The characters, each by each—are guilty, though generally not of the crimes that they believe they have committed. I feel sometimes that I am doing nothing more than infusing air into air, exhausting myself with meaninglessness—and most inauspicious, most ironic of all, the sooty air I feed to my ghosts serves not only to animate, but to poison them, blackening their lungs. To live fully, they must immediately be sentenced to death. The sentence is death. Dear Lizzy, I envy you, out there in the bright loud world. Will you write back and tell me what dresses the clever girls are wearing this year? Tell everything, the handbags, the shoes, the stockings, leave no seam unstitched. What a tiresome coal miner I have become in my darned socks and woolens. When I finish I promise I will fly directly, using my own wings if I must, to New York, and we will get together at that café you like and have bright green juleps. Until then I will mind my metaphors, I must mine deeper, coal dust and all, if only for the sake of finishing and returning home to you.* To her brother William in a letter of the same year, she wrote: *Dear Will, wherever you are, there is a way to get through the maze. How I have lost myself in this story! It is a labyrinth that I daily wander; as though I find my way out every night but am doomed in the morning to return and still not to remember how I found my way previously. But I think you will enjoy it, and have a great laugh at the foibles of us mere mortals. It is about the silliness of people—there is sadness too—as in Restoration Comedy, we laugh at the exaggeration of our own weakness, desire, and idiocy and so should learn a lesson. I shall compose some great moral ending to suit your philosophical inclinations. Johnny looks a great deal like you; his fingers are simian-long and his gaze quizzical. Owen says you must come visit when your semester ends. Give all of your studious undergraduates As and come loll in Eden under our apple trees.* And then the letters slowly tapered off, until by 1963 they had almost entirely ceased. William never came to Ireland to visit; Franny never returned to New York. She was left alone to wander the pages of the manuscript. By six-thirty on those winter mornings the sun was rising over the snowy fields. Ice hung on the bare boughs of black trees. She sat at the table where once, twice, hundreds of times, Brigid and I sat talking, using our coffee spoons to carve out the space where Franny Lieb used be.

In the chaos of Owen and Brigid Lieb's return home, in the maze of bags and baggage, you could still find traces of Franny—there, the window seat with the velvet cushions where afternoons she had sat and watched the trees unleaving; the kitchen counter where she had severed the tip of her right index finger while slicing a loaf of bread; the floors she gave up on scrubbing; the windows she ceased to wash; the mirrors she avoided as though the last two years of her life were spent in an endless ritual of mourning; the books she did not read; the pens and paper; the cotton nightshift draped over the bedpost; the winter oranges delivered with the last of the groceries; the laundry, the whites and flannels, the baby's embroidered blanket, just washed, left unfolded in a basket in the nursery. In the end and after the fact, the things she did not do became as important as those she did. She was jealous, prone to rage, picked fights, broke dishes, once threw a pot of failed soup against the wall of the kitchen screaming, too salty! as though the simple fact of confusing table- with teaspoon was an indication of all her suspect failings. *Too salty,* she cried, *I might as well drink the ocean.*

She sat at her kitchen table and planned grand dinner parties, scripting out the menu, parties that never happened but at which she would have served up on fine china and etched crystal: rack of lamb, roulades of beef carpaccio with caramelized onions, chilled cucumber soup, fresh mint and wild tarragon dressing drizzled over Belgian endive salad, twice-baked aubergine and butternut squash, crème brûlée, nectarines au glace, and a roasted chestnut sorbet flecked with black walnuts. The guests—artists, painters, poets, mathematicians, magicians of logic, the demimonde—they said great and fascinating things, told stories that had no end; their heels worn down, their fashions outlandish, careless, frumpy—oh such funny hats and ancient frocks! They would have place cards at the table with their names in curling calligraphy, red wine all through dinner, coffee with dessert, and afterward when they retired from the dining table to the living room they would remark on the charming woodwork, the beveled glass, and the stone fireplace devised of a masonry handed down by the Druids themselves; while others with teacups filled to the brim with blackberry brandy from Poland would wander outside into the orchard where the constellations were clear and true, where Orion hunted, and they would talk, these beautiful guests of hers, about how wonderful the evening had been, especially the tomatoes which were so much more fresh than the ones you get in the city markets, why you could practically taste the green, and the brandy, had it really come from Warsaw by packet boat? Until one by one, her guests became ghosts and drifted homeward remarking on the perfection of the sunrise, red, pink, golden. The woman sitting at the kitchen table in the dark of the morning while the snow fell and winds raged outside, while the promise of day offered little sun and less relief, the woman wrapped in two sweaters worn over flannel pajamas in the lamplight paused, rested her face in her hand, and speculated on whether perhaps at her next party the guests might enjoy a bitter chocolate fondue.

Soon after the publication in 1960 of Franny's novel, *The Bright Corner,* and the subsequent success of Owen's prosaic parables in several reputable and high-toned magazines, the young couple bought a Georgian country house in Ireland on the remote edge of the Western seacoast. Franny had grown up on the water and so in some grand sense felt a kinship to her new home. It seemed that maybe out here they would be safe from the world and all its various horrors and temptations. They would devote themselves to work and to each other. This was the fabled beginning when she typed his stories for him on the battered Olivetti, and they walked together to post them talking of probabilities and outcomes; of brilliance, their own, combined, and the sun's, solitary, and the stars, innumerable. She ironed his shirts and he read her fortune in tarot cards. On their honeymoon years before in Italy they had gone one day into a bakery and found there an old woman, the baker's grandmother, seated in the back of the store out of the heat, reading palms. She took Franny's hand. A shadow passed over the fortune-teller's face. Lieb shrugged his shoulders when Franny asked him to translate; he said he could not make out the rough dialect. Franny, who had no purse with her, gave to the woman the silk head-scarf she had been wearing. When asked years later by a biographer to comment on allegations that Owen Lieb had something to do with his estranged wife's death, Liz Warren reportedly replied: *Everything that they say he did to hold her back, everything that you think was done to hurt her was really for her own protection. You are looking at their lives from a completely upside-down point of view.* Owen led Franny by the arm out of the store into the afternoon heat where in the sun, without the protection of her scarf, her blonde hair seemed white-hot, shined platinum-bright. Later they ate the rustic bread they had bought and went swimming in the evening.

Sometime after the elopement and honeymoon stay in Umbria, sometime after plunging headfirst and barefoot into the ocean with both fists crammed full of raspberries, sometime between Percodan and black coffee, between poetry and prose, in the space between the dog and the wolf, in that twilight hour when friends come to visit

disguised as enemies, Frances called Franny transformed herself as so
many others had before her; from good girl to honor student, from
college graduate to wholesome housewife. It was only that with each
incarnation, with each new hairstyle, the trim, the cut, the dye, she
never quelled the desire to undo everything in her life, to run away,
to escape, to disappear. She learned how to bake soufflés that were
light as the suspirations of a Muse; creamy egg custards; peppered
beefsteaks still pink and bloody, iron-rich to the palate. She left the
fruit on the vines in her garden until the moment of lurid ripeness.
She was in the habit of drinking in the orchard at sunset, first with
Owen in the haze of summer warmth and then wrapped in a sweater
in the fall, and still sometimes alone in the winter after he had left
her when only the snap of branches under the weight of snow and
the cold bite of her bare fingers around the glass reminded her that
she was awake and not in the barren landscape of a nightmare.

Owen Lieb met Franny Warren in November of 1955. She wore
pearls and a black sweater-set, a gray flannel skirt. She smelled of
Chanel No. 5 with the musty undertone of the library stacks and carried under her arm Propp's *Morphology of the Folktale*. She stopped
by the Friday afternoon tea of a campus poetry club. She nibbled the
hard edge of a cookie, set her book on the table, twisted her charm
bracelet around her hand casually, as though the jewelry and long
sleeves of the sweater when a three-quarter length was in vogue were
not in some way devised to cover her scarred wrists. She scanned the
room for familiar faces: a girl who wrote tiresome verse about everlasting friendship; several young men, essayists or Marxists, although
probably both, and so laughably attired in brown and blue. She wore
heels, towering over the girls and many of the studious young men
at the party, so she had no recourse but to seek out others, the boys
in the corners who rose above the din to look down on the sloppy
cast of tea-drinkers. An exchange student from Spain was pouring

whiskey from a silver flask into his cup; he offered her some and she accepted. They shared, after a refill or three, a moment of dizzy carnival bliss as they together watched the earnest conversations swimming about them; and then they separated, and someone put a record on the phonograph. And with the voices speaking all at once in the jittery undercurrent of iambs, trochees, and secondhand quotations, and with the dancing, the room became a great wave, tidal. Franny was caught in eddies of the crowd pushed along and up against the biggest, brightest, most cornered boy in the world. And without speaking he took her by the hip and they danced, which she found a bit forward, but she was just drunk enough not to care. And when he leaned in close, his face pressed against her cheek, his mouth to her ear—to whisper his name? to ask hers? to incautiously opportune a kiss? He pressed his mouth to her ear and she met instead his ear with her mouth, and opened her mouth, lipsticked, just lightly as though to admit to some secret but no words followed. Instead she clamped her teeth against his earlobe and bit down. She bit him to draw blood. And she laughed too while doing it. And they stood for a moment like that, still arm-in-arm, in the light of the candles lighted by presumptuous poets for mood, for effect when afternoon turned to evening, and the tea was replaced by watered-down wine poured out in polite cupfuls. He pulled away from her; she saw his face and was astonished to find that he too, hands covered in blood, was laughing. She felt suddenly seasick, and rushed, as best she could away from him and through the smoky throng, stopping to locate her Propp, jacket, and handbag, from the room. But the story does not end there, not exactly. While they were dancing, he had reached two fingers deftly, delicately into the pocket of her sweater and stolen a tube of lipstick. We are in the realm now, you may find it ugly or enlightening—the place where every action has meaning and consequence. Later he was to write a short story entitled "Mulberry Red Night" about twins separated at birth who develop a psychic cryptophasia; it was an ode perhaps to the name of the exact shade of the pilfered lipstick or to his own drawn blood. Later that evening, after she paced her apartment restlessly unable to sleep, still before she had even learned his name, she documented in her journal the night's events: *Why is it that to give in to others, we must first overcome ourselves? I clutch fingers bruise-blackened at something or for someone who will smash me into pieces. To give in crashing, to give up shattered as a shipwreck, a disaster with no survivors. He, him, the one tonight at the party—I am certain I will be the ruin of him. I have seen it a hundred thousand times in my dreams. He is a vampire; I brought him over to the other side. There is no going back. How I long to crash and careen, to sink into him and wash up anonymous, a blood-less body broken on a foreign shore.* She was unaware until much later of the lipstick removed, fingered from her pocket; when she learned, she was delighted.

Liz Warren took in the romance from afar. She was eighteen and the letters she received from her sister in graduate school, narratives full of dark ideological longing, so Brontë-packed with brooding, disaster, and desire, captured her imagination. Franny even in child-hood had belonged to a different sort of world where duels of honor were fought over mud pies; and in their teens how many hours did they spend analyzing, poring over the minutia of sock hop romance? And if Elisabeth was not fully a conspirator in her sister's dream-world, neither was she immune to its charms. It was no surprise to her when Franny eloped with Owen Lieb. In fact, Elisabeth met Owen on a visit that winter. She took the train, and Franny met her in the station. It was snowing; there were delays all along the line. Franny without hat or gloves was oblivious to the cold. She took Elisabeth's hands in her own, freezing, and said: *When you meet Owen don't look directly into his eyes; you'll fall in love with him—and if you do, I'll die of jealousy.* Liddy hugged her sister and promised not to fall *too* much in love with him. Still, it was hard for her not to admit his perfection. Owen pulled out their chairs for them at lunch, and devised witty comments comparing the rice pudding and the viscosity of the Thames. None of the three had ever been to London but they all laughed. He lost himself in the telling of a funny anecdote and picked at his salad, eating cucumbers and carrots with his fingers. He was tall and slim. In his dark well-worn clothes, he seemed infinitely older than he was. He had read absolutely everything and could recommend several better translations of their favorite foreign novels. He wore black corduroy trousers and a cardigan sweater under which his white shirtsleeves dangled. He knew about wonderful wicked things like the Kabbala and Communism, astronomy and astrology. He understood the stars and could recite the Canticles of Solomon from heart. Franny, who was five-foot nine in her stocking feet, later wrote that she fell in love with him the moment she saw him at the party: *hovering over the heads of those second-rate poets, reckoning, judging, vindictive—*. They were not unreasonable or frivolous girls, the Warren sisters; they had only read so many books with tragic endings that they had come to expect, even long for disaster.

So how did it happen that 1933 became 1964? In fits and starts? Poems and nightmares; Shetland wool, Scottish tweed, in handbags that matched patent leather pumps? Elisabeth Chloe Warren never stopped seeing Franny as a crusader, an eight-year-old leading treacherous explorations through the blackberry brambles, cautioning her young siblings about the purple flowers of Deadly Nightshade, identifying morels, wild sassafras, stringing together with force the green fuses of dandelions on chains, while they all shouted, wild, drunk on the sweetness of berries, scratched and bruised with bee stings and mosquito bites, screaming together with stained mouths: *Mama had a baby and its head popped off!* When she was fourteen Franny Lieb wrote in her journal of dark moods that came over her, circling: *like birds without trees on a winter afternoon.*

When she was sixteen she published a short story in a popular girls'
magazine and turned the page to discover *how to lighten your hair for
summer fun!* She used lemon juice to bring out the brightness. At
seventeen she took a razor and slashed her wrists. And although no
one in the family dared speak of it, the incident was blamed on ado-
lescent passion, a love affair gone bad. The scars didn't heal well. She
spent three summers as an au pair for old money families on
Martha's Vineyard. Her own mother taught typing at a secretarial
school; her father was a psychiatrist born in Vienna of ethnic
German parents. He was a shadowy silent figure to his four children
who took care not to disturb his studies or make too much noise,
even on those summer mornings when they woke at dawn and
began their daily plots and palace intrigues over toast and butter. Dr.
Warren was fifteen years older than his wife. He had once been considered a brilliant prodigy, but soon despaired over the hopelessness
of his patients. He spent the last years of his life locked away in the
lamplight of their damp basement reading books about primate soci-
eties. He died of coronary thrombosis in 1956 while Franny and
Owen were on their honeymoon. In fact, because of the sudden
elopement, he never met his son-in-law. On those August nights
when she was baby-sitting for the summering set, when the children
had been put to sleep and the parents too had succumbed to martinis and tennis elbow, Franny headed down to bonfires on the beach
and sat in the haphazard circle of students earning their keep and
freed briefly for the night from the responsibilities of child-watching,
bartending, or giving sailing lessons. She drank beer or whatever
sweet substance was in the bottle that was being passed around, listened to dirty jokes, suggestions, improprieties, impossibilities, until
breaking from the group she ran into the ocean in the darkness.
When she was seventeen she went to college and studied the
Modernists whose fragmented and elliptical narratives captured her
restless longing to smash up the world around her. Her hair was

honey-blonde and her lipstick was Mulberry Red Night. She married Owen Lieb on a day in June too cold for the season, and wore a pale lemon suit of wool bouclé. Her first novel was published when she was twenty-six. Her son was born two years later. Her husband would abandon her soon after. Still, she would and did become for a while the perfect housewife in the last house left at the end of the world; with her marinated lamb medallions in the oven, fat tomatoes and snap peas on the counter awaiting the descent of the knife, her garlic cloves hanging by the window in the kitchen to ward off unwanted vampires, her vodka in the orchard at dusk just as the crows became insufferable so that to sit, to drink there as peaceful as it should have been under the heavy branches laden with apples, tart and bittersweet hanging from boughs lush and full, threatening to fall and upset her glass of vodka like clear burning water—as perfect as all this should have been, it was not; the crows screamed and seemed to herald in the gathering darkness the nightly procession of the dead.

In the end the pieces of a life should add up to something; a Rosetta stone, a semantic key, a decoder ring, x-ray spectacles for backward-looking. Marcel Proust was fond of admitting that he preferred the telescope to the microscope. The only thing of which Liz Warren remained certain over the years was that despite how it may have seemed to the outside world, Owen Lieb loved Franny as much in the beginning as at the end. Perhaps it was Elisabeth's vehemence, her unwavering belief in undying romance that led some followers of the affair to suppose a scenario in which Franny Lieb did not die, but finally and with the aid of Owen escaped her life to live anonymously in a village in Italy. It is a wild supposition. But if Owen Lieb couldn't have saved her, could anyone? Her parents, Frederick and Delphine Warren, opposed her marriage, not because of Owen per se; it was only that she had always been such a serious girl, it was hard to believe she had grown so silly for a tall, dark, poetry-quoting stranger. Her mother, who after her husband's death began to pore over his psychology texts as though searching for him in the pages, continued his study until her own death in 1970. She asserted to Susan Rhys, Franny's first biographer, that her daughter's fixation on Owen Lieb was the ugly result of an obsession with the Holocaust admixed with and heightened by being the child of a German father at a particularly difficult time for Germans. It was not so much a problem that Owen was a Jew; it was that Franny loved him not despite this failing, but for it. Elisabeth when describing years later her first meeting with Owen, that fateful lunch when they had all breathlessly agreed that it would be wonderful to one day live as an expatriate in Paris, in London, or among the canals of Venice; she recollected that Franny even then called him only by his surname. *He is my fate,* Franny wrote. *He is my heart. Is it not perfect? One of us will destroy the other and be made a better person for it.* Owen Lieb, twenty-four when he married twenty-two-year-old Franny Warren, was cursed from the beginning, everybody said, with Cassandra's gift. He from the beginning foresaw the terrible end but was unable to stop it, so he gave himself over to the inevitability of the cards he did not need to read. He had loved her once. No one doubted this. This was impossible to doubt.

Galapagos Islands

It may have come to your attention that sometimes when I address you my mind is elsewhere, that is, on someone else. And I'm not referring to the notion of an idealized reader out there hidden in the stacks of the library moistly thumbing pages, but I am speaking, or rather, writing this for the benefit of someone for whom you are the unlikely replacement. You've been a good sport, standing in, always a little suspect but willing to give it a try nonetheless. Haven't you ever been alone at a party and seen someone on the other side of the room gesturing to you, mouthing words, and you turn to find it was not your attention he was seeking but the girl standing behind you? Or the one off to your left? Someone *almost* but not quite you? It was nice, wasn't it, to briefly stand in place of that stranger, to intercept the message through the grenade-like popping of beer tabs? Do you remember how I said that I didn't copy or cheat? That all I had to commend me was my honest albeit ugly nature? Well, I lied. And how I may have mentioned that when the story is over, finished, the book slammed shut, we might get together you and I, and have drinks on the veranda of a hotel with fashionable striped, perhaps green and deep maroon, awnings? Well, to be truthful, that wasn't exactly you whom I was addressing. It was someone else, already a memory. We did sit and drink coffee, and I remember being utterly miserable, the way one is at the end when there has been no middle, only a prolapsed beginning. We talked about books, I think, and politics. In the beginning there is always time to stop, although it is difficult to discern, to separate out a minute or moment from the rest and say authoritatively: this is when I should have turned back. How could I have known that it would be from this disaster that I would stumble across an ocean to the next one? We sat on the veranda. It happened like this. I was twenty years old and trying to seem worldly as I spooned sugar into my coffee. The click of the silver against the china announced the silence of an unsurprising ending. Newton Graves sat across from me. Do you recognize his name? Have you read his books? He is insightful, though perhaps too unremittingly negative for some personal tastes; his outlook is grim but his prose style is infectious. He had recently published a book on journalistic ethics in a fame-craving culture. He was lucky, people said, to have found both appreciation and success at an early age. And his popularity had led to a lecturing tour of colleges and universities. Only he didn't feel particularly lucky; he felt rather sick, in both the meta and physical senses. He sneezed into a handkerchief. My spoon clinked the cup. He coughed. He wore awkwardly the mantle of spokesman for a disenfranchised generation. No, that's not quite right. He wore it like a noose. Newton Graves, he was barely thirty and was already considered an expert on so many improbable topics. He was working on something, he intimated, having to do with the inherent pornography of disaster narratives.

And what, you may ask, could be dishonest or disingenuous about such a scene? Did we skip out on the bill? Fail to tip? When, please tell me, when does the noose tighten? We stumbled upon each other by accident. Antihistamine packages lined his pockets in preparation for the treatment of myriad and mysterious symptoms. Sore throat? Chest congestion? Sinus pressure? He was a disaster waiting to happen: a shipwreck, midair collision, an avalanche, an epidemic. And I was caught up in what seemed more like a battle than a romance with a pedantic graduate student who valued the very morals that Newton Graves espoused but in such a convoluted context, such a perverted manifestation that it is safe to say the only thing the two had in common was a belief in truth. My spoon hit the cup. Newton Graves swallowed his bitter pills with coffee. This is a sad scene indeed for two young outcasts, rife with guilt and allergies, with desire and obligation alike. It was a chapter for his book. Who could imagine it would come to be one in mine as well? Say that with all of our beliefs and theories, with his ethos of ethics and my self-right-eous circumstance, either of us could have walked away at any moment. He wore my secondhand guilt like the curiosity it was; a hairshirt, a plot twist, a science experiment, a complicated bouton-niere of blue daisies, a beauty queen's tiara. I may in the future ask you to play the part of my accomplice, or rather my stunt double, to stand in at the top of the stairs and in place of his kiss please insert a memory of your own; one that, say, could have changed the course of your life if only you had turned your face toward him instead of against, if you had not pushed your way past him down the stairs and through the lobby which once impressed you as so grand and stately; now it seems only an inconvenient blur. The piano, velvet sofas, and bellhops form an obstacle course as you dash to the door. When one speaks of betrayal and deceit, is it best to put it in con-text? Is it a justification or an obfuscation to say: I was young and miserable. Or better to be philosophical and ruminate not on who did what to whom, but on the nature of the invisible boundary crossed? Perhaps it is true that for all of my sincere imitations of the world, I know that I am not to be trusted. And him? Newton Graves? He's no better than a ghost. If I address him through you, if my mind wanders, it is because of our shared guilt and complicity, nothing more. Do you believe me? No? No, I don't either. Maybe it's time to put it all behind me and get back to the real story. Brigid and I surveyed the house, room by room, and decided to begin with the dust. I left his hotel room. He followed me. It was late, past three in the morning. No other doors opened. He caught me on the stairs and kissed me and I turned my face to the wall. I ran through the lobby of the hotel whose awnings were striped forest-green and wine-red. And after that we saw each other any number of times and never again mentioned it, and we talked about books or politics or acquaintances in common and once even had dinner. The service was awful. He said that living out east had made him impatient. He was leaving the country soon; was restless to go. He complained about the collapse of the world. I was drinking wine and taking it upon myself to feel pity for the overburdened waitress. He lighted a cigarette. He buttered a piece of bread and handed it to me, a gesture that I multiplied into a thousand kisses in the stairwells of a thousand hotels while a thousand bellboys in gabardine jackets typed for a thousand years the complete works of William Shakespeare. I unwound the crust from the bread. There were wars. He talked about them. Men do that sometimes. Butter clung to my fingers. I was drunk. I picked at my food. I wasn't hungry. I had seen him take girls by the arm and whisper to them. I knew it was the most ridiculous of gestures. He paid the bill and the waitress made some cheerful comment or other to which he responded rudely, but with such stern authority that I felt I would follow you, no, no, *him,* anywhere. We walked then, not arm-in-arm, not so much as touching, not discussing our destination but knowing that all roads lead to Rome; we walked slowly, methodically from the restaurant as the evening darkened to the same hotel where the maids had long since changed the linens on our disheveled bed, and we sat on the veranda even though it was too cold for it and ordered coffee. He looked out at the lawns. He dared me silently. It was just as ridiculous as it sounds, scrawled textwise across his face: *just mention it, just say it, and I'll leave.* I said only: *the cream has gone sour, I think.* He flagged down the busboy. And he ordered fruit that we picked at with our cold fingers like the ones in the Melville story, disembodied, unbanded, stripped clean of gold and rings. You would have been proud of me. I held my own in the conversation even though I was young and had not been anywhere or done anything. I talked about how men write too many books. He smoked. He pretended he didn't care. He said that once he had met a deaf girl on a train in Austria or was it Germany? And that one should travel and how she was the most beautiful girl he had ever seen, but he wouldn't go on about that. He said that one should see the world. And that if men sometimes had to write books for the sake of money, how could I understand that? The coffee was rather bitter but the boy came back with fresh cream and I poured some in my cup and into his until the coffee became something else entirely, rich and sweet; evening was darkening until we could no longer see the wide lawns and the busboy lighted the candles on the other tables but not on ours as though he knew not to disturb us. There was no one else there. It was October. All of the other tables were empty. The candles flickered like a thousand fireflies, like the rockets' red glare, the bombs bursting in air. He didn't like jokes. There were wars. In all the hot dry countries of the globe people were suffering as we spoke. There were serious things in the world. There were disasters that we watched on television in our living rooms for entertainment. He said the world was no place for a girl like me, and I had to agree with him. He was already becoming someone else, *you,* in fact; he was becoming less and less like himself. While I became an exaggeration, a badly timed punch line, miserable and cold and no longer even drunk enough to take pity on myself. Unwilling to leave, we sat for a long time in silence. The clash of my spoon against the china. His coughs and unapologetic sneezes. He said it was the dust, the autumn damp. He said he would drive me home. And we left the veranda together for the last time. We walked down the street lined with elm and yew and willows. He studied me with the concern of a spectator. I was his disaster; not because of any of the reasons that a girl hopes for, not because I was young or pretty, tragic, complicated or mysterious, but because I was unreliable. He never knew what I was going to do next. I was like a soldier in an old movie sneaking across enemy lines. I did not think before I acted. We stood beside his car. He searched his pockets for the keys. He said something sympathy-eliciting about how it was a rental like everything else in his life. This was the beginning of a well-worn farewell speech. But I didn't stay to hear it or to watch the gentlemanly way he would certainly open the door for me. I took off running. Before he could call out, before he could wave good-bye, I was running homeward without looking back, breathlessly through the black night all the way home along those wide tree-lined avenues of the Middle West where behind curtains houselights dimmed at eight and were extinguished by ten, where October was damp and dark and dismal and already ripe with rotting pumpkins on porches, where the only thing left to do was to run home without stopping. I ran because while he was so many things, a displaced, no, a misplaced person who had been a good many places, knew people, had read important books, written highly regarded theories and could speak with calm authority on any number of topics from postcolonialism to predetermination, I ran because I was young and had only in my favor the element of surprise.

I should have been relieved when he finally as promised left the country. It should have been easy, a matter of postcards briefly exchanged and summarily forgotten, the inevitable lost addresses, smeared ink on holiday cards. How difficult can it be, I ask you, to quietly fall out of the world? But Newton Graves was careful about documentation; he was preparing for the arrival of his inevitable biographer. He sent me a krone strung on a chain as a good luck charm: *In case you ever need bus fare out of Elsinore.* I suppose he told jokes after all. I never felt that we were alone together, even on paper. I always felt the force of history, the book-strained eyes of a thousand researchers looking, peering through the windows, reading between the lines, peeking over my shoulder to see where he paused to rest his pen. Was I paranoid? Self-aggrandizing? Did I await the future he prophesied: *a boot stepping on a face forever?* I took care in my letters to strike the right tone, careless and irreverent, never implying anything beyond the common connection of our mutual disdain for the disheveled marriage bed of the Western world, once rose-petaled with promiscuities, now threadbare and soiled. He left Denmark for Germany. In Berlin the Wall came down. He wrote to me: *It was a colossal fraternity party. Sausages were sold. Mistakes were made. We are sewing up the raw rape of the twentieth century and expecting it to bear the force of a billion brutal fistfucks.* His impending arrival in each destination seemed to herald turmoil, collapsing regimes, floods, hurricanes, riots, bombs bursting in air. I wrote to him: *So you've gone and done it? Slipped the noose of the country? Left me here in the mournful Midwest to await word of safe passage? And what will I do to bide the time? Watch professional figure skating, diagram sentences, knit tea cozies, leave trails of breadcrumbs, cross days off the calendar, begin tunneling out of the basement with a soupspoon? Have pity. I'm trying, as you can see, to be cheerful, to be high-minded, to keep from tipping over from the weight of the world. I think I will not move from this exact spot until you return. Please hurry back. As someone will have to feed the cat.* In Paris there was a garbage strike. From Barcelona he sent a postcard: *I saw the Pope perform Christmas Mass in Rome. A shower of Holy Water rained down from heaven, and I caught the flu. I seem to be composed entirely of antibiotics. Where can we go? Is there any truly hot, dry, and amoral place left in the world? Tangiers? The Gobi? It's hopeless, Fern, no? Let's disappear. Let's get lost. Let's sell the farm and move to Hollywood.* I suspected that each letter sent would be the last. I tried to be serious, to be like one of those letter-writers who discussed not herself but the brave ideas of her time. Or characters in novels who over the span of generations let unfold the narrative of their lives through the exchange of penned confessions. But I kept forgetting that that was the stuff of fiction, and we, of course, despite and in spite of our best attempts otherwise continued to exist in the real world. I wrote: *I have tracked down and read the article that you suggested. In regards to the impending rise of the technological novel, the best one I can think of is already a hundred years old. It is very sad indeed that Dr. Frankenstein must chase his monster to the ends of the Arctic because the delete key had not yet been invented; but the assumption that the monster is a mere typo makes me wonder if it was a special radioactive ink developed in the lab of Bruce Banner, belted by gamma rays. I think suspension of disbelief is a specious notion that undermines the random nature of events that compose what we have come to call reality. I think it is an insult to imply that we expect from fiction the unexpected; and from life presume, no, demand the expected. Is it so hard to see the leap from mild-mannered Dr. Banner to his alter ego? Is it so difficult to believe reality is the alter ego of fiction, capable of all the same crimes? Or the worst crimes of all, inconsistency and lack of plot? Hulk smash it.* He responded: *Are you testing your new theories on me or watching too much Saturday morning television? Either way, how flattering. How goddamned interesting. Please tell me what, if anything, you are wearing.* For each letter I sent him, he mailed a response. Sometimes as little as a week passed for a letter to make it halfway around the world; a month or more would lapse without word. And with each letter that for me began to symbolize the absence of what was once so briefly, so unsuccessfully, so, so, *us,* I longed for the lack of letters just as I longed for the lack of his absence. I feared that even though we existed through distance and could discuss only the space around ourselves, he felt an unwarranted obligation to me. Perhaps we mistakenly believed that letters would and could come to replace the people we had once been until we were fictionalized versions, replacements of ourselves. And slowly by degrees (was it the gnawing guilt? the ragged infection sewn raw?), the way one reconstructs a story or reconstitutes frozen orange juice with cans of cold water, it was I who began to feel obligation. Perhaps not even to him, perhaps only to our narrative. And I wanted no more of it. I couldn't imagine what he looked like beyond the photos on his book jackets. *Dearest, I wrote, I am concerned about you. Are you taking your vitamins? You don't sound like yourself. Where's that joie de vivre, that je ne sais quoi, that preapocalyptic postcolonial desultory sang-froid murder-and-create fuck-and-smash-it-all bitter-best-bested wit and charm on which I could so depend to get me through the dark damp winter? I am tired of politeness. I am tired of words. Do you have any charts, graphs, or Venn diagrams instead? Do you have any photographs in which you do not look deep in contemplation of the woes of man? Surely, you must have one or two from spring break at Fort Lauderdale—wearing a neon muscle T? Dancing with a life-size beer bottle? Symptoms of endless winter include: dry mouth, shortness of breath, disorientation, abdominal cramping, and déjà vu. Are you following the lead of the great Dostoevsky himself and going underground? Do you write before the firing squad in the village square? I emulate creepy Mr. Kafka, who wore a hard candy shell, an insect's husk hiding a rich chocolate center, torturously sitting at a desk lost amongst other legions of likewise desk-sitters. Yes, I am here, right where the latest plot twist has left me, right where you found me; in the library suffering from a cold compounded by a fever, from the gray of the season, from as dear Jacques Lacan himself would readily announce, from the absolute lack of you.* He was undeterred. *Poor Ophelia,* he wrote. *Are the nunneries full up? Hardware stores out of mortal coils? Surely there must be a pill that you can take for your condition? A topical ointment? A plane ticket? Tired of tuning your dial to the oldies station? Longing for a little latitude? Poor bride of Frankenstein, fed up with white dresses and drafty castles? Shall I send you some grand palliative from Copenhagen? Something sweet and dry and flammable? A volume of De Quincey perhaps? I am writing this at three A.M., so you will excuse, won't you, my gauche and left-handed late-night intimacy when I ask: did I detect a note of honest-to-God fondness in your last missive?* And then. Letter after letter. We were bitter and entangled. We could not break free from each other. It was sickness. It was addiction. It was disaster. I couldn't tell his words from my own. I wrote: *We at home in the US of A are growing fat on our dreams of betrayal. We will hereafter follow our Teutonic cohorts to the chopping block speaking only in the passive voice. I give up. Everything was denied. Nothing was revealed. Mistakes were made. As the girls say as they stumble out of the frat house with their panties crammed in their purses: up was given. In Italian the verb "piacere" (to like, to prefer, to enjoy) is a passive construction formed with an inverted subject and object. Did you know? We come by pleasure so passively sometimes we forget being forgotten.* I don't even know what I meant by any of it. I lost track of time. His letters ceased. How long had it been? One month or six? Before I left for my own trip, my disastrous European adventure, I sent a letter to his last address. Still, I imagined that I would run into him, stumble upon him as on some ruin of the past, a cathedral, the Coliseum, the Spanish Steps, and it would be so funny really, to become in person the people who wrote letters rather than the ghosts who existed in and as only letters. I wrote: *I have begun to think that you are a figment of my imagination, assembled entirely out of spirit gum and balsa wood like those model airplanes that flew in loop-de-loops over our heads in grade-school classrooms. Assembled bravely by your own invention of crabapples, ferrous sulfate, and the ground bones of the innocent. Where are you? I receive no word or answer. I take it as some grand cosmic practical joke. A chair pulled out beneath me. Chewing gum that tastes of pepper. A sign. A portent. A trick done with dry ice, rope, and mirrors. To whom it may concern: I am writing this to the invisible man. Please send word when you find the antidote. Please send a message when you wash ashore.*

Maybe I had the wrong address. Maybe he moved. Maybe he imagined that it was I who stopped sending letters. Someone had to. Maybe he had grown tired of me. Maybe he suffered from dehydration, fell on a land mine, joined a revolution, lost himself in a hurricane off a tropical coast, embraced socialism, hurled gasoline-soaked rags in a breakaway republic on the other side of the world. Maybe he was writing screenplays in Hollywood. Maybe he had long-since ceased to feel that catgut fine thread of obligation that had sewn us together. Maybe he simply forgot about me. After all, what is the space of a few adulterous hours against the timepiece of life? We were drunk together on the bed in a hotel room. He read to me from his latest ink-scarred manifesto. You lifted my dress over my head. Up (we collapsed down on each other) was (forgive us these idiocies, these sometime sins of textual intercourse) given. I was not aware until later that I had memorized the words. Your trousers lay for a long time in a heap on the floor entangled with my dress until little by little, your shirt, the typewritten pages, my black bra with unfastened catch, a fallen wristwatch that had silently tocked the untimely undoing began to untick; all these things began to disappear. It was almost as though none of it ever happened. No striped awnings. No beginnings. No letters to re-create the way we used to speak to each other about books or politics or acquaintances in common. No cocktail party after his lecture when I was the girl so briefly, so suddenly into whose ear he whispered: *Wait?* No staircase. No part A inserted memorywise into part B to light and to fuse and to assemble and to create and to dissolve the drama and trauma of an idiotic chain of events that comes to mean, actually mean, less and less, the more I reconstitute it with leaking cans of cold water. The waiter, no, no, the busboy brought the cream and lighted the candles. You suffered once, twice to run your hand the length of my bare hip like a train on a track which carried as a passenger a beautiful deaf girl home to Austria or was it Germany? You stopped sending me letters. I graduated from college and my parents who were morally upstanding and financially secure sent me to Europe to separate me from the harmful influence of the boy I had long since betrayed, because as everyone agrees, it is so important to travel and to see the world.

Hollywood

"Why cleaning?" asked Brigid.

I found a ladder and with a long-handled broom untangled cobwebs from the ceiling. In the chaos of the sunny and once-grand great drawing room Brigid sat in the window seat looking out at the orchard. "Have you ever seen a day like this? It's pure decadence. It's almost obscene, don't you think? And I don't mean 'why are you cleaning this house.' I mean how did you become the sort of person who cleans houses in general? Am I prying? Is this too personal? You should tell me if I'm prying, honestly. You are being careful up there, aren't you? I don't want to have to explain to O how it is that you have been with us for two days and already I've broken you to bits."

I found spiderwebs, shriveled flies, hard blackened knots of indecipherable soot.

"Why cleaning?" repeated Brigid. "My mother," she continued, "was, is, an absolute clean freak, like in the commercials—scrubbing the bathtub in pearls and a tennis skirt. I think she may have been addicted to Lysol. She may have chewed cakes of bleach to brighten her smile. They say the cleaning gene skips a generation. I don't have any patience for it. I wouldn't have started with the ceiling. I never look up when I can look down. Do you know what I mean? I would have started with the floor. So was your mother one of them?"

Dust dislodged downward.

"One of what?"

"Oh you know, are you enacting some ritual of childhood? Did you have to vacuum the family room every Saturday for your allowance?"

"We had a cleaning lady," I said.

"How many days?" she asked.

"How many days?" I repeated.

"A week," she said.

"I don't know, three, maybe? Does it matter?"

"It all matters," said Brigid.

She paused, chewed on her thumbnail, frowned, smiled, continued.

"What do they do," she asked, "these clean-housed parents of yours? What do they do for a living?"

"My father is a lawyer," I said. "And my mother, she teaches—" I set down the broom for a moment, crosswise on the top of the ladder. "She teaches conversational English to foreign businessmen."

"Really?" said Brigid. "Where?"

"Where what?"

"Does she hold her classes, where?"

"At home," I said.

"Well there you go," she said. "There you have it. You had to have a maid, didn't you? Your home was a workplace. My mother had no excuse."

"For what?"

"For her addiction to Mop & Glo, her torrid soap-operatic affair with Mr. Clean, for," she waved her hand, "her germ-free existence."

"I used to watch them," I said.

"Who?" she asked.

"The businessmen—"

"Yes, yes," she said. "Was it just like in the movies? Did they wear lovely dark suits, drink Earl Grey tea?"

"She taught them business clichés, you know, self-help talk and sports jargon. I don't even know where she learned those expressions, from a book probably, or she took a class in it. I think she took a class in it. I don't think anyone really speaks that way, do they?"

"So she untaught them," said Brigid. "*Unschooling,* that's American, isn't it? You forget things like that when you are away for a while. It's amazing what you can forget if you set your mind to it. What else are you trying to forget?"

"I didn't say—"

"Of course you didn't," she said. "But that doesn't mean it isn't so. Sisters? Brothers?"

"Brothers," I said.

"More than one?"

"Four."

"Good God," she said. "That's a lot of bacon to be brung, brought, home and fried up in the pan. And pets? Cats, dogs, reptiles? Ferrets? Turtles?"

"My brothers were, are allergic."

"All of them? One out of four? Two out of three? And to everything? To turtles? My mother, aforementioned clean freak, didn't like animals in the house, but finally conceded to allow a cat if it was very, very, very white. In the end I think she grew to admire Snowball, who spent so much of her time involved in feline hygiene, although my mother would never use a phrase like *feline hygiene* because it sounds far too much like *feminine hygiene,*" she paused. "But you're not allergic?"

"No," I said.

"That's good," she said. "Because we seem to have had a cat adopt us. Have you seen the cat?" she asked. "Do you think we should name her?"

I said, no, I didn't know where the gray cat had gone to.

"Am I being too exacting, too penetrating?" she asked. "I'm so sorry if I am. I just haven't had anyone trapped in my presence long enough to bestow a good old-fashioned brow-beating. Do you promise to tell me when I get too insufferable?"

The cat crept unnamed into the room.

"I *am* bothering you," she said. "I can tell, but I'm afraid that it isn't in my nature to stop unless you ask me to, and I can tell that it isn't in your nature to ask. So what can we do but continue?"

The cat leapt onto the window seat, stared at the ceiling, crawled onto Brigid's lap, closed her eyes, and yawned.

"Isn't she lucky," said Brigid. "Do you think that you are?"

"Lucky?" I said.

"I sometimes wonder if I am," she said.

There was no question for me to answer. I picked up the broom.

She continued, "I've got it now. The thing is, I've been thinking about it all backwards, backwardly, it isn't *cleaning*. That's the point. You aren't doing it because you like it, but as punishment. You see, you see, I was thinking about my mother and why she cleans and I might have missed the entire point. Isn't that awful," she said. She rested an elbow on her knee and her face on her hand. She rubbed at the mottled gray fur of the sleeping cat with her other hand. "Isn't it horrible—to be so trapped by the past?"

"I fell into it. I didn't plan to—"

She tilted her face, chinwise, from side to side, still held in the palm of her open hand. "But don't you see," she said. "There is always a reason behind the lack of reason. Sometimes it's a matter of going back far enough to find the circumstance that put you in the position to allow random circumstances to be a guiding force in your life." She picked up the cat, kissed her ear, and then set her down again full in the afternoon sun. "Do you think we were destined to meet?" she asked.

I fumbled trying to reach a corner. The broom slipped from my hands and fell to the floor with a clatter. The cat opened her eyes, seemed to consider leaving, but decided after a moment that her present location was too wonderful to abandon. She closed her eyes and curled sideways.

"Don't let my questions bother you," said Brigid. "It's only a game. I'm afraid that we, that Owen and I have gotten so insular, that any hint of the world outside of us, ourselves, stuns us. Really we came out here to work. Owen wants to be far away from civilization. Do you want to know what sort of book it is on which I am working? For the completion of which he has dragged me away from the bright lights of Paris?"

"A novel?" I said.

She shook her head. "Do you promise that you won't tell anyone?"

I said, yes; I promised that I wouldn't tell.

"I trust you," she said. "I don't know you, but I trust you. And, of course, you don't know us yet, but somehow I can tell that we will all get along perfectly, the three of us. I feel quite safe in announcing that there is now a *three of us.*"

Brigid placed her hand up against the windowpane.

"Tell me something," she said. She turned slightly in her seat, palm still flat against the window. "Tell me what it's like to be Jewish?"

Owen came down the stairs. He was dressed in funereal charcoal gray.

"You aren't leaving already, are you?" asked Brigid.

He came to her. He took her face in his hands like a doctor studying a mysterious complaint in a young patient.

"How are you?" he asked. "You're flushed," he said. "Do you have a fever?"

"No, no," she said. "I'm sitting in the sun, that's all."

"And you'll be—"

"—fine if you go, honestly, if you absolutely must go then I'll resolve to be fine," she said. "At least until you get back."

"Has she been," he turned to me. He paused as though uncomfortable repeating his wife's choice of words. "Does she seem *fine?* Will you make sure she doesn't get over-excited?"

"Owen," said Brigid to me, "talks about me as though I am not here."

"Brigid," said Owen, "talks about herself as though she is not here."

"Fern is being absolutely wonderful," said Brigid. "She is toler-
ating my interrogation. She will promise, won't you, to take perfect
care of me?" And with that Brigid picked up and again kissed the cat
who suffered this indignity with a sleepy open-mouthed yawn. "We
have been reminiscing about the good gone days of white girlhood.
Do you know that every time a lucky contestant spun the prize
wheel on *The Price Is Right* I thought that it would never stop spinning? Honestly. Can you imagine? Do you remember that commercial where Madge says that she is smoking in it—"

"*Soaking in it*—" I interjected. "I think."

"Really?" asked Brigid. "Soaking in dish-soap? Why would anyone do that? It's insane. It's idiotic. Are you sure? Owen, is she right?"

He looked at his watch. She set down the cat. He kissed Brigid
on the forehead and spoke low into her ear. He turned and said
good-bye to me. It was not an unpleasant good-bye. There was nothing unusual to it, and yet his accompanying parting glance gave me
pause. It was a slight, sharp look. He left, and Brigid rose from her
orchard-facing window seat and went to the other side of the room.
She watched him drive away.

"He told me to be sure to take my medicine on time," she said.
"That's what he said when he whispered. He didn't mean to be rude.
It only means that he trusts you, because he doesn't like to leave me
alone. He's going to pick up supplies, you know, shoring up for winter and all that. We are going to try our best to be good recluses,
dutiful hermits and shut out the world, did I mention that part
already? Did I tell you that I am writing a book?"

"Yes," I said.

"Owen has left us for the day," she said. "He won't be back until
tomorrow and tomorrow and tomorrow. He thinks," she crossed her
eyes, "can you believe it? That I am crazy. And it's hard to fault him,"
she said. "I mean, with his history. It can't be easy, can it?"

And with that, she smiled and said she would be right back and left the room, but only for the kitchen. She returned moments later with two glasses of lemonade. She handed one to me and sipped at hers while wandering the length of the room. She paused to touch the wallpaper, the windowpane, the time-faded tapestry of an upholstered chair. It occurred to me that she had not yet had a moment to believe this house was her own. She had not been free, not until Owen had left her there alone, to finger the dust, to rub a thumb idly against the length of the sofa, trace the engraving of the staircase banister. I turned back to the work into which, according to my host and employer, I had fatefully allowed myself to fall. Brigid studied the wine-dark wallpaper. It was patterned with crimson and gold flowers curling into green vines. It peeled majestically around the wooden baseboards. At the far end of the large room a sheet was tacked over the wall. Brigid looked at me. She looked at the sheet. She went and stood before it like a magician's assistant or like *The Price Is Right* girls just at the moment before the big prize showcase is revealed to the studio audience: ahhh! Brigid reached up, tugged at a corner, and with one gesture the sheet fell away to expose its concealed secret.

A great stone fireplace with a carved mahogany mantel appeared where the sheet had been. Above the mantel, itself supported by two smooth wooden pillars, was a large bevel-edged mirror framed on either side by iron candle sconces wrought into the shape of Cupid with arrow poised upward. The intention was such that when the candle was set in place the light would be drawn upward from Cupid's quiver. The mottled mirror was inlaid with a border of stained glass, grapes intertwined with stars and flowers. The hearthstones were soot-scarred. And the twin Cupids grinned. I saw the room—its golden-vine entangled wallpaper, the weary worn chairs and glass-domed lamps, the windows facing the orchard, the dust and decay which was composed, or rather decomposed, of the substance of biographical mystery, hair and skin, eyelashes, sordid mementos of other lives.

"It's so beautiful," said Brigid, "that I can hardly stand to look at it. Or do you think it's ugly? Maybe it's not beautiful at all. Maybe it's hideous."

She ran her hands over the cold stones. I came down from my perch on the ladder to stand there with her on the sea-green hearth tile before the grate. Still, the size of the fireplace and mantel was so great, so outsized that standing there before it we could barely see the top of our heads in the mirror. Brigid dragged from across the room a velveteen chair, and I understood. I followed her with its mate. We stood on the chairs before the fireplace. We stood there like two naughty children when mother was away.

"I'm getting old," said Brigid.

"Me too," I said to her reflection.

She laughed. She leaned over and lightly kissed my smudged cheek.

"Hey grimy," she said. She watched herself wipe the dirt from my face with a spit-dampened thumb. She smoothed down my hair and then her own. It felt oddly as though we were awaiting our school pictures. "Are you ready," she asked, "to go through the looking glass? Are you afraid of what, of who awaits us on the other side?"

I didn't answer. I looked at us. Her fine face tightened in anticipation of the clicking of an invisible shutter. Nothing happened. No sign. No portent. The afternoon continued to be unremittingly sunny. The cat continued to sleep. The Cupids did not blink. And just when I was most fearful for her, for Brigid, when it seemed that we had stood there forever, for hours and hours, but it was really only a moment—she sighed and said we would never get through the mirror this way; that things never happen when you want or expect them.

"We will have to wait," she said. "Maybe you only know you've gone through it when you are on the other side, when it is too late to go back. Does that make sense?"

"No," I admitted. "Not really."

She stepped down from her chair.

"The truth," she said. "Finally. I don't mind hearing the truth. It's all this whispering, the intimations—that I find so damned annoying. As though it's easy, any of this. As though—" She broke off. "Are you thirsty?" she asked. "Would you like more lemonade? I would. I mean, I am. I do. I'm absolutely parched."

Owen would return the next day in the late afternoon. He would arrive bearing bags of groceries, with dry supplies of flour, sugar, oatmeal, and salt; fruits and fresh vegetables; the trunk heavy with canned goods. And while Brigid was organizing her kitchen and the adjoining little pantry, he asked me to help him in the garden. Brigid at first protested, insisted that she needed me indoors, but then she became caught up in the drama of her cupboards (tins, cans, glass jars of jam certainly shouldn't go on the high shelves. What if they fell and smacked right down on someone's head? What then, she lamented. And what about sugar? She used so much of it that Owen suggested she should fashion a little sack to wear around her neck and spoon it up immediately as she so desired.). Brigid lost track of time. She lost track of me, and I went out to the orchard where Owen was splitting wood. He set me to work collecting tinder in the form of dry twigs, sticks, and bark. I proceeded in silence to do his bidding, heaping up my splinters near the woodpile. After a while he stopped and asked me with no preface, "What did she tell you?" And in the orchard while the afternoon sun began to wane until it was almost too cold to sit among the trees, I told him what Brigid had said to me in the kitchen over lemonade the previous day. He nodded and we spoke then as though we had known each other for a long time and there were no secrets between us.

Brigid poured out the lemonade. She had mixed it up herself from bottled lemon juice and sugar and so apologized if it was one or the other, too sweet, too sour. I thanked her for the glass.

She rapped her fingers against the table distractedly.

"I think I'm sick," she said. She placed a hand on her forehead. "Feel," she implored. I reached across the table and rested a hand briefly on her forehead.

"Well?" she said.

"No fever," I told her.

She seemed disappointed.

"Do you want to know about my book?" she asked. She lowered her voice. "It's a biography, you know."

"A biography?"

She nodded. "I have to be so careful these days. You wouldn't believe how competitive biographers are. It's a shame, really. I think biographers must be the most bloodthirsty species on earth, like the vampire bat but less charming. And they can eat twice their own weight in human flesh, like wolverines, but less, you know—"

"Charming?"

"Exactly," she said.

"Do wolverines eat people, really?" I asked.

"The funny part of it all," she continued, "is that I never liked biographies myself. I found them tawdry. It always seemed to me that the authors, the *biographers,* stood behind, hid behind the idea of the truth of their subject as though to shirk the responsibility that comes with dreams, you know, with fiction."

"Then how," I ventured, "then why are you writing a biography?"

"That's a good question," she said. "That is the best question. Is one born a biographer or does one have biography thrust upon her?

Sometimes you feel like a nut," she shrugged, "sometimes you don't."

She graced me with her smile.

"One day out of nowhere—it just dawned on me: biography. I hadn't been looking for it. Of course, *biography*, as though there had never been anything in my life before it. It was like falling in love at first-sight with someone you've seen a million times, and yet you can't imagine never having not loved that person. There is no need to ask *why*. It is simply *of course, of course*. Maybe that's how cleaning is for you—cleaning, *of course*. Something that you fell into because it was awaiting you. Does this, does any of this make sense?"

I nodded.

"Do you remember a book," she asked. "I was thinking about this on the plane. Owen was no help at all. About two children, a brother and sister, who run away from home and live in a museum? They sleep in a Louis Quatorze bed and bathe in the coin fountain. Does it sound familiar?"

"And they pack their clothes in a violin case?" I asked.

"Oh exactly," she agreed. "Owen kept insisting that I was talking about Nancy Drew. He was only doing it to annoy me. Can you imagine Nancy running away from home, let alone washing in a public coin fountain? And from what would she ever have to run? The haunted clock tower? The phantom tollbooth?"

"Ned?"

"Ned and Nancy," she sighed.

"Yes," I said.

"That's how I feel," she said.

"Like Nancy Drew?"

"As though I am living in a museum."

"But the children loved the museum, didn't they?"

"I realized," she said, "that I had everything backward. I didn't hate biography. I hated fiction. I hated the pretense of the novel—an excuse to fill pages with endless details about the past—or present—

either way, an excuse, a device to describe in detail corsets and shoes or illustrate the shores of exotic beaches. At least in biography there is no pretense. It is the story of a particular person in the context of a particular moment in history. And so history is a character, not an excuse. Although there are still good novels and bad novels, good biographies and bad biographies, but that is another issue entirely."

"Whose biography," I asked, "are you working on?"

She put a finger to her lips. "It's all very hush-hush."

"I'm sorry," I said.

"I'm joking," she said. "Actually I'm not joking, but I trust you. Just promise me that in return you'll tell me sometime your deepest, darkest secret. Is it a deal?"

"I'll try," I said. "But—"

"You don't have any secrets?" she asked.

"Not good ones, no. Not deep, dark ones."

"Well," she said. "Then it will be that much easier for you to hold up your end of the bargain, won't it? It's hard to believe anyone these days. Do you know that back in Paris we have this lovely flat—with a maid who cooked, who baked for God's sake, the most perfect flourless chocolate cake—but Owen was so suspicious of, of, of, I don't know what, of her *perfection,* I suppose, that he fired her. We were helpless without her, and worse, lazy. And then we, he, decided we'd be better off getting out of the city. So here we are. Here we are in this house full of horror stories. You can feel them, can't you? Practically seeping out of the walls, the stories? I'm so happy that we have found you. I'm afraid that I am going to have to tell you everything."

"Isn't cake without flour really just pudding?" I asked.

"Don't try to change the subject," she said. "I think you are trying to change the subject. What is the point of having a secret if you don't reveal it? What's the point of having a story if you can't tell it?"

She reached across the table and put her hand on my arm.

"Do you like stories?" she asked.

I nodded. She removed her hand. She traced with a finger the damp ring left by the lemonade glass on the table.

"Here is a story then. Are you ready?"

"Yes," I said.

"Did she tell you about her grandmother?" Owen would ask me.

And in the rot of the garden where the last of the sunlight diffused through the leaves of the trees to speckle the path and woodpile, Owen lighted a cigarette.

"Yes," I said.

"And about her grandfather?"

"That too," I said.

"Do you believe her?"

I waited a moment.

"I can't have you judging her," he said.

He tossed his cigarette to the ground.

"Have you read her book?" he asked.

I shook my head, no.

"Brigid," he said and paused, "can't cook. So you will pardon my heavy-handed analogy—she writes as though she is cooking a huge feast—but she tries, she has always tried to cram the entirety of the banquet into a lunchbox."

The dog came bounding through the apple trees.

"If she says anything about," he waited and looked at me in the deepening dusk, "about Jews, don't take it personally. She doesn't mean anything by it. She doesn't understand what she's saying. Do you understand?"

We watched the dark birds alight and circle the trees. He said something about how they would pick off the seed and kill the fruit long before it had time to flower in the spring.

"When I was in graduate school a million years ago," Brigid said, "my grandmother died, and I went home to Iowa for the funeral. By the time I made it home, my father had brought all of her things, boxes and boxes really, to our house. He filled up the basement, and mother was unhappy with this. She didn't mind death, but disorder was something else. And my grandmother had, well, a lot of junk. My father was an only child, and his father had died even before I was born. So our basement was full of this lifelong accumulation— dishes and jelly jars, china trolls—I'm trying to remember what she had—Santa Claus saltshakers, ships in bottles—I had never seen anything like it, not as the representation, you know, of one life, of what was left behind. My mother didn't like antiques. She's a firm believer in progress. Why buy something old and dirty, that's what she used to say, when you can buy something clean and new? And because I showed interest when I saw all this stuff heaped up in the basement, I was relegated to sorting duty. You know, I was supposed to go through the boxes and decide what should go to charity and what was worth selling and what might have "family" importance of the heirloom variety. Of course, I couldn't imagine parting with a single tomato-shaped pincushion or state-fair shot glass. And the basement seemed the perfect place for me to hide out. I wanted to be alone and suffer my separation from my sensitive boyfriend of the moment, Klaus. Klaus, who used to wear a sport coat with jeans and looked like a German version of Robert Redford in *Three Days of the Condor*. Have you seen it? His jacket is a little too small and it gives him an air of, you know, painful integrity. That's what poor Klaus had, painful integrity, an almost characterless passion, if that makes sense. Does it? I couldn't stand being away from him. But, of course, I felt guilty about my grandmother—is this boring you?"

"No, no, go on," I said.

"My mother," she continued, "didn't want to go through the boxes herself. And my older sister was visiting with her children. It was around Christmas. I think it must have been around or before Christmas because they were upstairs doing the tree and all that, and I was confined to the basement longing for Klaus whose name of course elicited funny seasonal jokes from my mother so I didn't mind hiding. I was digging through a box loaded down with a full tea service. It was all crammed in very tightly, wrapped in newspaper. It had probably been packed away like that for a million years. I kept reaching into the box and unwrapping piece after piece, cups and saucers, creamer and sugar dish, but when I got to the bottom the box was still heavy. Do you ever try to make sense of a moment while it is happening, as though it has already happened? You know, put the sequence of seconds back together and try to remember what you are feeling even as you still feel it? I was in my parents' basement in Iowa. I was listening to a call-in radio show where listeners were describing their fondest Christmas memories. I think the winner would get a box of ammunition and a hunting rifle for the most tear-inducing story. I was drinking eggnog and rum. Upstairs the children were arguing about something, about toys maybe. I picked up the box and turned it upside down and began shaking it—mercilessly, crazily shaking this poor battered box—until the bottom broke. Or what I thought was the bottom, but it was really a false bottom; there was a cut-out square of cardboard fitted inside over the bottom to hide—"

"Something hidden?" I asked.

"And this square of cardboard shook loose and then the box collapsed and out fell—"

"What?" I asked. "What was it?"

"Out fell a book."

"A book?"

"A book," she said. "A diary. My grandmother's diary hidden there under that tea service for who knows how long, out it fell," she said. "Just like that."

"Did you read it?"

"Not right away," she said. "But I realized, I had this horrible realization that I knew nothing about her, about the woman who had taken so much care to hide her diary, and why? Here she was, my own grandmother for God's sake, and I knew nothing about her, let alone why she would go to the trouble of constructing a cardboard hiding place. Why not destroy it? Do you know what I mean? She wanted me to find it. Who else could have found it, if not me? It was a leather-bound diary, about forty pages—but the problem was that it was written in German."

"Please tell me," I said, "that Klaus was fluent?"

"Oh absolutely," she said.

"So he translated it for you?"

"Maybe the story should end there," she said. "Or begin. But since I couldn't read the notebook and didn't know really what it was, I was uncomfortable handing it off to someone else. It was pure superstition. I waited. I didn't tell anyone about it. I went back to New York and hid it in a drawer—nylons and stockings, I think. I let it sit."

"Until?"

"Let's not talk about how or why, that's another story entirely, but let's say that one day Klaus found the book on his own. It seemed so fated."

"You were together a long time?"

"For a while," she said. "Long enough."

"But he, Klaus, he translated the diary?"

"Oh yes," she said. "He was nothing if not dependable. The book was, the diary turned out to be an account of when she, Greta, ran away from home to Paris to escape an arranged marriage. It spanned about six months, ending in November of 1922. She was sixteen and fresh from Danzig."

"It's like a romance novel," I said.

"It is," she said. "It was. The entries in the diary weren't very detailed, not what you would call *narrative*. But I could piece together the story. She found work as an artist's model and that led her to certain salons—the diary at points is simply a date book—who she met, who she worked for. She was—" Brigid trailed off.

"Popular," I offered.

"To be tactful," she said. "Yes, but imagine it, what a life. Sixteen and alone in Paris—and suddenly to find your dance card overflowing."

"Now it's a *best-selling* romance novel."

"And it seemed that she had one particular patron, a writer, who she identified only as M.P., and this, along with the time period, her reports of his illness, his frailty, their meetings, even the location of his apartment, um, *flat*—it led me then, it leads me now to believe—"

I waited.

"My grandmother," she said, "was the mistress of Marcel Proust."

"Oh," I said.

"I know, I know," she commiserated. "I was just as shocked as you are, but then I couldn't ignore the evidence."

"Oh," I repeated. "And then?"

"There is always more," she said, "to every story. The romance ended badly. I suppose if it hadn't, it would be well-known, even celebrated, not hidden in a box in a basement in Iowa. M.P.'s brother persuaded Greta that she was a detriment to the writer's failing health and he convinced her to leave. He paid her to go; he paid her way to America in November of 1922."

"And that's where the diary ends?"

"She left Paris without seeing him again. She sent one last letter, but never heard, never received a response. Marcel Proust died in November, 1922. Greta came to America, landed at Ellis Island, married a mild-mannered Scotsman named Pearce, and gave birth to my father in June, 1923."

"Are you saying—?" I didn't know if I should ask.

"Am I saying that everything skips a generation? Am I saying that my grandmother hid that journal where only I would find it? Am I saying that I understand now why I have always felt such a kinship toward Jews? I am saying that I am the granddaughter of Marcel Proust."

The afternoon of the next day passed into evening. Owen would carry in an armload of logs, and I the tinder. We started a fire in the great stone fireplace. Brigid poked at the cinders with a stick and asked if O had perhaps stashed some marshmallows for her in his newly captured loot. He would say yes, and she would be delighted. But we did not speak of anything else that evening. We turned on the radio and listened to BBC news from around the world. And I would feel very sad and small, but safe. Brigid fell asleep on the dusty sofa with the dog curled at her feet.

Her story told, unfolded, Brigid said that she had grown sleepy and was sorry to leave me with such a mess and everything unfinished and I should not forget about our pact and I owed her one very delicious and wicked secret and she would accept nothing less but would have to wait because she had gotten up very early this morning to work on her book which now I knew all about and could perhaps understand the importance of and please I wasn't going to tell anyone, was I? I assured her and she seemed content with that and yawned and said that maybe she was going to find someplace decadent to curl up for a catnap. I went back to cleaning although I tried to keep my distance from the fireplace and its ridiculously high mirror in which it was impossible to see yourself unless you were a God or similar giant. I picked up my broom and caught at cobwebs. It was past six when Brigid reappeared with her cheeks flushed and hair loosened from the knot that she wore knotted around itself. She said that she had fallen asleep in the orchard like Claudius and had I seen anyone lurking about with a vial of poison? And barring the fact that she just might drop dead of ulcerous wounds at any moment now, would I like to join her for dinner or did I prefer to call it supper or did I have some wonderful boy waiting for me somewhere or could I please stay for a while with her for dinner at least and she would not presume to keep me until sunset because she saw my bicycle outside and didn't want me riding down the remote stretch of just-barely road into town in the impending darkness but we must have an hour or so before darkness sets in entirely, don't you think? Two hours at least, she said, and are you a vegetarian because Owen and I bought fresh snap peas and tomatoes, radishes and endive at a lovely outdoor market on the drive here and it was sad that he had left her alone just as they had barely arrived and she thought she might make us a salad as that was the extent of her culinary abilities but we could have apples and she could offer me wine but then she would worry about me riding home because wasn't that my bicycle outside, wasn't it? It is terribly awful to ride a bicycle when you are even the least bit tipsy because sometimes she used to do it in college but we could have vegetables and slices from the round loaf of black bread and would I rather, that is, was I the sort of person, a sweet person or a salty person? Would I rather have jam with bread or take mustard because they happened to have both because she and Owen had stopped at the most quaint stand and bought honey and strawberries, and I was, she was pleased to announce, doing such a wonderful job with the living room or was it a drawing room? Either way it was wonderful work to begin with the ceiling and work my way down but I needn't be in a hurry because we had world enough and time to work, she and I, or there was also butter and if you put butter on your black bread it would be sweet and salty both so there was no need to hurry really and we could have strawberries because it was that very sad and fateful time of the year when she could not help but think of poor Persephone who died for our sins and girls like us in September when there are still the last of the strawberries and the first of the apples together, one beginning to be born and the other sweetly dying, and if I would stay with her until dark she wouldn't presume to ask for more than that although if I wanted I could stay the night and we could have wine and talk as she wanted to hear all about me and was tired of talking about herself and we could call it a good old-fashioned sleepover or slumber party and we could do each other's hair and talk about television commercials like the one where the little boy eats margarine and suddenly finds himself anointed and crowned King of England and it was already getting so very dark you could see it along the horizon beyond the apple trees and since it was dark and looked like rain why didn't I stay with her just for now for the night and we could start again as one always can and does in the morning?

This is the end of the first day of the telling of my story.

It is January second, 1999.

It has begun to snow. It is snowing.

This is the beginning of the second day.

Ivory Coast

When asked how exactly she came to be a biographer, Brigid Lieb recalled driving across the endless scorched stretch of the Middle West in the summer of 1971, driving past fields of wheat and corn, past grain silos, grazing cattle, and the grim gray clapboard of Apostolic Lutheran churches, all the while her mother applying to her arms a tanning oil that smelled of coconuts and reading aloud the names of cities from the map; past national forests, scenic turn-outs and orange-jumpered work crews working to keep America beautiful while her father drank coffee poured out in tiny, almost graceful, almost tea-party-like cups from a plastic thermos; through four states with her little sister, Jojo, wearing a flowered halter-top that revealed the bones of her back just as clearly as the anatomically correct model of The Visible Man they had at home on the unreachable upper shelf in the rec room; from Iowa to Ohio with her older sister, Lydia, painting her toenails and borrowing back and forth from their mother a *Redbook* magazine with the newest installment of the serialized romance novella, *The Ghost of Desire:* it was the story of Kyle, the amnesiac young widower, and Kimberly, the student nurse who nurses him back to health after his tragic horseback-riding accident. From Indianola to Sandusky they drove, the fair-haired Pearce family, to visit the girls' maternal grandparents, but also, and more to the point, to spend a summer day in an amusement park, to ride the roller coaster, the merry-go-round, the Ferris wheel, to eat cotton candy, saltwater taffy, to get sick and sunburnt and lost in the crowd, to briefly and thrillingly separate before they piled back into the car and headed together homeward.

Brigid was ten. Jojo was six. Lydia was thirteen. Her sisters sat in the middle seat, while she, Brigid, had carved out a corner of the mysterious third tier of the wagon that faced backward so that you could see only where you had just been, never where you were going. Brigid faced the driver of the car behind them like Kyle meeting his evil twin in episode four. She sat in the back with the suitcases, sleeping bags, board games, and coolers. She slept and woke and rested her head on the bag of towels that her mother had packed because she did not trust hotels or motels even though they promised *sanitized for your protection,* just as she did not altogether trust the homes of friends back in Iowa even though everyone was wholesome, Methodist, and germ-free. Being ten, having only just turned ten in May, Brigid felt that she owned the decade. Still, she was not nearly old enough to understand that this wood-paneled station wagon driving through an impossible drought of a summer carried them as an arbitrary collection of characters: her business savvy father, Steve, who sold insurance against fire, flood, and natural disaster; Jane Anne, her bright and outgoing mother in the front seat; her two pretty blonde sisters, Jojo and Lydia, in the middle seat. Brigid couldn't have known, she couldn't have suspected, she couldn't have had much more than an inkling that none of them really liked each other. She couldn't have anticipated that her sister Lydia, after losing the Miss Teen Iowa Pageant 1975, would at the age of seventeen elope and then just as abruptly divorce a young marine from Dill, Mississippi named Chester Apollinaire; that Lydia would drop out of community college for cosmetology school and drop out of cosmetology school to marry Philip Phister, a dim but devoted student barber, former member of *Up with People* and sometime make-up artist involved in stand-up comedy, and after a few supposedly romantic but surprisingly bleak months of coldwater newlywed struggle they would accept a loan from his parents and move to an upscale suburb of Des Moines; or that Lydia would never abandon her dream of running into Chester Apollinaire years later, someplace incongruous, someplace accidental, the grocery, the emergency

room of the hospital, JCPenney, until she came to the conclusion
that some people do fall out of the world entirely, irreplaceably, and
nothing can bring them back; that of her two children, the oldest,
Philip Jr., would have a penchant for dousing Frisbees in gasoline
and lighting them on fire before hurling them at dogs; or that her
daughter, Pauline, who would be called, due to some paternal whim,
Pepper, would have no interest in Little Miss pageants, cheerleading,
or country club cotillions and instead find herself fascinated by the
workings of the combustion engine; but Lydia would evince a happiness, no matter how undignified, through the cult success of her
husband, Philip, known affectionately to fans as Flip, who would
rise to local celebrity as the bumbling but affable weatherman on
Channel 12, an ABC affiliate, and although often the butt of the
anchorman's jokes took it all with the cheerful malapropism of utter
oblivion. Brigid couldn't have known at the age of ten in the month
of July when everything was burning brown and dying in the heat,
that not only are all unhappy families alike, all families are unhappy.

Jojo was curled sleeping in the middle seat, her head on Lydia's
thigh. Lydia owned Jojo, the way that Steven owned the station
wagon, and Jane Anne owned Lydia, and Brigid owned the decade.
Jojo slept on Lydia's thigh, bronzed and sticky with coconut tanning
oil, while Brigid, the middle sister, was banished into the back seat
to stare into the lovelorn faces of strangers in Volkswagens, vans, and
convertibles. Brigid drank Seven-Up and read *Tales from the Crypt*
comic books of which her mother did not approve, but this was the
hidden pleasure of back-seat exile, to be unnoticed, to be like the
Invisible Man just at the moment when he removes his bandages:
Gone! Vanished! Disappeared! The women in the drawings, the
good girls and she-devils alike, had breasts that rose from the pages,
heaving with fear, desire, or blood-lust. Brigid had never known
women like this in real life, so beautiful, so mysterious—well, except
perhaps in the person of a girl who worked in her father's office who

was called Daisy Bright. The vampire villains had gaunt ash-gray faces and tortured hearts. They lived in cobweb-tangled mansions that overlooked graveyards. They mourned forever the loss of a long-dead true love and so exacted vengeance on the world for this cruelest of deprivations. The undead minions who did the vampires' bidding had no light of humanity in their eyes and feasted on the flesh of the innocent. Jojo wore her hair in pigtails; each one fashioned into a perfect corkscrew ringlet. Lydia had long hair that she brushed smooth and parted down the middle. And it was true that sometimes Jane Anne, when she was shopping, at PTA meetings, or at bake sales, courted the *Brady Bunch* analogy with her three blonde daughters, the youngest one in curls. Lydia and Jojo didn't mind, and Brigid was oblivious; she had already begun to construct in her head intricate escape plans. She could not, as yet, being only ten, describe the sensation that she felt as unhappiness. It was only that sometimes she saw herself like Snow White in her glass coffin, not quite sleeping and not quite dead while some dashing stranger with hair as blue-black as printer's ink leaned in to offer the kiss that would save her.

Brigid was too tall for her age. She had a habit of tripping over her own feet, and Jojo laughed and said she looked like one of those dancing skeletons at Halloween. Jane Anne had begun discreetly to ask other ladies in the neighborhood if she should try to keep Brigid from sleeping so that she would stop growing. Jane Anne had been born in Findlay, Ohio, and had lived in Iowa for fully fourteen happy years with her husband, Steven, himself a native of Dubuque. She found things like war and politics and hippies and free love distasteful as well as not very hygienic. She did not particularly like this new decade. She and Steve went to church every Sunday and Bible study on Wednesday evenings. Steven sold protection from locusts, cattle blight, and arson. He spoke with authority on the dangers of property damage when the study group read about the ten plagues

in Exodus, although he felt obliged to offer the cautionary note that
a good life insurance policy is essential for every homeowner. Steven
was having an affair with a secretary in his office, but was going to
break it off any day now. Lydia read with flushed cheeks and freshly
seashell-pink fingernails as Kimberly and Kyle's passionate embrace
was once again thwarted by the mysterious figure in the black velvet robe who may or may not have been the ghost of Martinique,
Kyle's dead bride. The secretary with whom Steven was having an
affair was called Daisy Bright. She was part Indian, everybody said;
although some people claimed Spanish. She had straight black hair
all the way down her back and could type 115 words a minute,
which was Steven's explanation for her utility around the office to
his wife Jane Anne, who thought that Daisy, although she smelled
of strawberry shampoo, always looked, for want of a more discreet
word, *dirty*.

Steven offered compensation for electrical fires, windstorms, and
Dutch elm disease. On the desk in his office was a photograph taken
at the Sears Portrait Studio of his wife and three daughters. It was a
Christmas present to, the card had said in Jojo's looping hand: *A#1
DAD!!* And while no one can really say whether Daisy Bright had
loved Steven Pearce or not, it is safe to acknowledge that she often
looked at, studied the gold-framed photograph on his desk of his
wife and three children, and one day after work she bought a bottle
of peroxide and a box of Miss Clairol at the drugstore and took it
upon herself to bleach all the darkness from her hair. She stripped it
clean like the locusts on the green leaves of Egypt. It was as white
and dry as the chapped wheat that Steven insured against root rot,
powdery mildew, and soil-borne viruses. The plot thickens,
announced Lydia to her mother, from middle seat to front, yelling
over the voice of the baseball announcer on the radio: Reginald, the
fiancé of Kimberly's half-sister, Brittany, has arrived from London
with an urgent letter from her wealthy dying grandmother.

On the day after Daisy Bright dyed her hair blonde, Brigid and
Jojo went to their father's office to ask about going to the movies, but
really to see what everyone was gossiping about, what Daisy had
done to her hair. Steven was out on a call to a client, and the girls
suffered to sit beside Daisy's desk in the reception area and paw
through old copies of *Field & Stream.* Daisy asked them if they liked
comic books and pulled a stack of *Tales from the Crypt* from her file
cabinet. Jojo stated that her mother didn't allow them to read such
filth and asked if she could go next door to the laundromat and
watch the clothes tumble. Daisy said yes, yes, she supposed that Jojo
could, but not to talk to strangers. Brigid took the comic books from
Daisy, who also offered her a bite from her square of green apple
bubble gum. Brigid leaned over the desk and damply nibbled off an
edge of the gum from Daisy's outstretched hand. The Bible study
group might have used their exegetic skills to speculate that it was
like Eve tempting Adam only with apple *gum* instead of apple *fruit,*
and with two women instead of a woman and a man. The group was
very specific about analogies and the meaning to be drawn from
them. And Brigid asked Daisy Bright why she had done that to her
hair, why she had dyed her hair like that? And Daisy who was still,
and perhaps even more so despite her new hair color, dark and mysterious, Daisy who was Russian or Lebanese, paused and smiled and
said it had seemed like a good idea at the time. Brigid nodded and
tried to blow a bubble with her original-sin flavored gum that was
sweet and delicious and tasted to the less-discerning Christian only
of apples. *Let me see your hands,* said Daisy to Brigid. *They're clean,*
said Brigid. *To read,* said Daisy. And there in the State Farm Property
and Casualty Office on Fourth Street and Lafayette in Indianola,
Iowa in the summer of 1971, Daisy Bright read Brigid Pearce's fortune while her little sister Jojo, who would soon demand to be called
Josie, would meet a cross-eyed boy named James Samson whom she
would not see again for several years until one day they would meet

and sneak off together to smoke cigarettes behind the Hy-Vee grocery store right near the dumpster where peaches and pork loins
were sweetly rotting among the flies, the fruit rinds and filth; that
this Jimmy, who would grow up to own Uncle Sam's Used Furniture
Territory, the largest independent retailer of custom-designed
Western-style home furnishings and waterbeds in the tri-state area,
and forget all about the blonde girl with the pigtails twisted into
curls even though he would be the one to lead her down the primrose path from as the poets say *innocence to experience,* from pot to
painkillers, from Demerol to despair until the years would become a
blur and waking in a stupor on the poured concrete floor of a gas station in Topeka, Kansas in 1987, she would see a vision of the Virgin
Mary carved in a grimy cake of Dial soap and subsequently demand
to be called Josephine, move to Seattle and devote herself to working with runaways, the indigent and addicted. While Jojo watched
the clothes tumble in the Spin-A-World and a mean-faced little boy
helped his mother fold undershirts and unmentionables, Brigid let
Daisy Bright read her palm. *You are going to die in a foreign country,*
said Daisy. And Brigid who had perhaps thought about death more
than other girls her age, and certainly more than any other Brownie
in troop 227 with the exception of Paige Braun who would be found
dead in her parents' basement at the age of nineteen with a plastic
bag over her head and a cryptic note reading: *Now is the time for all
good men to come to the aid of their country,* which turned out not to
be a farewell letter but a beginning typing assignment from secretarial school, Brigid said, *A foreign land? Yes,* said Daisy. *Will I be happy
there?* asked Brigid. The phone rang. Daisy answered, *Good morning,
State Farm Property and Casualty!* Brigid looked at the comic books.
The girl on the cover wore a low-cut wedding gown and was stifling
a scream as her groom emerged from the shadows of their bedchamber joined at the hip with a Siamese twin. *May I borrow these?*
asked Brigid. Daisy put her hand over the receiver and nodded. *I*

can't tell you, she said, *whether you'll be happy.* Brigid suspected it was best not to know. *I'll bring them back when I'm done, I promise,* she said. And she put the comics in her backpack because her mother did not approve of such things just as she did not approve of Daisy Bright or public laundromats or the honeymoon habits of Siamese twins, or, for that matter, foreign countries which were hot and dry and dirty.

And they all piled into the station wagon very early one morning in July: Steven, who would never again touch the bare breasts of Daisy Bright; Jane Anne, who would become a certified real estate agent for Century 21 and wear with pride her gold blazer while showing affordable new suburban homes with central air-conditioning, attached garages, and maintenance-free siding to young couples just starting out in life, and she, tennis-trim Mrs. Pearce, the number-one seller in her office for three years running, would at a luncheon for the League of Women Voters have her picture taken with Nancy Reagan herself, and this framed photograph would replace, finally, the one on Steven's desk that Daisy Bright used to study with an expression on her beautiful foreign face of bemused loathing; Lydia, who after Phil Jr. and Pepper had grown too big to fit into doll clothing, would adopt a Chinese orphan named Zhijian whom she insisted upon calling Jack and dressing in sailor suits; Josephine, called Jojo, who would come to be known as St. Jo by the derelict and disenfranchised, by junkies looking to swap needles, by runaway girls who sought her out to ask if it was true, really was it true? That she had been a sinner too until the Virgin Mary came to her in a soap-bubble vision of cleanliness? And Brigid, what would become of Brigid Pearce in the back seat? She who had worn the decade like a Burger King crown, paper-bright, jaunty, bejeweled, ill-fitting, and ironic? Brigid who was to die in a foreign country, happy or not, with a vampire groom in a mournful graveside manor, she would grow up to become her own biographer, forced endlessly by strength of will alone to live in the past, to play out the stories of lives deemed more important than her own, to prove until the end of time the premise that all happy families were truly as unhappy as her own. And on a day in July the Pearce family packed their bathing suits, shorts, sun hats, inflatable starfish floats, blue jeans, sweatshirts, and teddy-bear pajamas into suitcases. They packed their maps and magazines and coolers full of soda pop and sandwiches and headed for Sandusky, Ohio, which was such a pretty name after all, like *sand* and like *dusk* and at the end like the beginning of *key lime pie*. Off they drove to Ohio and the promise of the Blue Streak, that thrilling roller coaster which took you up, up, up impossibly high on its clickety clack wooden tracks and plummeted back down to earth. And one morning very early, maybe on the same day that they left, Daisy Bright woke and saw in the bathroom mirror the black roots of her brittle blonde hair and took a scissors and cut it all off and packed her bags and left Iowa forever. Steven always imagined she was heartbroken, and Jane Anne was just plain glad, and Brigid saved the comic books for a long time until her mother found them one day years later and she took them away from Brigid and threw them in the garbage just as the family was going out the door to pile into the station wagon to drive to the church ice cream social and charity bazaar where Lydia would meet a boy on leave from the Marines named Chester Apollinaire with a tattoo on one arm of a mermaid and on the other of a dancing hula-hula girl and that night they would go to the drive-in which has long since closed down and in the dark decide that they would love each other forever, which after all, maybe they did. And Jojo would share her banana split with a boy called Jimmy who she was certain she had seen before only she couldn't remember where it had been and as a token of thanks he slipped a beer tab on her finger and called it a wedding ring. And Brigid would sit alone away from the latticed cherry pies, Rice Krispies treats, devil's food gooey cupcakes and apple tarts, the

twenty-five-cent bangles, bracelets, blue glass bottles, and old-fashioned dresses for sale or swap as the afternoon darkened into
evening thinking about their trip to Ohio years before and how
when the Blue Streak plummeted for one brief thrilling moment
she had hoped it would crash and kill them all. But she knew that
she wasn't going to die that day because while Ohio is very far away
and in some ways foreign, it is not specifically a foreign country, not
really. And on the final page of the story Kyle and Kimberly kissed,
once and once only, passionately, deliberately, and Kyle placed
exquisitely one hand on the small of Kimberly's small back just
before the words ran out: *the end!* But there would be a new story
next month. And Daisy Bright let her hair grow and went to
California where she starred in B-movies under an assumed name.
In one she played a zombie queen and in another a feckless girl
motorcycle bandit on the run from a corrupt sheriff. She made
movies, who knows how many and in what disguises, until she
saved enough money to move to New Mexico and paint the faces
of the future on ceramic pots, plates, and decorative vases that she
sold to tourists on vacation. She might have been Persian; she may
have been from Salem, Santiago, or St. Petersburg. Who can say
and what did or does it matter? She could see the future just as surely as Brigid could see only the past as she sat in the wood-paneled
station wagon staring into the sun-strained faces of ghosts who
looked forward while she was resigned to forever looking back.

Jericho

Able was Owen in the orchard. There among the rot and ruin, the skeletal remains of carrots, wizened tubers, dried up, desiccated, wrenched from the earth with his bare ungloved hands; there among the seed and sap, the sallow dark-eyed mystery of the crows, cawing jays, red-jacketed cardinals, sparrows, hummingbirds, wren, thrush, goldfinch, and the gray cat creeping along and through the tangled grasses to stalk and spy and move on; Owen knelt with trowel, spade, and knife cutting through the sun-warmed strata, dirt upon dirt—so much dirt—each shovelful containing all the past, the root and dislocation, rock, rust, famine, fragments the wind had blown far off-course, cinnamon from the Spice Islands, crystals shaken from the Great Salt Lake, the jawbone of Job's overburdened ass blown a hapless million miles from the fertile crescent to bury itself in our backyard. In the ground, in the soil set on Owen's silver spade, he found all the things the earth had solidly fixed and buried within itself: broken glass, fossils, fibrous tendrils, the fat fingers of grub worms. And at an upper window, Brigid leaned out, suddenly, unexpectedly, and waved, calling down to us: *find any buried treasure?*

Boolean, the gray cat's sunny morning proceeded undisturbed. She sneaked into the house through an open window and then unable to decide: either/or? here or there? climbed back outside to loll under a bittersweet tree and paw passing field mice on the garden path until without warning she ran back through the kitchen window past the dog sleeping on the hardwood floor before the stove upon which a pot-au-feu was simmering and made her way to the staircase, rubbed her ragged fur and bumped her head two or three times pleasantly

against the wooden balustrade before making a frantic-paced run up
the stairs and then back down and then up up again and down down
to pause at the foot of the stairs, give a leisurely look around the
sunny stairwell and run again in the opposite direction.

Cloistered and closeted, Brigid with her books in an upper bedroom
drank coffee and corrected manuscript pages. On the undersized writing desk sat her typewriter. Over and across the keys ASDFGHJKL went
the light long-fingered touch of her fingers breaking down and adding
up letters into words. To this, the smallest of the second-story rooms,
she retired each morning. The breeze from the open window had the
underside of coldness to its over-upside of warmth. The sunlight was
diffuse, the air rich and rotting. Across the small single bed with its
bleak metal frame that put her in mind of wounded soldiers in some
long-ago war, Brigid spread out her papers if only it sometimes seemed
for the purpose of allowing the gray cat a further playground. Into the
room the cat bounded and immediately went to work digging hiding
places within the papery substance, the residue remaining of the life
and loves of Marcel Proust himself, long gone, long committed to the
earth. Imagine him as snug in his grave as he used to be in his bed, as
dry as a stalk of Indian corn adorning an Iowa doorway. Brigid sat at
the desk. She shifted her face from right hand to left, reread the page
caught in the carriage, rose, went to the window and looked out to see
her husband laboring in the garden. *Laboring?* Or was it *toiling?* More
ominously: *searching?* And she watched for a moment the girl who was
me working nearby picking apples from the low branches of the trees
and dropping them each like a tiny guillotined head into a wicker basket before reaching up again and disappearing into the branches.
Brigid returned from the window to her desk and shooed away the cat,
caught incautiously chewing up and coughing down a morsel of chapter five that concerned the beauty of cathedrals.

Dirt was devouring Franny. Her body had been converted by fire
into ash. And these ashes were cast upon the water to float and to
drown; to be swallowed by fish who were eaten by birds who were
shot by boys with slingshots to fall to crash to the ground and be
roasted on sticks over bonfires, the ash to return to the land blown
and displaced and taken by the wind to mingle with the earth and
become through harsh seasons so much muck and mire. The earthly
absence of a grave was marked in memory of Mrs. Lieb by a cairn
monument heaped up low of bare stones in the shelter of fruit trees
in the orchard where I collected apple after apple, some ripe and
worm-worn, others raw, ashy, red, wrinkled and rotting, to be sorted
later for the baking of sauces and savouries in the kitchen where
John Paul Jones slept on his belly dreaming of the stewpot.

Eggs for breakfast Owen ate that morning. Empirically dropped each
by each sunny-side up into the frying pan, the work of my own hands.
Eerie under the spreading apple tree hours elapsed as I continued my
epic examination of gravity and let fall each fruit from my hand into
the awaiting basket with the sheer force of the Earth's pull. Who but
Einstein could have supplanted Sir Isaac Newton? The apples continued to fall. Earnest in her endeavors, Brigid sorted through ephemera:
old stamps, dead letters, stubs of railway tickets, pressed flowers, candy
wrappers flattened, brittle and faded empty envelopes containing no
remnants of their former epistolary sweetness.

F-e-t-i-s-h, typed Brigid. She was thinking about a particular passage in
her grandmother's journal in which Monsieur M.P. dotes over a pair of
Greta's dancing slippers sewn with seed pearls to glitter bewitchingly as
though damp with dew. It would be no great stretch to say that a foot
fetish is not so far removed from logomania, a sordid passion for words
themselves, as "feet" are the rhythmic substance of poetry. One poetic
foot is composed of toes, tiny digits, words, letters, the knuckles, joints

both flexible and arthritic, stops and starts, desire and utility going two by two cobbled together in a matching set: right foot, left foot, forward march! Yes, yes, Brigid was certain she could make a case for it, work it all together—although she was not sure that this grand sexualized analogy of shoe leather to sordid syntax, this very unbuttoning of words could explain sweet young Klaus who had translated the diary and thus inadvertently started her on a genealogical odyssey while he was searching one evening in her dresser for a particular pair of thigh-high mesh stockings—oh, and how her parents had doted on Klaus when she had brought him home that Thanksgiving! They exhorted him: *Speak in German! The language of science! The language of our past! The language of the future!* And Klaus obliged them. He blushingly quoted Rilke and then, realizing that it didn't matter what he said so long as he said it in the paterlingua, that they couldn't understand but wanted only to hear the hard edge of foreign syllables, he aimlessly recited a grocery list broken up between compliments to Brigid's mother on her candied yams and nervous sidelong glances at her younger sister Josie. He dropped his fork under the table and in retrieving it lingered a moment to notice Josie's shoes, black combat boots, laced, his heart ached, tightly. Oh Klaus! He was small-boned, bespectacled, and selfless, really, caught up in the mysterious transcription of one language to the next, the replacement of one word for another in the same way that one stands before an open closet barefoot studying the selection and begins by slipping on red ballet flats but finds them unsuitable and so substitutes a candy-apple pair of anklestrap pumps for crimson slingback heels for open-toed pomegranate sandals for Bordeaux flannel mules for burgundy suede clogs for riding boots of Italian oxblood, until, with each successive stylistic darkening, a little bit of meaning is deferred, replaced, re-created, and an entirely new connotation is gained until gradually the poetic foot grows accustomed to the height of the heel or elevated arch of the instep and the mouth sounds out the vowels and diphthongs with rounded lips, ahhhh, like confessing to a priest or a good Freudian doctor. And on that Thanksgiving day years ago as they had stood in the doorway in the darkening gray of the snowy afternoon, her mother had announced in her dramatic stage whisper just loudly enough for everyone to hear and for Klaus, dear that he was, to smile not unsympathetically and pause to wipe his wire-rimmed glasses on his sleeve: *Bee,* she said, *I think he's a keeper!*

German? Why not Spanish? Mandarin? Aramaic? Fortran? Finnish? Why did and does, why must every twentieth century evil and woe, story and cautionary tale alike boil down to a brute ugly German root? A misshapen and septic toe sticking out of a worn boot? Let the imagery suit the crimes. We need more ugly words for our ugly world: geld, gelt, guilt, guillotine, gulag, gung ho. But who could blame Greta who had walked the streets of Paris in slippers embroidered with all the tears and broken glass that were to come? Who could blame Greta who begat Steven who begat Brigid who in turn begat an entirely new Proust? Or perhaps Brigid was re-creating the *Marcel* whom Marcel had always wanted to be? A Marcel who didn't dote on boathouse boys, one who didn't take more interest in the styles of ladies' dresses than their ample décolletage? One whose legacy did not die out with the turning of the page but continued in the improbable golden beauty of his granddaughter? Brigid begat the ghost of her grandfather as surely as her grandmother birthed her father on the red-and-black checkered tile of the kitchen floor in a small apartment in Brooklyn before lighting out with her fair-haired husband for the wild territory of Iowa. *I owe ya,* joked her husband, the young Scotsman who didn't mind the language that came between himself and his pretty pink-cheeked Greta. In fact, in the years to come he would consider it a consolation, the best artificial boundary between amicable partners who shared little more in common than cheerful temperaments and having purchased tickets, having taken passage from Cherbourg to New York across an ocean on the same steamer. They never had to blame each other for silence at the breakfast table, there was always the language to indict. And so each felt no acrimony toward the other. They had gotten on famously and in near-silence for some thirty years together. They cheerfully, proudly let their one child, that big strapping blond-eyed blue-haired American boy, Steven, fill in the blanks with words. Ah well, so it had been German. In fact it now seems impossible that it could have ever been anything else. Brigid trusted Klaus's translation of the diary in perpetuity not because she had loved him so terribly much, no, he was long forgotten except for his kindness and the curious crossover nature of his nocturnal inclinations— but because, despite fears that sometimes overtook her about the details of the story, she knew that she must faithfully follow no other translation because she, Brigid Elizabeth Pearce Lieb, was wholeheartedly monogamous, fixed and steadfast in thought and deed and desire. Why, so sensitive was Brigid to the cosmic laws of monogamy that she was certain that if she ate a carrot a nearby celery stalk in the salad bowl might become jealous. Honestly. So she was content to stick to a given routine in which her hours were arranged and orderly; she ate the same food every day not only for the comfort of familiarity, but for the sake of containing the rioting that surely occurred in the vegetable crisper whenever the refrigerator door slammed shut.

Hero killed herself for love of Leander. Hemlines are rising by the year. Hope springs eternal. Haberdashery aside, Owen had begun to resemble the actor who would play him in the movie. It was impossible to discern whether he was performing the tried and true role of a misanthropic writer or whether all the cliches from pen to ploughshares rested quite weightlessly on his flannel-clad shoulders. Did Atlas hold up the whole of the world? Or was it the other way around? Did the heaviness and heft of the shouldered globe keep him tethered to time? For heroes one should look to the classics—for those hearty fellows who were tried by fire, by the wiles of witches, the will of winds. For haberdashery, try a tunic, a turban, tuxedo? Or perhaps the simple unconstructed line of the toga more suits your fancy? At the Acropolis there was nothing in the least risqué about showing a good deal of manly knee while wrestling with moral dilemmas and arguing the distinctions between anima and animus. Hope waited impatiently packed away in the bottom of Pandora's purse. Leander drowned in the crashing waves while swimming the Hellespont to his awaiting Hero. And sometime in the midst of this adventure the ball rolled from Atlas' shoulders to bounce away on its own. It was like a toy for the children of the Czar. No one bothered to go after it. Sometimes I am certain we will all flutter, fly, hiss and disappear if we do not keep to the parts that providence has penned for us. Other times I drop apple after apple into the awaiting basket with absolute and boundless hope that one speckled yellow flecked red misshapen prodigy will defy both reason and order and take it upon itself to fall upward and never be heard from again.

Inflamed along the garden path, morning glories succumbed to sunny urges. I too have taken some liberties. Note for example how easy it is for me to know what Brigid thought years prior to our meeting or what she did when locked away alone in her room. It gets worse. I know things that happened before I was born. I am in the habit of meeting up with sages and sibyls, prophets and poets who know everything there is to know about the study of the study of the future of history. Each one tells a different story. I have long-since come to realize that I am invisible to everyone. Save you. Save me. So here I go, tripping from story to story in an idiotic attempt to set things right: elude plot, defy oracle, outrun Smokey, foil Bandit, save the day! One more tale will turn the tide. One more confession cures all. One more sentence of the styptic pencil will stanch the bleeding. Nothing ever begins or ends with me. I am all fingers and toes, a very fetish of perpetual motion and movable parts each one clamoring and with its own inkpen writing a declaration of independence. Why, my ring finger alone has announced secession from the union that is me. And now the rest are rioting: the liver biliously seething with rebellion; ankles awaiting marching orders from the Achilles' heel. What will I do? How do I become one nation indivisible? Shall I stitch a flag emblazoned with the family crest: a crossed mop and bucket? Shall I plead incompetence under the protection of my patron saint Lady Macbeth? I command my kidneys to remain renal; spine to stand tall; toes to tread lightly. The protein presoak is breaking down the stain. The residue of the past, drop by good-to-the-last drop begins to dissolve. Fancy that! There is hope. You can *Shout* it out. I'm absolutely soaking in it—a brave concoction of vinegar and Mr. Bubble, the same brand endorsed on the label by Marat himself for the soothing of scabies. Brigid would stick to one story for the rest of her life; knowing that it was either true or false would neither diminish her faith, attachment, or belief in said story. It was important only that she had chosen. She cared only that she had picked a card. The deck itself was irrelevant. Either/or. The window or the door? Klaus or Owen? Proust or Hitler? Carrots or celery? Iowa or Ireland? After all, who cares which or what you chose just so long as you call the new territory a land of your own invention? Raise the flag! Declare independence from doubt and live with the serenity prayer as your motto: God grant me this day my daily dose of surrender. Write your own life story replete with all the twists and turns, forgiveness and dispassion, frantic mouse-chasing, reckless destruction and fickle back-alley peccadilloes just as the gray cat with her mottled sun-warmed fur speckled and crackling with dried leaves, twigs, cobwebs and spiders alike goes tramping across the keys of Brigid's typewriter pounding in rapid and confessional succession her long-awaited, highly anticipated unauthorized autobiography: ZXC!!@I

Jonathan Warren Lieb was born the first and only child to his awaiting parents, Owen Gamliel and Frances Mathilde, on December 3,
1962 at 4:41 A.M. under the sign of Sagittarius, the truth seeker, and
ascendant Scorpio, at the maternity hospital at St. Sebastian's
Crossing, delivered, wrenched forth of his mother and into the
world with the surgical steel forceps of doctor of obstetric medicine,
unlimited conundrums gynecological and maladies miscellaneous of
the feminine variety, Patrick C. Brunty, lately of Perth, Australia,
who cut the cord and handed the infant into the arms of Christ in
the form of his nurse, one Sister Martha Ignatius who summarily
washed, swaddled, powdered, and peekabooed under the aegis of the
order of the Little Sisters of the Assumption of the Virgin, and
though not herself prone to sentimentality noted to her dear friend
Sister Mary Lucia what a big fine strapping crying blue-faced two-
fisted boldly brash-lunged bawling brute of a blessing was this one!
Owen was brought from the waiting room to the window of the
nursery to stare at row after row of fat little citizens of the human
empire, androgynous and baldy-headed, who would grow up to play
ball, pour tea and pay taxes, to break and breed, to mull mundane
mysteries, pilfer from the petty cash drawer, to deny logic and
endorse horse-sense, revere homily, honor tradition, concur to caste,
to discover the joys of self-expression through the reading of self-
help books and penning of volumes of poetry which would be purchased by similar verse aficionados who knew it was bad poetry but
still took solace in the bosom of its badness and to be sure found
good poetry vaguely antisocial and thus to be avoided at all costs,
and if not through *poesy* then perhaps *pictorially* they would choose
to render inspirational oil paintings of shipwrecks, sad clowns, dogs
playing poker, bullfighters, the Lord their God with flowing yellow
pin-curls, foreign ladies of the culturally informative bare-breasted
variety and homespun landscapes of snowy barns, radiant sunsets,
starry nights, and seashore holidays; children who would learn from

their parents how to breach fully nine of the Ten Commandments in general and five of them on a near-daily basis without getting caught, at least in this mortal realm. Children destined for lives of desperation, mediocrity, compliance—oh oh oh, Owen was no cynic—let it be said he saw with sagacious sadness something else, buried beneath the mire—brief goodness, agape, mild hearts and meekness, forgiving natures, selflessness, and passing passion of either the saintly or sinful sort, children who were the children of the children of the children of the parents of the children who plucked the first apple under the auspices of the public's all-encompassing ahistorical right to know nothing less than everything. He looked through the nursery glass at those hapless creatures composed of wiggling limbs and uncontrollable emissions, spring offsprung, yolk, zygote, quickened fetus, tiny tot: in the holiness and beauty of the grand design, for now at least, simply filed under: *miracle.* See also: *survival of the fittest.* And Franny, sedated, nauseated from the gas anesthesia but unable to sleep, whispered to Sister Mary Lucia, who though not a nurse herself brought magazines, clever books of baby names, *The Lives of the Saints,* orangeade, and congenial pillow-fluffing services to new mothers. Franny leaned close to muse not on the fabled wonder of childbirth, but the brutality. Her body had not yielded up the boy easily but held vigilant defense of the citadel for thirty-two hours before relinquishing in attrition the unwilling hostage, and even then not submitting to expel the child forward with uterine contractions but suffering to split, to tear apart. And this was no neat rent like the unseaming of a skirt's hem; it was cross-wise and jagged, a trail of forty-seven stitches inscribed as the covert path of an army traveling unevenly and in darkness across a danger-ous perineal territory. And so Jonathan was brought forth, like the rest of us measly sinners, of war and ruin, of pain, protest, and embrace; braceleted and bundled in blue, the bawling baby Lieb. He arrived two years after his parents set their bags on the drive which

led and wound up to the great blind face of the Georgian house.
This fine walkway in front was lined with lime, yew, and chestnut
trees—and around the back a neatly plotted kitchen garden gave
way to a wild expanse of fruit trees loosely deemed an orchard. An
orchard *and* a garden? Yes, although sometimes it was difficult to tell
where one began and the other left off. For Jonathan, who afternoons often napped on a blanket under the trees with his mother,
the only distinctions were the blue of the sky, the green of the earth,
and the barking of the sheepdogs. The apple needs the loneliness of
cold night air to come to crisp and knowledgeable fruition. And the
carrot, though hidden snuggled down in the dirt and offering only
a green-tasseled umbel, a hint of vegetation to the upstairs world,
demands for survival the kindness of strangers, the wrathful recrim-
inating gaze of the scarecrow to keep away the unholy legions: chip-
munks, chirruping hummingbirds, raccoons, squirrels, mice, the
pests and beasts of our nightmares who lurk, who bear down and
bore fang-first into the fruits of our cultivation—dear God, protect
our house of splendid isolation, see that it still stands, and our garden, that joyous Eden, demi-paradise, keep it safe though we are all
long-gone and faraway. Protect it from weevil, woodchuck, and water
snake! Amen. And he had grown, Jonathan, up among the tubers of
this garden, the books and bedtime tales, the smashed dishes, parental
accusations, the stuffed froggies, the egg cream custards and snowy
snowstorms like the most normal of expatriate American boys until,
of course, the evening of the snowiest snowstorm of them all when his
mother bathed and tucked him in and read aloud a story about a
sleepy rabbit being read a sleepy bedtime story and then she stopped
reading and disappeared entirely so that he was certain she must have
fallen right off the edge of the bed and into the pages of the book. He
searched for her in the pictures. He hunted for her like a rabbit catcher
at night among the trees of the orchard, his ridiculous oversized
galoshes cutting a path at first new, then familiar, oft frequented, and

finally, forgotten. Goodnight moon! Goodnight room! That was 1964. Goodnight Franny! Doesn't it—will you tell me—and please be candid, speak from the heart: doesn't it become more difficult year by year to recall the once-familiar faces of the past? And after all, life goes on, hey? Other faces have a way of replacing the ones we find ourselves forgetting. Good-bye kittens! Goodnight mittens. He is all grown up now, baby J, that once-cranky crawler, his royal highness who disdained the proffered bottle and demanded with open-mouthed and toothless howls the breast, or rather both breasts—one for feeding and the other for companionship, for clutching, clasping, cleaving, kissing, condoling, and plaintively caressing with his tiny curled fist—his majesty the rival, circumcised scion, successor, primogenitured heir upon whom daddy doted and called kiddingly: Johnny Cake Kid, Johnny Come Lately, Johnny Appleseed, John Barleycorn, Johnny B. Goode, John Bull, Little John, The Johnstown Flood, John Jacob Jingleheimer Schmidt, Johnny Jump-Up, Johnny on the Spot, and most wicked of all, John the Baptist and Blesser of Nappies—all of which made the boy coo delightedly. How long ago it seems. He is now a respected geoscientist, Dr. J.W. Lieb, Ph.D., specializing in the extraction and analysis of prehistoric fossils embedded in ice, and so I have been told, spends a good ten months of the year anonymously, peacefully, and perhaps even happily in a research outpost near the Arctic Circle.

Keys were given, two. Each key strung suspended on a silver chain. Allotted by Owen to the girls, the keys were worn around their necks brimstone bright. And one day Owen said to me, commanded: *Come live out at the house with us.* And so I did. And I went forth from the house of Marie where I had lodged in a cheerful little room and was awakened promptly every morning at six A.M. by Miss Beatrice who turned the handle of the door with jammy fingers to announce a new discovery of linguistic or scientific importance:

Today the sun is orange like an orange not like a pumpkin and just as round. Do you want toast? I'm Capricorn; what are you? Marie conceded that it made more sense to move out to the house with *them,* she supposed, since I was out there every day as it was. Beatrice begged a visit now and again. And Tommy, not one to be left out, sealed the deal by spitting up strained peas onto his corduroy jumper. It was all agreed upon and on a day in October some two weeks after I made the acquaintance of the Liebs, I came to stay with them in their fortress. I slept in the garret, not because it was the former maid's quarters in the days of yore, but for the sake of privacy, mine. Of course. I could see down on the orchard from my attic hideout. And Owen gave me a key to the great front door of the house. And he gave one to Brigid. And she squeezed my hand and said, commanded, rhymed: *How happy we three will be!*

Lord grant me the cloak of disguise that Athena loaned to Odysseus so that I may meander through the ruins taking stock of chattel and charnel before the spell breaks and my all-encompassing swath of darkness is transformed back to wool. Lord grant me but a secure hour, a sandbagged story, a nimble pen, a wandering eye, a leper's lassitude, a loner's intemperance, a fetishist's foot, a poet's prudence, a pen pal's prurience, a playmate's provocation, a pornographer's persistence. Grant me a sensitive syntax, weak-roped gallows, safe Southern passage, and a face impossible to remember. Forgive Eve the pseudocarp and regret Adam both stamen and pistil. Allot to Lot the Franklin Mint commemorative saltshaker in the shape of his wife ever backward looking. Admit into evidence the blood-spattered sword with which Judith slew Holofernes; the tears of Niobe; Salome's seventh veil; the mottled feathers of Philomel; the abandoned bed of Oenone; Agamemnon's uneaten last supper still set cold at the banquet table; a bucket of Marat's crimson bathwater; and here, these grisly crime-scene photos of Leda's talon-scarred thighs. Forgive me my sins: the cracked looking glass, the

glue-pot, forged signature, the unfastened blouse. These are but the
infidel's manic diversions. Forgive me my cloven hoof, forked tongue,
my tattler's prehensile tale. Allow this day to last unending. Grant me
the strength to deny the permanence of even those things which are
penned in invisible ink; the perseverance to serve out my sentence; and
the wisdom to know the difference. Amen.

Milky into the coffee goes the cream. From the kitchen I returned
with two cups. I brought Owen black coffee in the bone-white
china. He set it solidly in the dirt and resumed his digging. The del-
icate-handled cup looked like a little colony, an outpost of British
pride and progress in an unsullied new wilderness. Tiny men in pith
helmets rallied their forces. Ladies lived inside the white china dome
alternately fainting and reviving themselves with the aid of smelling
salts and cordial liqueurs. The cat could not resist. She ran by this
new empire and after two or three sideways attempts quite success-
fully tipped the cup. I declare you free! Meow! Emancipated!
Liberated! Be free to return to the liquid siftings of the earth: sink,
seep, ooze, sail out to sea or sewer. Owen said nothing. I stated the
obvious: *Oh, look what the cat has done this time.* And I rose and
returned to the kitchen to colonize another cup from the coffeepot.

Nursery rhymes and fairy stories papered in cloudless blue, Florida
orange, chicky-wicky yellow, wax-fang pink, blackbird black, bean
green, riding-hood red—the walls of Brigid's study. It had once been
Jonathan's room, he who had fallen asleep all those nights of his
childhood to the cracked-up soufflé of Humpty Dumpty, the sight of
which in turn evoked the rumbling tummy of Jack Sprat who could
eat no fat while his wife could eat no lean. The King's men arrived
with grated cheese and frying pans. The fork ran away with the
spoon. And there too sat Little Miss Muffet like a petticoated Lady
Justice weighing the virtues of a bowl of curds against the contents of

her other hand, a rather pleasant-faced spider wearing a bowler hat. Jack climbed the beanstalk; Jill came tumbling after another Jack entirely. In the end many crowns were broken. Sugarplums were duly savored. And who could forget Bo Peep scandalously napping under a willow tree with Rip Van Winkle, both having succumbed to the pastoral pleasures of counting sheep? Jonathan was not yet two when his mother died. Snow White contemplated a bright polished apple. Rumpelstiltskin danced a jig. Hansel and Gretel watched as the witch shingled her cottage with gingerbread. And three little pigs smartly attired in top hats and cutaway coats revealing their delightfully sausagey shanks and curling wiggly tails took tea and marmalade cakes in a snug brick cottage while a wolf lurking nearby waited for darkness to fall.

Oozy, life arose from the mud, the slush, the soup and silt. Amoebae, squirmy organisms, shape-shifters, protozoa sending out armies of arms: fake, pseudopod, temporary tongues and spindles into the muck to feed and grow, to locomote and thrive. Oligocene: monkeys and apes appeared across the earth. They foraged, they groomed, they hunted, they reproduced; multiplied by the laws of the covenant and became as numerous as the stars in the heavens. They took up sticks and learned to dig. On paper in longhand, cursive, line by line, Owen was writing a book. A book of the old stories once singsonged by blind men, scrawled on papyrus, chalked on cave walls. Owen was obdurate. When would old lessons be learned? Five thousand years of progress and the semantic cautions of the Tower of Babel still apply? It's absurd. When can we hope to defy our legacy of disaster? He retold the stories of Narcissus, Minos, Icarus and Daedalus. He used as digging stick a silver inkpen. Owen sprawled out on the Procrustean bed that had trapped so many travelers before him; he stretched out to the full length and breadth of his limbs to find that he was the only one in the whole of the world who fit like Goldylocks in the bunk of the littlest bear, snugga-dub-dub, just right, no dangling participles, no banging against the headboard during fitful sleep. Onus: the burden of time and tide on the backs of storytellers. Obverse: the opposite of reverse. Oceanic: the sensation described by Freud as akin to religious ecstasy felt without belief in God. Onionskin: the peeling away of layer after layer. One million: the number of licks it takes to get to the candy center of a Tootsie Pop.

Potatoes in the stewpot eyeing the dog with suspect reservation. Portents in the shape of blackbirds gathering in trees against the sky. Premises, promises, predictions, predilections, the present tense presents itself in the plink plink plunk of the shovel hitting stone. I hand Owen a new cup of coffee, black, and he places it into the earth defying history to repeat itself. I sit and sip from my own cup. I stir and sip and listen while he tells me the story of Prince Paris, the passionate shepherd, the secret son of Priam and Hecuba, the brother of Cassandra, the neglectful groom of Oenone who abandoned her for a discordant apple which he exchanged for Helen, who was the daughter of Leda and the sister of twins Castor and Pollux who cracked open from the egg of divine rape to shine constellation-bright in the heavens serving to guide sailors home across wine-dark foreign seas in ships destined to be smashed to bits on the rocks of unfamiliar shores. Owen sets down the shovel, sits on a stone, stares out at the fields and cautions me: *Incidit in Scyllam, cupiens vitare Charybdim.* I wait. The apples ripen a moment more on the trees. Worms are turning. The birds hover darkly at a distance. He translates as prophetically as Cassandra herself: *He runs on Scylla, wishing to avoid Charybdis.* We speed to our fates. There is no stopping us.

Quoth, quote, quoted, quotidian, quixotic. Winston says: *The one thing that matters is that we shouldn't betray one another, although even that can't make the slightest difference.* Julia says: *They can make you*

say anything—anything—but they can't make you believe it. They can't
get inside you. Brigid kept her bedraggled paperback copy of *1984*
bedside bookmarked at page 137.

Regarding the reversal of sentences into the passive voice, note please
this: untold revolutionary rewards can be found in the denial of subjects and the prominence of objects. Look at this sentence: *I ate cake.*
Invert it. *Cake was eaten.* And suddenly the "I" is gone. Suddenly the
cake was visited upon by absolutely anyone: a horde of hungry wedding guests, two escaped convicts wearing striped pajamas and leg-
irons, three brokenhearted teenage girls on prom night, four lords-
a-leaping, five failed dieters, or perhaps the one face you face daily
in the mirror. There is no "I." I am an implication. I exist only in the
margins. I have been exiled to the land of context. I have vanished.
I commit no action. I allow action to be smeared upon my body like
Betty Crocker frosting with a great oversized spatula. I am one or
one hundred thousand. But the cake remains. A hundred honey
cakes were set out for the tea party. A slice of day-old lemon cake sat
encased under glass on the kitchen counter. An anonymous fork and
knife approached in silence, a disembodied set of hands and count-
less ensuing sticky fingers devoured by mouth the evidence: icing,
marzipan rosettes, pistachio splinters, all seven colossal layers until
neither the spun sugar bride nor the licorice-bedecked groom
remained standing. Think on that lovely slab of cake that was baked
and decorated and displayed on the best of china plates to be consumed by drunken revelers; that confection of butter, milk, and eggs
that existed for a while as subject only of its own epic-comic-tragic
culinary marshmallow drama: *Die do I?—Alas—I digest.* What of the
existential deathbed questioning of the pineapple upside-down cake:
Eaten am I upped? What of the tearful eulogy delivered by the
scullery maid: *Here lie the plate and pedestal, the mouthwatering*
remains of dear departed Devil's Food; Children remembered, but only

a few and down they forgot as up he was chewed. A moment of silence. The oven timer chimes out the funeral march. *Beaten were eggs and folded were butters. Batter to batter and crust to crust.* Consider the buttered crust of bread on which Brigid nibbled and picked into pieces until it was broken down into a speckle of crumbs across her typewriter keys. Presently she grew tired of typing. The crumbs remained alphabetically arranged. Think of the object as the subject and let the verbs disperse like cinnamon streusel topping. Dirt was dug. Books were read. Dug were days. Bread was broken. *I Am,* the Lord proclaimed himself for he needed no name to prove an axiomatic existence crying in the wilderness. *Am, am I!* Am I? Unwound were hours. Melted in the desert heat, the icing on the golden calf gave off the strange sweet scent of honey. Bees swarmed. Lost were hours, unregained. Cake was eaten. *Who am I?* cried the Lord, *to be so forsaken?*

September fell by the wayside. It crashed down headlong, sans senti-mentality. It lost itself somewhere on the thirtieth day of the ninth month under a layer of the first fine frost and the hardened earth. The solstice passed. The days became short and cold. Still, on that morn-ing, on this morning, on the morning of the particular day which in some miraculous manner becomes the signature, the stand-in, the synecdoche replacing the unwieldy sum of all the days we spent together, the sun was bright. Brigid shivering a bit, having grown tired, distracted, looked out the window, rose to find her sweater, then from her perch saw Owen and me in the garden: he pausing on his shovel to sip coffee and I sitting before a heap of updug dirt lis-tening to his narration. Before us stretched the flat green world, browning, as though no one had yet devised a vision of its oviform peculiarity. She hugged herself in the warmth of her oversized woolen sweater. Her concentration sorely broken, her mind jumping on to other mysteries, she switched off the typewriter, slipped from the

room, made her way down the hallway to the third bedroom on the
second floor, a room which we had not yet had time to clean and perhaps never would as Owen had taken it as his study and would neither allow nor brook access. Still, all this said, there was no lock on
the door. Brigid turned the handle. She opened the door like the last
of Bluebeard's wives. Dusty cretonne curtains shut out the light. The
walls were painted Balmoral red. She saw Owen's work, in the form
of eight stacks of index cards, each rubberbanded, atop the mahogany
desk, beside a manuscript. Each story or rather myth or rather parable or rather fable or rather legend or rather story that he was using
in his collection was outlined, explicated, and traced from ancient
origins to popular interpretation on numbered cards in a handwriting so tiny and cryptic it seemed designed to present itself as a new
language. Brigid later told me that she felt as though someone, a
ghost whose name she dared not speak took her at that moment by
the hand (See! Feel! How cold her fingers were still!) and led her into
that forbidden room. While Brigid searched through the study urged
on, impelled by the vengeance of an uneasy ghost, in the garden
Owen held forth on the history of the world by way of the coinci-
dentally Germanic origins of both his first and second wives.

Thus sprach Owen: *What a mess this Christian millennium has been.
In the year 1096 German soldiers in the First Crusade while on their
way to take from Islam the citadel of Jerusalem made the tactfully utilitarian, ultimately zealous decision that it would be inefficient to wait
till the Holy Land to purge the infidels when so many lived among them,
and so these soldiers of Christ took it upon themselves to burn and destroy
every Jewish village along the length of the Rhine. And it was eight hundred and forty years between those purges and the rise of the even more
efficient German gas chambers. Or more ridiculous, the gas vans that
offered drive-up genocide service. Nearly nine hundred years that saw
the Renaissance, the Enlightenment, the birth of scientific reason, logic,*

*secular humanism, not to mention centuries of art—oil paintings, icons
to abstractions—eight hundred and forty-odd years of disease—leprosy,
plague, cholera, consumption, influenza, pox, and polio. And the
national mindset, whatever justifications one can construct about following orders or obliviousness or self-preservation, in eight hundred
and forty years the German mindset did not change: they were still in
1936 constructing efficient ways to cleanse the world of the unclean. So
how, tell me, should we presume that if they did not change or learn or
develop a moral consciousness in eight hundred years, that they have
changed in the past fifty? And please, excuse the clumsy analogy—I still
prefer the method of pen and paper—but I refuse to believe that the rise
of technology, the age of plastic, or the invention of the computer chip
can change the human heart. No, no, don't try to answer. Of course, it's
a rhetorical question. Of course every rational person knows not to judge
a people as a monolithic whole, a wall, if you will. That in the masses
there are those of moral virtue hidden among millions of monsters. And
Abraham would have had Sodom saved but for the strength of one vir-
tuous man. It is as easy, is it not, to rationalize anonymous goodness as
it is to quantify amorphous evil? Some questions have no answers. While
every noun or date in the history book is an answer to a question not yet
proposed. Tell me why I, a rational man, no? Why should I hold in spite
of my education and rationality firmly to the irrational belief that
Germans have a genius, an inbred addiction to collective murder in
which the deaths of faceless millions are perpetrated by faceless millions
in an endless obscene anonymity? Have I earned the right to espouse this
particular heresy; am I exempted from, outside of reason on this particular topic because I am a Jew, a victim not only allowed, but sanc-
tioned, expected to be irrational? Or are some crimes against humanity
so atrocious that rationality toward the perpetrators is, should be thusly
suspended in perpetuity? Tell me what great act of contrition could
expunge the historical guilt of any nation? A monument? A statue? A
round-table discussion? A returned suitcase packed full of stolen gold*

teeth? Whatever are we, Jews, five thousand years in the making? Secondhand infidels still? Or exiles, outcasts, worse, genus species: Wandering Jew, subset Americana? None of us is free from our guilty past lives. As Americans we crave a more intimate sort of frontier mayhem, the crime of passion committed with the kitchen knife—the lover brained with a frying pan—the gun accidentally discharged fifty-two times from the bedroom window into the schoolyard below. A nation of hunters and collectors. A nation who values the abstract ideal of beauty so deeply that it doesn't know what to do with it, but kill it. Mooseheads on the wall. People magazine in the rec room? Think about it: all over America, in kitchens, in bathrooms, in bedrooms, that wondrous nation of troglodytes, noose-necked wrestlers are breeding with fashion models in a bone-breaking crush to create a new race of Visigoths—let's hope they leave us all in the dust. The best hope for Jews is the ultimate martyrdom of extinction. Let a nation of brutes rule the earth preaching the Good News. The Good News? Do you know what the Good News is? Christianity spreads like an infection. It dispersed across the earth like a contagion and killed what it could not assimilate. When Princess Anna of Constantinople saw the ragged illiterate band of thugs that was to be the first wave of two hundred years of Christian Crusaders she wrote in astonishment: "the whole of the west was bursting forth into Asia in a solid mass, with all its possessions." What a picture—like the tourist-besieged ticket booth at Disney World. And how many more pictures there are to come. And still the most beautiful and enduring image man has constructed in the history of art is the sadomasochistic torment of a Jew nailed to the crossed planks of a wooden gallows. Our very suffering is a thing of beauty. Is it any wonder we marched ourselves into the gas chambers? We had only our collective suffering as a weapon. So this was and is our battle plan: to suffer. We do it exceptionally well. We stand as a grand artifact, a museum piece, testament to a time before the birth of time. We are the great cautionary tale, the mild David who bore the mighty Goliath; and so this is our collective and astonished guilt—to

suffer the knowledge that our worst oppressors were born of our own chil-
dren. Our guilt is nontransferable, based on the myth of Exodus, the
story of communal escape, so that each and every Jew is taught that he
himself is interchangeable with a historical version of himself. There are
always two selves. The one who is me and the one who went forth from
the house of bondage as me. And we the undersigned, signatories of
bondage, carry this inestimable house around on our backs like the shell
of a turtle plastered with a "kick me" sign. But what can any of this pos-
sibly matter to us? As Americans we tell ourselves that we must live of
and for the future. That no one is responsible for the past or its seismo-
graphic eruptions of slavery, genocide, and ethnic cleansing. No past? We
have bathed in the River Lethe to forget even having forgotten. And all
over America in a weak-kneed love of beauty men are loading shotguns
and women are baking cinnamon rolls that pop mysteriously out of card-
board tubes. And children are growing fat and dull and glassy-eyed from
staring at so much beauty and gorging themselves sick on so much whole-
some dairy-fresh goodness. So tell me, who can blame Brigid? How can
I presume to either blame or not blame Brigid, who has never done any-
thing efficiently or maliciously in her entire young life—for having con-
structed a fantasy to both condemn and absolve herself of inherited
responsibility? We are none of us free from the sins of our fathers, and if
Brigid can wrench and render and rename something from the squalor,
whether it is true or false will matter very little in the end. True or false?
What are we? Something ridiculous? The stuff of which dreams are
made? We split atoms. We sling phrases. True? False? We are only in the
end the stories that we tell about ourselves. He looked up toward her
window. He did not know, neither of us could have known that
Brigid had left her room led by the ice-cold hand of a specter down
the hall into his room where she went immediately to the closet and
without prompting was possessed of an uncontrollable desire to
remove a certain loose panel of wooden baseboard which she could
not have known in advance concealed a small cubbyhole barely large

enough to fit her hand, but into which she reached and felt then against her fingers the substance of something light and dry and secret. Brigid removed the bundle. The ghost abandoned her, and she found herself unexpectedly and suddenly alone, huddled on the cold floor in the otherwise empty closet cradling to her chest the yellowed letters, long lost, fabled to the point of being fabulous, the missing letters of Frances Warren Lieb. In the orchard Owen stopped in midsentence, looked up again at the empty window, dug his shovel in the ground, and asked: *Where was I?*

Understand that I did not know that Brigid had at that exact moment found the letters. Understand that I did not know that Owen was searching in the dirt for those selfsame letters; he being of the unwavering belief that the letters, having been lost for nearly thirty years, were long-gone—destroyed, no doubt—but also of the superstitious inclination that only through ritual searching would he keep them from ever being found. Understand that when he asked where he had left off in his essay against the sins of Christendom, I did not answer as such: *You were saying, Professor Lieb, that all the world's a sewer and we are merely sewage—the flotsam and jetsam, rags, cans, bottles, the ignoble crap floating along its capacious and briny depths to the tune of old standbys and show tune ditties: "Sam, Sam the lavatory man, picking up the tissues and the paper towels, listen to the rumble of the human bowels, down, down, down beneath the ground!" Or more prettily put: we have fallen asleep among the poppies, in the asphodel fields of forgetfulness. History is then an, um, sort of combination of hell and home spa: a whirlpool and cesspool and geyser all in one, a grand embarrassment that sucks in crap but can't make it go away, and all the old stories, the woes, even the minutely trash-compacted miseries simply churn and churn until suddenly spewing up and spraying out unrestrained all the submerged detritus of the centuries, the hours, unleashed, upchucked! Undenied! Oh well, if we*

can't sink it, we can burn it, hey? And if we can't burn it, we can raze,
implode, tear everything down and leave in its place a gaping maw
over which will be erected a giant Kmart as a monument to a generic
freestanding future sanitized of the ruins of the past, a great un-Babel,
a divine Ur-text, a concrete box free from guilt or responsibility, style
or substance, faith or faithlessness. With a parking lot the size of the
summer palace, the length and breadth of a billion thousand football
stadiums lined up from here to the crispy onion rings of Saturn. Open
twenty-four hours. The only thing left for which to live is brand loyalty!
Sweat equity! The Jew, the Christian, the Muslim, all of us obsolete
inventions of the ancient mind, mousetrap-like devices in the war on
things that go bump in the night; all of us trapped in the gutter of his-
tory, pushed along by each great flush, dredged up, borne backward by
tidal eddies of filth, bearing the taint of our origins to each new stop
in the recesses of the underground septic circuitry. All aboard the
garbage barge! What? Wait, no. What happened to those poppies? It is
our same cesspool from which up above grows this delirious field of
flowers into which we fall sleeping to forget everything? That's better.
Dear Sir, I wholeheartedly agree. I concur. I follow your logic. It jumps
in fits and starts. The token of all living creatures is their response to
stimuli. Your dialogue lives, dialogic! It reproduces line by line into a
thousand arguments until each of those divides, breaks off to follow
and chase its own crazy teenage dream: forms a militia, joins the Peace
Corps, feeds the impoverished, burns a cross, breaks hearts, buries a
loved one, buys a beach house, prays without ceasing, paints a master-
piece, starts a business, dies in a rest home, dims the lights, departs for
the infinity of space in a satellite. Is never heard from again. Your tau-
tology aches in tropism toward the light of goodness shining like a bea-
con in the heart of man under a rainbow on a Sunday drive in the
country with the radio playing oldies tunes all along the macadam
back roads of childhood. It fills me with the abject contented hopeless-
ness of hope. But it seems to me that the key to understanding you is to

*understand that you acknowledge no difference between now and then.
Between say, 1096 and 1996 and 1496. Between the Battle of Hastings
and the Battle of the Network Stars; betwixt the moon walk and the
first cockroach creeping off a Spanish man-o-war to bite deliriously into
a fat New World tomato. But does such a thing as responsibility exist?
Or blame? That is, is anyone ever to blame? Is it true that Columbus
was a crypto-Jew who sought the freedom one finds only when drifting
far off course? And that the Pope himself has secret documents hidden
in the Vatican basement attesting to the veracity of this supposition? Is
it true that there is no basement at the Alamo? Was it a navigational
mistake or a suicidal attempt to fall off the map? And that in Latin
"columba" means "dove" or "columbinus," "like a dove"? Do you see the
pattern? The dove sent by Noah from the Ark to find land? All coinci-
dental? What if Christopher was on the run, getting out of town fast,
escaping the black-hooded wrath of the Torquemada Inquisition, and
what if he unwittingly brought in tow enough filth, rats, bacilli, small-
pox, and tuberculosis to conquer a foreign shore even without the aid of
firearms and the Good Book? Is he to blame? Is anyone to blame? And
what did his men receive in return: corn and chocolate, potatoes and
peanuts, vanilla, indigo, tobacco, sunflowers and syphilis. Do you imagine that there is an unending patronymic disbursement of blame so that
one father blames his actions on his father before him? And no individual is ever more than the sum of historic parts? As for Germany, sir, I
admit, I've never been there. If I ever get there I'll send along a postcard.
A funny one with a picture of a beer garden or a concentration camp
turned theme park attraction. It was on my travel itinerary but then I
got waylaid in and along and around the bays and beauty of the Aryan
Isles in autumn. So I'll take your word for it. I'll defer to your better
judgment. But then I'm the impressionable type. Unleavened,
unformed, somewhere between uncouth and unctuous. We are not so
much, are we, the stories that we tell about ourselves? Rather, we are the
dreamy lard-laced middle between the wafers of before and after; we are*

the mysterious doublestuff with which Oreos are filled. We are the flesh
of the kid seethed in the milk of the mother. We are an abomination.
Understand that in answer, I did not, in fact, speak. I was afraid of
Owen Lieb.

Vindictive, vengeful? No, Brigid was neither. She felt impelled by
some external force, she swore to this, not only to search out and
find the letters, but to protect them. But really, was this force a
ghost? A shade? Perhaps yes, maybe no. No one who has felt the
cold fingers of a specter creeping along the back of the neck ever
again doubts the horror of such a sensation. Or simply an icy presence in an otherwise cozy room? Let's forget grim ghoulies and
move on to the substance that quieted Brigid's nightmares.
Valerian blooms in small flowers delicate of pink and white, but
when the root is ground into a fine powder and encapsulated in
gelatin it promotes the sort of sleep that lingers hazily past the
necessity of night and on into the next morning. And this, the taking of soporifics, left Brigid still in a dreamlike state, so that when
she found herself on the floor in the closet, she gave a silent count
of ten before averring to the belief that for the second time in her
life she had found artifacts of literary importance. First her grandmother and now her predecessor? Astonishing. Brigid did not at
that moment read the letters. In fact, she was uncertain whether
she was ever going to read them. She knew that she was no vampire. She didn't particularly thrive on the blood of others, did she?
She didn't need the sustenance of the past to survive. No, rather
she was going to hold onto the documents for safekeeping. So up
from the floor of the closet she rose, valiantly. She went then not
to her writing room papered with oranges and lemons, nor did she
remain in her husband's study, but into their shared bedchamber
where stood an enormous unmade bed, the sheets in a heap, pillows flattened, quilt thrown wanton-wise to the floor, a bed of the

sort that was the marital secret between Penelope and Odysseus, not fashioned in the Lieb's latter-day myth of the trunk of a tree but rather framed now with greened-brass. Brigid was overcome by vigilance, protectiveness. How else to explain why she did not leave the papers in the nook where they had been safely stashed for decades? She placed the letters, hid them where her husband would not look, in her velvet vanity case that sat discreetly, forgettably beneath the bedside table. She lifted the top cosmetics tray and set the bundle in the bottom on a silk voile scarf patterned with the signs of the zodiac. How bold was Sagittarius! How bullish Taurus. Brigid arranged the vesture within the case, folding, fluffing, setting the edges just so, nicely, cozily, very comfy indeed, until she was satisfied with her little vault. And so among tiny bottles of French perfume, lipsticks, cotton balls, trinkets, here and there hard candies of butterscotch and lime, keys to rented houses of which she had long forgotten even the street addresses, earrings and charms, on a bed of pilfered hotel soaps in the shape of seashells, the hidden letters nestled, fortress inviolable.

Wait, wait, there's more. Brigid walked outside to meet us in the garden. She said that she had gotten ever so much done that morning and were we going to play all day in the garden without her? She didn't think that that was nice at all. John Paul Jones came out into the air with her, and he ran a few spirited laps, nosed rotty apples, prodded the cat playfully, rolled, wallowed in the weeds and demanded his due honor: attention and ear rubs from each of us in turn. And as the petting progressed, the cat stalked a hummingbird. We talked with great gravity about dirt, and then with some levity about air. On the subject of water, we were fluid. The discussion of fire proved inflammatory. Brigid bore on her face no hint of recent bewitchment or mark where the ghost had gripped her arm. Owen hinted lunchward. Sandwiches were in order. And we all agreed that the day, thus far, was progressing wondrously. It felt like all the days of a life rolled up and wrapped into one winningly wistful morning. What a pity to see it end.

X marks the spot where we stood against the autumn afternoon, tableau vivant: Brigid's red sweater, the spotted apples, gray cat, the chocolate dog, Owen with hands dark-dirt-darkened, I carrying cups. Exeunt all characters. Owen placed the shovel against the side of the outbuilding, a glorified shed loaded full of the rusty implements of earthy excavations, and awaited Brigid who turned her face up to the sky with eyes closed in a sort of ecstatic acknowledgment of the sun deity, but only for a moment before allowing Owen the gentlemanly grace of following her into the kitchen, not before the cat slipped her way around Brigid who entered before Owen, but after the cat and before the dog who waited while the first three had vacated the scene and ran a thrilling set of circles, loop-de-loops, crazy-eights into a panting exhaustion before joining me, bearer of cups, our lady of situations, into the house after which I shut the door. We exchanged nature for nurture. But you remained in the orchard, glad to have a moment to wander about alone, free from our company, yes, I entirely understand, but still I watched you from the kitchen window and saw you place a twisted apple, windfall sweet, along the monumental rocks of the first Mrs. Lieb's overgrown memorial.

You can't quite get oriented, can you, to the house itself? Does it face the sea? Can one see the sea? And in which direction should one walk to find the fields of sheep herded by the heartbreakingly diligent black-and-white dogs? If one continues in this direction will one come upon a charming small town just like the tour books promise? Complete with church steeple, crowded breakfast café run by a nice plump lady and her red-cheeked daughter who is either a

great deal younger or older than one would expect, where the exactly
three tables are taken by men eating platefuls of eggs and smoking
intolerable hand-rolled cigarettes, but don't despair, the ladies do a
bustling take-away business especially on mornings when the heavy
cream and currant scones are baked fresh on the premises. Which
house belongs to Marie, and can I meet the kids? Where exactly is
the orchard in relation to the garden? And when did the shed
appear? Was it there all along? Is something ominous hidden inside
or are there only garden tools, not that they can't be ominous—the
axe! The pruning shears, the cruel heft of the whetstone, not to mention insecticides so bland, odorless, colorless, tasteless that they
could be boiled into soup and no one would be the wiser. And what
of the story of the woman who dealt a lethal blow to her husband
with a frozen shank of lamb and then cooked up the evidence with
pearl onions and mint jelly and served it to the police when they
arrived to investigate? But perhaps your imagination is getting the
better of you? Which way does the kitchen door face? North or
south? Does it open into the kitchen properly or is there some sort
of porch or out-room for the hanging of raincoats and removal of
muddy boots? Is there anything particularly Irish about this house?
Could we remove, dig, extract it with a giant crane and place it
someplace else entirely—Belize perhaps? What would be the
difference? Would one nibble on cinnamon crackers instead of
shortbread? Would the tea be iced and served with generous wedges
of lemon rather than sugared and steaming? Or Baghdad, where, on
the sunny shores of the Tigris, one could linger over sesame seed
slices of halvah and sip coffee pressed through a filter of honeyed car-
damom? Have you ever been to a place that you had so long imagined and dreamed of only to find that it was just like the place you
had recently abandoned? Can you find your way at night by the constellations or when lost in the woods do you prefer to get your nose
to the dirt like a good groundhog and snuffle along snout-wise? Do

you consider yourself a creature of air or earth or fire? Water? Borne
on a tall clipper ship across all seven seas and the greatest of lakes
even if only in your daydreams? Ah, is that you bedecked in a ruffled
shift and leather breeches swabbing the deck? Singing in time with
the rowing of the galley slaves: *All we owe, we owe her.* Well I can't
tell you how to best find your way through this particular labyrinth;
the keys that I have are useless, the birds immediately devoured the
breadcrumb trail, my astrolabe is fractured, and the wool skein, once
unwound, proved far shorter than my original calculations had
promised. But, still, don't despair. Go on now and get pen or pencil;
you are going to draw yourself a map. You are the cartographer of
your own destiny. Set the dimension to be synonymous with the
timeline of the standard geological scale. One inch represents ten
hundred thousand years. Draw the water in crimson blue! The warm
climate melts the glaciers. The sky is xanthic yellow! And the substance of the air is pure milk black. St. Eulalia prays for the safety of
sailors. This is your treasure map. Mark *Z* where you stood alone to
survey the scene after we abandoned you to your own devices. Place
A whence the first apple fell. In between the alpha and omicron
somewhere all the necessary letters to the serving of your sentence
come to represent characters, scenes, moments, memories placed on
the flat surface of paper. Symbols to represent symbols. I know, I
know, it's a maddeningly indecipherable cryptology, but you've
always been good with spatial relations, with fitting the tiniest ship
into the most ridiculously narrow bottle. The trick is that you build
it piece by piece, the mast, plank, stern, the leering pirates bran-
dishing a built-to-scale Jolly Roger. And with the aid of the tooth-
pick, tweezers, model-airplane glue and magnifying glass you construct from sticks and slivers a minor miracle. When it is finished it
looks remarkably of one piece, complete! Thar she blows! You have
a density of thought, an architectural eye, an ability to force big ideas
into tight airless spaces like elevators and soda bottles. Your hands

may be small, but your grip is mighty. Your reach is out-and-out obscene. Use these God-given skills to your advantage. Draw the house for me, then. Use a compass, protractor, T-square, and tablespoon. Remember your conversions: there are 2.2 pounds per kilogram. Orient yourself to the four winds, the four humors, the foreign faces that people your imagination. And set adrift in your little two-masted yawl you begin to despair, *I know, I know,* as you coffee-tin drain out buckets full of sweet saltwater, sinking, until suddenly, unexpectedly, no—yes—the shore appears, landfall hazy in the burning morning fog, and you cry out as did all your ancestors before you with the grand unstoppable barbaric yawp: *Yahweh!*

Zymologists educated in the art of fermentation understand what you and I are only learning, that from rot and ruin comes wine; from summer comes winter; from zeal elation rises, and conversely, declines. From zenith to nadir, the downward slope is ever more slippery than the uphill climb was treacherous. Which is to say that I have fallen upon the unlikely and abrupt ending of our morning's activities. It became all of a sudden, afternoon. Which is to say all stories bear the burden of ending within their first lines. Do you like your stories long and littered? What of afternoons that seem endless over crumbs, cookies, quotes, and conversation until the sky, by the pull of tides and most celestial of inclinations, turns black. I used to read books in the half-light of evening and through squinting changed the words on the page to other words. We entered the house. When you think about us, be kind. Be forgiving. Be not unlike the Zen master who opined, *when life gives you lemons, make lemonade.* For lunch Brigid spooned soup. The dog danced for scraps. Zwieback, oven-warmed, maple-rich, and sprinkled with nutmeg was taken with apples. Owen ate a sandwich. There was some talk, I recall, and laughter about the euphoric sensation of bodies under the influence of zero gravity.

Kafiristan

I began with the most simple of motives. I wanted to tell the story of my time with Owen and Brigid Lieb and how I became, by virtue (or lack thereof) of their hard-earned fame, one of those overlooked and forgettable girls who tells all because she had the experience of being briefly trusted to live in their stellar orbit. She knew everything. They kept cinnamon vodka in the freezer. Owen sometimes sneaked a cigarette in the orchard. In logical progression Brigid divested herself of America, margarine, brassieres, and diet soda. But this is just too much: long-limbed high-breasted, and blonde as an Iowa cornfield, Brigid Lieb proclaimed herself to be the lost granddaughter of father time. *Marcel Proust?* Maybe I would have believed Faulkner or Fitzgerald, even Ibsen. But Proust? That tiny doe-eyed Frenchman, that insomniac who could barely leave his bedchamber, who spent his life in a hypochondriac's limbo always awaiting the vindication of terminal illness, the chrysanthemum-bearing boy to whom the society ladies prettily referred as *our pet Jew?* Never mind that, never mind that no previous biographer had turned up or tumbled or stumbled across stalwart Greta from Danzig who arrived in Paris in worsted wool stockings carrying a suitcase full of sausages and who departed in silks, concealing beneath her corset the secret to the legacy of lost time—a child who would grow up to wear lightly the crown of this empire as a purveyor of property and casualty insurance in Indianola, Iowa. Never mind any of it, perhaps it's true. Stranger things have been known to happen, right? Didn't motherless Romulus and Remus suckle their strength from wolves? Didn't Alexander the Great conquer the world before we would have allowed him to toast his own victory? Didn't Marco Polo return from

143

the East with a take-out order of spaghetti and meatballs? Didn't
Lizzy Borden endorse the wholesome drinkability of milk products
from the eponymous Borden Dairy? Didn't she have a tattoo of Elsie
the cow engraved on her shoulder at one of those wharfside bars, a
dive, a shack, a shanty just like but not quite the one where Mrs.
Paul met in secret with the Gorton's fisherman in the dark, their forbidden love painted in tartar sauce, smeared in evidence on a thousand discarded lobster bibs, played out in waltz-time against the
romantic siren's song of the foghorns? Didn't the right honorable
Reverend Arthur Dimmesdale on the sheer burning force of his own
guilt brand a scarlet letter across his chest? Do I mix fact with
fiction? Myths with the mythic? The sweet with the salty? Fine—but
wasn't Elvis Presley recently sighted speeding away from the drive-
through of a Burger King in Kalamazoo, Michigan? Isn't the road to
hell paved with fast-food joints? When the first Crusaders heeding
the call of Pope Urban II reached the holy city of Jerusalem in July,
1099 and slaughtered 30,000 Muslims and Jews in two days flat,
didn't an ecstatic onlooker praise God and announce that the blood
of the infidels reached up as high as the horses' knees? Didn't fraulein
Greta, that little linzertorte of a girl with the straight seams of her
netted stockings running like chocolate-cherry icing down the
sumptuous curves of a Black Forest cake, didn't she offer the anonymously French M.P. protection from the world, solace crushed
against the Wagnerian beat-beat-beating of her timely Teutonic
heart? And speaking of hearts, let's not forget about Owen. What's
he up to? He's digging graves. He's excavating catacombs and plotting tunnels for a life underground. Even John Paul Jones, no
stranger to buried treasure, is dumbfounded. Autumn is counted in
days that don't match the date on the old calendar. We consume
cakes. Sugar, flour, egg. Subject, verb, object. Brigid writes in her
wallpapered room in the morning. Owen retires in the evening to
the red room. Like an off-time metronome the tip-tap-tapping of

typing, the scrawl of stories punctuates the progression of days. They pass. They go. The days are shorter, the mornings cold, the essence of decadence is distilled into the last few hours of light when we sit, no, no, *sat* amongst the dishes and crusts of bread while Brigid talked aimlessly in her honey-sweet tangle of this and that. I swear it is illegal in Iowa to live through September after September as though there is no winter in sight, as though no one had ever invented December let alone snow, let alone the thousand words for snow in the Eskimo language. We lived with no future tense, with nothing but the next pot of coffee and the books in a heap on the table and the papers scarred with red ink and the potatoes on the cutting board. No future, but of the past we could not speak except in terms of generalization, of wars perhaps and the names of kings, but never of what had happened not so long ago in that very house. Franny was gone, and yet she seemed to continue to inhabit her former rooms. Was it dream or desire when I turned my head quickly and thought I caught the glimpse of a retreating shadow on the staircase? It is only now after the story has long since ended that I wonder about the details as though the outcome could still prove different. Will Owen unearth a pirate's cask brimming with skulls, bleached bones, Confederate doubloons, manuscripts which neither begin nor end, good luck charms and mother-of-pearl trinkets pilfered from ships on the high seas? Are the sands of the hourglass so like the days of our lives? Will Brigid stuff a sixteen-course meal— braised grouse, bitter herbs, bread of affliction, candied yams and charlotte russe—into a lunchbox and call it a biography? And what does it matter these days, what you call anything? Here are some details in raw form to be cataloged and interpreted: Owen was an avid astrologer. Brigid was homecoming queen in high school. No one knew from where the gray cat came. She arrived the moment they opened the door to the house. There she was, the gray cat, unnamed. She appeared with the turning of the key in the lock and

she happily though somewhat apathetically in and after the manner
of all great cats submitted to domestication in exchange for a bowl
of cream. I would have done the same myself. And perhaps I did.
There I was, bleach-blighted to my inelegantly callused fingers, a girl
regrettable, forgettable enough to blend into any backdrop. Owen
and Brigid spoke, lived, complained: her tummy hurt; his eyes were
weakening. Was there ever an autumn as damp as this one? They
sympathized. They commiserated. Owen told stories that began
with the unquestionable premise: *have I ever told you about the
time—?* And no matter how many times the story had been told
Brigid laughed. And I crowded the corners of this happy domestic
life they had created for themselves. I was washing the floors or
combing the cat's matted fur. I was scraping grime from the brass
doorjambs or polishing the wood. How could I not doubt that they
needed me if only to silently witness and thus later give testament to
the artifact that was their beauty? I was your American girl-on-the-
guilty-go. Pretty soon we can all go home. Let me repeat that for
those of you seated in the back row: *pretty soon we can all go home.*
My story. Lost in the rubble. A trick done with dry ice, rope, and
mirrors. It gets more ridiculous by the moment. I told you about my
own letters, do you recall? They were exchanged most romantically
across a dark and stormy sea, spirited by carrier pigeons, sealed as
bottled messages and set bobbing on the waves. I'm afraid I wasn't
altogether forthcoming with the source of that situation. To really
understand you have to know that at the time of those events, I was
living with a graduate student named Alexander Piltdown. He was
never called Alex or Al, but always by the fully four syllables of his
Christian name. He said he saw in me *great potential,* not the greatest compliment a girl has ever received, but still he set about the
battle plan of saving me from myself. Oh, but don't start to get high-
minded and sympathetic about his messianic goodness, don't inform
me that missionaries are only thinking about the immortal souls of

savages; don't paint the halo over his head before I tell my side.

Alexander taught history to freshmen and delinquent sopho-
mores at the very bucolic university we both happened to attend.
History, I was hungry for it—the details, the dates, disease,
battlefields, bayonets, bandaged limbs, the speeches, the sentences
handed down and heretics strung up. I was a one-woman war crimes
tribunal. I found mapped from the beginning of time the legacy of
my own unhappiness carried from peasant to peasant like the
plague. So please allow me to plead ignorance in the court of your
good opinion. I fell in with Alexander. Others followed him. But I
feel that it is fair to say that I fell. And it's true that I was charmed
by his arguments. I wanted to be a better person. Really. Honestly. I
know that sounds ridiculous now. I know it should be followed by a
laugh track and a pie-in-the-face pratfall. But I did harbor the hope,
the possibility, that one can actually be saved from oneself. Did I
plead *ignorance?* I think I should amend that to *innocence.* So with
Alexander along I went. At first I thought it was funny when he disagreed with Darwin. He condescended to Camus. He snickered at
Sartre. Whose theory did he willingly embrace? He was fond of the
writings of a historian with a philosophical bent by the name of
Vines who presented tangled theories about the necessity of
Christian violence in shaping the culture of the twentieth century. I
think that Mr. Vines has long since left this world behind and his
books have thankfully fallen out of print. You can still find them in
used bookstores. Alexander himself would probably loan you a copy,
but his penchant for underlining in yellow nearly every sentence in
the book might grow to annoy you. I speak, you know, from experience. Oh well, it all seems a long time ago, and what did I know
then about the world. The world! It rolls across the floor like a boiled
potato. None of Alexander's students could find fault with his theories, so how bad could he have been? I was dark and decadent by
nature. He was tall and bore a striking resemblance to a popular

actor known for his tear-inducing death scenes. He did not drink
alcohol; he was abstemious and abecedarian. He was hale, healthy,
and historic. He did not smoke. He didn't swear or otherwise curse;
he did not even write in cursive. He was, by his own admission, a
teetotaler. I was eighteen and he was twenty-two. I was nineteen and
he was twenty-three. He was twenty-four and I was twenty. There
seemed to be no annual or superannuated end to us. We totaled a
great deal of tea. Alexander talked about the brave new world not
built on the ruins of the past, but excavated from it, wrenched from
the belly of the Old World, a return to the Classics! I nodded and
waited for the end of the world, new or old. The punch line to that
old joke is: I'm still waiting. So why did I stay? No, no it's all right.
It's a good question. Why did I stay with him long past the time his
student study meetings began to take on the well-organized fervor of
a Nazi Youth rally? Did I really read page after page of a dissertation
on what he called *the biological imperative of history?* He said that a
Jew could never be anything but ironic; he didn't mean this in the
pejorative sense, he assured me. It was simply a fact. And that being
ironic by nature a Jew couldn't help but lack a certain quality of faith
or even faithfulness. I hope my quandary has become clear. If I was
unfaithful to Alexander (I was! I was!) it reflected not only on me but
upon a population who for some inexplicable reason was represented
in its varied entirety in me. And while I grew to understand that
Alexander's logic was specious, I knew that he would not see the
error. He could not be moved. He had sworn faithful allegiance to
nothing so much as his faith in himself. And what could I do? I
couldn't let him believe that I stood as some kind of proof, an ambu-
latory testimonial to the sundry vices of irony, lust, and infidelity.
He said that the only loyalty a Jew could have was to the past. Did
I mention, through all of this, that he looked like that movie star,
what's his name again? The one with the winning smile? And that he
had the pervasive perversions of a Christian soldier when the lamps

were unlighted? And God knows, Jerusalem was a long way away; there was always next year. I might have been able to hold my own— teabag for teabag—against Alexander if only I hadn't made the acquaintance one day in September, if I hadn't literally stumbled over Newton Graves as I came out of the library on a rainy autumn afternoon. Moses moaned. Solomon sighed. Atlas shrugged. Proust was pensive. And in the course of a few hours, I became guilty of all the various moral crimes that Alexander had promised were my ignoble birthright.

There is no going back.

We will press on ahead, and then we can all go home.

Alexander Piltdown and Newton Graves: I will have to keep them separated from each other offstage in soundproof booths. Or they could be like the twin blue-haired Dr. Seuss monsters, Thing One and Thing Two; yes and no; matter and antimatter; proton and elec- tron rushing about like frenzied circus clowns tricycling a high-wire singing "You're a Grand Old Flag," while balancing a goldfish bowl on an umbrella. I may have to obscure their identities, supply them with false passports, monocles, bowler hats, and handlebar mous- taches. Oh Newton, have no fear; I will make a hero of you yet. Send out a casting call for leading men. Start with D: despairing, disheveled, distant. The other details are less relevant. We will apply his face later with a putty knife and spirit gum. His sickness came as an almost pleasant afterthought, a shock of mortality. He had rheumatic fever in childhood and it left his heart weak and wanting. His lungs were on the verge of collapse. Each country he left stamped a souvenir illness in his passport: conjunctivitis, shingles, whooping cough, scarlet fever, dysentery, walking pneumonia, strep infections, pleurisy, ptomaine, pox. He contracted ailments without names and suffered on past the point of recovery—but somehow he always survived. He rose from what those solicitous nurses and nuns in foreign hospitals were sure was his deathbed and made the next plane out. All that blood and bile. All those bandages and pills, those syringes shot full of antidotes, elixirs of mysterious origin adminis- tered sublingually—wouldn't you, in light of these woes, expect to hear that he has long since died? But he lives. Yes, I too marveled at it, wondered if he himself was the angel of death passing blight from land to land, growing sick yet never succumbing. The outcome of his struggles is more ridiculous than I could have imagined. I saw him on television. He was standing in a bombed-out village talking about genocide. And then the story ended and he was gone again. When I had given up finding even the ghost of him drifting aim- lessly from station to station, well, there he was—this time on one of those Sunday morning shows. With spectacular authority and rev- olutionary aplomb, he discussed the importance of his forthcoming new book: a socioeconomic/ethically-oriented study of the wreck of the Edmund Fitzgerald in the dark waters of Lake Superior in November, 1975. Was he healed? I got up close to the television set. He disintegrated into a billion pixels. I noted that as the show came back from commercial (Fred Astaire dancing with a vacuum cleaner? John Wayne endorsing beer?) he coughed into his hand. Poor Thing Two! *The sun did not shine. It was too cold to play. So we sat in the house all that cold cold wet day.* He is now only another passerby and even his signature begins to look world-weary and bedraggled. You've read the letters. You've had your moments of confusion when you were sure that the sum of your life meant less than the individ- ual pieces. Here is us again, briefly, immodestly revealed for the sake of voyeurism, solipsism, scopophilia, and what you would do while you mother was away, for the sake of going backward through the mirror to have a lookseedo at us resting there for a while before dis- appearing. Here I am at age twenty with mopsy-top curls, with flushed cheeks and furrowed brow, with a white sheet scrolled

shroud-wise like that bleached relic of Turin found a thousand times
a thousand years later still with a lover's face impressed in the fabric.
Nothing ever goes away. Everything exists in the space around itself.
This is me rolled in a white sheet on a day in September, face
propped on elbow, his hand steamrollering, bulldozing and blazing
a trail from hip to heart and home again. All aboard the Empire
Builder! Stops in Fargo, Billings, Butte, and points west! He smokes
cigarette after cigarette, in coughs and hacks, a pack, a carton, a
truckload as though through sheer ridiculous volume he could undo
the supremacy of the cliché. The ashtrays overflow. Burns speckle the
sheets. Cinders singe the carpet. He hates the world. None of the
sparks take hold. The world will not burn. How long must he await
the destruction of this room, of all rooms and times, all places? He
won't admit this until it is late and he is drunk. The well-wishers and
party-crashers, the hangers-on, the department chairs, the board
members and buyers, the hands that feed him, the student suck-ups
and dirty-joke-telling ideologues have disappeared homeward. *Fuck
them all,* he says. *I've read their books. I've been to their schools. I've
cashed their checks. I've fucked their wives and daughters. Fuck it all,* he
says. The Empire Builder slow and steady rolls its way through
wheat fields and snowstorms, blue waters, forded streams, urban
blight, and dining-car doldrums, from Seattle to Chicago and all
points in between. And look! There I am. I have no photographs to
prove my story. Get your face up close to the page and watch me dissolve into tiny blots of ink. Watch me disappear. He takes my face
in his hands. You'll have to make do with words. *And in what do you
believe?* he asks. *In God? In Country? In equal pay for equal work?* He
is only half-sardonic. *In Manifest Destiny? In Norman Mailer? In the
Heisenberg Uncertainty Principle? In tastes great, less filling? Arbeit
macht frei? What slogan will be pinned on our generation by those who
have come before us? A spoonful of sugar makes the medicine go down?*
He is going to lose himself in the ruins, the clutter, crap, the contagion.

We are already an impossibility. A moment among all the other moments like the little olive-jeweled hors d'oeuvres on silver trays, like the books heaped on the table beside the podium, the pen he uses to sign every one, mine included: *Warmest Regards!* So what was my answer? In what did I believe? *Nothing,* I say, I said to him. I repeated it for dramatic effect. *Nothing.* I wait in line to purchase my ticket, take my seat, and travel back through the mirror to arrive at today, January 2, 1999. Snow falls. We are having a nice time, aren't we? Ambling, rambling, chatting, remarking on poignant parcels of past. So how will I ever reach my destination in the allotted time? If I don't finish this story I may miss my connection, and thus be stuck in the station, not quite here nor there, stranded between *before* and *after*. Still, I wish I had time to listen to some of your tales. Trials and tempests, taxation and tribulations? I'm sure you could tell some stories. Yes, yes, that's exactly the point, isn't it? You must help me stay on course. Don't forget, if you could bring a trowel and some dry cement—I need help finding a certain vintage cask in my wine cellar. No, no, I'll go in and get it. You start mixing the mortar and laying the foundation. Have I been writing this confession for hours or eons? Newton has lost himself in front of a camera crew. He is on the steppes, the plains, the savannas, while I am brick-by-brick bricked-in by the most secure and immovable of walls. Can you imagine? The world traveler and the shut-in? I think it's a new television show on NBC full of laughs, tight sweaters, and heartwarming hilarity. A real must-see. To think we have passed through so many places and not once run into each other. Not in the corner grocery store where I paw paperbacks: oh, the hopeful diamonds of Elizabeth Taylor! The rough magic of Harry Houdini! The consumptive genius of Julia Child and Franz Kafka! I have long since come to understand that we will never Rome our roads back together based on the sentimental and sad impenetrability of matter: *Two bodies cannot occupy the same space at the same time.* Together we were

absolute, axiomatic, so unfailingly devoid of belief that we wanted
nothing more than to collapse together into nothingness and rest
there for a while and stay there and never again move or care or
unshroud, never to wash or wake or attend parties where books are
signed and cheeses sampled and wine swilled, never to do anything
but wallow in darkness. The absence of everything. Or am I wrong? Do
I have it reversed? Was it the overwhelming presence of absolutely
everything all at once contained in the close darkness of a locked
room? While collapse is certain, the moment of collapse remains
infinitely uncertain. *Thing Two and Thing One, they ran up! They ran
down! On the string of one kite we saw mother's new gown!* He drank
the remains of a glass of wine, red, which tasted suspiciously of
spoiled cider like the vinegar swabbed on Christ's dry lips as he
suffered on the Cross before disappearing. And lookee here, I'm so
free and forthcoming with the details today that I don't mind if you
now feel the need to interrupt and ask a question or two with a hint
of well-earned outrage. Ask this: Do you mean to imply, do you
mean to say that your frail body imprints the holy shroud and that
his disbelieving mouth which has sworn and sinned and needs from
your cider-sodden kisses a thorough soaping, a necessary de-Jewing,
a gargle with Epsom salts and syrup of ipecac, that this mouth of his,
lip for lip, has something at all to do with Christ on the Cross? Do
you mean to tell us that this is how you see yourself? A photon spinning toward collapse? A child left alone on a cold cold wet day? A
body in motion tending to stay in motion? A cat in a hat? A girl going
from sin to salvation and back again with the undone catch of a
brassiere? Say this, sing like the girls in the schoolyard dreaming of
ponies used to: *Under the spreading chestnut tree, I sold you and you sold
me.* You see, I am aware of my conceits, my mashed metaphors, eli-
sions, faults, foibles, flaws, and digressive misrepresentations alike. I
could, I suppose, regale you with other stories, ones that would be nostalgic, background-building, lesson-teaching, and character-educating;

stories that would rely on the funny forgotten clothing of lost time, broken-down bygones, on yellowed ephemera, on appliances, appendages and vestigial tails rendered useless by the slash-and-burn march of progress: manual typewriters, hat pins, amphorae, abacuses, silvery clamping devices for the curling of eyelashes, knitting needles, chastity belts, metal ice-cube trays, silly string, transistor radios, wedding dresses, rakes, yo-yos, record players, pencils, pipe cleaners, straight razors, wooden matchsticks, postage stamps, Valentine's Day cards in the shape of hearts and doves, pillories, Pullman cars, penknives, poke bonnets, Pomeranians for petting, incisors for puncturing, prose for parsing, cauldrons for boiling, Zyclon B for delousing, Red Dye #2 for prettifying, Thalidomide for deforming, Nembutal for numbing, department stores for displaying, aerosols for de-ozoning, peroxide for discoloring, eighteen-hour bras for supporting, station wagons for herding, crayons for melting, rec rooms for roughhousing, sundials, moon boots, kaleidoscopes, kilts, candlesticks, keepsakes, kerchiefs, cameo frames for photos of faces forgotten, free will, Frisbees, funnels, fake fur, fountain pens, frozen cokes, the funny pages where Marmaduke battled nobly with valiant Prince Hamlet for the title of greatest Dane of them all, Ferris wheels, flip flops, fluted madelines, the jack-o-lantern face of ignis fatuus—that false fire of memory that causes every story to catch fast and then smoke miserably under the weight of its own damp tinder until sputtering into ash. My story? As old as the hills! As deep as the rivers! As directionless as Oedipus at the crossroads. Gertrude Stein sez: Jewish girls do it with reservations. My story? Thanks for asking but I couldn't eat another morsel. Here's the thing—maybe Brigid really was the granddaughter of Marcel Proust. I am worried that everything has reversed. Left has become right. Sinister becomes dexter. We are living on the other side of the mirror where impossibility is realized. And there is no going back. Besides, these days it is beyond useless to talk about *guilt* or *innocence*. It is so damned old-fashioned;

it's like going to town in a horse-drawn buggy to buy a bolt of fabric or spooning up lard straight from the bucket. One can get a nice fresh and bloody *A* tattooed anywhere on the body—the hip, the heart—for only a few dollars, and it's good quality work. So little pain, so many shades of crimson from which to choose, such a brief window of infection—and the imprint lasts a lifetime! I know a twenty-four-hour place where we can go and have it done. As soon as I finish with my story, we'll go. I'll put on my snow boots and we'll trudge there together. We'll take the back alleys where the ice shines sinfully under the streetlamps. We'll get matching *A*s. *A* is for Asbestos. *A* is for Apple. *A* is for Absolute power corrupts absolutely. Maybe Frances Warren Lieb died an accidentally natural death by electrocution in the tub. And maybe Owen found happiness with his second wife, Brigid Proust Pearce Lieb, of the Iowa Prousts. Maybe. And maybe I threw myself into their lives because I was haunted by my own mistakes. Only I couldn't, as I say, identify which of my actions were mistakes and which were not. That is, if you believe that some statements are true, then must others of necessity be false? Owen ate carrots. Owen loved Brigid. Neither of these sentences logically follows the next, but when placed beside each other by virtue of time, subject, space, and the way we cause effects, these sentences begin to form a story. A story of love among the tubers. A story of hidden letters. Sometimes I slip back into the darkened room in that hotel with its awnings of green and plum-red, which although genteel, bore, as all hotels must, traces of anonymous corruption. And in that selfsame room I never fail to notice the disarray. The maids refuse to enter, to empty the ashtrays, clear away the cups, soiled towels, the sheets. You would think I would have barged in myself with a bucket of bleach, a vacuum, mop and broom alike, and with steel wool scrubbed the whole damn place down. Oh, and a drum of gasoline. Let's go, let's go, we'll get our tattoos and torch everything in our path. We will be our own holocaust, a moving fury, a portable vengeance cutting a swath through the snow in search of a guy who will draw Daffy Duck on the hip or etch in detail the martyrdom of St. Stephen across the breadth of our backs. The truth is I haven't scrubbed anything in a long time. The truth is that by the time this story is over I will give up cleaning. I am announcing this in advance. Don't think there is any symbolism, allusion, or redemption to be found in my one-time profession. There is nothing left to be scrubbed, scraped, saved, or restored. I confess, I confess. Give me a crime and I'll sign my name to it. Let's not stop at *A* but inscribe ourselves with the whole damn alphabet from heels to hairline. I'm a sport. I'll go first. I'll try anything twice. What do you think will work better—an ice pick or a carrot peeler? I know now that given two choices, given before and after, I will refuse to decide, but given no choice, I will demand that I want nothing less than everything A to Z. I thought telling this story would be the right thing: a full confession. In exchange for three days of fever, a lifetime of immunity. An open-ended train ticket to the end of the line. Isn't it all supposed to come out with the wash? *A* is for Absolution. *A* is for Antiseptic? While Owen is digging in the garden, while Brigid constructs with Popsicle sticks, corks, and glue a scale model of Proust's bedchamber, let's sneak away. Let's leave them to their own devices. I am going to do exactly what I promised I wouldn't. Offer the past as a pretty picture. Please consider, please consent to have a look at these snapshots that I salvaged from the scrap heap.

PICTURE ONE

This was taken on my eighteenth birthday. The girl on the right with the straight black hair and kohl eyeliner, the girl grinning at the camera and offering a cheerfully raised index finger to the world is Dory. The girl on the left is Dory's friend, Megan. She's the one with the long red hair tied off into two braids, her face bent and obscured as she performs a seemingly lewd act upon a beer bottle. And, of

course, that's me scrunched in the middle—the one who looks a
little lost, blinking and stunned by the light just as the flash goes off,
the one who is going to be blamed by the other two girls for ruining
the picture. This is the summer of 1987. I started college in the summer term—the dormitories closed, I sublet a room in a house with
only one other occupant, Dory. I tagged along with Dory and Meg.
I was a minor annoyance, hardly noticed, barely noticeable, I think,
subsumed into a ragged band of summer-sunburned, patchouli-sod-
den rich kids: hiding from their parents, bitter about the future,
shoplifters, scene-stealers, class-skippers, a legion of students hovering perpetually on the boundary between a C+ and B-, they only
came out after dark. At night we went down to Lake Huron, whose
garbage-strewn banks were crissed and crossed like all the back alleys
of the Middle West with railroad trestles. We sat drinking and smoking and saying unremarkable things until eventually the drunkest
and smokiest of the bunch, the boys, talked it up and took it upon
themselves to climb the great iron edifice and swing high above the
water shedding their clothes, a T-shirt, cut-off shorts, a falling sneaker
kerplunked into the darkness below as they rose higher into the
darkness. And the girls on the shore watched and laughed. We
thought they were crazy. Boys were cray-zee. We cheered and awaited
a disaster that never happened. They climbed one by one and each
by each, stoned and sedated, up to the tracks at the top of the
bridge and naked in the moonlight performed miraculous swan
dives, belly flops, and belated suicidal tumbles into the murky lake
below. And the viewers, we held our collective breaths in silence
until they rose up again, reappeared through the dark surface of the
water screaming for air. Dory had a transistor radio tuned in to a
lovelorn call-in show. She thought it was funny. And Meg, with her
henna-bright hair, wore halter-tops and stretched out staring up at
the stars with a beer can resting on her bare stomach. The boys
emerged from the water delirious and shivering to fall into the leaves

and bottles and dirt, to rest their wet faces cold against Meg's mosquito-scarred skin until she pushed them away. She pointed out constellations. The summer wore on. They called out to us from the bridge. Come with! Jump! they called to us. They sang it like Van Halen: *you might as well jump!* Dory and Meg ignored their pleas. They braided each other's hair and gave their own answers to the brokenhearted radio callers. They were tiny pretty girls. They didn't have any interest in climbing, in running across the railroad trestle in the moonlight because it would spoil the mystery of their bronzed skin when they fucked individually each and every one of those boys as they would by the end of that summer. So who can blame them for not baring all that beauty in one fateful high-wire tumble. But what did I care? Look at my face in the photo, so squinted and corkscrewed. I am a veritable jigsaw puzzle of moving parts. A sideways nose. A closed eye. A hand clawing the air pleading with the photographer: stop! And one night in August when the boys were calling, I followed. Dory and Meg sat on the shore reading an astrology book illuminated by the dim circle of a flashlight. I don't know what the planets promised her, but the future held for Meg a room with her name on it at a rehab clinic run by the Church of Scientology. But on that night she was small and perfect with her gray eyes and strawberry honey-streaked hair. She didn't know how soon everything would change. I left the embankment. I climbed up the iron bars, up even though I could see nothing, no light in either direction, only on the shore the shadows of the flashlight caught against the white pages and wet skin. I followed by sound the boys above me until I got to the top only to find myself alone in the darkness. They had already jumped, their splashes lost far below. And me? Did I jump? Did I fall? Did I turn back? These are fine points of semantics when compared with the gravity that pulled me down to crash breathless through the hard spectacular surface of water, to pull me under and down to crash through to the other side. And I recall the boys still swimming around and circling; suddenly it made sense, didn't it? On land they were idiotic. They were sweaty and clumsy, fought, cursed, complained, lumbered, lurched, and struggled to put one foot after the next, but in the water, swimming, they became something else. We all did. We belonged if only briefly to that element that defies speech and demands silence—green, trapped, even the most graceless thrashing became fluid—until the open-eyed moment of the tightening of the lungs, the great either/or? Float up or force yourself under? I broke back up through and heard their hard gasps for air and saw the white glint of Meg's bare midriff and the space around Dory, her black eyes and hair engulfed in night. So I jumped. Just once. Or maybe I fell. Or I took a leap that can be categorized years later as a jump into the void of either faith or faithlessness or perhaps more relevantly unfaithfullessness. We collected our clothes and wandered to someone or other's house where we collapsed in a heap and slept like that, muddy, befouled, sour-sewer smelling, until late the next afternoon. Sometimes I wish I hadn't made it back up through the surface. Sometimes I think my stay with the Liebs was an extended visit back below and through the surface of the water as through some grand metaphoric mirror, a place in which for a short time one thrived on the absence of air rather than its necessary presence. But I suppose that's crazy, right? Everyone knows that only witches float while the righteous sink weighted down by their goodness. This is me just before the fall. And after. A few weeks later Meg's parents checked her into the rehab clinic after one-too-many of her late-night trips across the Canadian border left her with a pierced navel, a mysterious black eye, three large contusions on her hip, and what looked like a wedding band on her finger, although no groom ever appeared. Dory, as promised and prophesied by the sign of Pisces, took up one by one with each of those boys who jumped naked from the trestle. She abandoned each one of them for the next in an unending succession until she had to find an entirely new set of boys to befriend. But by then the summer was over. Dory ended up moving to California. But that winter I met a serious-minded graduate student named Alexander Piltdown. *A* is for Antediluvian.

PICTURE TWO

Consider this one. The only photo of Newton Graves and Fern Jacobi together. It was taken after his lecture, by one of those roving campus newspaper photographers. Newton is caught at the moment of saying good-bye to someone leaving the reception, his head turned and his arm in a half-wave. That's me standing next to him. I look surprisingly more young and awkward than usual, my innocence emphasized somehow by my borrowed black dress and strand of fake pearls. I am also unaware that the photo is being taken. I am looking off in the same direction as Newton, not quite saying good-bye to that forgotten guest but tilting my head slightly, curiously, as I watch the departure. What you may not notice about this picture unless you look closely is the placement of Mr. Graves's other arm. This arm should be, I suppose, doing what arms and hands do—resting at his side, holding a glass of tepid wine, clutching a pen ready for the next demand for his signature, perhaps even thrown casually around across Miss Jacobi's shoulder to suggest camaraderie with a party guest he has had the occasion to meet once before. But if you lean in, look closely, you will see his arm circles my back and his hand, or rather a trace of fingertips really, emerges locked not around my shoulder (Liberté, égalité, fraternité!) or even my waist, but three fingers appear at the level of my ribcage. I've studied it myself a million times. It seems audacious. I've tried to remember the casually drunken familiarity that caused him to place his hand just so while that anonymous guest was departing; Newton is smiling and waving good-bye and daring to graze just below the breast in a room full of his dutiful and devoted readers who pride themselves on noticing nuances and undertones, the symbolism of their own dreams manifested outward into the real world. No one notices. And anyway, it looks like a picture of a happy couple, don't you think? You can imagine summering at our place in the Hamptons. The sea, surf, the surrender! It is as though the photograph has its own future, separate from the girl in the slightly ill-fitting black dress and the man caught in profile. The picture, still, it's a good likeness, no? We were netted like lobsters oblivious to the steaming hot pot of the future and so damned happy at the moment of our capture. The date written on the back of the picture is September 22, 1989.

PICTURE THREE

This is the Saturday after Thanksgiving, 1974. I am standing outside in my front yard with my mother. While my little coat and stockings are patently adorable, the expression on my face is one of belligerent perplexity. My mouth is twisted into a frown and eyebrows quizzically drawn together. The snapper of this shot is my oldest brother who has just been given a Polaroid Instamatic camera for his birthday. He is saying something funny meant to elicit a smile from his subject but I am standing in the cold and having none of his holiday bonhomie. I am five years old and going shopping with my mother. Do you remember her? Do you recall? Her hair comes in dessert-tasting colors with names iced on the box: Clove Me Tender, Burnt Caramel Bridges, Cinnamon Sinsation! Her pretty face is round as a Moon Pie. Her eyes are rich toffee brown. She has skin the color of cocoa butter and her freckles are hazelnuts toasting over a roaring fire. She wears a plaid winter coat. It is a wet wet cold day, but she wears neither scarf nor hat. I am always in a state of misery spinning toward my own collapse. No season offers relief. Her coat is almond and coffee and eggplant. She favors earth tones and wears White Linen perfume. Some of the wives of husbands on our street wear White Shoulders or A Night in Paris. The teenage girls smell of

Love's Baby Soft. Those legions of perfumed ladies who do not work, who get together for potlucks and Tupperware parties, for quilting bees, craft projects, child-swapping, or fence-mending, those ladies who sip Tab with my mother, they eye me with recrimination like a perpetual *before* in a world of *afters;* they discuss best-selling novels, scandals, cases their husbands won or diagnosed, thrilling new ways to unskin, debone, or stew birds, how best to clarify butter, where to vacation, how to spice up a loveless marriage, murder a cheating spouse, reaffirm faith in a lost God, and likewise Scotchgard shag carpets against the genuflecting and bloody knees of their perpetually punished children. My mother wears her plaid coat with the belt looped tight. Slung over her shoulder, her purse is calfskin and demure. She is slim and short and pretty and small-breasted. She has five children and remains disturbingly pert and girlish despite her daily chore of waking at dawn to pack sack lunches with Fritos, pudding cups, celery stalks, candy apples, and heart-shaped sugar cookies. We each demand a different item from the menu. Tuna salad with sweet pickles for Ira. Olive loaf for Ezra. Crunchy Jif peanut butter spread on rye bread with grape jelly for Si. Hebrew National hot dog, cold, dry, and wrapped in a bun like a baby in a blanket, an adulterer in a bedsheet, or a savior in a shroud for worrisome Walter. And what about frantic finger-nibbling Fern? A pint of O-negative in a thermos, of course. To the less discerning vampire it looks like tomato soup. My mother smells of White Linen, or is it White Shoulders? Even her hair and fingers. We park on the street and walk to the department store that carries exactly everything necessary to the survival of the human race in three stories, a mezzanine, and a bargain basement. My mother does not hold my hand, but clutches her purse to her side. Muggers hide in alleys. We've never seen one, but the neighborhood ladies thrillingly swear they exist. They'll tie you up, strip you naked, take your wedding ring, talk to you like they love you. At the cosmetics counter the girls in white lab jackets like professional beautyologists with sable brushes and triptych mirrors produce from invisible depths below the counter palettes of colors to study against my mother's crème brûlée skin, testing a blue here, a russet there, drawing tiny stripes on her unclenched fist until retreating back below the counter to find an umber more honest or melon more merciful. The girls in lab coats look down at me curiously. My mother's hair is cinnamon-stick red today, smooth and straight, pulled back with a velvet headband. The boys are at home playing football in the yard. They are turkey-tough and scream against the wind with bruised knuckles and shins knee-deep in mud. They crash to the ground in a heap. They are glad that I have gone shopping with my mother. They don't like to play with me because I bite and claw instead of bashing, breaking, and barreling. I can never remember which team I am on or which way to run to score. I have no allegiance nor sense of direction. And worst of all indignities in the world of little girls, they won't let me play cheerleader because I chant again and again the only rhyme I know: *It is fun to have fun but you have to know how! I can hold up the cup and the milk and the cake! I can hold up these books! And the fish on a rake! I can hold the toy ship and the little toy man! And look with my tail I can hold a red fan!* So off I go in my little green jumper and woolen tights, in my cloth coat and black beret like a diacritical accent over an impossible foreign word, off I go into the world of disappointment stores like the pint-sized slice of apple pie that I am, off I go into the wild blue yonder and my mother lifts me high on the chair and the cosmetic counter girls pretend to be impressed with my imitation of an honest-to-goodness human child. I can walk and talk and parrot cute phrases in pidgin French. My mother purchases lipliner and eyegloss, a talcum powder that produces pleasant sneezes, a balm from Gilead and hand lotion that smells unselfishly of violets. The cosmetic counter girls, exquisite professionals, wrap and admire her choices. They agree, as I am so matter-of-factly adorable, to watch me while my mother runs for just a sec upstairs to lingerie. And why is it not busy in cosmetics on this busiest shopping day of them all? Where are all the country wives and cross-dressers? Lost in menswear? Sorting through racks of ingenious pajamas and neckties that double as nooses? Eyeing sporty colognes, herringbone hacksaws, swimming trunks displayed on headless mannequins of the male variety, golf pantaloons and pet rocks of skull-smashing smoothness? The girls tell my mother they will watch me and off she disappears, plaid coat, cinnamon skin, pannacotta coiffure, velvet headband, up the escalator and off into the invisible promise of ladies intimate apparel. The girls paint my eyelids with glitter. I sing for them: *London Bridge is falling down, falling down, falling down.* They sing for me: *There was something in the air that night; the stars were bright, Fernando!* Serious shoppers begin to line the counter. I slip down from the chair. *They were shining there for you and me, for liberty, Fernando!* The girls have already forgotten forgetting about me. I wander off. Here is what I think. I think this now as a fully functioning adult who has been a good many places and seen the world from ports and piers and plane windows. I think my mother was trying to lose me. I think she wanted me to wander off and disappear forever. And off I go from sporting goods to electronics, from houseware heaven to hell and back. I follow one plaid coat to the next until I attach my crabby pincers to the wrong mother entirely. I hold on tight. I cling desperately in hope that this plaid coat will take me home and tuck me into a canopy bed and rename me Susie or Annabelle. But she extricates herself and throws me back in the ring. And little by little I grow up. From plaid coat to leather handbag until I Hansel-and-Gretel my way with a trail of Stove Top Stuffing breadcrumbs back to my very own mother who does not seem happy in the least to see me and does not, in fact, take my hand painted finger-by-finger with discontinued shades of Pretty Politics brand nail lacquer: Plantagenet Purple, Jonestown Punch, Free Love Fuchsia,

Emerald Empire, Black Panther Blast, Sun Myung Moonshine, William of Orange, Chicago Seven-Up, Crimson and Punishment. She allows me to trail behind her. What is the point of this story? Is all this hidden in the photograph, the picture of a child standing alone on a cold November day? This digression suspended upon the tail of digression like an umbrella supporting a book and a toy boat, a fish and a dish, a mirror, cup, and slice of cake on the toe-end of a jackboot? That my mother never loved me and so I grew like a character in one of her romance novels to seek solace in darkened hotel rooms? That my father was remote and so I sought stern replacements who would save me from myself? Perhaps. That they preferred their winning sons to the cheerless misleadings of a daughter? I don't know. I honestly don't. I think she was trying to get rid of me. It seemed to happen more than once. I was left behind and not remembered until long past dark. I don't know. I know nothing. Newton asked me, *In what do you believe?* And I knew it was a trick question. There was no answer he would accept. There was no answer without fault, flaw, or fissure. *Nothing,* I told him. And for the chocolate star of each nothing to which I plighted my troth he offered me one more nicotine-rich kiss until there were no more kisses to be had or hours to be lost. He smoked on in silence. *I saw her your mother! Your mother is near! So as fast as you can think of something to do! You will have to get rid of Thing One and Thing Two!* He knew that if it came down to it, we would betray each other, and he found this fact tragic and hopeless and appealing. Briefly we must have seemed less like two dullards on a Midwestern college campus than deux Parisian faddists passionately fornicating in one of those closed cabs that came to be known as a Bovary; that is, we were secondhand fiction. Anything that was romantic or sad, either worthwhile or worthless, was inherited. We were each an accumulation of someone else's past. It does not, I admit, seem like fiction. But then it is hard to tell the difference or to know whether difference matters.

In school there was always some sad stinky little boy who survived on paste-and-paper sandwiches, who walked two steps behind the bullies and ate the refuse they cast off. He gobbled mittens and galoshes, tater tots, substitute teachers, and colored chalk. Well, that wasn't me. But I probably had a crush on him, a human anteater, a garbage disposal in moon boots with a missing front tooth and a lazy eye, a junior G-man gulping the gluey evidence at the scene of the crime, breast-feeding on Elmer's straight from the bottle, and for dessert, saving the best for last, a mud pie chock full of asbestos shavings, lead paint chips, and silver buttons. Is a life story made up of the bright tinfoil bits you tell, the tragedies, the passion, the beauty? Or is it every ugly cut and scrape and rash? The eggshells and coffee grounds, the wasted hours, dirty jokes, abrasions, petty obscenities, crumpled Kleenex, the meanness of self-preservation, the gracious gloating over pennies tossed to strangers, the knot of hair caught in the teeth of a comb, flakes of dead skin, Band-Aids blotted with brown blood, the trash can upended, overturned? I doomed us from the start with my confessions. But ladies and gentlemen, please, please, rewind the tape and watch how deftly he heaps doom on his plate, in place of cream crackers, salmon pâté, and ash blonde faculty wives.

Here I am: writing. Raw and cooked. Dirty and disheveled. I can't keep from alliterating as though the not-too-distant past is composed of a series of twenty-six matching pairs marching in step. From chimpanA to chimpanZ fill in the blanks and follow me! Full fathom five our narrator lies, once alphabetical, once denied, these are the pearls that dot her eyes: abject and abhorrent; bitter and bested; contagious and corrupt; distracted and dim; entropied and ectopic; fierce and fin-de-siècle; game and gamin; hermetic and helixed; inky and intolerant; jinxed and jeremiad; kin and kind; lovelorn and ludicrous; moping and maudlin; nomadic and nocturnal; opulent and obscene; pornographic and pearly; quotidian and quixotic; roped and railing; sandbagged and salty; tortured and ticklish; untried and untrue; vapid and vehement; wandering and witness; xenophilic and xeroxed; yesteryeared and yo-yoing; zeitgeist and zebra-striped.

I am writing this for three reasons. 1. Because we do not have to assume that Sisyphus is happy, only that a body in motion tends to stay in motion. 2. I want you to take these pages and follow this instruction: burn them. Mix the ash with rubbing alcohol; siphon the resultant liquid into a jelly jar with a label that clearly states: *drink me to grow tiny.* This new liquid we have concocted is the glue that stoppers up the escape hatch. You can't get out now, but look, we are in this together. We've bricked up a wall. Sealed off the pipes. I can't get out either. This time calling it a dream won't save me. If only this story would end happily with a sleeper slamming an alarm clock and speaking aloud to an empty room: *And then I woke to realize it was all a crazy dream!* This time I fear I'm in too deep. I stopped bumping my face against the mirror. The quotation marks fell off and I slid right through. Go on, you try it this time. Look in the mirror and tell me that the face you see is not that of the greatest magician of all time. Your life has been a colossal disappearing act! A transformation! A rabbit out of a hat. A sword from a stone. Water rushing from a rock. You've sawed yourself in half and then used needle and thread to sew on a mermaid's glittering fins in place of your own knobby knees. You've been a flexible amphibious creature with no joints or hinges to impede your fluid vacillations. You've told stories that have no end. You must know now after passing through so many trap doors of your own invention that the rules of the game are for everyone else, not for you. You vanish when the lights go out. I dissolve with the turning of a page. Turn forward. Turn back. I am here. I am gone. I am trapped in a book clamped shut with a hook. 3. I imagine that someday he may or will read this and know that I exist, that I once existed, that I remember, that I may in the future choose to assume various disguises: a half-drunk

novelist besotted with old grudges, the night porter on the lonely
Siberian line, Snow White in her glass coffin. *Then we saw him pick*
up all the things that were down. He picked up the cake and the rake
and the gown, and the milk and the strings and the book and the dish,
and the fan and the cup and the ship and the fish. And he put them
away. Then he said "that is that." And then off he was gone with a tip
of his hat. And we in our ridiculous guises, pilgrim bonnets, Gogol
overcoats, wooden clogs, corsets, bandoliers, tin drums, and powdered wigs, we will continue to exist until our collapse. I exist today
as myself only, the grimy and chipped remnant of a girl who once
had creamy skin and zodiac-blue eyes, but I don't give a damn. I like
it better this way. I like it underground with no windows. I like it
dark and subterranean. I demand more night. And believe you me,
while we are on the subject, why not say we loved each other? I
know, I know, it's utterly absurd, a conjecture, a catchphrase. Why
not say: the moon is made of green cheese? Or Rome was built in a
day? Why not skip words and say it with flowers? Why not say the
lives of two small people don't amount to a hill of beans in this crazy
world? Why not say: all molecules exert a force of attraction on other
molecules? Is there anything or anyone left whom you truly trust? If
you were the weakest of the herd, do you think you'd still be a pro-
ponent of survival of the fittest? If you had a cleft palate, a clubfoot,
a lazy eye, a loner's loneliness, pigeon toes, premature gray, a tied
tongue, simple chronic halitosis, the heartbreak of psoriasis, creeping eczema, a reach that exceeded a four-fingered grasp—? What
then? Would you do as I did? Deny the future, destroy the past?
Newton and I could not suffer to exist in the same place at the same
time. That is, mournfully misquoting each other's plagiarism, we
could see no solution but to part before dawn on that cold cold wet
day in the darkness as gentlemen with drawn pistols at twenty paces.
I wish I knew. I wish I could calculate the proportion of time to
energy, of reprehensibility to regret that allows one moment of the

past to be transcribed into a page of prose. Poor Thing One! Without Thing Two he seemed so lonely and useless. I thought he would wither up and die. But he didn't. He read books on the Peloponnesian War. I don't want to spoil the ending for you, but Sparta won. He pumiced rough languages. He thrived on the dust of history. I tried to be good. I tried to repent, but I kept finding myself peering over his shoulder in search of his blue-haired twin. And then one day, was it cold? Was it wet? I packed up my books and my cups and my plates. I picked up my dish and my fish and my rake. I know it's wrong. I know it's not right, but sometimes when I am thirsty I don't want water or wine, I crave only vinegar.

Love Canal

I suspect that it is the nature of novice storytellers to dwell on outcome rather than inception. I keep finding ways to obfuscate. And you, obligingly, politely, continue to stick with me—but I know that sometimes in spite of your charitable nature, you can't help but flip a few pages ahead to see if things will improve in the not-too-distant future. So let me state for the record, I am going to restrain myself. Yes. Honestly. I am going to crunch down another spoonful of instant coffee crystals while I try to explain how it was that I met Newton Graves. Confession #72: I sneaked a peek some time ago, a day? A week? (How to tell? I measure hours against snowflakes to estimate the passage of time. Three feet of snow on the ground: my calculations indicate that I have been working on this manuscript for approximately thirty years.) That is, when it occurred to me that I was going to have to write this story (certainly more to rid myself of its stigma than to impose it on others, but still—one so wants to make a good impression, no?) I stole a glance at the pages of a book charmingly titled: *How to Write like a Writer Writes, Right Now!* at the bookstore and found the following rule: *the most complex events are best told in a single concise and informative sentence.* For example:

I came out of the library into the rainy afternoon, tripped and dropped my stack of books at which time a man sitting on the steps rushed up to help me collect them.

There. That's it. That's exactly how it happened. That seems very clear indeed. Because even within the limited boundaries of this one sentence I know the small forgotten details trapped between words.

They come to mind, rise up like bedsheeted ghosts on Halloween. So *afternoon* does not mean any hour between morning and night, but a specific moment on a day in September right down to the darkening quality of the light and the arabesque sprawls of the drunks on the burnt university lawns. It implies not only that afternoon in particular when a certain "I" comes out of a certain library—but all the events that led up to that moment from the long-dead foppish young man in the frock coat after whom the library was named right up to recent weather patterns which had left the lawns piebald and bleak after a dry summer and lent to the afternoon a brooding secondhand Brontë quality that precurses the arrival in romance novels of mysterious strangers. Or distant dead-and-buried subtextual psychological details like the fact that this "I" had always looked to libraries for an outcast's sanctuary. I'm getting ahead of myself. But I am only just learning the strange process of translating memory into, can you believe it? *Specifics?* To be precise. To tell a story. To begin at the beginning instead of muddling and mucking about hip deep in *whys* and *what happened laters?* Because it must now become your story as much as mine. You must be able to slip specter-like into one or both of the characters' skins. And in the face of unadorned factual narrative it does not matter so much, does it, that my specific and informative sentence is not really a good sentence, not really as far as sentences go? It doesn't say when this happened or where. It clumsily lumps an action *(I tripped)* with a consequence *(he helped)* by the crude and vaguely pseudo-legal use of the phrase *at which time.* And how can one sentence afford the myriad outcomes of his retrieving a few fallen rain-damp books from a tumble down the stairs? *At which time* could we have stopped ourselves? *At which time* should we have turned back? *At which time* did I (I'm just a girl—I'm not Ernest Hemingway for God's sake. Don't blame me for saying this and then drawing a strawberry pink heart around the sentence. In June of 1961 Hemingway wrote a very nice

letter to a little boy in praise of the beauty of Midwestern summers.
Two weeks later he put a shotgun to his head. Bestest wishes, Papa)
fall just as surely as the books, one, two, three, on the steps? I dropped
the books at which time a man who had previously appeared and
asked me for cigarettes helped me collect said books. But beginnings
are funny things, and I think we (I, I, I) cannot help but go back to
them and try to find the endings encrypted in those first moments.
Should I have imagined that books (objects composed of paper, ink,
and glue) as they tumbled down the steps would be our inevitable
downfall? Would the symbolism of each detail of that scene play itself
out over the course of months, year after year, only to find its meaning multiplied and more complex with each retelling? Can it be told
in three sentences? Can it be undone in three thousand? Can we (I)
really go back to that first moment which at the time meant nothing, nothing at all, but would serve to be remembered later with the
nostalgic and sometimes acrimonious belief that subsequent events,
the outcomes, the inevitable finality was and were all and utterly
encrypted, blue-printed, road-mapped into the actions of two
unsuspecting and otherwise minor characters?

*It was a raw, rough September day in 1989; the darkening sky betrayed
the Midwestern late afternoon, the branches of trees, the golden gray of
the red and rust remnants of maple, oak, and ash dispensed by the
northerly wind, leave by leaf. I came out of the library into the rain,
tripped and dropped my stack of books at which time a man sitting on
the steps rushed up to help me.*

I don't have that handy edition of *How to Write like a Writer Writes,
Right Now!* with me today. If I did I might have a little more luck
and less devil with the details. You might instead be turning pages
with spit-dampened fingers edging closer to the moment of obscene
revelation. An argyle sock falls to the floor. A strap is unslipped.

Buttons hastily unfastened. Oh, sadly I only leafed through the book in the crowded store. *How to.* Tell it like it is. Or was. Or isn't. Or never was. And how! How to tell until the telling itself becomes an addictive substance. Ink and graphite are protein-rich and laced with nutrients. And paper has a delicate flavor, like star anise or frog legs. And if a story is not strictly true, perhaps it becomes true through the act of telling. But honestly, do you feel comfortable enough alone here with me to go about being a "we"? The two of us lumped together in the closed-door slap-and-tickle intimacy of the first-person plural? It's a little creepy, but at least I'm not one of those old men pretending to be a girl. I'm the real thing. The genuine article. I know enough to know that I don't know anything. I secretly have to consult *How To* books to get even this far. As I was eyeing the pages of that book, a certain roving store clerk was suspiciously eyeing me. Could I be that low, that abysmal? To be suspected by clerks of stealing *How To* manuals? Has it come to this? As I studied the book and attempted to duck low and hide from the gaze of my accuser, I came across this pronouncement (and please, I beg you, excuse the clumsy paraphrase): *Always describe your characters as though the reader is a Border Guard comparing a passport photo to the traveler at the gate.* And the clerk, a mealy-faced young man, glared at me. I am certain. So you see, I didn't get far with the reading of the rules. But I do recall that the more complex a story is the more clear (transparent? crystal? see-through?) the storyteller should be. And that one should be as generous with descriptions of setting, time, and place as one is with butter on a slice of freshly baked bread. That is, don't forget the meltdown factor! Everyone loves rich buttery characters. In Wisconsin they enjoy an extra dollop of sour cream. For readers in the Chicagoland area, please substitute gravy. Whenever possible mention color, textures, and authentic details that will pin the time period firmly to the gentleman's lapels or to the lady's peekaboo undergarments. A little more. A little time. A

little tide. A little song. A little dance. A little seltzer down your
pants. Also strongly suggested: the use of smell. If possible put a
familiar scent into your first line, to draw the reader in, to let him
know that this new world he will share with you is comforting—cinnamon wafts, grass is mowed, hay is baled, curry is cooked! The bar
reeks of gin and sour defeat. You lifted the lid of the pot just as the
hissing lobsters succumbed to a watery death and you could feel all
at once in a flush of steam the happiness of childhood days on the
beach collecting shiny pennies with your uncle's metal detector
while he wooed a lady in a yellow polka-dot bikini; the salt, the sea,
the surrender. Delightful! You are halfway there. Tell me how you
feel and leave no detail undetailed. Or perhaps you may find it help-
ful to interview your narrator. In this technique, the two of you are
locked together in a cement-walled interrogation chamber. A bare
lightbulb sways with a gentle creak, or is it an insistent moan? Ask
and he will answer; you've got him on the ropes; he wants a Pepsi
and will do anything, tell you everything, delve into the depths of
his briny and barnacled soul for an icy cold beverage. He will tell you
about his lousy childhood; the trailer park; the trauma and terror
alike; the man on the beach was no uncle but a stranger who gave
him a sno-cone to play the part of a well-attended kid so that he
could attract the sympathies of beach-blanket ladies who smelled of
cocoa-butter and ate with their slim tan fingers grasping plastic cut-
lery egg salad sandwiches so impossibly delicious that it is almost
better to be able to recall it, to recall the sloppy sun-warmed may-
onnaise, the hard-boiled whites mixed just so with the yolk. The
dusting of pepper and red speckles of paprika, better to remember it
than to risk the disappointment of having one on a plate in front of
you today. Ah, you ask, this is how we begin? We begin with the
things no longer on the plate? We begin with place in respect to
character. In the telling of my story, of this chance encounter on a
rainy afternoon, we have both a place and moment. There is an "I"

and a "he" and the great marble steps of a monumental library which seems to grow more Jovian and outsized until it is a veritable Parthenon plunked down in the middle of the wheat-shocked flatlands. And what can one do when faced with the promise of a September day but think of Septembers past? About new pencil cases, the damp of woolen sweaters, fearsome taunts of bullies, the bite of the staple gun, the swishing of plaid kilts, the long breathless run home through the alley—? The ugly parts sink to the bottom and the bright things rise to the top. And the leaves come swirling from the trees, wet and golden. Red and brown. How all the days of the past form a sort of collective September rushing toward the thick rotten brokenhearted bog of October. *Think of your narrator as an actress in a movie. She will ask you sincerely: what's my motivation?* How will you respond to her query?

Fern came out of the library on that raw September day to find the sky was dark with rain. Out on the university lawns the red and rust of the stately maple, ash, and oak trees were victim to the rough northern wind. The leaves fell fiercely to the ground and left the bare black branches ominously swaying as blackbirds circled. Students scurried to and fro. Fern paused on the library steps, burdened with an armload of books. And while it may have appeared to the casual observer that her face wore the careful concern of a co-ed worried about how to best get her books home in the rain, she was, in fact, thinking more specifically about the lovely borrowed sweater that she was wearing. It was a wine-red cardigan with silver buttons shaped cleverly like horse heads. It belonged to Fern's friend, Dory, and she had conceded to lend it to Fern in exchange for an undersized pink angora sweater with three-quarter-length sleeves and buttons of tiny faux pearl. "Do you have a match?" asked suddenly a man sitting below her on the library steps. How strange and mysterious he was! He called out just at the moment when Fern was considering turning back into the library for shelter, when she was lost in the universal "why me?" of the perpetually umbrella-less in the rainstorm that is the life of the busy undergraduate. He asked politely if she had a match and she, despite the genuine civility of the request, despite the inherent evils of tobacco and its users, immediately tripped and dropped the stack of books at which time he, the owner of the once disembodied voice, now embodied in the visage of a mysterious stranger, rushed up to help her.

There we go. She pities herself. He helps her. Whether knowingly or not he speaks a single line of dialogue that evokes both the best romantic clichés and the worst of childhood jokes. Here we have two characters propped up against the backdrop of a rainy September afternoon. There are any number of outcomes. They may each leave in opposite directions. They may leave separately in the same direction. They may leave in opposite directions with thoughts still sharing a path together. Newton Graves sits on the library steps, a visitor, a mysterious stranger taking in the darkening afternoon. We begin with Newton Graves and then note that the great brass-edged doors swing open and a girl clumsily fumbles out with an armload of books. Or we could begin with the girl herself, the girl in the wine-red sweater who neglected to wear a jacket. Let's start with Fern a few moments before the story really begins, let's follow her as she goes from the high-ceilinged reading room on the second floor, its walls painted with a mural of mythology: Persephone with a palm of pomegranate seeds; Helle hugging the golden fleece; Icarus riding roughshod toward the sun. Under the canopy of Bacchus bashing grapes, Fern descends the winding staircase to the desk on the first floor where, with her mind still captured by a certain painted picture of scheming Discord watching Paris take possession of a Hesperian apple, she asks the girl at the desk for books being saved on the hold shelf for Alexander Piltdown and then (again: clumsily, fumsily) produces her library card, drops it, shifts nervously from foot to foot while the transaction is being completed, looks at her watch, accepts finally the books and nods ceremoniously or perhaps apathetically as the due date is announced to her. So off she goes, arms full, in her wine-dark sweater swapped for a pink angora with pearly buttons (it was too small anyway; what a trade!), pushes with her shoulder against and out the heavy door to arrive outside on the library steps where she notes with dismay the pouring rain and she pauses to weigh her obligation to protect borrowed treasures against her desire to run home in the rain. And when the exact action of our story, when our beginning begins to begin, Fern is standing under the great library's marble edifice waiting to make a decision or, conversely, to have a decision thrust upon her by fate.

We looked out at the rainy afternoon. The trees were bare of leaves. There were still hippies playing hackeysack and drunks sprawled out across the lawns. Did he ask first whether I had a cigarette or first if I had a match? I dropped my stack of books so that they fell idiotically, dramatically, end-over-end down the steps. It was at this time that he rushed up from where he was sitting on the steps below and helped me. He collected them in a heap, then picked up the one on top. He studied the spine. He opened it. "You can't," he said. "You can't be serious? L. Manning Vines, A History of the White Peoples in Cold Climates?" *I was embarrassed and I fumbled to take the books from him and mumbled something clumsily about how they were books that I was picking up for a friend and not really mine at all and that I preferred Romance novels, that is "Romance" with a capital "R" in terms of the age, you know, the nineteenth century, not Harlequin although one could make a logical leap from one style to the next but I understood neither the appeal nor the ideology of the books I was holding that he had rescued from the rain, and no, I did not have cigarettes nor did I have matches because no I did not smoke. And then I stopped speaking. And he said nothing, nothing at all. And we stood for a moment watching the red paper flag that*

denoted the books had been saved on the hold shelf, the red paper flag
that connoted the beginning and ending of everything all at once,
watched the wind take it down the steps and through the summer sun-
burnt grasses, past the elm and oak and ash, through the trees and gar-
dens and dirt slowly but surely converting itself into rain-sodden muck,
through the quadrangle and past the drunks and hippies and through
the autumn afternoon until we could no longer follow the flag's path and
we remained in silence awkwardly us, for the first time, two characters
crowded into one pronoun. And we stood on the library steps in the rain
trapped between the howling imperious marble of two grand rococo lions
who guarded the building. Those great figures wore upon their brute chis-
eled heads Detroit Lions caps, the result, no doubt of some fraternity
prank. The hats sat rakishly, tiny and ill-fitting on the carved manes.
The wind blew. The rain raged. It seemed that the hats should have long
since fallen away. But strangely they had not. And the result was so sad,
so idiotic, so unnerving and ominous that no one had bothered or dared
to remove the blue caps from those growling outsized felines.

He has asked for a cigarette or matches, and she has tripped in one
of those comedic gestures that implies an underlying moral stumble.
But does it pass the passport test? Is she specific? different, or somehow distinguishable from the host of co-eds in the second floor reading room pausing before open chemistry texts to gaze upward at
Paris paring apples or Daedalus at the drawing board? Does knowing the year help to set Fern in her surroundings even though the
library and trees have survived a century? The year? 1989, the month,
September, tipping top-heavy out of a decade of craptacular excess
with nowhere to go but down. Fern, with her arms full of books, is
twenty years old. She is dressed in her borrowed sweater (the
exchange of which for the pink angora was so amicable between
both parties that the items were happily kept by both girls). A
straight avocado-green-and-mustard-yellow plaid skirt (side-zip,

sans waistband, kick-pleat, hemmed by hand with a sloppy running stitch already tearing loose to reveal an eggplant-purple acetate lining) hits demurely at lower-mid-calf to meet crimson tights which lead down to sturdy black shoes whose thick-heeled severity recalls either lonely spinsters or the corrective booties of pigeon-toed playground outcasts. Her hair is growing out or in, a mess of bobby pins, unruly endings and confusion. In fact, with her inky hair, bedsheet-skin, and an unforgiving shade of red lipstick, this character, Fern, has the look of a black-and-white celluloid creation come to life and then whimsically hand-colored, haphazardly painted into Technicolor brightness with the most forlorn hint of obscenity. It would seem that knowing this about her, picturing the exact oddity of her, it would have been difficult for Mr. Graves to miss, to avoid, to overlook this chaotic character who bumbled through the library doors. But then this type of girl is not for everyone, is she? Perhaps the still-anonymous Mr. Graves could have looked on with bemused amusement and noted how funny girls were these days. But for some reason forever unbeknownst to us, he asked for a cigarette. Or was it for matches? He engaged her. We could even say he accosted her. Perhaps he really needed them, cigarettes or matches? Perhaps he had left his hotel room without them and was weighing the option of making a run to a drugstore or waiting out the rain. Perhaps she looked like the kind of girl who always has in her possession cigarettes or gum; mints or matches? And after all, let's have a look at this Mr. Graves. What a godforsaken Cain in a world of Abels. Banner headline: *Clark Kent sez I just flew in from the coast and boy are my arms tired.* In his battered suitcase the shirts have a candy-counter sweetness worn down and out into sepia-toned respectability: green apple gone rotty, lemon platt soured, crème fraîche curdled, grape grown raisin, blueberry blotted. He wears black serge trousers once knife-pleat sharp now pathologically wrinkled; a shirt of indistinguishable shade, perhaps yellow or ecru, maybe ochre? His jacket, a thrift-store masterpiece with narrow lapels seems awkward, anachronistic, and no match for the elements. And yet, he has an utterly American aura of utilitarian irony. There is something useful about his vestments—as though if needed he could fashion a sail from the shirt, boil down the jacket for ink to write his next great thesis. What seems amazing to me, what I must convey as amazing to you is that these two unlikely characters are a matched set. It now seems impossible that they should not have met that day. For whom else was he waiting in his dark bargain-bin attire, if not for her in her borrowed sweater and war bride's boots? Who would have found them if they had not found each other? Her carnation stockings and his bleeding heart? The show must go on. The show can't go on.

And when I said then that I did not have cigarettes, he asked if I had a match. And I, having grown up the only girl in a house full of boys had to stifle back the immediate response. You want a match? How about your face and a (fill in the blank)! Do you remember September and October and the cut and scraped faces of boys and the bruises and split lips, the ragged Frankenstein scars of stitches and the bronze taste of dried blood? And how they called out loudly, chanting like a chorus of castrato sailors, fortissimo, adagio: *if I had a dog that looked like you, I'd shave his butt and teach him to walk backward! I've got a match: your face and a horse's ass! I've got a match, Mr. Newton Graveyard: your face and a train wreck. I've got a match: the march of time and a hall of mirrors. At which time did the screaming singsongs of schoolyard boys become jokes? At which time did those jokes become funny? At which time should we have turned back? Did we always know that those horrible boys, those warbling monsters of secondhand sit-com conception and insult would come to rule the world? And I dropped my books. As I, we, hastily collected them from their Odessa steps tumble, I suppose I said, no, that I had neither matches nor cigarettes. At which point he said that he had both somewhere or other and ruefully patted an inside pocket of his old-*

fashioned jacket. "And is," he said, "this friend of yours for whom you're
picking up books, is this friend an unenlightened ethnologist or simply a
brute?" The day was September, or was that the month? The decade was
on decline. I said, "A historian and a bit of a brute to boot." The rhyme
was unintentional. He asked lighting the cigarette, "A boot in the face?"
And it was then that I noticed his face all around us papering the kiosks
and bulletin boards, his picture on flyers of pink and green and sky-blue
promising a lecture by Newton Graves entitled, "Experience to Innocence:
the New Puritanism in American Popular Culture." The flyers were rain-
soaked. The likeness, his picture was blurry, so that he became an anony-
mous shape, a sort of Rorschach blot, an abstract formation on a lime-
green backdrop. The wind picked up and let down the tattered edges of
paper. He was plastered alongside posters promising term papers for sale;
Rush Tau Beta Gamma! Fly to Europe cheep! And his face lost amongst
the ruins. I held my stack of books. "How old are you?" he asked. And we
watched as from across the quad a troop of Greenpeace kids in plastic
rainslickers of Dolphin-safe yellow, maybe five or six of them, armed with
staple guns, headed to the kiosks and began to paper over his face with
flyers for their latest rally. And we found ourselves walking together down
the library steps and he took the stack of books from me and wrapped
them in his jacket and carried them even though it was pouring and cold
and he had the look of someone just coming back to life after a long ill-
ness, a strange battered quality, and it was that first raw rough day of
autumn, the day that you so long for during the summer. And we crossed
the lawns, first walking, then going a bit more quickly, faster, without
speaking until we broke into a run. Past the elm and oak and ash, past
the drunks, the hippies, and Greenpeace foot soldiers, through the mud
and muck until we too disappeared from the picture.

I now have all the pieces of the story spread out before me like a great
jigsaw puzzle: character, dress, passport photos, motivation, time,
place, texture (reminder: rough and woolen), the smells (rotting

leaves, cigarette smoke, wet paper) the sophisticated palette of colors (mustard, umber, pumpkin, port, passion fruit, pink), and I have even some bonus factors like allusion. Imagine, if you will, that the massive marble lions poised regally before the library are *emblematic* or rather *symbolic* of Owen and Franny. And I fear that all along I have been the prankster slapping silly hats on them. Of course, nature is responsible for the punch line; no matter how furious the rains, nor how persistent the howling winds—the hats refuse to fall. I fear I have come to believe that the life stories of the famous are no more worthwhile than those of the drunks passed out on the palatial university greens. I fear that we all tell the same story. You want a match? My future and a locked door. In fact, one does not really need a story so much these days. Every story hangs on the thread, hitches a ride on the hips of all the stories that have come before. These days one can get by, make do with a few symbols, a few signs. These days it is best to do away with the words altogether and let the narrative unfold as a picture, a rebus, map, centerfold, a paint-by-number passion play in which all the girls and boys alike are fighting for the role of Scheherazade. Her costume is the best! A coconut-shell bra and bandolier, Corinthian leather breeches and conquistador boots. Imagine Brigid as Persephone pondering a six-month split between feast and famine. And Owen is Prince Paris. Franny is Helen. We may even scare up an extra or two among the cast to play the role of the slighted Menelaus, victorious Aphrodite, and brotherly Orestes. Just maybe. And me, yes, what role suits my mercurial mood? I've memorized the lines and am trying out for waxwinged Icarus in my clever jalopy with its thousand-ton steel hull, a modified dune buggy gilded golden with shellac. The wings are balsa wood and propeller fashioned of spun sugar. I tell you I've got the greatest flying machine ever, but I can't seem to get it off the ground. If I could, I'd gladly relieve you of my presence and go gallantly galloping into the sun, but damn it all, the wings won't lift this two-tone two-ton pure gold baby. And I'm wondering if the bookstore has any clever *How To* manuals on the design of sun-bound self-immolating crash-on-impact flying time machines. I bet they do. There is a book on absolutely everything, I tell you, these days. But I don't want to see that wormy-eyed bookstore clerk, so I am going to figure out the secret of flight on my own. I'll hang out here holed up in my hideaway recalibrating the instruments on the control panel of my immobile contraption, mixing up a super space-age polymer fuel of Nile basin mud, pilfered plutonium, and Petrograd potato vodka. I'm ready to take off at a moment's notice. I'm ready to leave everything behind. I've got aviator's goggles, a white scarf, and a leather flight jacket. I'm waiting for the first spark of combustion to lift us up, up, and away. Until then I've got all the pieces of my story arranged by size and color and shape. Now it should be easy. Now I should be ready to begin.

Micronesia

It was, I admit, very nice to be inside with the rain pattering on the roof and the fire crackling in fits of brightness. A glass-domed lamp shone dimly in the corner; the room was darkness, the flowered wallpaper, the flecks of gold, the drawn curtains shutting out the dismal damp of evening. The dog nosed toward a plate of almond macaroons on the low mahogany table. Brigid announced that she would for a little while, until at least she conceded to sleep and succumbed to medication, talk.

Do you mind, she said, *if I ramble on for a while? I feel so very awake. It comes over me every once in a while. I feel awake all along my skin. Do you mind very much,* Brigid asked without waiting for an answer, *if I just talk and talk and talk until it goes away? Do you know that when I wrote my book, you know, my first book, I was thinking about 1984—about the one little room that Julia and Winston share— the only safe place in the world, and even that place, they will come to find out, is not free from observation. What was it? A camera hidden behind a picture on the wall? I suppose I was thinking about how there is no place left without some secret recording equipment—oh, perhaps not literally, not yet—but the evidence of our lives that we leave behind, intentionally or not, the way that nothing ever goes away—there are always letters, photographs, and witnesses. But then I wonder if it matters, if in the end it mattered at all that the room Julia and Winston shared was not as secret as they believed; perhaps we exist only when viewed by others, perhaps it was the unconscious understanding that their illicit afternoons became magnified from loneliness to pure rebellion because they were being watched. I mean, that's the story of Adam and Eve in the garden, isn't it? The eye to the keyhole. That's Owen's Old*

185

Testament God? A great storm cloud that sees and hears and records all in the book of life? Who endlessly punishes man for choosing a woman over an invisible father? The hammer of vengeance? The Angel of Death? When Owen says that we've lost our right to pure fiction, I know what he means, and I know why he says it; but I'm afraid I don't agree. If there is always a camera behind the picture or a microphone in the potted plant, then the only thing that we have left, as ridiculous as it sounds, the only thing is the egg shelled in the cranium. We can save of ourselves only what is incommunicable. Everything else spreads—like words, like disease, like germs. An unstoppable game of telephone—the original message long submerged, lost in the whisperings, the interpretations, mutations. He is writing a book ripe with moral sustenance, modern-day, no, contemporary parables. And I feel so terribly locked up, like Proust really, a self-created invalid. Did you know that Proust lived to fifty-two? That despite his professed chronic illness and weak lungs, he lived longer than any Brontë sister, longer than Joyce, Poe, or Kafka? Years beyond Dylan Thomas, Fitzgerald, or Kerouac? Why, for a writer, he lived to an absolutely ripe old age. When he turned thirty, he mourned that he had done absolutely nothing with his life, and so climbed into his bed and waited to die, and to wile away the hours of sleeplessness between indigestion and asthma, he wrote the story of an entirely different Marcel, one who was and was not himself; the one he dreamed himself into being—do you know—there are people, and I won't name names, but people who discount the book I am writing not because of the ridiculousness of it, and I grant you, it is ridiculous—not because it seems strange that a girl from Iowa should one day discover that she is the lost granddaughter of Marcel Proust—but because it is generally believed that Proust was gay, homosexual. But I'm sure you know that as well, and you are being very polite, and it's the first ques-tion that came to you. How in the world has delusional Brigid devised a scenario in which she is the only living link to Marcel Proust who so changed his beloved Albu into the immortal Albertine? But look, don't you see, I wouldn't have made up a story this ridiculous. And I wouldn't discriminate against reality and so say: this could not have happened. Who knows what kind of solace Greta provided him? Biographies are rewritten every day. Biographies about the lives of people who died hundreds of years ago are rewritten even though those lives in no way have changed. It is only how we view them that changes. It's the knowledge of the viewer that makes Winston and Julia's trysts more meaningful; this one incident recorded in a diary hidden in a basement for fifty years in no way makes me disbelieve Proust's homosexuality. I believe that exceptions prove rules; aberration is the locus of fiction and reality. And I don't mean his homosexuality was in any way an aberration, that's not at all what I think, that was—him, I suppose, part and parcel of what made him see the world as he did, isolated, an endless outsider footing the bill for a party to which he was too tired to attend; it is Greta's story, that's the glitch, the anomaly so out of place that he, Marcel, suddenly becomes real, not simply a character from the past, a face in a gallery of great authors. How could it be that we would know everything about his life, about any life? It only makes sense that in him, as in all of us, there are hidden moments; it is only a matter, as awful as it sounds, of turning the right pictures on the walls, looking for the place where the garment gapes. I hate and love at once the perverse necessities of biography. Does that make sense? I was at a party just before, a week or so, before we left Paris, and there were writers and biographers celebrating someone or other's book, one of those awful parties where I become immediately a cliché, a boiled-down lowest common denominator of myself, relegated to sitting with the pretty young wives of distinguished old men—there was a great discussion going on about the sort of bleach that Proust's maid used to launder his linens and to yellow the bed lace, and whether he had an allergy or adverse reaction to this particular solution. And I understood suddenly everything that Owen had tried to keep from me, the world he had tried to protect me from, the detail-hoggers, those cocktail party collectors of the mundane, those people who knew not only more about Proust than I ever would or could, but who knew more about my husband than I ever would; those nameless faceless endlessly smart fascinating chatters who would come to know more about me, me, myself, than I ever would. And I went home from the party in a fever. I was sick and couldn't get out of bed. I was like a character in a Henry James novel, some stupid wide-eyed American girl who gets lost in the ruins of Europe. There are such colossal absurdities in the world—how can it be stranger that Marcel Proust would have a child than that Michael Jackson keeps the bones of the Elephant Man in a cookie jar? That Stephen King purchased at auction a vial of Charles Dickens's blood and drinks daily exactly one measured drop in his morning orange juice? Or that Barbra Streisand uses the Shroud of Turin as a bedspread? It's true, you know? I heard it from her biographer. I'm saying that just as this life, this reality, is full of improbabilities, so are the fictions we create. Nothing follows. Nothing makes sense. So why demand that the title of a book explain the contents? Does your name describe you? Or is it part of you? There is probably some funny story about why your mother chose that name—a dead relative, a dear friend, a bitter rival? Does it matter? Our titles, names, are not the key to decrypting our-selves—they are only the first word—a splotch of ink on a map that has nothing to do with a faraway landscape. The Place-Names, that's how Proust phrased it, so that the words themselves become as lovely as—but separate from not only the location but the events that transpired— Imagine him in his bed thinking of the names of places he would never see—so that the word itself became completely detached, disattached from the location on the map. So that the words he spoon-fed himself were not fetishes, but medicine. Words to replace all the places he would never go; the places he had once been, the details, flowers, the dresses, the things of the past—haven't you a million times in your dreams taken that same walk around Swann's Way to notice the hawthorn roses in bloom along the garden paths? Or is that ridiculous? It seems I'm back in the garden again; it always comes back to that, doesn't it? The old stories,

*the same old monomyths and morality plays? So maybe dear O is right,
we have not yet learned our lessons from the past so how should we ever
expect to move on to the future? We are in a constant limbo of the present tense: Moses in the desert allowed to see but never enter the Promised
Land because he was born of slavery. Can't you almost feel the future?
But aren't you certain you will have to watch it from the distance because
you will be too old by then, born out of a different sort of slavery entirely?
The future is a children's crusade. We are already too old; we already
know too much of the past and have to bear its burden upon our backs.
Owen imagines the solution for the myth of Babel is that one day all the
voices of the world will speak one language; but I tell him I think the
story should end with everyone, every voice speaking a different language, but that everyone will understand implicitly and be able to translate for themselves all the disparate languages. He calls it chaos. He says
it's a worse scenario than the original story; I've out-babbled Babel, he
says. Oh, he doesn't say it in a mean way. Honestly, he's amused, befud-
dled by it. Sometimes I call him the Angel of Wrath—for the way he
rages against the whole of history and the dominion of Christianity. And
yet for all his rage against the messianic hordes of missionaries and leaflet
passers on the street, he still sees the answer to the world's problems as
monolithic. One language will cure all. Maybe not one language literally, but then, then at least figuratively—it seems ridiculous to him to
have a thousand disparate voices crying out from the tower and each
voice is unique and each voice is understood; why have that when all the
voices can cry out as one? Do you see what I mean? That even to our
advanced and enlightened minds, we who know absolutely everything,
we still believe the taboos that anything pluralist is in some way a throw-
back to polytheism? That is, if we don't believe in the immutable force of
one, we will immediately find ourselves naked dancing before a fire and
praying to a pantheon of kitchen gods and fertility goddesses. As though
they didn't already paper the pages of our magazines or stand a thousand
feet high on movie screens. Neither Moses nor monotheism could or has*

kept us from devising any number of golden calves. So we aren't dancing around a pyre or worshiping a stone. I tell Owen not to be so literal about false Gods; he equates God with invisibility, with what always cannot be seen, with what goes unseen, instead of with the visible— what is disseminated bit by bit in everything we see daily around us, with what converts and conquers us bit by bit until we have no choice but to desire it madly, to pray for it, and then in rapid succession succumb to it: Playboy, *recipes for glazed chicken in* Better Homes and Gardens, *the red sports car speeding happily along in a TV commercial. He looks for idols in the clay, but I find them wallpapering the fabric of our lives. Is that very ridiculous? More ludicrous even than a poet, well-known, I won't name names, a poet who bought from a survivor a striped concentration camp outfit that he wears now nightly as pajamas? He swears the dead speak to him in his dreams; he says the quality of the tailoring is impeccable. And his poems have improved greatly. I used to go to those cocktail parties with Owen. And we would get our drinks, our wine or martinis, something seasonal or daringly out of season—say hot rum toddies in July, so that we would all congratulate the host or hostess on such invention, such imagination—how awful, how endlessly awful, it, we, it all was—and Owen would link arms with one of his friends in a circle always introduced as from the "old days," men and women who were politely sizing me up against Owen's past, against Franny, there I said it, Franny. Who saw me as either a diminishment or replacement of her. And after some small talk of this or that, the weather, the funny sly jokes and double entendres, the inappropriateness of sangria in December or mint juleps in January, I would slink off to the death row of young wives, sidle up on the velvet sofa with my vodka blush and wait out the hours listening to the talk of women my own age and feeling foreign to it, lost in it, listening as well to the seductions of second wives by angry young men trying to unseat and upend the beds of their literary gods. How awful, to become a symbol that replaces a symbol that replaces a symbol. Like a bad translation of your favorite book retranslated by a good translator from the bad translation into another language. Nothing of the original remains. Except maybe the names. I was sick, did I mention, for a week, maybe two? It could have been longer. And when I was well Owen brought me here, and I suppose it was a good idea after all. I worried about being alone, but look, now I've met you. Now Owen doesn't have to worry about me. He can write his parables and offer meaning to the messy world and not worry about me, because I have you to suffer through my endless babbling. And I have said all this and not told you what I meant to say when I began, when I began to have the feeling of burning in my fingertips, under my skin. Am I flushed? Can you imagine? I wanted to tell you, to show you something that I found. I should have showed it to Owen, and perhaps I would have if you weren't here, but then you are here, and that changes things, doesn't it? It changes everything. I found something that I wasn't looking for, and that makes it, things, even more difficult. And I didn't, don't know what to do exactly. I haven't read—I haven't opened—done any more than hide what I found. I was, I don't know how to explain this—I was led to it, but having been led to it, I don't know what to do with it, with them—*

And here she broke off. Her face, as promised, as described, bore the traces of a burning flush across her cheeks. The dog rolled onto his back awaiting a belly rub that never arrived, and so sadly, mournfully completed the rotation of his circle to rest his face on the rug. She left the room, up the stairs. I waited. It was raining outside, not so much heavy as persistent, a cold drizzle of miserability so that the morning would be mist and soft gray fog. But that was still such a long dark while away. I added wood onto the fire. I poked at the embers. The clock struck the hour. Brigid stood at the top of the stairs. She wore a red hooded sweater and long skirt of black-watch plaid. At dinner Owen had remarked, was she on her way to grandmother's house? As one should avoid travel during the hour of the wolf. And I asked him what he meant by that, the hour of the wolf?

He said it was a folk expression: the twilight hour when even the most friendly dog is indistinguishable from the predatory wolf, when enemies arrive disguised as friends. Brigid had said only that it was a very warm sweater and the rain made the day seem much colder, didn't it, than it really was? Brigid came down the stairs in her red sweater and long skirt that scraped the steps behind her each in succession and after the next with the lightest swish of fabric. And she sat on the sofa and set before her on the table a bundle of papers. And I came to her. And I sat beside her. And we looked at the bundle without touching it. It sat as a curiosity before us. We studied in silence the handwriting on the first envelope. A line of letters once made by a pen. The way a snail slides leaving an indecipherable trail of muck. Or the rain seams and scores the packed dirt along the garden path. Or a child picks up a pencil and copies an oversized A after the shape of the great pyramids of Egypt. This writing was feminine, to be sure, but not at all rounded or marred by girlish loops. It bore the curious backward-seeming back-slash of the left-handed; the elegant spires alike of F, L, and lowercase B high yet tilting like flags of surrender on an already sinking ship. We did not speak. Brigid, delicately, with dry trembling fingertips, opened the first envelope.

Nagasaki

From here on out everything will grow a shade darker: our clothes, our hearts, the sky above and backdrop behind. Do not adjust your television. It's me, not you. It's me, not the world. From this point forward the symbols will overtake the metaphors two to one. Everything will grow a little more ugly, dingy, and dirty-white. Do yourself a favor: trade your Bible for a drum of bleach. We are going to have to learn to live by our wits, hide out, hole up, build fires, keep dry, and stay warm. From here on out gloom will coat my story like Shake 'n Bake on a chicken leg. Disaster is impending. It will be relayed in dialogue, that delicate art that once we used to call politely, *conversation*. Those days are long gone. There is no time for white gloves, for roses; it is all rope and razor. There will be partial nudity of both the male and female variety. I may lapse into memories of Alexander Piltdown and Newton Graves who inadvertently and embarrassingly have come to symbolize the alpha and omega of history, who each in his various ways failed me through nothing more seductive than the sheer strength of his convictions. I am going to press darker for night. I am going to set the brewing dial for extra-strong. Stay with me a while longer as I may need your help dragging the bodies onto the stage in time for the climactic denouement. You've helped me before and know what it takes; you grab the ankles while I bind the wrists. Oh, this darkness that falls upon us nightly, a plague, a diversionary tactic, a trick done with dry ice, rope, and mirrors. From here on out I will trust my memory less and less and rely on momentum alone. Soon I am going to sit in that kitchen again with Brigid as we did so many times, but this will be the last time. It will be the morning of Halloween and she will have only just come in from the rain, soaked and sopping, a thin rain slicker covering her nightdress. From here forward everything Brigid does will be infected with double meaning like a monarch who refuses to commute her own death sentence, like Marie Antoinette marching to the guillotine in velvet slippers. Each word the second Mrs. Lieb utters will come to resemble an heirloom vase willed away to a distant ill-tempered nephew. I admit that I delay approaching that moment. Are you ready for it? Are you waiting to see her rain-damp shift fall to the floor and the cold blue five-times-two chronology of her ten toes before she slips her feet into a pair of her well-worn husband's socks? I'm not. I've lived in that world and I don't want to go back. I ran my fingers over the papered walls. I vacuumed up the fragmentary remains of ours and us: slivered fingernail parings, clots of hair, the dust of skin, eyelashes, ash, mud and muck, the only proof, really, scripted in genetic code that any of us existed. I searched for direction in the darkness. I saw my hosts at their most bare and private, their most wordless moments. I saw them naked. I saw them clothed. I lie. I speak only the truth. I saw them fall upon each other like Grant and Lee in the firelight. Let me tell you, let me say: it's no place for a girl like you. We are coming to a tollbooth up ahead, a new page, a white space, a clean place, an undiminished hour. What is the fee for passing? The price for continuing, for confessing, for expounding, undoing, unshoeing, for unknowingly stumbling across the border between desire and discretion with an out-of-date passport? To be marked like Cain? Overboarded like Jonah? Strangled like Isadora Duncan on the fine silk of her own winding shroud? We lead lives, I think, of necessary desperation. After the coffee and cupcakes, the confetti and catchphrases, the swapped misdeeds and squandered hours, what's left to do? One either ploughs ahead or meanders backward. Not me! Not me. I tell absolutely everything. Step right up. You ask, I'll answer. I'm a walking Ouija board. There is no stopping me. After all, who keeps secrets these days? Not me. Not me! I find the winding silk of a story in every hangman's noose. Oh Alexander, my alexicacon, you couldn't have been as bad as all that, could you? How could I have been led so far astray? It seems impossible. Mr. Piltdown, you fraudulent relic, with your name more ridiculous and sublime than any cognomen that I could construct for you, you had only my best interests at heart. I was a grand experiment. A borrowed liver. A brain stolen from an open grave. A secondhand monster, a cadaver awaiting her wedding day to come to life to become the bride of. I was asleep. I hardly noticed the armies who bunkered with us; those undergraduates whom you taught and took in, suburban lonelyhearts, tough-but-tender city kids; those quiet boys fresh from the farm, theoretical as the gears of a combine, clean-cut, spendthrift, science-fiction savvy, those a-penny-saved-is-a-penny-earned rope-a-dope dreamers with crop-top snapshots of their girls back home tacked to the walls; those History 101 hordes condemning themselves to their father's mistakes that they would surely repeat in an endless system of con-voluted incest; those boys with their comic books, with shirts that buttoned and shoes that laced, with skin that refused on principle to brown, with fine hair that did not curl, Nazi-neat, they were spec-tacularly unspectacular save for the fact that they all loved you. They all believed in you. You gave them the history of the world in three easy verbs. I came. I saw. I conquered. I can see now how oligarchies, how empires are built one slutty girl and stupid boy at a time. I have no excuse. I went along with you. For a while. Blame it on youth or apathy, on curiosity, disgust, or more curiously, self-preservation. At times I felt like a spy. At other times an accomplice. But along I went nonetheless. Sometimes it was easier, Alexander, to imagine myself a character in a book who lived in a different time and place. And so I took to spending hours in the library for sanctuary, for escape. I gave up on the books you recommended. The students who hovered in those stacks were too creepy. They clicked their boot heels with

the turning of each page. I found peace in the aisle lined with forgotten books of gentle lady novelists. I learned how, with only the
aid of a few spare adjectives to turn you into someone else. I apologize. It was rude of me. But what did you expect from a Jew if not
the evils that you preached as their birthright? Shiftlessness, secrecy,
and betrayal. Look at it from my point of view: what could I possibly want with the past? Nothing. It's ugly. I don't want a minute of
it. It's been burnt to the ground, kicked to the curb, baseball-batted,
molotov-cocktailed, mangled, maced, mutilated, bombed-out, and
bullet-riddled. There is nothing left to salvage. Your history is a
world of ghosts. They have cold bony fingers and howl and haunt on
January nights. Alex, Alex, you said that work would make us free.
We could become the antidote to our own affliction. You said the
problem with Jews is that they never could understand that the best
defense is a good offense. You said start on page one. I read all the
dusty tomes you could trowel out, but it didn't do me any good. Do
you know why? Because I'm a twenty-first century girl! I can't
remember yesterday and am always looking bravely to the future:
robots, desiccated pellets of astronaut food, equal pay for equal
work, the house-arrest bracelet as a bold new fashion accessory for
the girl on the go. Alexander, le temps perdu, you were mad for it,
the past, lost time, the Jew's backward obsession. You claimed with
pride that you had never actually read a book written by a woman.
We laughed and laughed. You said that while men *appear,* women
only *seem.* What happened to it all? Those cobblestone streets, ladies
in bustles, gents in togas, tots under tuberculosis blankets, teens in
trenchcoats arguing the fate of the world in the rhymed iambs of
choplogic? Where are the empire waists and bound feet? What happened to modesty, morality, polygamy, public hangings, and parson's
picnics? We choked with delight and the host of pale undergraduates
reading Milton by guttered candlelight paced the floors above and
below us with the pounding resolve of the jackboot. You spoke in

slogans printed on bumperstickers: *My other car is a Trojan horse! The masses are asses! I'd rather be smoting Philistines! My boss is a Jewish carpenter! From Paw Paw to Climax to Hell, visit southern Michigan!* I thought you were joking. *Truth is beauty; beauty, truth.* I thought it was hilarious. *Let them,* I said, *let them eat cake. But let them also specify whether that cake will be for here or to go.* We laughed so hard that books, dishes, framed testimonials and family photos, forks, spoons, decanters, inkpots and peaches fell from the shelves and rolled and broke and shattered and collapsed. The robots came in to sweep up the pieces. Do you remember the last days of our first summer? And the Manifest Destiny of those hot bedroom afternoons like a Western saloon with the blinds pulled and the darkness settling in at eight or nine, lazily, soppy and sloppy as raspberry jam coated over us into the sticky hours of the morning when the player piano sounded suspiciously like a clock radio? I know, I know, it seems ridiculous to credit you with a Svengali's power. You? Alexander? Part of your charm was your humble simplicity. The all-American sincerity. You were unassuming and sympathetic. You collected those willing to confess during office hours. Oh, you seemed so out of place in the hallowed crusty halls of the history department amongst those bespectacled professors and guilt-ridden grade-grubbers. You never stooped, nor weakened. In fact, you seemed to grow fat on history, more hale and hearty with each year you ingested, more fit with each student you failed. Robust, I might venture to say, passingly prince-like, if not legitimately regal. You saw. You came. There was something a little off. You blended too easily into crowds. And worse, you seemed most content when lost in a gaggle of onlookers gawking at a crime scene, a train wreck, a child fallen down a well, the confetti-strewn bliss of a Thanksgiving parade. You conquered. Alex, it's all true. You know it is. You saw it for yourself. But if I'm aging in dog years, you must be a thousand by now. Where are you tonight, Alexander? Have you become one of them? A ghost, a zombie, a nightmare of the past relegated to a place on the bookshelf? You can claw the window with the best of the undead. And I'm stuck here, trapped, feverishly sending out word to the outside world: save me. Send supplies. Please send hardtack, pemmican, musket balls, and recent copies of *The National Enquirer.* Find an exorcist. Forward, freight, or Fed-Ex to me a metric ton of butter-flavored Crisco. Help me before it's too late.

Dear Charlie Bucket: I am trapped on a desert isle and have run out of Everlasting Gobstoppers. Please send reinforcements. You know, you knew, you must have known all along that I scuttled from the light like a retreating roach. And who would have me anyway? Gone green-skinned and aphasiac, patched together from dinosaur bones, Greek graveyard tragedies and sticky fingertipped globs of Dippity-Do. I seem to be composed entirely of CliffsNotes and wax.

Dear Doctors Frankenstein, Freud, Mengele, and Bones McCoy: can you fashion from this mess of scars and scabs a real live, working, breathing, bouncing, anatomically correct girl? I have a store on my shelf of livers, hearts, kidneys, and spleens packed in pickle jars. I've swaddled all of my baby teeth in cotton for the preservation of those indentured pearls. Please feel free to choose the fairest as a souvenir for your keychain.

Dear zookeeper: do you have an extra cage? One with cement floors, track lighting, and a scratching post? One rife with the dung-damp perfume of a thousand homelands burnt to the ground by cross-bearing crusaders?

Dear Inquisitor General: I believe I may be something of a Jew. I have begun to talk like a Jew. Do you have any ointments for the alleviation of this hereditary chronic condition?

Dear Doctor Salk: oh Jonas, I eagerly await immunization!

Dear Captains Crunch and Cousteau: what of the rough and silent seas we sailed with you boys masterfully ministering to the mermaids and me alone manning the mizzen-mast? Hey? We were near and neaped and netted like starfish.

Dear Mr. Robert Louis Stevenson: my treasure map has fallen overboard. Could you have your agent fax me another? I navigate by the stars and find myself listing ever westward. Hollywood-ho!

Dear Lassie: please guide my way.

Dear Sisters B: your advice to the lovelorn helps. I scour the moors with steel wool in search of mysterious strangers.

Dear Brothers K: it was Professor Plum in the parlor with a pen knife.

Dear Marcel P: Why did you throw your alarm clock out the window? Is it true that you wanted to see time fly?

Dear Alice: stay back from the ledge. Wonderland awaits!

Dear Snow White: you've heard all the jokes. The ones about an apple-a-day. The ones about girls who live in glass coffins. The one about the huntsman and the hatchet. But have you heard the one about Walt Disney, Henry Ford, T.S. Eliot, and the farmer's daughter?

Dear Count Chocula, Frute Brute, and Yummy Mummy: the villagers never liked you. They were craving Booberry, and you just wouldn't do.

Dear Mr. Marx: the fact that you got so fat made Communism as a system less credible. I know it's not nice to say, but who was buttering your bread if not the proletariat?

Dear Alexander Piltdown: I am a scrolling roll of tracing paper. There is nothing left save the lines I can barely suffer to misquote. If this were a poem of lost love, I would say that you were a wax pencil and history was a pretty pony in a picture book that you needed the overlaid film of my clear, invisible-seeming surface to more accurately copy. But thank God, this is no ode to lost boys. This is a brave manifesto on the nature of darkness, the ink of undoing, the gestures that our hearts no longer make, the sweetness of jam, jelly, and the preserving power of pectin.

Dear Smuckers Co.: I like razzledazzleberry the best. It glows. It shines. It pulsates with vine-ripened plutonium. It is one-hundred percent fortified with calcium-rich goblin hearts.

Dear Chef Boyardee: I've been eating paste-and-paper sandwiches just like the label recommends. At first I was suspicious, but now as little Natalie Wood says: *I believe, I believe, it's crazy, but I believe.* And then one day people started asking: what kind of wood doesn't float? I trust in God, country, and the ladies in the Sara Lee taste-test kitchens. I'm not hungry anymore. I'm not lonely anymore. To tell you the truth, I'm not even *me* anymore.

Dear Phone Company: I am chaste, but disconnected.

Dear Folgers Co.: I eat your aromatic crystals dry. I spoon them up and chew and chew. As the bride confessed to the groom: I do, I do.

Dear Mr. Lévi-Strauss: good news! I am almost civilized. Only 114 more lessons until I get my correspondence school certification.

Dear Mr. Clean: I find your new Mountain Fresh scent to be narcotic and fever-inducing. I'm not sleepy anymore. I felt for one fantastic moment that I was clad in lederhosen and frolicking mit the von Trapp kinder on the Alps. But then I stoppered the bottle and realized that it was all a crazy dream.

Dear Madame Curie: Marie, please see my compliments to the Smuckers folks and take your fair share of the credit. Regards to Pierre!

Dear reader of this sticky confabulation of memory, memoir, and molasses: please know that I am going to soon reveal the stupid secret candy center embedded in this narrative mishap. It is buried beneath a heap of junk mail. It awaits you in a plain brown wrapper. It is lost at sea. It is smothered in special sauce. It is the scene of the crime. It is the bottleneck near the smash-up, the icing on the cake, the calm before the storm, the fly in the ointment, the frost on the pumpkin, the telltale heart, the purloined punch line, the one that got away, the last best hope, the great white way, the final frontier, the long and short of it, the pie in the face, the carrot and the stick, the slap and tickle, the force through which the green fuse drives the flower, the penny dear penny brown penny, the hide in plain sight, the catch as catch can, the can of worms, the can't you take a joke, the curiosity killed the cat, the every dog will have his day, the bell, the book, the candle, the lost weekend, the last picture show, the locked room, the step by step, the pay to play, the ill-gotten gain, the golden rule, the glass house, the cooked goose, the upped jig, the needle in the haystack, the moment on the lips an eternity on the hips, the poet on payday, the coin in the fountain, the drop in the bucket, the picture is worth a thousand words, the good fences make good neighbors, the home sweet home, the hobgoblin of little minds, the baby with the bathwater, the dead men tell no tales, the stop in the name of love, the moon and sixpence, the cakes and ale, the days between stations, the Bermuda triangle, the back east, the down south, the out west, the up north, the middle of the road, the shot in the dark, the time and the tide, the open book, the asked and answered, the banker's holiday, the end of the line, the give them enough rope, the in dreams begin responsibilities, the shut-up he explained, the turn that frown upside down, the don't worry be happy, the chair kicked from under the noose. The chalk outline. The crime of the scene. I'm tired of fighting it. I give up.

Dear Mr. & Mrs. Lieb: I enjoyed so briefly your company during those deep rainy green days that we spent together, but enough is too much. Consider this my letter of resignation. The white flag, the olive branch, the dove. Dear Mister and Missus Lieb: I hate to be the one to tell you this, but if you lived here, you'd be home by now. I surrender. I give up. I give up! Up was given.

Odessa

Dear Liddy,

Every year I think the world becomes more ugly. Or is it a case of us unbecoming the world? Why is everything so much less familiar, so different from the way I seem to remember? Take for example last night. An awful couple, the Kimbroughs, "friends" of ours from Boston who are now living in London—but traveling in Ireland for, I swear, the express purpose of quoting Yeats into and out of utter nauseam—came to the house last evening. I call them "the Chaucers," and Owen laughs although he insists that it is not funny, not funny at all. They came to Boston like Owen himself from some landlocked burb in the Middle West and yet they have tiresome accents that vary from high Brahman to Queen Mother. Impossible! They were oohs and aahs for the dilapidated charm of our haunted house. They swilled gin without ice because they didn't want to risk "bruising" it; they took it upon themselves to get drunk and move beyond poor Mr. Yeats to feverishly declaim each other's poems. They gobbled up everything A to Z: aspic to yams. And after dinner drank Irish coffee minus the coffee and worked through an entire batch of cream sherry cookies (from a recipe mother sent) saying all the while—what lovely biscuits—!

Oh Lizzy, have you ever felt strange all along your skin?

Have you ever woken in a familiar room and not known where you were?

Have you ever said to yourself: the world would stop if only I could close my eyes?

Have you ever picked a scab only for the pleasure of seeing what festers below the surface?

Here is the story for which you begged and that I so coldly, so wickedly refused to tell you over the telephone. I could not speak the words. I am too exhausted to speak the words but find that my fingers are more than ready to clatter out the chatter of details. We were all a-frenzy to pack up and get out of the country—we had found the house, this house, the perfect house. I was shipping boxes. L was teaching Spring term at Rosewood. He had final papers to grade (ponderous undergraduate essays on Poe), and I, pleading fatigue (and knowing how impossible he is when buried under stacks of freshman insights on the unending theme of man's inhumanity to man), drove up to spend a long weekend with mother and Freddy. But for one reason or the next, because I was anxious about packing or Mother was on a tear about Wills wasting his life away instead of going to medical school (she so wants to make him into the image of Daddy, doesn't she?), as I say, for whatever reason, I drove back a day early. Ah, you are nodding, aren't you darling? You see trouble looming on the horizon, as the kids in Poetry 101 inelegantly yet inexorably phrase it, "shining like a beacon in the night." I didn't call to let him know I was returning early. I didn't announce myself, silly me, silly us girls and our notions of romance. Every day is Valentine's Day replete with bloody slings and arrows. I was going to cook a horrible big dinner and surprise him. Surprise!

To make a tiresome escapade more terse: when I got to the apartment, I found the place (which was in a disastrous state due to the combined packing and paper-grading) strewn with unmentionables of unfamiliar origin—cheap things, gaudy, obscene if they weren't so damn sad: stockings and a small white patent leather handbag which, of course, I riffled through (as was certainly my right as the wronged wife?) to find a vulgar shade of peach lipstick (a blonde this time? or a redhead?), clove cigarettes, and a date book with Owen's office hours notated with a giddy hand-drawn heart. I felt my rage welling slowly, a dull boil; rolling, roiling, working its way up to the surface, burning along my skin—rage, vindication, violence—electric. Oh poor Lids, do you remember how we feared electric eels and Daddy said they would bite us if we swam out too far from shore? And summer after summer we searched up and down the beach, looked underwater, opening our eyes against the salt in search of eels?

There I was in our apartment, our quaint and overburdened love nest littered with papers and poems, the typewriter perpetually in need of new ribbon, dirty dishes, soggy crusts of toast and coffee-stained teacups; the bohemian charm of our life is a disaster. And how my anger rose as I imagined her, some tarry-fingered co-ed who had left the imprint of her mouth stained orange on a wineglass (a wedding gift!) or a trail of ash across the bathroom tile—a young, stupid, innocent, foolish girl whose crime was not only to own a white patent leather clutch, but leave it behind in the apartment of the most brutal, jealous, self-possessed and possessing wife (do people still call us newlyweds? How charming. How ridiculous) in the world. Is it wrong to stand on ceremony? Some things must be true and others false or else we would all go quite mad. And to tell you the truth Liddy (because I always do, to you, if to no one else), I didn't want to hear his excuses this time. I couldn't imagine they would be different than before—could they be possibly more inventive, inspired, sympathy-inducing? I didn't want to hear his explanation. I could practically construct it myself and then hand it to him on a little silver tea tray: tutoring . . . a rainstorm . . . thunder and lightning . . . a distraught student in need of a shoulder on which to shed tears . . . did I mention, a rainstorm? . . . Candlelight . . . the recent death of a dear dowager aunt . . . an unslipped stocking . . . a Herrick poem . . . a warm thigh . . .

I left, went out to search the places I might expect him to be. I had to find him if only to let him know that I knew. By this time it was getting dark. I searched the campus, his office, coffee shops. It was night, darkness by the time I crossed the path to the library; I heard him before I saw them. I heard his voice through a grove of linden trees. We used to walk this path ourselves and sometimes laugh and argue if they were in fact lindens or whether I called them that simply because I liked the word better than "oak," or "elm," though not half as much as "ash." I heard a girl's laughter. I stepped back off the path and hid myself in the shadows of the lilac bushes just coming into bloom—so sweet I was lost in the tangle of purple. Had I been embraced by a thornbush or nettles, I might have had the angry momentum to leap out and reveal myself. But I did not do this. The lilacs were sweet, like some maiden aunt's palliative for a broken heart. I saw them arm in arm walking away from the library down the cinder path. She was wearing a skirt with knee socks. I did not see her face, only his arm encircling her hip, his hand at her waist. And their voices talking lazily about the death of the novel.

Poor me! Poor deluded Fran. Mother's magazines reprove and pronounce through their recipes for Pork & Beans Luau and Polka-Dot Spaghetti, through cunningly devised gelatin molds in the shape of American flags and the Easter bunny, that it is my own fault. How inevitable are the infidelities of my husband—don't you grow tired of them? Have they become a tiresome B movie, and you sitting alone in the theater shouting at the screen for a plot twist? No, no, not you—despite my confessions you remain so woefully on his side. You always find the best in people and assert on his part, on the part of all would-be brutes, a brave and boyish innocence of intent. You would believe that it was raining; that sometimes a handbag is just a handbag. L says that my suspicious nature is going to be the ruin of us. He was, as you have already imagined, "tutoring" the girl . . . and yes, it was raining . . . and so she slipped off a stocking or two and let them drape over the bath. After all, he says, wouldn't he have taken greater pains to hide a crime? Worst of all, he says the girl is a fan of my work and they discussed Corner *in exhaustive detail. Oh, so you see how it is? The days grow a bit more ugly daily. Mother's mags say if I could concoct a budget lobster-and-asparagus bake with the aid of Campbell's cream of mushroom soup, my husband would be too happy to roam. And how then could I not be happy? Wasn't there a time when we searched the shore for starfish, and one day Billy said—if you have never seen an electric eel how will you know one*

*when you find it?—And we thought he was the most brilliant little boy
in the world, and we knew then that we would never find the eels, but
still we did not stop looking even though we did not know for what or
for whom we searched the waves.*

*So L and I had a great row, plates were broken, accusations hurled.
He stormed out only to come back later, contrite but rebellious. And
look, see for yourself: we continue to exist. We have made it across an
absolute ocean into our new life. We are devoting ourselves to devotion.
And last night, it was only last night that we had the Chaucers over.
They were intolerably drunk, and she, the missus in an Indian print
sarong sprawled across the divan and began to channel the Brontë sisters.
Did I mention that the couple brought with them two young sons and a
nanny in tow? The boys played in the orchard with the dogs while the
girl, the nanny, sat quietly under a tree reading a mystery novel—I
caught a look a the title, but can't recall—something pulpy. The three of
them ate dinner in the kitchen. The drunken parents held court in the
great room (as we call it—for its outsize fireplace and high ceilings)
while L and I suffered their anecdotes and aphorisms. At some point I
became aware that L had been gone for rather a long while and I was
left alone listening to Mr. Chaucer (Geoffrey) expound on the virtues of
spaniels over setters. Or was it the other way about? I excused myself
under the pretense of loading a tray with more cookies, ahem, biscuits,
but instead of heading back to the great room, I took a detour upstairs.
Why have I such a suspicious nature, I ask you? Such a knack for the
rack and the screw? I found L "tutoring" the nanny in our very bed (her
book fallen to the floor) while the boys napped in the next room.*

*And for my part, Liddy, I must be growing older, jaded, either more
refined or simply worn down, because I returned to my deplorable guests
with a silver tray of grapes and sweets, port cheese, brie, and shortbread.
And later I set them up very nicely in guest bedrooms. And I fed them a
breakfast of black coffee and cream, eggs and sausage. And when they
finally left, I threw my requisite fit and banished L from the house. This*

is the last time. I swear to you. I will have no more of it. I am too tired to feign delusion or pretend that I don't know about the students, the girls, the nannies, the wives of friends, and daughters of acquaintances. And L, for his part, acts much put-upon; he chafes against my "imperial" nature. He must be "free." I am impossible. And this because he knows the truth. I am a thousand times better than he is—more honest, bitter, brutal, a better writer, a less-promiscuous soul. Oh, while I do not wish that we had never met—I wish sometimes that he simply would not return. And I would live out here forever as a hermit and free myself of the union that is so nauseatingly called "us." He needs me only so that his infidelities have importance and currency. He feeds his guilt off my anger. And I, for my part, ache to be rebelled against. Are we not perfect? A chipped cup and cracked saucer. Mister and Missus. As you see, this is an impossible situation. I have unwittingly stumbled upon the most strange and ugly and foreign creature in the world. And before I found it, I could not have imagined what it looked like. The irony is not lost on me, although perhaps the humor is.

Do you remember the eels and starfish, Liddy? And the summers that we were left to ourselves, and so became mermaids, seaspawned and seawracked searching the ruins of sunken pirate ships for gold doubloons? Full fathom five, my father lies: do you remember? Oh Liddy, I long for the tiny world, when we were miniatures of ourselves, when the fishes were pink, and I can still—please don't make me, no, stop—recall the screams of delight in the summer that we cried among the garden at the sight of the ants, big and sturdy, crawling deliriously over the peonies. How sweet to smash it all with my fist if I could. I am drowning in him. It is an impossible ugly death. To fight back I must claw and rend and disfigure, make ugly all that once was not. I find the suggestion of reconciliation an affront. One of us will die before I take him back. We grew, he and I, too big for ourselves. We were monsters, outsized as gods, and we smashed whole towns, villages, small animals in our colossal footsteps. You will ask me to forgive him because that is your sweet nature. But it is not mine. I do not forgive. I cannot. I would smash it all.

I must stop now. But remain yours,

FWL

P.S. 6/25, Lizzy, wrote it all yesterday evening and then slept for hours and hours. Have reread and find it, myself, terrible. Was in a rotten mood. Too much to drink, drunk, the previous day. Was trying to bake a pie and the crust, as Mummy used to say, sogged on me. How all occasions do inform against me! Owen has just returned home and we have had a terrible crush of apology and kisses. Ignore the previous ramblings and take this letter instead as a sign of my devotion to you—that I can and will and must tell you honestly everything as it happens— melodrama, paranoia, and ecstasy. What a shameful big sister I am. This was to have been a birthday letter, and I have gone on and on, confessional and sloppy, again about myself. You deserve so much better than this. More happy birthdays to you, Lizard, endless happy birthdays, my darling girl. Xoxoxo, Franzi

Brigid held the letter, pages unfolded and delicate, flat on the palm of her right hand.

"You can't blame people," she said, "for what they used to be, how they"—she trailed off, smiled, resumed falteringly. "We can't know what it was like—"

"Before we were even born—" I said.

"That too," she said.

"I don't know what polka-dot spaghetti is," I said.

"With green peas," she said. "Green peas in the sauce," she said with distraction, her hand shaking slightly. She folded the pages back into their envelope. She ran a finger over the handwritten mailing address.

"Did you know that they cut up the letters?" she asked. *"They* being Owen and the biographer, they edited them for the *Collected Letters,"* she said.

"Why?" I asked.

"Why?" She set the envelope on the table before her. "Who knows why anyone does anything? The reading public has limits on its right to know."

"Then why publish them at all, the letters, if you aren't going to—?"

"Maintain the integrity," she finished my question. "Because the public has a right to know some things, but not everything."

"So what did they cut, edit out?"

"I couldn't be specific," she said, "but Owen told me—"

"He told you?"

"He told me," she said. "He tells me everything. He told me before we were married. He wanted me to know what was true and what was rumor."

"So then you knew about these letters, the missing ones?"

"Yes," she said. "But everybody who followed the story had *heard* about them."

"But you knew they were real," I said.

"I knew," she said, "that they were once real, and that they were misplaced, displaced, when he was working on the collection, nothing more sinister than that."

I didn't ask her then what I really wanted to know: if there were no secrets between them, why didn't Brigid tell Owen that she had found the letters?

"He edited them for the sake of privacy," she went on. "And even if it was his own privacy, doesn't he, don't we have a right to that?"

"I guess," I said.

"That's how it is in biography; you have to balance what you tell against what needs to be told," she said.

"I guess," I repeated.

"This letter," she said. She ran her finger along the edge of the envelope. "It's impossible to imagine my husband as the person she is writing about in this letter. It seems like a million years ago. And it's only one side of a story, isn't it?"

I nodded.

"I think you would agree with anything I said right now just to help me feel better," she said. "I think if I said that Groucho Marx was the illegitimate son of Karl Marx you would agree, wouldn't you?"

"Maybe," I said. "But why do they have the same last name?"

"Who?" she asked.

"The Marxes, if the son is illegitimate?"

"I don't know," she said. "Tax purposes? Brand loyalty? Coincidence?"

"So you can make up a story to fit the characters?" I asked.

"No, no," she said. "It's not like that at all. The most logical, the most rational supposition based on, drawn from the existing facts is usually right."

"*Usually?*"

"It is horrible," she relented, "to think about someone taking bits of your life after you are gone and shaping them—"

"I guess if you're dead you don't mind," I said. "It doesn't matter."

"Oh, but now you're wrong," she said. "The ghosts care. I believe in ghosts and I believe the ghosts care—"

"Then we shouldn't read any more of them, the letters," I said. I wanted to reach over and touch the yellowing paper, but at that moment I feared the ghosts who sat beside us in the sagging arm-chairs, lounged on the divan, curled up in the window seat.

"It is, this is a little like Hamlet's dilemma, isn't it?"

"How's that?"

"You know, whom do you trust? Ghosts or real people? Ghosts are untrustworthy, but people will betray you for personal gain. Ghosts can be spiteful, capricious, even vindictive—but they won't do *that*, betray you," she said with such authority that I thought she was going to produce on the spot a ghost to affirm her assertion. No ghosts at that moment made themselves known. She picked up the bundle of papers. "We should," she said, "I think we should read them. I think we should read them and call ourselves intermediaries between this world and the next. What do you think about that?"

"Maybe just one more," I agreed. "Just for now."

"I don't know that I'll be able to stop," she said. "Is that too horrible of me? Of us? Are you with me? Are we going to be like the fat little boys in that Pringles ad? Now that we've read one letter we won't be able to stop until we're stuffed sick? *Once you pop you just can't stop?* Is that how it is going to be?"

There was a sound, a creak. The rain pattered against the windows. Or was it a thud? A doorknob turning? A book slammed shut? An otherworldly presence in the otherwise worldly room? The noise came from the stair and we both froze, uncertain whether to turn and look or bury the letters, stash them under the cushions of the sofa, hide them from sight. I was afraid to see Owen—worse to have him find us bent like spies guiltily over stolen documents. Brigid did not move. I had to be the one to look. I did. I turned to find, to see that it was neither Owen nor some bedsheeted specter. John Paul Jones lay at the top of the stairs chewing on his new bone. He picked up and dropped heavily against the wood floor the sinewy and delicious hoof of a cow.

"I don't like keeping secrets, not from Owen, not from anyone," said Brigid. "We'll read one more, and then we'll decide what to do."

"It's a deal," I said.

"It *is,*" she said. "Isn't it?"

December 15, 1961

Dear Lids,

Here we have no snow. The damp hangs in the air, more bothersome to me than the cold. The gray trees are melancholy; I think they miss their apples. If I have not written often enough, please don't take it as a sign of my dispassion. It is because I am sinking into the new book. It is not an easy book to write. This seems a silly thing to say, but I swear I am losing weight through the exercise of typing. I am always starving, ravenous. I feel that each adjective weighs fifty pounds, each noun one hundred. If the first book was full of all the things that rise to the top when you are growing up—then this one is composed of all the dark and heavy jetsam that sinks in ugliness to the bottom, to the very ocean floor. If that book was tin, this one is iron. Oh, here I go: not a paragraph into the note and already I have abandoned you.

Since I do not have the fortune of you sitting here beside me, I'll do the best I can to write you, not simply write to you—but create my own companion version of you for the sake of assuaging loneliness. I think when I am hungry I would do better to simply write myself a meal than cook one; when I am heartbroken, I can write a better version of Owen than the one who exists. But I could never truly compose a better version of you—only a replacement, a copy. I have only to close my eyes, no, not even that, I have only to place my fingers on the keys and see you sitting in a pleasant little café while a blizzard cheerfully rages outside the window. There are books, papers, a plate with one imperfectly perfect raspberry croissant (an edge worn away by nibblesome fingers), a cup of coffee (light with cream, dissolute with sugar), a spoon on the saucer; your tweed coat is thrown over the back of the empty chair across from you. I think you are waiting for someone who is delayed by the weather. It doesn't bother you to be alone, not on this snowy afternoon when—oh, pardon me for not noticing your new haircut! It's clever and sweet; I am absolutely envious. Oh Lids, you should see me: a mess, an absolute mess! I am partaking lately in the very Jewish ritual of avoiding mirrors: though there is, as yet, no death in the family. Nothing as concrete as a body to mourn. My hair has lost all remnants of blonde and has returned to its habitual, its "natural" and naturally woeful mousy brown. I should say field-mousy brown because I see them sometimes scurrying across our desolate orchard. They fear fierce barn cats. It is indeed a very natural life that I lead here—studying the brutality of blackbirds, the stentorian owls, all manner of herding dogs who possess such intelligence that they roam free and unfettered by leash or chain; I expect soon during one of my walks to stumble upon a pack of them, canine impresarios dressed as gentlemen in hats and spats, smoking cigarettes and discussing the fate of Parnell with grave authority. So I walk through the fields looking for mythical dogs and cats and field mice; I take trips to town for postage. I have come to believe the less exciting one's life is in reality, the more passionate is the page. That is, when reading a book one would do better to imagine the author is lying than telling the truth, don't you agree?

Well, perhaps that is a question for another time. I'll pose it, ask you again when we are sitting in the café together—although I feel sometimes it will be difficult to return to a world where I do not write all the dialogue, where chatter and chaos and commotion reign. Where no story ever begins or ends. It will be, I think, a hard thing to get used to a world that I do not own in its entire entirety. The best I can do to entertain you now and from such a prodigious distance is to tell you something of the story I am writing. Here is how it progresses. It begins with a young couple in love who rush into something—who do not consider the consequences of their actions. He is English, a poet, fair and brooding from the bleak North. She is an innocent American girl abroad. They seem at first so perfect for each other. But she begins to sense something is amiss. And she loses, she is losing, perspective, and cannot say objectively whether she misjudged him or misrepresented herself. And after and with apologies to Henry James, the simple American kid is beaten up by the bullying Old World. In the end, I think she never had a chance. She felt suspicion keenly. It is awful to use words like "keenly." It is said to denote the knife-edge of suspicion that cuts through the butter of domestic happiness. They are in

*London together. They see girls on the street and his eyes follow them
for a fraction too long. It starts, it begins slowly. Nothing happens. She
does not trust her own fears; for most of all she fears in herself jealousy,
possession, desire, rage. How does it sound so far? A romance primer?
Should some hapless young American, a banker on holiday perhaps,
swoop in and rescue her? Or shall it be one of those books in which the
naïve girl is subsumed into immorality and then by turns becomes the
worst character? Let's only hope it doesn't end too horribly for all the
poor characters. I write slowly these days; even I do not yet know how
it will end. I would send you a chapter, but I'm afraid it is all scrib-
bles and nonsense. L will send you some of his new stories when he gets
back from Paris. I am alone here and use the time well—planning
and penning and plotting. The dogs and blackbirds are my constant
companions.*

Please send me word and news from the outside world,
Yours ever, Franny

"This isn't right," said Brigid. "You understand that, don't you?"
I nodded.
She unfolded the next letter from its envelope.

Here is what I know. Everything undoes itself.
*The eyelets and lace—the ribbons, the strings untied, hair slipped
loose of the clip, the stockings and underthings unfastened to reveal the
mystery beneath the mystery. No one could have stopped us. We undid
ourselves. More and more until it was less and less and there was nothing, more or less, left to undo. We stood on the bridge and I remember
thinking: jump. Jump now while you have never been more happy.*
Ah penny, brown penny, brown penny.
I am looped in the loops of her hair.
Everything undoes the next thing.

"It's bad luck," Brigid said.

"Bad luck how?"

"It's backward. The last page first—"

Brigid unfolded the typed pages, one by one.

"Don't you want to know how it begins?"

"I do," she admitted. "But I don't."

She found the first page.

May 10, 1962

Dear Lizzy,

I am all apology, my darlingest! I haven't written or sent word to you since March, before L's birthday party. Now you will think we lead a very decadent life, what with drunken guests trampling the flowerbeds and Englishmen pontificating on the sorrows of Keats versus the joys of Byron. In truth, it is such a rare event to have visitors and for such a long while—some stayed for more than a week! I believe even now that I may stumble over an owl-eyed old gent lost in the library. I felt as though I was in one of those films, a murder mystery, in which the characters gather in the drawing room during a storm—the lights go out! And when a taper is lighted, the guests are horrified to see an axe buried in the hostess's skull! Oh well, you know I have always been a morbid girl. Alas, no one died; only a few obligatory sorrows were drowned.

Imagine this, dearest. I spent so much time in preparation for the party—moving furniture and appointing guest bedrooms with sheets and blankets, finding the most lovely embroidered linens and napkins from a dear and near-blind old lady in town, what else? oh, chopping carrots and stirring sauces, whipping cream and beating eggs into sub-mission—that moments before the first guests arrived—even as the first car wound up the drive, I was in the kitchen wearing a work shirt and flour-dusted dungarees up to my elbows in a chilled tomato and aubergine bisque that lacked—either cumin or chili powder—perhaps both—so there I was dashing cayenne and sneezing with no thought in my mind, no consciousness whatsoever that I was the lady of the manor and not some scullery maid. I hadn't given a thought to what I would wear—yes, I know, for the first time in my horrible life, me, the girl who finds herself drawn to parties and crowds if only for the sake of ogling the morbid spectacle—I wanted to hide up in the attic or worse, spy on the goings-on from the banister rails like an orphan looking for prospective parents on visiting day. Oh, country living has made me plain and boorish! The less I have to do, the more each tiny intrusion infringes upon my being. What to wear? Dear Liz, I made do with the black crepe de Chine, you know the one, don't you? I think I wore it to Aunt Ludmilla's funeral. Poor Lootie! How sometimes I miss her, but that is in another direction, that is the past and we must move forward before I run out of paper, before the ink runs dry, before this tale merges into the next. It is no small commentary on the nature of my world that funeral fashions pass quite unobtrusively in the company of poets and painters. I ran a brush through my hair—hopeless! Futile! I ended the battle in abject defeat, twisting it into a braid and then pinning it up like a German washerwoman. I dug out my neglected cosmetics case to find my once-favorite lipstick dried out to a stick of chalk, a cake of red clay. I did my best—salvaged eye shadow and kohl, found a shade of less-flattering bronze lipstick still intact. I painted on the face, a face which did not seem anymore to belong to me, surveyed that face in the mirror just as I heard from downstairs Owen ushering in the guests. How horrible I was. What a mess of gobbledy goo! It seemed an absurd disguise, a bank-robber's moll. I didn't recognize myself in the mirror. Who told us to do this to ourselves, Lizzy? Who told us to cover our freckles with powder so that we look like porcelain dolls? Do you know what I did? I washed it off with soap and water. I scrubbed until my skin hurt—trying not to remove only the current layer of soot and gloss, but all the years of it. I washed until my face was rough and raw and wondrously chapped. And then I went downstairs in my out-of-date black dress and greeted my guests who between the wine and the house took very little notice of me anyway. And as I was collecting coats, Owen pulled me into the hallway closet and kissed me among the tweed and macintosh and galoshes. He said, he whispered, have you always had such a sad face?

I suppose I have, haven't I?

You might suppose that this could be construed as a moment of happiness, but with us it is no longer a question of being happy or unhappy. It is the fact of being too irrevocably tangled together to know the difference between each other, let alone draw distinctions between "happy" and "un." And both of us so egotistical that we hate the other for being so damned necessary. How many times did I during that evening alone catch his eyes with an unspoken and symbol-less symbol? See, we seemed to note in unison from far corners of a room full of chatter—notice how Charles Eveleth's third wife in nearly as many years hangs on his every word as though she is going to spill it all in a book? See how Harris prattles on about animal husbandry and the Queen's own Welsh corgis? We notice and give signal with no sign, no smirk or wink, no rolling of the eyes or untoward grimace. It is simply mute understanding. How can this be? How can it be that we are at once so hateful and so exactly understanding of each other? Could it be that we are monsters of the same invention? And that no matter how great our sympathies, it is in our very monstrous natures to tear each other apart?

I saw him on the sofa with the wife of a young painter or poet—a girl in an oriental dress of red satin glistening like a fish. She wore black stockings and sat with legs curled beneath her. She was not like the others. She seemed infinitely older although her face was young. Her hair was a rope of dark brown, black in the lamplight. She did not laugh in the manner of young wives in the company of other women's husbands, fascinated and intimate. In fact, I do not recall that she laughed at all. She seemed exhausted by life in general and bored with us in particular.

*Yet she was comfortable enough, immobile, unmoved, unmovable on
the sofa in her shimmering red dress. Under black lashes her sleepy
ashen eyes, bistre-circled, took in the room. Everything and everyone
swam around her, drawn as into a great swirling whirlpool. She was
oblivious to the interest she inspired in L. And he after a moment of
chatting her up and perhaps down, grew petulant. He excused himself
to play bartender to two young ladies who laughed immediately at his
first no-doubt witty comment in a way that was appropriately fascinated and intimate.*

*The woman on the sofa didn't miss him. She sat, the quiet sphinx-
like center of the room, offering neither judgment nor reproach.
Someone introduced her husband to me. He was nice enough, though
rather spectacularly unspectacular—Canadian, I think. She sat alone,
silently after L left her, and then in a bit her husband brought her a
glass of wine. I would like to put her in my book, but I wouldn't know
what to do with her. I would write a party scene and perhaps have her
sitting quietly awaiting her wine, her head nodding sleepwise onto the
arm of the sofa. Someone told me they heard that she had been in a concentration camp, but I don't know if this is true; someone else rumored
that she was a descendant of the fallen Romanov dynasty. It is hard to
know what is true when in the company of so many drunken liars. She
and her husband sat close and spoke low. I was, I admit, envious of his
devotion. I placated myself, my plain-faced, out-of-fashion self, that
fashion and faces fade away, while books sit on shelves and outlive us
all. I know it is nasty of me—to be so malicious, to content myself that
while the entire party moved around her as a calm implacable thing of
beauty, history wouldn't note a trace of her, or her red dress, or her
world-weary exhaustion.*

*Oh, Lids, I've become a clawing craven creature out here in the
wilderness. I have lost all vestige of social grace. I'm left to defend my
little plot of land with scarecrows and my ragged fingernails. And in the
end the party did end without too much incident—a row between rival*

editors over the proper footnote form, a few amorous matrimonial recou-
plings, a brief downpour of rain. The next morning, preparing breakfast
for the overnight guests, I sliced off the absolute tip of my right forefinger
while grappling with a loaf of bread. I took the most insensate and mori-
bund delight in watching exactly how much blood could drain from the
wound. I wanted to collect it in a measuring cup or a bucket like rain-
water. But instead L bandaged it up and rushed me off to hospital for
stitches. At least I still have use of my formidable left. L says ominously:
everything happens for a reason.

Our guests have long-since cleared out and left us alone. One so wants
to be left alone to get work done; I resent so much tiny intrusions: the ring-
ing telephone! And yet when the awareness comes to me, the fact of the
loneliness of life out here, I resent that as well. It is hard to think about it
rationally—that you give up one life, trade it in for another, which must
be, objectively, no better and no worse. It is, I think, a matter of turning
the past into the present and forging the present for the future. Quite a
conundrum, isn't it? And L is always running off somewhere—leaving the
telephone to ring in his absence. I have given up answering. It is always a
wrong number, a crossed line, an anxious and breathy silence. And I am
left alone in the company of my poor typewriter as though we two were the
real couple. Sometimes for the sake of perverse occultism, I pretend my
typewriter is a Ouija board pointing me letter by letter to the revelation of
strange and dangerous mysteries: where is Amelia Earhart? What became
of the lost dauphin? Is Anastasia an impostor? Did Eva Braun really take
poison in the bunker? Will I ever end this letter?

Still, you must not find me too morbid and withdrawn (please,
don't tell Mother I've gone maudlin; she'll fret—she'll send recipes for
fortifying tonics—for that objectionable palliative mixture of broth
and soda water that she calls "beef fizz"—oh!). To prove my point, that
I am not composed only of moody ruminations and do sometimes ven-
ture out into the world—just last week L and I went to an antique
market. I had the most curious sensation of déjà vu—the way one can

and does when touching objects that have survived the past and long outlived their owners. So many things do not survive that it makes me terribly want to know why, in a clinical, scientific, and nonsentimental manner, why these curiosities have remained whole while others have since shattered, rusted, been burnt to ash, set aflame—? How should one teacup stand perfectly formed, unbroken, neither marred nor chipped, while its mates have landed in the dustbin? I was eyeing a nice enough teapot when I heard a sort of gasp from two ladies nearby. They had found a tea set very much like the one I was admiring, and yet theirs was far more fascinating for being miniaturized. Imagine! The same, but not the same; tiny, scaled-down, precise, and useless. Tea could not be poured, nor anything more than crumbs served on the elegant little hand-painted plates. And one of the ladies placed a saucer and teapot and cup all on the flattened palm of one hand. Her friend cooed most deliriously.

No matter how perfect an object is, it is made imperfect by the fact of its utility. Among dollhouse furniture, tea sets, and doll beds, one feels like a giant, a god looking down on his own private landscape— everything so easy to control—no wonder the nice ladies preferred a tiny teapot to that of a functional size. And in the car on the drive home, I said to L this is what art is, this is what a story is—a miniaturized version of the world that we can turn over and over in our palms. He said it was only women who adore the fetish of tiny replicas. But I said, don't men like to build model airplanes and mass armies of little soldiers? And what of ships-in-a-bottle? And then he relented and laughed and said he supposed that I might be right after all—that we all lord ourselves over something tiny—dogs, dolls, spiders and ants, children and words. We build our own invisible empires and appoint ourselves kings. He called me a tyrannical genius; no, he called me "his" tyrannical genius, which made the statement sad and funny both in a manner he had not intended. He talked most passionately of the new story he had started writing about the semiotics of the golden calf. He took his hands from the wheel in emphasis and gesture. I told him that he was a magician at making plot disappear into story. We talked and argued and disagreed, exhorting, confounding the real with the unreal—useless endless ideas each spoken and then replaced with another useless endless idea—all the while speeding down the most perilously narrow roads lined on both sides with ancient stone walls. We should have crashed and died. We didn't crash and die. It remains a mystery to me how we so often elude the disaster we court. Instead of dying broken in an auto crash, we were hungry and stopped off at a pub for dinner and had terrible salmon and boiled potatoes, but a nice enough bread pudding for dessert.

I call this book Ten-Twenty-Seven. *Happy Birthday to me. And oh, yes, after the ladies in the shop moved on to the next curiosity, I bought the tiny tea set. But no more stories for tonight, I'm afraid. The white page is making me weary, or is it bleary? I have not been to a doctor nor yet said anything to L—but I fear the signs—headaches and morning nausea, a craving for sometimes salt and sometimes sweet? I have counted the days on the kitchen calendar a hundred thousand times. I didn't want to lose myself in L, in this world of our own construction. And now I am ill-tempered and restless—to have to give up even my body to a new monster? A colonist? A pilgrim on the path? I wish I did not have to see things this way. I wish I could be one of those tickled-pink-or-blue respectively girls, but I am not. I see only disaster. So this was my real news for you. Is it natural, do you think, to feel so terribly unnatural? I should have a long time ago run from him but I could not resist the challenge. I would not be threatened; I could not be overcome. Oh well, I suppose I was stronger back then, in the murky moldy past. I needed nothing and wanted everything, or was it the other way around? And now I feel inside of me something so irritatingly tiny, a little vampire sucking the life out of me. What sort of horrible hybrid is this? What sort of strange new monster? Or do I remain the worst monster of them all?*

In Italy he took my arm.

Can you see us then?

And in Dublin walking the gardens of Parnell Square, he took my arm. And on the street the girls clattered their way to work in the shops—those beautiful seaside girls—so tall and grand with their chestnut hair bound into braids or hanging about their faces in a riot of red curls. And their skin pale and perfect just flushed from the damp morning cold as they walked along the Liffey where we stopped and threw pennies for luck and he took my face in his hands and kissed me in the cold as the girls queued up for the buses with their thick tangles of hair, golden, pinned up loosely and falling askew as they hurried to the bus stop and the whole of the world spun, spinned, spinning around and around as we stood at the rail and crossed the Ha'penny Bridge. Let's never leave, he said. Let's not leave. It began to rain, and we were cold. We walked into the crowd and became, as I see us crossing that bridge, less and less ourselves, less Owen and Franny, less and less; we are lost in the crowd and in some strange manner immediately become passersby.

I do not know if I will ever be free of him.

Here is what I know. Everything undoes itself.

The eyelets and lace—the ribbons, the strings untied, hair slipped loose of the clip, the stockings and underthings unfastened to reveal the mystery beneath the mystery. No one could have stopped us. We undid ourselves. More and more until it was less and less and there was nothing, more or less, left to undo. We stood on the bridge and I remember thinking: jump. Jump now while you have never been more happy.

Ah penny, brown penny, brown penny.

I am looped in the loops of her hair.

Everything undoes the next thing.

Forgive me if I've rattled on. I'll sign and stamp the document, kisses, F.

P.S. You must promise to keep my secret for a while, at least until I am certain. And further you must swear that if anything happens to me

you will burn my letters. Liz, I am not asking but demanding. I would
hate for L to see me revealed as such a revolting desperate creature. Please
promise? Say it aloud now. I promise. I would hate L to believe that he
had defeated me. Let him believe that I was never anything less formi-
dable than a rival miniaturist.

  Yours, F.

Shadows crept ghostly along the flowers of the ancient wallpaper.
The fire flickered. Brigid and I read no more letters that night. Only
John Paul Jones was tireless. Long after we had folded the papers
away, we sat in silence in the dimly lighted room listening to the
sound of his gnawing, the grinding of tooth against bone.

Pompeii

Appomattox, explains Owen.

This is surrender, he says. We are sitting at the kitchen table. It is the next day. Or maybe the one after that. The precise day has ceased to matter precisely. Brigid is ill in bed. Arranged on Owen's plate, a late lunch, an apple, red-skinned halved in half white-fleshed and halved again to become not twice but four times itself and smaller and more numerous with each successive division. He lifts a sandwich, cheese and tomato on dark bread, holds it aloft for a moment before presuming to bite. He bites. He chews. He bites. He chews. He says, *this is how beneath bloody battles a war was ended in an exchange of notes between Grant and Lee. It seems innocent and naïve. Perhaps in the end they were love letters? Perhaps there is no other kind of letter? Perhaps there is no other mode of surrender?* He lifts his glass. *A toast,* he announces, *to all the letter writers and their reasons for using pens when swords might have been mightier.*

Byzantium, sighs Brigid.

I am reading a book on the Crusades. I like the place-names the best: Antioch and Outremer, oh, oh, but I am sailing to Byzantium! The very word twists like a stone street. It tastes like smoke and cinnamon. The jewel of the crown, the unrolled saffron rug, the samovars, the bazaars, the Turkish delight. What have you brought me? Tea and honey? Lemon tea, is it? And gingersnaps? Owen has given me this book on the Crusades, she says and lets the heavy tome fall to the pillow beside her. *It is an important book. Why, just look at the prodigious blurbs! Still, despite these ringing endorsements, beyond the places and Papal machinations, it is a book that makes me sleepy. The most important books are so often the most tiresome, don't you agree? It is a book that tastes like medicine. It is a book full of important words about an important time. Poor awful awfully important book! Poor Byzantium!* She settles the tray upon its little metal legs over her lap. She wears a plain white nightdress, sleeveless. The windows of the room are open, and she shivers, but smiles. *I am like a patient in a hospital,* she says. *I am like a patient etherized on a table. And this book is meant to be my medicine.* She holds her teacup in both hands and blows lightly. *But I need a spoonful of sugar to make the medicine go down.* She sips. *Still, I am resolved to be healed. I must finish this chapter,* she says. *So you must go away now and when you come back I will tell you all about the jewel of the crown, the rolled saffron rug of the East.*

Canary Islands, John Paul Jones dreams of.

On the floor beneath the table where he dozes devoted with territorial love sprawled out upon his master's shoes or rather boots and wakes awaiting the appearance of a hand to match the foot, a sleight hand to appear as though out of nowhere holding something wonderful: a crust of bread, sweet or salt, a pinched bit of cheese. He eats tomatoes and apples as well, when offered. John Paul Jones catches grapes tossed, lobbed, pitched from across the room to land with a delirious pop right in his mouth. He chews carefully on carrots, pensively on peanuts, casually on cashews. Onions cause sneezes. There is no food objectively, fruit or vegetable, meat or grain, legume or dairy, upon which he does not dote. Once he ate half a spice cake left on the counter. Once he caught and fell immediately upon a boiled potato, hot, hot, hot, that fell from the pot to the floor. He gobbled it in one gobble and then just as quickly made it reappear magically, regurgitation-wise, intact and unchewed, still steaming upon the kitchen floor. It does not, however, in the future diminish his enjoyment of potatoes. He dreams of them. He likes them twice baked and buttered. He likes them mashed, scalloped and au gratin,

fried with garlic, vinegar, and coarse pepper. Potatoes ripe-rotten in
the garbage. Potatoes with sour cream.

Danzig: fort da.

It is sunny all afternoon. It is bright but chill, no, not quite chill, the
moment just before, almost. Owen at the table wears dark attire,
chocolate-brown corduroy trousers and an ash-gray cardigan sweater
over a black-and-green checkered shirt. The cheese sandwich is everdiminishing. He says, *on his deathbed Grant wrote: "I would like to see
truthful history written."* It is a tart day. Apple-skinned, red and bright.

El Dorado: mythical city of gold and amusement park. Call now
to voice your reservations. Treasure maps, T-shirts, souvenir
postcards, keychains, gold nail polish, eyelash glitter, sun-
shades, serapes, sifting pails, pickaxes, etc. available at the gift
shop. Make memories happen.

*Truthful history? Ask yourself this: whose truth? Whose history? Take
Brigid for example,* he pauses, wonders aloud about a fresh pot of
coffee. *Take my wife, please.* Eating is Owen an apple. I am putting on
the coffee. Out with the old grounds and in with the new. *She's not
exactly as German as she believes. Danzig became Gdansk. It was ceded
back to Poland in 1945. Her family comes from the Polish side of the ever-
shifting border. And so she calls herself German based on a map of a different world; I suppose we can take some grim irony in the idea, the spec-
ulative notion that her questioning of her "German" inheritance only
proves her lack of—what's a good word for it—Germanity? Germaneness?
But I suppose these days people can be whatever, whomever they choose.
Has she shown you the diary? No? That's the beauty of it. Her belief in
belief proves her belief. Pick a story,* he says, *any story.* He pauses. He
relents. Owen asks, *how is she?* I tell him that she is fine. Her word,
fine. He says not in contradiction but rather contradistinction, *ah
then she's only having a bout of proust. Prousting, is she?*

Fairbanks: when it's springtime in Alaska, it's forty below!
The thing about Brigid is—

Galapagos, declares Mr. Darwin darkly.
When we were in Paris, Owen says, *she was considering, thinking about converting to Judaism—for no reason more cogent, more important to her than realizing her connection to Proust. She read books and studied. She was happy about the idea, determined. And then one day she decided that, being fractionally Jewish to begin with, on the evidence of her fractionally Jewish Parisian grandfather, conversion itself was superfluous. Why convert to what one already is? And I suppose I thought, ah, another drama averted; we are done with this one, onward to the next. And we were fine for a while at least*

Hollywood, hooray for.
until the idea came to her that being the unhappy admixture of Aryan and Jewish genes, she could feel the sides warring, embattled within— encamping in her kidneys, punching her liver, pummeling her lungs. She couldn't breathe. Doctors were consulted. Specialists made house calls. How, she asked them, could one resolve such an internal struggle? I'm guilty of calling a psychiatrist. I'm guilty of this much at the very least. He visited and pretended to be a specialist in rare diseases of the blood. How could she live, she asked him, with the history of a German past plaguing a Jewish present? Do the platelets tell their own story? Can one find history in blood cells? Is there a vaccine for national disgrace? The doctor prescribed a sedative. She said her greatest fear was that she might not win the war. I know, he says, waits while I pour out coffee into the china cup, hand it to him, *that all of this sounds absurd, but*

Ivory Coast: chief agricultural exports: cocoa, palm kernels, palm oil, cotton, groundnuts, rubber, sugar, coffee, bananas, and pineapples.

finally, the illness passed. She was herself again. No more talk of battling blood cells. And then one morning over breakfast she announced her intention to petition the French government to dig up Proust's grave for the purpose of DNA testing. That is when I thought, I proposed, that we come back here, to the old house. And here we are, home again, home again, how does the nursery rhyme say it? Jiggety-Jig?

Jericho Jericho
Joshua fought the battle of Jericho
And the walls came tumbling down.
You may talk about your kings of Gideon,
You may talk about your men of Saul,
But there's none like good old Joshua
At the battle of Jericho.
And for my part, Owen continues, *I'm not willing to say that she is altogether wrong. As I have always subscribed to the philosophy that there are more things in heaven and earth.* He taps his spoon distractedly against the china cup. The dog opens his eyes. The cat peers in from the doorway.

Kafiristan, coughs the cat.
Now he's gone and done it. With the spoon tap tap tap on the cup. John Paul Jones is chewing anxiously on a paw. The cat is scratching at the door: *Let me out! Please release me!* As though herself the representative of a nation of unsuccessfully domesticated cats she cries in coughs and migalkos: *let my people go!* Brigid has tried to keep her inside, make a happy house cat of her, but oh the kitty-kitty escapes. She finds her way out of second-story windows. She shimmies along drainpipes and cat burglar-like on cat feet scrambles across the roof toward freedoms unspecified and achingly perverse. Each escape brings Brigid to tears. She cries. She worries. She will never see her darling kittykins again. She sits in the orchard with a bowl of cream

awaiting her return, poor kitty, where are you? Here kitty! Bad kitty! And the cat always returns. And the cat always escapes. And Brigid always waits with a bowl of cream in the orchard under the apple trees calling here girl, here kitty.

Love Canal: I miss home when I'm away. I miss away when I'm home.

All right, okay, yes sir, yes master, says Owen as JPJ pushes his face, rests his snout with frantic aplomb right upon the wooden table to gaze imploringly upward. *Shall we go then, you and I?* he says and pats canine on his head. *For a walk? Is that it? Before it rains you say?* He scratches dog ears. And to me he adds, *will you check in on Brigid? Will you keep her company? I know she misses the company of girls her own age. I know she misses the outside world. And I know,* scratch scratch on doggy chin and pat pat pat ribs, *too well how the world is too much with us.* And when only moments later the door opens by the hand of Owen to walk the dog, what do you know, the cat slips by and escapes into the apple-bright afternoon soon to be dampened by downpour.

Micronesia, so tiny! A masterpiece of miniature detail!

Brigid is not sleeping. She calls out from her bedroom at the sound of my tippytoe footsteps on the stairs. *I'm awake,* she cries lightly. *Come tell what you two have been confabulating about. Did you talk about me? Did he tell you that I'm crazy? He tells everyone that I'm crazy.* She runs a hand over her hair, disheveled and sleepy, the hand, the hair. *Not that I mind in the least. I've been thinking about Byzantium. I've been thinking about the mad murdered pope, what's his name? I've been thinking,* she lowers her voice, *about the letters. I suppose we have to talk about,* she says, *about them, you know, the letters. But first tell me what did he say? What did you talk about?*

Nagasaki, no, no, nuances Brigid.

Grant and Lee? Really? Like the way girls sign yearbooks? Remember Grant, remember Lee, to hell with them, remember me? She laughs, falls back upon the pillows. *No, no, don't go. I'm not tired at all. Maybe close the window a little. I'm only homesick and dislocated. Which is why maybe, perhaps, why Owen and I get along so well—because at heart we are embarrassingly Midwestern. He's from Minnesota, did you know? I know, I know, there isn't a trace of an accent. Someplace far and northern, one of those places like Frostbite Falls, colder than Alaska itself, herself. Although before that—his grandfather, well at least one, was Russian, I think. Although before that? I suppose if you keep going back infinitely you are always going to end up someplace—a desert, a salt sea. At some point you must simply plant the flag and call yourself home.*

Odessa: pearl of the Black Sea, mild and dry with average temperatures in January of -2 °C (29 °F), and July of 22 °C (73 °F). Odessa averages only 35 cm (14 in) of precipitation annually.

Tell me what he said, she says, *and I'll tell you my side of the story.*

Pompeii, the last days of. No sooner does the second day end than the third begins.

He's the crazy one, she says. And for some reason, this vicissitude delights her. She finds it hilarious. *Did he tell you, for example, exactly what is wrong with today's young writers, the young writers of today? Did he say that they write as though they were raised on a steady diet of Ex-Lax and* The Art of Fiction? She is grinning. She pulls back her hair, twists it into a knot. Then she says, *the sad part is, he's right*

Qumran Valley: I dream I am in rats' alleys where the dead men have lost their scrolls.

about that. But did he say, did he tell you that every story should take exactly three days to unfold? And how that is based on a careful calculation of thermodynamic, no, a ratio of, what is it again? You take the seven days of Biblical creation and divide by the inverse of—the number of fathoms in a league? Invert the space-time continuum? Does that sound right? Oh, I can't recall. I think it also involves a gerund, a nun, a priest, and a sailor. But if you can work out the mechanics, you are assured of ending up with a story that walks, talks, and frets its weary hour

Rome: down with baroque, long live rococo!
on stage.

Samara: see Kuibyshev.
Oh, and a rabbi. A nun, a priest, a sailor, and a rabbi, she sighs. *I always forget the rabbi. Isn't that just like me? To forget the rabbi. Do you think it's because I'm German?*

Thebes, sings the Greek Chorus, gypsies, tramps, and.
Do you think there is a reason that I found the letters? Do you think there is a reason why I can't bring myself to tell him about them?

Ulster fry, though primarily a breakfast dish, is popular at any time of day with a few additions like chops, steak, kidneys, liver, tongue, tomatoes, and mushrooms (Serves 1):
Ingredients:
2 sausages
2 bacon rashers
2 slices black or white pudding
1/2 farl soda bread
potato cake
1-2 large eggs
oil for frying
When I close the bedroom window (now that the afternoon descends toward evening and reaches, has reached, is within reach

and grasp of the moment when one can say without reservation: it is chilly!) I see Owen in the orchard with John Paul Jones.

Verdun: dites-moi, pourquoi la vie est belle?
Brigid, hair knotted in a knot, face composed, implacable, studious, astute, takes the letters in their tied bundle from beneath her pillow. She sets them before her on the blanket. *What are we going to do,* she asks, *today and tomorrow and the next day?*

Waterloo: trains from London leave from the station, roughly twice an hour.
I have an idea, she says. *About the letters. Because I have been trying to read this book on the Crusades but it is so objectionably boring and my mind wanders, which is not such a bad thing, just a wandering thing. Oh, could you, because I'll forget if I don't ask now, could you find me a different book, something from the shelves downstairs? Oh, anything, anything at all but this—you know, maybe something Brontë-like if not Brontë itself. Anything in which a young heroine wastes away from consumption. Oh right, my idea—we should read exactly one word a day for the rest of our lives. Like a vitamin. And with each word we read we will take a black magic marker and obliterate the one that came before. And if we want the story to work we will have to remember the sequence of letters by head, by heart. Do you think it's too dramatic? Do you think there is such a thing as too much drama? I have a terrible habit of leaving books half-read because I don't want to know how they end. I never finish antibiotics. I leave one pill in the bottle and it renders the entire course of medication useless. The infection always returns, which is to say, it never quite leaves me. And I have to start the damn book over from chapter one. I feel so terrible about*

Xenia? I've been there. You name a place, I've been there. Go on, name a place, I've been there.

reading Franny's letters. Haven't you ever received a letter, she asks, *a love letter, a letter of surrender, that you didn't open for a few days? You took it from the mailbox. You turned it over in your hands, studied the stamp, the postmark—and left it like that—because in being sealed, in being unread it was so much better—and even if it was the best letter in the world offering news from someplace or someone long lost—still, the possibility of that unopened letter is so much more painfully wonderful than—oh, than anything in the world. I must not tell Owen about them. I don't want to read any more letters. But I know that I can't stop myself. Because I know, I see, I seek, I find myself in them, in her. Is it wrong? All these places I've never been, all these places I'll never see,* she drops the book to the floor. *It makes me,* she says, *sad. Even though they long ago ceased being one place and immediately became another.*

Yalta: Roosevelt and Churchill sitting in a tree. K-I-S-S-I-N-G, first comes love, then comes marriage, then comes Stalin in a baby carriage, sucking his thumb, wetting his pants, doing the hoochicoochi dance!
Her letters, she sighs, *we will read them, I suppose, but not today. Let's not read them today. Let's sit here and pretend the world is civilized. Promise me that we will read them, won't we, tomorrow and tomorrow and tomorrow?*

Zion: I love baseball, hotdogs, apple pie, and Chevrolet.
If three actors attempted to play the part and parts of us on this imprecise autumn day, they might assume familiar poses. Owen sitting at the kitchen table. Owen out the door with the dog. Brigid in bed with a boring book. Brigid holding the heap of letters, still half-read. Fern leaning against the marble-topped counter with kettle in hand. Fern sitting on the bed beside Brigid and pausing to pick at a gingersnap left forlorn on the plate. The actors would be, no doubt,

blue-eyed, beautiful, bruise- and freckle-free. The actors might be more persuasive; sad at moments of sorrow, bright where brightness counts. But this said, they would not be us. They would fail, the not-so-Owen version of Owen, the I-can't-believe-it's-not-butter Brigid, the fake Fern. They will never be us.

Qumran Valley

And so Owen met Brigid by chance in New York during a January snowstorm. Brigid Pearce—a peculiar girl in an oversized Navy-surplus peacoat wearing a knit stocking cap pulled down low over her lank blonde hair—wandering the aisles of his particular favorite imported and exotic grocery lingering, pausing to hold a glass jar of candied green cherries up to the light studying the emerald color, reading the label, imagining the endless uses for such a rare product. She took her time, touching and marveling the endless miracles of confection. Who could have conceived such grand impossibility? Tarragon cream cheese? Bottles of blood-orange pancake syrup? Behind the delicatessen glass fine smooth heaps of smoked whitefish lay stacked and silvery. Tin drums of olive oil announced in scrolling italic script that each individual olive had been tramped by the bare feet of Sicilian schoolchildren. She did not know that she was being watched.

And Marcel met Greta through the introduction of a mutual acquaintance who suggested that the German girl who was a new favorite of the demimonde might provide an afternoon of cheery gossip to the nearly home-bound gentleman who had been claiming to be dying for as long as anyone could or cared to recall. Fevers kept him bedridden; his stomach ached; the slightest odor, the smoke of a fire in the grate or the breeze from an open window caused apoplexy. He remained in his rooms at 44 rue Hamelin where the fire was never lighted nor the windows opened. The world was locked out.

And the author, feeling one day a bit more strong than usual, had written to the girl in his own hand on cream stationery a rare invitation to visit him in his rooms. In accompaniment he sent to her a bouquet of chrysanthemums although he knew they were out of fashion. While he could no longer suffer the scent of botanical or perfume, he had a love of the rich chinoiserie that filled and overflowed the drawing rooms and dark-papered parlors of the past before the fad had changed to Louis XVI and walls of stark white and Delphic blue. And girls were wearing shapeless tunics as though they had only just alighted from a phaeton or stepped off of the picturescape of a Grecian urn. It was a horrible new world!

And so this Greta came to sit before him, a great handsome girl who stood a head and a hand taller than her host; even in her pale pink summer dress of watered silk, she carried herself with the jostling frank and friendly gait of a farm boy. Monsieur found it odd that in the wake of the Great War the fickle Parisian ladies had chosen this good-humored, big-boned girl as their pet of the moment. She was, like himself, a curiosity. How the wicked mesdames must have mocked her behind closed doors! She had a wide face and accepted the proffered cup of chocolate with only a nod. He apologized for the disorder of his sitting room; it was only that he so rarely received or invited visitors. His coat was a remnant from an earlier era. He apologized, anticipating, expecting that she might judge him on his lack of fashion; he was shabby but he had once been elegant. And she was said to be a girl who posed for artists. It was rumored that hers was the body of the mythic queen Juno in a celebrated oil painting, and that one irreverent artiste had copied her visage onto a canvas, took her face and broke it down so that her eyes, nose, and mouth fit like the jagged pieces of a jigsaw puzzle into the wrong spaces. Greta frequented salons where witty things were said and reputations were made. Marcel feared that people who mattered would cease to speak his name. He feared that he would cease to know the names of people who mattered. He asked her word of so-and-so. But she answered with a shake of her head implying: sir, I do not know him. He asked after Madame whositandsuch, but the girl signified with a pretty shrug that she was unfamiliar with the lineage of that great and inestimable family. He asked her then to tell him a story of the world outside his self-imposed prison-house; a crumb of gossip, a morsel of who was doing what to whom. She paused. She smiled with her full lips fastened shut. Her lips parted. She spoke. Mon Dieu! She broke her silence finally in a giddy girlish rush of guttural low German admixed with broken French. Sacre bleu! Oh, how his eyes rolled back into his head and the breath rushed up from his lungs. She could barely speak a word of his beloved language and when she attempted, it drove him into such an asthmatic paroxysm of chokes and gasps that he fell back in convulsion. The girl in the pink dress rushed to his aid. She upended her chair. He lay shaking among the pillows of the sofa, lost amidst the yellow lace and coughing for air. She gathered him up in her arms and held him, and she rocked him back and forth until his tremors ceased. This great strapping Greta held the tiny rag doll of a man in the once black now paper-worn pepper-gray coat on her lap, and he buried his ashen face crushed deep in the silk flowers pinned to her bosom. He fell, he tumbled into sleep in her arms and had a dream, blurry and lovely, in which he was a boy again—on a seaside holiday he was sifting the sand for oyster shells and splitting them open in search of black pearls; he watched the blue-green water part and suddenly chere Maman no older than a child herself rose from the waves in a black bathing dress and cap. She waved to him on the shore. Allez, allez, she called laughing. And yet she used the formal address as though she did not know him, did not recognize him as her petit Marcel. He wanted to join her but could not find his way. When he woke it was past ten in the evening. He had been dressed in his nightclothes and tucked into bed. The girl in the pink dress was nowhere to be found.

And so Fern stumbled upon Newton on the steps of the library during a rainstorm. They ran through the downpour and past the edges
of the page, out of the picture to enter a new picture. They took refuge
from the gray afternoon in one of those cramped subterranean coffee
shops where indiscreet professors go to seduce students and students
stumble in search of seduction. They entered through a street-level
door and wound down a steep and narrow stairwell. It is said that the
descent to hell is the same from all places. Fern missed a step, and
Newton caught her by the elbow before she tumbled. I'm sorry, she
said, it's my first day with the new feet. She rose. He took her arm.
They descended the stair. And passed through the doorway. In the
dark little room they were lucky to find the last empty table tucked
away in the corner beneath a student art display of haphazard double-
post-pointillism in which thousands of colored bottle caps were
affixed to a canvas to create from the distance the image of human
faces. But up close, the caps made no picture at all and seemed only a
promotion of different brands of soda. There was a candle on the table
but it remained unlighted; although it was dark outside, it was still
afternoon. Newton struck a match and lighted the candle which gave
a spark and sputter before catching full flame. At a nearby table a
young man was rolling a cigarette. The girl who sat across from him
said something and touched his hand. A chalkboard announced the
lunch special was chicken salad with mandarin oranges and sweet
grape tomatoes. We rushed in out of the rain and tumbled down the
steps to find a table in the corner just below a picture composed of
Seven-Up and Dr. Pepper caps, and the girl at the next table touched
the arm of her companion, and Newton lighted the candle and then
it occurred to me: *we are not moving.* The waitress took out her pencil and lightly licked its graphite tip before touching it to her order pad
and announcing that today's coffee was Celebes. *Sell-a-bees,* she said
with tart apathy: *the red wine of coffee, a light rich full-bodied roast from
the faraway mountains of Indonesia. Would you like to try it?* she asked.

Yes, we answered. She nodded. When she was gone he asked me: *what sort of story do you think she's writing on that notepad?* Our coffee arrived. We agreed that we would stay only until the rain stopped.

And Frances Warren met Owen Lieb at one of those tiresome poetry parties where boys quote Eliot like Jesus or was it Jesus like Eliot? Or Pound like Plato. What difference could it make? It was November and the campus paths were soggy with rot. The gardeners were burning heaps of leaves. But the fires wouldn't take and they only smoldered leaving an ominous cloud, a fine layer of grime that sifted down and speckled in a pall of freckles the skin and face, the hair and hands. She imagined the smokestacks of Auschwitz dispelling in great gusts the vaporous remains of burnt bodies. It was an ugly thought. Still, the evening was not quite cold yet. There was a warm dampness to the air that brought up from the ground the ripe and lovely stench of decay. The trees were bare; the sky was sooty and marvelous. It seemed that she should have been able to make out the skeleton figures of witches riding their broomsticks across the horizon. She was on her way home, but missed the turn on the path and instead found herself on the doorstep of Montcrieff Hall in which the poetry society was having a party. She entered. A boy was saying something about Jesus; a girl was telling a joke that ended mysteriously with the punch line: *in the room the women come and go; they do not speak of Michelangelo.* The room was terribly stuffy and close. Someone handed her a flask and offered a drink. And was it then or later that she saw Owen Lieb coming toward her?

And Lydia Pearce met Chester Apollinaire at a church picnic and white-elephant rummage sale. He was on leave from the Air Force and visiting his aunt who had brought him to church to show off to her snooty rival, Mrs. Joanie Van der Loop whose son, Timothy, went to college *Back East* and one never heard the living end of it.

Lydia, crushed from her recent status as third runner-up (why, absolutely three girls would have to die or at least suffer some demoralizing disgrace before she would wear the golden crown! And what were the odds of that?), was sitting at a picnic table commiserating with her best girlfriends, twins cryptically named Mary-Ellen and Ella-Marie, about the woes of life as a runner-up, when Chester Apollinaire in his airman's uniform appeared coming out of the doorway of the church carrying a lemon chiffon cake for his aunt who followed behind him in her best blue-flowered summer dress and a straw hat with clusters of plastic grapes affixed to its brim. And when his aunt, Mrs. Delphina Beauregard, called out: *ladies, let the cake raffle commence!* a throng of women in sundresses followed behind her like Moses leading the Israelites across the Red Sea. Lydia took the divinity cake decorated with halved strawberries that she had baked herself from the recipe in *Better Homes and Gardens* and rushed up (not *rushed up* so that you would notice—*demurely rushed*—less than a genuine run but more forcefully than an amble—) and found a place in line next to Chester Apollinaire who smiled awkwardly at her and said he hadn't really baked the lemon chiffon himself but his Auntie Bo had (that's what he called her—it was so sweet—Auntie Bo or more affectionately, Bobo—) and Lydia waved to her adoring fans and imagined that she wore the rhinestone tiara of the first place winner gracing her golden hair which fell in cascades down to her waist when she smiled back at him the smile that she had practiced for her final walk down the runway.

And Greta met Marcel Proust who was a funny little man with great round eyes like pools of ink and a tiny moustache that looked to be drawn on with a lady's eyebrow pencil. She was forewarned that he had the manners of a gentleman and the habits of a spinster. He served her cocoa from a silver tea set, and then judged her on just how she used her plump fingers to grasp the handle. He apologized for the confusion of his ramshackle rooms, and then proceeded to form an opinion of her based on her dress and the informal upsweep of her hair. Speak as little as possible, an acquaintance in common told her. But Greta was a romantic girl and knew that some things were more important than how one spoke. In fact, once when she was little, her father had taken her to a circus show where a man in a black cape sat a wooden dummy on his lap and asked riddles which the little man miraculously answered in a funny French accent. And the children in the crowd had laughed and laughed at the snooty wooden doll. And she did not remember this until only recently when she and some other girls took in a puppet show and although she could not understand all the dialogue, it was beyond words and funny indeed when the wife banged the naughty red-nosed husband over the head with a tiny frying pan. Greta and her girlfriends laughed and laughed. As Monsieur sipped his chocolate she found herself looking, searching for the marionette strings which must certainly have controlled his dainty arms and legs. Where, she wondered, was the mischievous master in the black cape who gave this little doll voice?

And Owen Lieb bumped up against Franny Warren by accident. He looped his way through the crowd to the punchbowl when he found himself smack hip to hip up against a tall blonde girl with gray eyes who held onto his sleeve for a moment to catch herself from being toppled over. She immediately let go of him. And then someone extinguished the lights. The music slowed; couples were dancing. He took her by the arm, and she followed with neither protest nor assent. They pressed close together. He placed a hand to her waist and slipped a finger into the pocket of her sweater where with an almost Houdini-like dexterity he lifted a small tube of lipstick without the girl noticing. And he was congratulating himself on this trick, this sleight-of-hand that meant nothing (it was only for a

laugh and he honestly meant to slip it back into her pocket, really—)
when during a lull in the music he leaned in close to her and she
reached up to him, her mouth to his ear, her teeth to his earlobe, she
bit down. She drew blood. He would not; he would never return her
damned stupid lipstick. And then he laughed.

And James Pearce (Call me Jimmy) met Greta Schott (he would later
adopt an affectionate habit of calling her with an Americanized cow-
boy drawl Gertie) on a boat sailing from Cherbourg. The waves
rolled blue-black. James had fought in the Great War and lingered
after overseas only to get into scrapes of trouble here and there and
then move on to the next place thank you very much. And it was a
whim that took him there, onto a boat bound for America. And he
happened upon a girl leaning over the rails in a bout of seasickness.
He braced her shoulders as she vomited into the ocean. It was an
ugly dark day. Rain pelted the deck in fits and starts. And then the
sun for a moment broke through the cloudy autumn afternoon and
the girl turned her face upward to see Jimmy Pearce. He handed her
his handkerchief. He stayed there with her in the rain. He had some
peppermints that he offered and she nodded. Her eyes were bright
Prussian blue.

And a boy named Jimmy Samson whose head was proportionally
much too big for his body crept up behind Jojo Pearce and indis-
creetly smacked her on the back of her own normal-sized cranium
with a toy Nerf bat. She, caught up in a discussion about whether she
preferred to be called *Jojo* à la Miss Jojo Starbuck or *Josie* after the
illustrious Pussycat chanteuse, turned around after being whacked on
the head and with a closed fist punched her assailant in his left eye.
And he, being overburdened, as some twelve-year-old boys are, with
a wobbly head resting on a thin neck and narrow shoulders—he took
the blow like one of those bobbling toys that sits on the dashboard of

cars—he tipped, he tilted and teetered until he tottered back into the grass while Jojo's friends Tangie, Angie, and Peyton broke out into a fit of giggles and ran to tell everyone what had just happened. Jojo, a humorless ten-year-old, stood curiously over her opponent before giving him a hand and helping him up. Then, seeing that her friends had deserted her, she offered her new companion-in-combat a spoon and they shared the remnants of a banana split and then used their fingers to finish a sticky scrap of pecan pie that Peyton had left on her paper plate. Jimmy produced from his pocket the aluminum tab to a can of beer and slipped it on Jojo's finger—her pinky to be exact. A small bruise like a splotch of strawberry jam lay on his freckled cheek as a testament to his devotion. And he was going to show her the packet of cigarettes he had hidden in his jacket when she ceremoniously shushed him because the cake raffle was about to begin and did he see that pretty yellow-haired girl up front near the soldier? That was her sister who was almost but not quite Miss Iowa 1975. Jimmy could have cared less about Miss Iowa, but tugged on the little girl's ponytail. She pinched his arm. He overturned a cup of Orange Crush left on the picnic table all over her bare legs. *That's it,* she announced. *No, you're it,* he called, poking her shoulder. She took off running and he followed her.

And Klaus Hoffmann met Oren Abner, a young science-fiction novelist on his way to premature failure due to his inability to commit to a verb tense. Though cursed with painful shyness, after two or six tumblers of vodka Oren might be cajoled into reading aloud from his unfinished epic, *Reverse Infinity*. He was very good, especially when drunk, at funny voices and foreign accents. But when he was not drunk he was morbid and mopey. Klaus, who did not drink nor do anything into rabid excess and generally prided himself on a moderate temperament, took to the doomed young artist and made it his cause to help Oren become funny when not drunk and learn how to match verbs to temporal context. And after a few fights and bottles of delicious coffee-infused vodka dumped horrendously down the drain, Klaus won Oren over and the two became inseparable. And if a nosy neighbor had placed an ear to the wall to hear the goings-on in the apartment next door, he might have been greeted with the tinny click of two typewriters clacking in unison as Oren wrote page after page and Klaus rewrote, subject by verb.

And Brigid met Owen in a funny little grocery full of exotic treats but empty of customers. It was 1986 and her book of short stories had only recently been published. In her black-and-white jacket photo her blonde hair was brushed smooth and twisted into a chignon at the nape of her neck. She wore a string of pearls over a dark sweater and stared out with jaded yet wholesome ennui. One would not have matched up the girl in the picture to the shady character in the baked-goods aisle with the wool cap pulled slouchy over her eyebrows. But she was the selfsame Brigid who had ten years before helped her sisters decorate the top of a chocolate divinity cake with strawberries while they quizzed each other on the merits of Shaun Cassidy versus Leif Garrett. Brigid had horrified her sisters by announcing with a lick of the frosting-coated wooden spoon that she greatly preferred Mister Richard Burton whom she had seen that morning on the Merv Griffin show—to either of the fair-haired teen singers. Lydia called her a retard. And then to add insult to injury called Merv Griffin a retard as well. She reserved her judgments on Richard Burton because he was married to the beautiful Elizabeth Taylor. And Jojo said it wasn't right to call people *retards* and so Lydia begrudgingly took it back and called Brigid a spaz, and Jojo, studying the symmetrical placement of the berries on the cake, decided that *spaz* was a name with which she would not take umbrage. Brigid wandered the store in her peacoat and woolen cap. Her basket contained two boxes of fig cookies. As she rounded the corner into the produce aisle, she happened upon the only other customer in the store. He stood before a mountain of out-of-season red seedless grapes. Outside the snow fell in great dizzying tumbles. He looked up to see her watching him over a bin of Valencia oranges. She turned away in embarrassment and began to head to the checkout when, for no reason that she could explain, she instead approached him and said without the least trace of forethought: *These grapes are so beautiful that they must have been grown on the sunny slopes of Mount Ararat herself and brought back into this very store one by one in the mouth of a dove.* He answered that he agreed with her assessment although he thought that Mount Sinai might produce a less sweet though more prudent sort of fruit. And she countered that those grapes would be too dear for mere mortals as they must be sold not by the pound but the tithe. They continued to speak in an argot of extended metaphors (he said something funny involving the transposition of the words *Decalogue* and *dextrose)* and cryptic allusions (she asked him: *is there any fruit as heartbreaking as the pomegranate?* And then she conceded to her own query: *perhaps only the strawberry who wears her seeds as skin.)* as together they approached the checkout. The cashier was reading with rapt interest a best-selling novel that had just been made into a film. There was a picture of a famous actress on the cover of the paperback. In fact, Owen and Brigid had to wait a moment for the girl to realize they were there. And she apologized saying she was lost in the book. And Brigid unloaded her little grocery basket and said, yes, yes, it's the best place to get lost, isn't it?

And Pepper Phister met Georgina Kohl, a girl who worked after school in her uncle's flower shop and smelled of mint and daisies. Georgina was shy with a drooping mouth that never seemed quite to close. One Saturday morning when Pepper was riding by the store on her bicycle, out walked Georgina Kohl with a box of flowers that

she had been sent to deliver because the regular delivery boy had
called in sick although he was nursing a broken ankle so he was not
technically *sick*. And Pepper asked Georgina if she needed a lift and
off they went with Georgina clinging with one arm to Pepper's hip
and the other to the box of long-stemmed red roses meant for the
unlucky Mrs. Ella-Marie Kinbote sent on her second wedding
anniversary from her soon-to-be ex-husband Guy, a displaced
French-Canadian, who was saying with flowers that he was leaving
her to realize his longtime dream of crafting chain mail on the
Renaissance Fair circuit. He had come to believe that he had married the wrong sister and carried with him a faded picture razor-
bladed from his wife's high-school yearbook of her identical twin
Mary-Ellen who had joined a convent of Carmelite nuns in 1980 and
soon after embarked on a mission of goodwill to Nicaragua from
which she had never returned. Although Guy had never met Mary-
Ellen, he loved the lost nun. Georgina carried the roses. And Pepper
thought her passenger, whose head rested against her shoulder,
smelled of mint and something else indecipherable that she would
later come to realize was chrysanthemum.

And Alexander Piltdown met Fern Jacobi in a cramped used bookstore. He saw a dark-haired girl in purple tights reaching for a book
on a high upper shelf. The girl was reaching very specifically, he
was certain for Frazier's *The Golden Bough,* and she seemed in jeopardy of knocking the whole dusty shelf labeled *Mythology & Occult*
down on her head. He extricated the volume and handed it to her.
She accepted, but said she in fact had not wanted *this* book. He
asked: *what in the world is wrong with* this *book?* He said his name
was Alexander Piltdown—like the city. She said: *Alexandria?* And
he replied: *the city in England.* And she asked: *the one where they
found the orangutan skull?* Alexander, who hated nothing so much
as evolutionary humor, announced that he had at home a complete

three-volume set of *The Decline and Fall of the Roman Empire* and would she like to come over and borrow it and then they might have something reasonably civilized to discuss?

And Phil Phister Jr. would meet in rapid succession: Andrea Winters, Minnie Grimm, Cindy Bronowski, Lisa Pennybeck, Dimitra Otero, Tina Brokowski, Jenny Anderson, Anna Schmidt, Freddy Crouse, Ola Anderssen, Missy Scott, Norine Robespierre, Abby Tintern, Thora Fjordstrom, Kylie Blood, Susanne Paisley, Happi April Stout, and Abra Keats before he would meet Viv Valentine who was born again and newly baptized and took him with her to see the good Reverend Jabes Branderham and his traveling salvation road show at the County Fairgrounds. Phil, who was called P.J. by his friends, and Vivian Leigh Valentine (her mother was a devotee of Margaret Mitchell and the glorious years of the Selznick studios) sat right up front. And P.J. emerged from the tent that day born anew into the arms of his Lord and the good graces of Viv who had strength enough to cure and quell the wayward wickedness in his young heart. Six months later Viv broke it off with P.J. because she found herself smitten with the memory of Jabes Branderham and could settle for no mortal less than the good reverend. She hoped that P.J. would understand. But he didn't. He couldn't. Instead Phil took to lurking in the shrubbery outside her house. But it all changed when he met Ardis Rabbit, a plain-faced girl who liked to do needlepoint samplers and sewed all of her own clothes from *Simplicity* patterns. She, Ardis Rabbit, had never had a boyfriend but was more than happy to let P.J., when they were coming home from the movies, walk with one hand clasped on the nape of her neck.

And the gray cat in one of her inestimable peregrinations through the wilds in search of field mice encountered a fierce barn cat of black and marmalade stripes who was called by the enigmatic appellation

Arthur Fonzarelli by the children who set out bowls of milk in return for his companionship. The green-eyed gray cat allowed the tiger-striped tom to bring to her by the tail a lovely lowland marsh rat. And these two feline warriors spat and hissed and curled up in the fields playing and chasing and fighting and murdering and coughing up bits of hair and grass and gristle until the sunrise when they valiantly parted ways. The gray cat would later drop her litter under an oak tree. The orange-brindled kittens were delightfully cooed over by the children who found and called them: Pinky, Princess, Curious George, Miss Crabbyapple, Whiskers, Baby, Hello Kitty, and Chatterbox. Baby was renamed Sneezy when he hachooed upon waking from an afternoon nap. Chatterbox, a white kitten with a golden T running from ears to nose was called Topper who became Bonnet who was in turn called Bonnie who became Bonbon before she was given away to a family who named her Maggie but called her affectionately Rumtumtummy and had her claws extracted so that she would not ruin their new love seat. But she went on to live a jolly life as a pampered house cat eating scraps of sardines from the good china and snuggling in bed with the babies on cold winter evenings.

Some of them lived and some of them died. Some went on to love feverishly in country lanes and fight in back alleys. One of them called Sydney Vicious went on to make her home in the basement of a city library where she happily shredded her way through the complete works of Mr. Jonathan Swift. She made a nice soft nest near the furnace out of torn pages. And anyway, even when she was finally discovered, the librarians didn't make a fuss as she was such a lovely black cat with orange boots on her feet and a white stripe on her forehead and no one really cared for the deplorable Jonathan Swift let alone his complete works. In fact, it would seem in the years to come that books of which the librarians were not fond were left in the general vicinity of the cat who came to be known as Gutenberg—and those books that displeased her were remorselessly shredded while others received from her clemency and were duly reshelved by old lady volunteers and high school students who petted the discriminating Gutenberg and brought her nibbles of catnip and fish sticks and dangled before her the endless loops of string and bright buttons of which she was most intolerably fond. And Gutenberg begat Socks, Cleopatra, Rosebud, Frodo, Micky the Mouser, Buster, and Mittens who begat Buffalo Bill who begat Tickles who begat a black cat as big as a dog who was called Poe who begat Jehoshaphat who was hit by a car but not before he begat Wee Willie Winkie who won a lifetime supply of Friendly Kits cat food available in liver, lamb, and chix flavors when his owner sent in a funny photo to a magazine contest; And Winkie begat Margarita who begat Taffy, Professor Plum, Zane Grey, and Niblet.

And Owen and Brigid took their bags of grapes and fig cookies and left the store together. They walked through the snow that lay thick and jewel-bright, which fell and was falling on the deserted city streets, still untrampled by shoes and boots and the skidding slips and slides of children. When they arrived at her apartment she asked him in, although she noted that this was not the sort of thing she was in the habit of doing. It was only that she had such a terribly good feeling about him. She didn't know that he was *Owen Lieb,* only that he was *Owen* who she immediately began to call O, and he was alone in a snowstorm. He was Owen and she was Brigid. They took off their snow-speckled winter things—coats and scarves and gloves and hats. *Oh look,* cried Brigid, as their boots collapsed wanton-wise alongside each other by the door—*how happy they are together!* A chenille bathrobe lay in an unceremonious heap atop the coffee table while pink bunny slippers peeked out from under a stack of junk mail. A lacy white brassiere trailed over the arm of the sofa. When Owen sat in the lone armchair, he found a stained cup still with an ancient moldering teabag crushed into the tapestry pillows.

What a dump! said Brigid in her best Elizabeth Taylor-imitating-Betty Davis imitation. *What's that from?* And Whiskers begat Bean. There were magazines with pages folded back to articles half-read and abandoned. Who begat Pooky who begat Luke Skywalker who begat Licorice. The bedroom was barely large enough for the modest queen-size bed, unmade; while the curtains were cut of red velvet, though perhaps it was velour, and beaded with mock seed pearls and sequins—Brigid told Owen that a girl she knew had made them out of a bridesmaid's dress—could he imagine how horrible it must have been for the poor thing to walk down the aisle like Scarlett after Sherman's march? But as curtains were they not wonderful? Did they not horribly excel in their second incarnation even as they had failed in their first? And Sasha begat Miss Marple who begat Tigerlily. Brigid and Owen were married by a Justice of the Peace within the year. And Marcel sent a lovely note and flowers to Greta saying he had so much enjoyed her visit and could she come around again very soon? He begged no reprimand when he admitted he did not care for the tiresome way that young ladies attired themselves these days and if possible could she appease his failing eyes and wear a gown salvaged from the lost years of his youth? Was that at all within the realm of possibility? When Greta came around to his flat the next afternoon, she wore a gown borrowed from a girl who was an actress who had pinched it from the costume room at the theater where she was an understudy in a not-very-funny drawing room comedy set some years back. It was one of those remarkable stage garments that seems to be real but is cleverly held together by a system of snaps so it may be torn away between acts and replaced snap snap snap with another costume. And being the good-tempered girl that she was, Greta didn't mind let alone notice the curious reproving looks of strangers as she arrived on his doorstep in a dress that might have been the height of fashion ten years before her own birth.

And Critter begat Mr. Peabody who begat Sweet William who was called Wonka. And Newton gave a lecture one autumn evening and discussed in part the Puritanical dichotomy in the American mind-set between intellectual freedom and the restrictions on the land-scape of the body: Mind colonizes muscle! The head ploughs the heart into submission. He demonstrated his point with a slide show featuring a history of the iconography of the Eden tableau in maga-zine and print advertising. See, there is Adam hawking 100% pure combed cotton briefs as a more comfortable alternative to the ill-fitting fig leaf, while in the background a naughty Eve, herself draped in only a peekaboo sarong of golden curls, holds a shiny apple. And after the interminable question-and-answer portion of the speech which lapsed into a tiresome explication and argument on the merits versus the demerits of Martin Luther and the so-called Protestant Reformation, there was a party where cheese (camembert, Neufchâtel, and a woefully ignoble brie that prompted a young boy whose progressive parents thought that it was never too early to inculcate children into the grand epistemology of hermeneutics—to poke the backward end of a fork into the runny room-temperature fromage and announce with objective glee: *boogers!)* was served on silver trays along with crackers (rye crisps were gobbled, the very popular Middle Eastern hearth-baked flatbread squares called collo-quially *open sesames* were savored) and white wine (it was rumored that it came from a box!) for the followers of Luther and red wine for the supporters of the Pope until finally all were so cheerfully drunk that arguments fell away into devoted slurs of ecumenical compromise. After all, what is an indulgence or two between friends? And Snickers begat Rosemary who begat Ivan the Terrible. Newton and Fern left the reception and made their way through the wet leaves and wailing wind of the almost-October night. And Fern worried that she had already forgotten his face. And Newton won-dered if every time he crossed his name off the title page of his book and signed his name again, in his own hand, underneath the obliterated typescript of his name, if he was, in fact, writing himself out of existence. Owen and Brigid moved to Paris because Brigid so longed to see her homeland. And Greta and James set out westward from New York to Iowa. And Marcel died on a day in November. And Greta passed away sixty years later leaving behind a legacy of tea cozies and china trolls and green soda bottles and *Photoplay* magazines and a collection of candles shaped like obscene leering gnomes and a hidden diary. And Franny sat at her kitchen table and carved, letter by letter, her story in stone destined to be shattered against the rocks of her own empty grave's monument. And Newton arrived in Berlin just at the moment that the wall collapsed. It was chaos; it was madness. It was ugly. Of all the gods nailed to the cross, Discord was the most beautiful. And Fern read maps as though they were volumes of Dickens; her eyes damp with tears over each anticipated yet unstoppable melodramatic bend in the road. And Bonkers begat Little Angel. Separation follows conjunction. For each meeting is a moment undone and each consequence obliterates the original action. And Tippy begat Tigger who begat Ronald McDonald who begat Lefty who begat the violet-eyed tabby called Miss Elizabeth Taylor who begat the undersized and soot-dark Blueberry Muffin who never grew beyond the size of a squirrel who begat the menacing Count of Monte Cristo who begat in turn Reuben, Simeon, Levi, Judah, Issachar, Zebulun, Joseph, Benjamin, Dan, Naphtali, Gad, Asher, Honey-Bunny, Billy Baloney, and Bootsy. And these are the generations of cats who went on to purr and prowl and procreate; and these are the generations and the outcomes of circumstance born of the chance meeting of a gray cat and a black striped marmalade tom in a field under the moon and stars one midsummer night years ago.

Rome

Dear Libby,

The days have become short and dark again. Even the birds are abandoning me. I am, as you may imagine, monstrous as I shuffle through the ninth month. Thank God the end is in sight. I have had a terrible argument with Mother (again) about the baby. She wants to cross the ocean to dote. While I understand her desire, I can't. I refuse any more house guests until the book is finished. She calls me selfish, etc. Asks in that invariably supercilious manner: what am I going to do, place the crib next to the typewriter and attend to both in turns? I say yes. I say there is no way around it. She demanded to speak to L who was endlessly patient and placating, promising visits when "everything is set-tled—" which seems to be some code hinting toward nothing so much as the fact that soon I will give up the frivolity of the book altogether and concentrate on maternal duty. And then, of course, when he handed the telephone back to me, Mother was sweet, having found herself a new and unlikely ally. I admit, I would rather have the arguments and smash-ups than all this tiptoeing around me. Anyway, don't say anything to her, to Mother, because I know that she will ask.

You know that I'm an absolute hurricane if I don't get my way. It maddens me to think of the smugness of tone, the knowing silences between Mother and L—they expect that I will transform into a soft milky creature. They keep waiting to see signs of change. But I remain the same. And so I am blamed more for what I have not become than for what I continue to be. If there has been any change, it is only a matter of having become more so. That is, I'm more secretive, more protective of the book than the baby. I haven't shown L any of the new MS.

Self-preservation, self-protection, or pure vengeance: pick a card, any card. And he, for his part, while he falls happily into the beds of any and all semi-literate limerick-writing girls along his primrose path, he faithfully follows the commandment: thou shall not read! Ah, see, what a man of principle! They are so difficult not to find these days. They absolutely line the streets, sincere and swashbuckling. L has vacillations of paranoia and ego. I know he believes the MS to be a manifesto of mistreatment. How could he believe otherwise? How could he imagine a novel that is not based on or designed for his own pleasure? And if I suffer to admit that stories begin with the germ of truth, of situational truth at any rate, it has long since moved beyond that point.

L calls women as a class, "victims," but he never has the tenacity of thought to follow through on any of his "theories." For if women are a class of victims, how do they exist without their requisite oppressors? Oppression is his second favorite word. He does not use it lightly. It is reserved for lofty topics. When he writes of history the story is invested with personal connection, with hereditary pain or passion—and yet, when he happens upon me writing a letter to you, he will ask: don't you have anything better to do than go on about yourself? Do you know, Liz, I cannot imagine us grown old and cozy. I can't see a version of us with the rough edges worn down. He is prone to anger by laughable abstractions; it bothers him that I do not cave in under the dusty presumptions of his history. I fear he is galled most by my firm belief that men should not dictate the lives or art of women.

Do I sound grand and pedantic? I don't care. It must be said. A better topic than the pitiful female self might be, he suggests, a fictional exploration of the Crusades from a female perspective. Why is there such a belief among "enlightened" men these days that the best (and oh, the most "useful," whatever this means—?) women's writing is a "version" of a male narrative told from a softer perspective? A second-best story meant to supplement rather than signify? Is there some horrid old man in a cave somewhere thinking up these wretched ideas and disseminating them to the literati through psychic waves and magazine articles? No? Yes? Perhaps it is being taught at University. I felt the horror of it myself when in Freshman Lit (oh, for that version of myself! Fearless! Unvanquishable!) I had the temerity to ask the professor why we weren't reading any novels by women. He curtly replied, "Miss Warren, any book that has been written by a woman exists as only a weaker version of a novel written by a man, cough cough, an author." He said that there were entire courses devoted to gentle lady novelists. How to escape such illogic?

Look at me, look at what I have done, have had to do to write this book. I have had to hide myself away from the world and the sincere academic smirks of both men (to them I am a hobbyist, nothing more) and women (who believe I will relinquish my pen for the joys of motherhood) alike. A pox on both their houses, sayeth I. Liz, what do you make of Franz? She is either waddling about in woolens or wailing on about the evolution of the species. It is only that I cannot quite escape the place between the two worlds, the land of "what if?"

Imagine this: you are waiting in line at the bakery. What if, as you are walking out of the store carrying your box containing one lovely chocolate cake, you run into a woman carrying a box identical to yours? And in the clatter, you manage, each of you, to pick up the wrong boxes and go on your separate ways? And you arrive home to find yourself cutting the strings on the box to reveal a lemon chiffon torte while she in her kitchen finds herself in possession of your Black Forest cake? What then? Have you changed places in the universe based on baked goods? And so the intersection of your lives continues in dream and possibility long past the brief collision; yet somehow it must have existed before the run-on, that is, everything in both lives respectively led up to nothing but that moment.

And if, let's say, your husband is unfaithful—who is to say that this woman in the bakery is not your rival, that is, already connected to your life? What if, what if, what if—? What if in trading places with her you become more of yourself, not less? Nothing is real or unreal in fiction; it is all in the realm of the moody subjunctive. "If I were you," people say, "I wouldn't put up with it." But I only half live in this half-world anyway; I have learned, I am learning, how to divest myself of its more tangible charms. When I want a better Owen, I'll write one.

So I've prattled on with my lesson for the day. I know that it's silly to go about this and that, about the real and the unreal, but you can't imagine that there is much else out here; I don't seek diversion. When I am downhearted, when morning passes to afternoon with an inevitability that never fails to surprise me, when I have forced a daily dose of words onto the page, I sit by the fire and neither asleep nor awake I allow myself to see us the way we used to be—and still I am shocked by my own inability to make these scenes truly happy when I need some modicum of happiness to get me through till dawn.

I see us. Wills, so skinny that he was our skeleton. And he and Fee did the pirate song and dance. You, draped in a paisley tablecloth and mother's clip-on earrings were Polly the pirate, or was it Moll the pirate's gal? And singing, you did, do you remember, in a hilariously frightful Shirley Temple parody, "On the Good Ship Lollipop"? I nearly fell on the floor with laughter but then I set to and worked the problems out of the production and rewrote the script, making the three of you act it out again and again until absolutely no fun was to be had and Fee began to cry in his cape and folded newspaper hat. Do all czars and tyrants remember their reigns beginning as such?

And now what have I become? Owen glares at me as though I am Madame Dufarge unstoppably knitting our lives into my pages. It is best now that he goes away so often, that his returns are infrequent, that his excuses are formulaic. He claims a fearsome case of writer's block as though between us there is only one shared allotment of words and I am being terribly hoggy with them. I have left, he claims, nothing for him.

Do you recall a dress of Mother's, dove-gray with silver buttons? Do you remember? She wore it on severe occasions and it had a familiar softness; when she wore it one knew, ah, this is not the black dress for

*funerals, this is the gray dress of quiet and penitence. I wrote a poem
about it the other day, but then thinking the poem was wretched in comparison to the fact of the dress, its smooth worn fabric between my
fingers, the clinging scent of her perfume—the poem was dry and sham-
bling. I tossed it into the fire. Owen needs a source, he says, to start a
story. And a dress is not a source, unless it was worn by Helen or poor
headless Anne Boleyn. He needs an authority to challenge, while I find
myself longing to be able to feel those silver buttons. It wasn't a good
poem, but this is because in part I suppose I am not a poet and feel con-
strained by such short little bits of writing. See, how a letter to you turns
into an exposition on buttons and baked goods? I only mean to say that
one does not choose desire; one sees and tells. One remembers and tells. I
admit I pity him for being lost in his sources, fighting this and that long-
lost battle if only so that he does not have to confront himself in the mirror. He cannot tell a story unless it is annotated and written in at least
six languages (two of them dead or close to dying). And for my part, I
take my medicine. I force myself to acknowledge that the baby will
change the circumstances of my life; and I do so hate change. But I will
not let it change me. It never ceases to amaze me that even when faced
with tragedy or memory, in the very face of ecstasy, we do not change. We
remain nothing so much as ourselves.*

*So Elisabeth, having suffered through another rant that has taken
probably more time to read than to write, I ask for your pity. Because I
can tell these passing thoughts, fears, dreams to no one else. Does Mother
show you my letters? I write to her and say how goddamned happy we
are and how the nursery progresses and I ask her all sort of bits of useless
advice about which I don't really give a damn. But it means a great deal
to her. And she sends back her lists of names and sincere recipes for
smashing carrots and mashing peas. I read somewhere that when Emily
Brontë wasn't doing terribly beautiful and tragic things like wandering
the moors with her hounds, she could always he found cooking in the
kitchen; she kept a book on a stand on the counter and read while she*

chopped or stirred. That is to say, we fight, all of us, against domesticity ruling and running roughshod over our lives. I don't have the luxury of distraction or writer's block. Those are diseases of the male animal. I do not have time to waste on such things. In better humor L jokes that the baby will be connected not with an umbilical cord but an inked ribbon threaded to the typewriter.

We are right now even on hiatus from a row about who will be god-mother. L protests (from no lack of love of you, only your objectionable youth) and demands his tiresome big sister, stately and married, Natalie with the respectable house in impossibly faraway Portland, OR. I have met her exactly three times and like her less with each encounter. She is quite regal and looks rather like Joan Crawford playing the matron of a ladies' prison. She is not my picture of a fairy godmother. He has told me to promise you the next one! Can you imagine? He is portioning and farming out his young before they are even dreamed into existence. How terribly sad and funny alike. You once said that when I was through with him, you'd be happy to take him off my hands. Is that offer still on the proverbial table? Why in the end does fate force such meetings? And did we ever have a choice? Was there a chance that we might not have met and if so how in the world should we ever have lived without each other? Oh well, more melodrama for me to ponder while changing nap-pies and hoping some day for the return of a waistline. See how damned jolly an extra forty pounds can make a girl?

Enormously yrs,

F

July 8, 1963

Dear Lids,

How good to hear from you! And that you have found a new apart-ment—all these things grab my attention and make me hunger for the world! Even the city heat! Does it rage on the way it is wont? Dull on the sidewalks, dank from the sewers, fetid, wonderful. Spreading disease, bright green flies delirious in trash bins searching for delicious rotten treats? I enclose some snaps of J. I cannot say whom exactly he favors. He has a penetrating gaze (mine?) and charms the local ladies with cooing (surely he inherits this trait from L?) but other than these details, he seems to be a tiny version of himself.

There is a girl we have met called Esther who does lovely sketches. She wants to do J and if she does I'll send that along as well. She and Owen are collaborating; she is illustrating his new poems, which are fanciful things, rife with Celtic ruins. It seems living out here has at least done him good. She and her husband have come to stay with us for a bit. Perhaps I mentioned her before? At one of the parties? Her husband is several years her junior and absolutely adores her. Dotes, can you imagine? I can't imagine what it would be like to be suffocated with devotion. I don't think I could bear it, bear up under the weight of it. She is strange and silent, rumored to have been in a concentration camp, though no one dares ask the truth. I can't discern even an age or locate a point of origin for her accent. And if you ask her, more than likely she will not answer. She does not even bother to make an attempt to change the subject. She simply does not answer. I suppose people learn to stop asking. I would worry about Esther and Owen spending so much time together, but her diligent husband is always two paces behind and cheerfully so. The taciturn manner with which she treats L is most off-putting. He favors girls who fall and fawn and swoon for him. And these days L is very caught up with J (I think he is as amused by the fort da game as is J, his majesty the baby.). Although the crying, L says, drives him to distraction which explains, this time, his absences.

Why do I wonder so about Esther? Is it because I am devoid of other society? Or is there something, some trail of clues, some hint of a story that I am failing to find, missing? I think I am fascinated by her expression— her implacable face. Aloof and sad. Mean and sympathetic at once. Quite, as I say, strange, surreal. J has had colic and though I grow inured to the cries, I am sleepless myself. Sometimes I find the cries reassuring.

And I am envious; when he is unhappy he cries until he can cry no more. When is it exactly that we are no longer allowed to do this and so must convert yowls into words? Perhaps I have always feared women like E; do you recall the line, "what some women only——, others truly feel"? It is not that in her darkness there is more mystery, but in her mystery there is more darkness. I find myself in comparison (and I do compare) mousy and pallid. And if my hair was again college-girl blonde instead of this brownish brown, I would find myself, compared to her, too-bright, gaudy and ridiculous. And if I dyed my hair black so as to emulate her, I would be ghoulish. One can never be, despite paint or dye or powder, otherwise than what is chipped and peeling beneath.

I am tired and so will keep this brief. One day you will show me this letter, these bundles of letters and I will laugh, I think, at my descriptions and ponderous pondering. I think there is a chance that E and I may become fast friends; I hope to learn something from her cool dispassion. I think my temper will lead me to consume myself in a fire of spontaneous self-combustion. How fine is the edge of fashion between sharp-witted and shrewish! How I so blame L for transforming me into this complaining and compliant wreck of a girl. And I blame myself for allowing his behavior to affect me, to effect change in me. I ask L if maybe he would like to stay alone in this drafty mausoleum, while I go out into the world for a while. He laughs. He says, ridiculous; he says I am, I have become a room in the house itself and so could not suffer to live without my foundation below and roof above. What does any of this mean? Oh well, these stories, these words, it's tiring. It's tiresome. And anyway, where would I go? There is no place else for me. And who would have me? Anyway, I'm too grand to simply be "a room"—I'm the entire haunted house—every creaking floorboard and tiny mouse scampering in the pantry. Do you ever think this—about the future? About someone living in your house after you are long gone? Will they hang the curtains as you did? That is, will a certain spatial prescience prevail? Have I only haunted these rooms myself as the ghost of the girl who came before me?

No wonder at home in America they build new houses from sanitary kits that promise to be 100% history-free—no else's dust, no fingerprints. And then when you move out of the house, they simply tear it down and build up another in its place in the newest suburban fashion. All traces of the past are collected and heaped in a junkyard far from the eyes of wholesome families.

It is sad to think of others inhabiting the shell of our lives after we are gone. The judgment cast upon us will be formed almost exclusively of things we have cast off. We shed words like the skins of a snake and yet through the indelible quality of ink, these skins, these words shape what we were, what we have been, and never what we are; the moment passes. I cannot yet make peace with the abstract nature of time and the concrete fact of being. It might be easier, everybody says, if I had a sense of humor. But I don't. And neither does this house, I think. It is serious and unironic. I am this house, I think. And the hallway and the doorstep. I am everyone who ever lived here before me whose names are burnt to bits in the fireplace. I am lost in the smallest of concerns; how to tell stories. How to lie. Every child knows how. Start a moment before the beginning; finish a little after the end.

I don't think that I want any evidence of me beyond this house to remain. I want everything burnt black. I would like to be a character in a myth whose eternal punishment, like Sisyphus or Tantalus, suits exactly their earthly flaws. I would be damned to being a flower on the wallpaper. It would be my punishment; I would be forced for eternity to watch the drama of domestic life play out in my house. It is awful to imagine such a purgatory, an immobile fantasy of voyeurism. Who would choose to live as a spectator? Who would be Horatio when he could be Hamlet? Maybe I mete out my own punishment because it is what I have been doing all along. Haven't I taken an immodest and immoderate delight in watching L prove his licentious nature? Don't I absolutely demand it of him now? I feed on it. I yearn for it when he is too good and devoted to me. Where else would I look to inspire my rage? And doesn't anger fuel inhibition? And in anger I can set down words with no fear, fearlessly, unafraid of the truth? I accept my sentence now, and can live no longer with a fear of what will come after.

Yours ever,

F

October 23, 1963

Dearest Lizzy,

The moon is slowly by degrees moving from Pisces into Aries. I can feel it all along my skin. It is imperceptible. One should not be able to feel these things, the tug of planets, the pull of tides, but I swear that I do. I felt it as I woke this morning to the gray sky. I didn't want to work on the book or clean the kitchen or try out the new recipe that Mother sent for sugar cookies or boil and mash the carrots for J or dress the Sunday goose or repair the ripped seam in his plaid jumper. Instead I ran a bath, pulled back the shade from the window, and sat in the scalding water staring out into the glass fogged over and then I rubbed a blurry spot on the pane and kept my vigil. I saw the orchard, all things dying in their turn and birds against the sky ready again to leave, ominous portents of things to come. I thought that I might fall asleep there in the water, my own element. Water into water. Air into air. Nothing into nothingness. L looked up my birthday in the taroc pack long ago and said that my card is "The Hermit." It suits me. I never understood until now the blessing of this curse. I mean, the curse of this blessing. I could sleep all day in the water. Nothing can move me.

And the moon moves into Aries today. I rose from the bathtub, cold, cold again, endlessly cold; even the water gone flat and tepid with its layer of sloughed-off skin and scum of soap. I cannot stave off autumn. I heard someone downstairs in the kitchen. It is E, I suppose, letting herself in because our palace has no locked doors. Esther coming over to drop off translations or the new sketches for L. I told him that her beauty will be his curse. He laughed and said that I made pronouncements like a carnival fortune-teller. Shall I cross your palm with silver? But I was not joking. And when he saw this he said, "It is already a curse." We used to argue about such silly things as verb tenses; that was a long time ago. We argue about Esther's beauty. Perhaps there is no difference between the two subjects. Sometimes the past is simple; sometimes actions beginning in the past continue into the future. And as such, they inhabit, they belong to no specific time. Esther belongs to no specific time. L says we owe it to her to be kind where others have not been. And when I ask who, whom he means by this mythical "we," he will only say das welt. "The World" is only another card in the taroc deck. Still, he is not altogether wrong. In fact, I think he is right. Early this Sunday morning I hear her in my kitchen. L is not yet awake. He is only here for the weekend. He will be gone tomorrow. J had a rough night. He could not be settled. L said, isn't he too old for this nonsense? L said, can't you quiet him? I do not say, but I do not want to quiet him. Let him howl. And finally, J slept and L slept. But I could not, so I sunk myself in the tub. And E pushed open the door. I was not hiding from her. I am not hiding. I did not hide. I do not remain hidden.

I tried to braid my hair before the mirror, but my arms were sore and tired. My arms fell and fingers fumbled with the braid. I sat on the edge of the tub—perhaps it was the humid air in the small room—the window befogged—I could not see the orchard anymore or out into the gray morning. I sat on the edge of the bathtub and the sickness I felt did not abate or dissolve. I slid down onto the wood floor and pressed my face against the cool slats—counting them until the nausea passed. I heard the door again—shutting? Closing, being pulled to a close. Esther is so quiet. Esther has been here and gone. She is nearly invisible. She leaves packages and rolled drawings in plain butcher's paper. She was here and now is gone. Owen is here and will soon be gone. She left the house, although I cannot be sure, because I did not go downstairs to look; I do not know if it was Esther who was here at all.

Here I sit at my kitchen table where I write to you letters. Elisabeth,

I feel the pull of Aries, brutish, along my planets—. I want to run from the house and through the hay-dry fields. Who was it? Thomas Hardy—? who described a certain landscape as having "a face on which time would make little impression?" Esther's face, if I sleep, when I dream, haunts me. She has dark circles beneath her eyes that other women would trouble themselves to conceal. Her hair is black and tangled—all the shadows of winter. I do not think she has ever gone to a beauty salon. No, this is not true. She must have had a mother. She must have gone with her mother as a child. I can see her in a little worsted wool suit, a beret, stockings, clinging to her mother's lavender gloved hands—but I do not understand the language they speak. It is bleak and guttural. It sounds like a train chugging smoke against a desolate January morning. Her mother carries a pocketbook, a small cluster of cloth violets is pinned to her cloche hat, and I cannot make out the harsh foreign tongue. Esther does not file her nails. They are ragged and sooty. L says it is nothing more dirty than India ink and charcoal. Charcoal? It terrifies me. I cannot suffer the touch or look of it. It is a substance of incineration; it is all that remains of burned bodies and charred landscapes.

Esther will do us no good. It is too late to stop her, us, him, me. Everything will from here out play its course, unstoppable.

I can do nothing more than close my eyes and run my fingers over these keys, sightless, seeing Esther, dark-eyed, disembodied, with crooked teeth and swollen split lips—not the face of the woman but the girl who keeps her past a secret. Liddy, you quote Freud and say, "We cannot fall out of this world." How can I explain, sweet girl, how it is that one must make an effort, a tremendous effort every day to continue to exist? When I am in the bathtub sometimes I pray to God to float me to the top like the witch that I am. And I float. It is a miracle. It is ridiculous. I am not to be believed. I rise to the top like cream. I am only learning to become more perfect.

F.

December 27, 1963

Dearest El,

It does not seem like Christmas to me—but then I was never great for holidays. I felt sad and silly chopping down a tree. Begrudging the birds a home. I felt more the stump than the branch. So immobile and stubborn. Gifts sadden me with the prospect of a receiver's obligation. I am bound up in sateen ribbons and green velvet bows. Carols and almond cakes were nice enough, weren't they? Weren't the school pageants morbid? All the boys wanting to play second-bested Joseph, king of the cuckolds? And we smartly chose to work on the set rather than play this Mary or that. Rather than take the part of the innkeeper's wife or sackcloth pilgrims. You once drew a backdrop, do you recall? Of Bethlehem? In which against a blue sky the myriad stars had faces and smiled out blissfully in a celestial narcotized haze, oblivious.

J thanks his aunt for the pajamas that she sent and calls you who are shadowy and faraway—Aunt E. I think we are fading into the shadows of our own initial phonemes. Mother sent monogrammed towels. So now I see letters everywhere; letters to signify possession: FMWL. I run my fingers over the stitching concocting new slogans. From Mother with Loathing. For Me Wanting Love. Fear Madly Winter Light. The house is drafty and cold this year, so much colder than last. Still, I cannot imagine leaving. It is now very much a part of me. I think that the house is *me*—the way a hermit crab's shell is foreign up until the moment that he crawls inside, up until the moment he casts it off again. I have not seen L in two weeks, more or less. I don't expect to see him today. Frankenstein Monster Wins Lottery.

But don't despair, Liddy, I am best like this. I am bare and stripped clean. I wake each morning feeling that I have passed the night in hydrochloric acid and my skin has been burnt clean. It is not particularly a good feeling—but then I am coming to understand that I am not particularly a good person.

There are things of which we never speak, Lizzy. Does it seem that I confess to you with salacious pride about L's infidelities? Words can *make things so clean sometimes, so damned tidy. We do not speak of details because we were raised good girls. Am I jealous that he cannot find happiness with me or that I do not have the daring, the audacity to be as unrestrained in my life as I am on paper? But then I don't believe that it is possible to have everything. And if one were stuffed with sugarplums and surrounded by caring friends, if one's pockets were lined with silver—wouldn't it be a fate worse than death? To be so content? There is a peculiar sensation in finishing the writing of a novel, a nauseating emptiness—but it is only the shadow of emptiness. I feel the lack of something, of a world that never existed. There is nothing, no body to mourn. There is only an empty grave. This is no occasion for pride. I hate celebration.*

There is a man who brings round the groceries once a week. And this week, I asked if he could find oranges. He brought them, oranges. I nearly cried for the poor furiously bright and beautiful things—how they must have traveled! From Florida or California, from some city that looks like a picture postcard—to arrive on this gloomy sunless isle. Sometimes I invite him in, a nice enough young man who brings groceries, who works for the grocer and makes deliveries to shut-ins and cripples, to widows and old spinsters.

What sort of person are you these days, Lizzy? Are you full of terror and pity? Are you still so good and honest that I cannot believe we are related by blood? I begin to look forward to the visits of the young man who brings the groceries. He accepts coffee while I unpack the boxes. We speak with the intimate dislocation of two people stranded by the side of the road. How do we ever know what sort of person we are? Or what great sins or selflessness unless or until tried? I think about this young man. Was I brought here by fate to meet this man in the woolen coat who brings milk and cheese and oranges? Am I so different from Owen? Shall I avenge myself on L? And why have I waited for so long? Why has it taken me this long to realize that given the slightest chance I would act against him just as he acted against me?

The young man has a name, common enough, but I won't put pen to it. He has a face, but I would struggle to pick him out of a crowd. He could be anyone. I see now that this is the point. Anyone. And everyone. All the faces that you pass and who pass you by, pass by you on the street whom you must of necessity make the decision to keep moving beyond. Or stop.

And I have finished the book. So how can it be that I do not know how it ends?

I have a sketch that Esther drew of me. I asked her, is this how I look? She answered, isn't it?

Billy sent Jonathan a stuffed bear wearing a baseball uniform. Mother sent a crocheted blanket and picture books—and a box wrapped in red and looped in plastic holly. It is marked "to Owen and Franny." I have not opened it, seeing as how I do not know where to find these people.

A good way for a book to end is with someone dying and someone else valiantly carrying on. I don't think this is how my book will end.

And when the man came by with the groceries, you see, I invited him in and we had coffee and talked for a while. It began to snow and he asked, he said, he did not want to be impolite, but where was my husband and why had he left his son and his wife alone? He saw the typewriter and asked me: are you very good at it? I said, I think I came as close to demurring as I ever have: oh, I make up stories, that's all.

He said: but are you very fast at the keys? How many words can you make a minute?

Shall I tell you a secret? He kissed me in the kitchen. Among the pots and pans. And it is not at all like the movies. It is horribly awkward to kiss a stranger in your kitchen even if he brings oranges. It is not easy to let yourself be kissed in the kitchen. And worse, how to traverse the distance up the staircase to the bedroom? One does not glide. Or float. One places foot after foot upon the stairs all the while with this thought: I am not this sort of person.

Am I?

If I keep rewriting the beginning, by the time I get to the end I will be ready to start beginning again.

All through the snowy afternoon and the blankets of the bed and fingers on the keys, we spent an hour. An hour? Who can say? Who keeps track of time anymore? Until the evening darkened and J woke calling out from a dream. And I woke crying out from a dream. And the young man who could be anyone and is, collected himself and his plaid coat and unrecognizable face and vanished against the fields. And it occurred to me that I have never not been this person, that each one of me has undone and replaced the next. How impossible not to believe that context creates us. What hubris to believe that we are anything but another shape in a shifting landscape. My tryst (call it that) was not pretty. It was not romantic. But it had to be done. I had, you see, to see what it felt like to be Owen. And now I know that it is the most horrible fate in the world. I am sickened. And he has left me. Owen has left me alone here. And the man whose face I cannot recall disappeared and left me here with a sack of winter oranges brought by boat or airplane, brought in crates from faraway sunny places.

Franny has taken a lover. And now she sits in her kitchen fearing that he will return or worse, that he will not. He is not coming back. One day passes and then two have passed, I think. The fields are white with snow. I scared him away. The crows flee in terror from the stupid hay-stuffed effigy in the garden. Why do they who have sharp beaks and talons fear such softness? In the summer it keeps the birds from pecking the seeds and gathering food. And in the winter they fear it still. The ugly snowman's face protecting the frozen earth. I fear that I am not like other girls. The ones to whom Owen turns. I am a terror. I lay claim to everything I touch. I am a disease. Others are not as I am. I am as I am. I bite, claw, scratch, and disfigure; I struggle like Jacob to be renamed. Call me Israel. I want no more fields or deserts crossed for me.

Where is he?

I fear I have killed him off, but I can't recall what exactly I did with the body.

I have become Owen. And one day he will become me. It is not a gypsy curse. Neither is it a blessing. It is the transformation of water into water. I have undone myself. There is no Franny. Her house will stand and her dishes and plates and trees and window and books will stand. But she will fall away. The words will outlast her and prove only her inability to endure. Look at me. A tree chopped and burned, a stump standing. Oh look, look at how I live, how I live through it. Fact Murders White Lies. Fiction Mothers Willful Loss. Father Mutters Wasteland Liturgy. Find My Winding Loom.

No action that one commits is ever an action that one is not capable of committing. I was that person all along. It was only that I needed to become her. And now having become her I realize that she has already shifted and become someone else, and I chase the shadow. She's the girl with the great sense of humor and hilarity; she moves left whenever I try to move right.

I must stop now, Liz. You won't believe this. He is coming back. Can you imagine! It was only that he could not live without me. He is infected with me. I think we are going to be happy together. I think we are going to run away together to the place where oranges grow.

No, of course not.

This did not happen.

He did not return.

And if there are certain gestures that his heart no longer makes, know too that mine still does.

I am uncertain if he was ever here at all.

I expect him back at any moment, any day now.

It was here that the last letter broke off, unsigned. Brigid folded the pages back into their envelope. She set the last on top of the six that had preceded it. She took care. She moved slowly. She bound the bundle with its faded length of ribbon. And she handed the letters to me.

Samara

I saw Brigid on the garden path in the rain. She made her way through the trees in the morning darkness to the stone monument, and she bent before it in the mud. I woke from a dream to the rain pattering on the attic roof. I pulled back the wooden slatted window shades to look out at the fields. I saw her there, a spot of yellow, a shape beyond the apple trees. I knew the color of her jacket. I dressed quickly—in the kitchen I found Brigid's garden boots and pulled them on. The paths would be muck and tangled weeds.

And I went out into the orchard. She sat, head uncovered, on her knees, the rain, the rain, her hands pressed flat, white against the stones of Franny's empty grave. When I saw her, when I came to her, she turned her face up to me. "It's haunting me," she said. She looked to the stones, water-smooth, and asked, "Do you think she will forgive me?" I took her by the arm. She did not resist. Brigid wore only her yellow raincoat over a thin nightdress, her head and feet bare. Yes, I said, and we walked back to the house. We weeded our way through the trees under a sky that did not cease to darken. She spoke too. I remember this. The rotting apples, tart and sweet, rolled to the ground; we crushed them beneath our feet. She told me in the space of those moments, seconds really, all that there was to tell, but it was lost on me because I could not hear her whispering over the rain. Lightning caught the sky in brief broken snaps. She did not stop telling until we reached the house. And once inside the kitchen she touched with wet hands the walls, the marble counter, the wooden table. The dog slept. Brigid allowed me to remove her jacket from her shoulders. I lighted the fire in the grate.

"I'm sorry," she said. "You must think that I've gone—"

The raincoat lay at her feet. Her white nightdress, sleeveless, was soaked through. She stood in the middle of the room, cold, alone, lonely, and yet vaguely comedic as she hugged herself for warmth with mocking exaggeration. I sat her by the fire on the hearthside bench. I wiped the mud from her knees, dried her feet while she watched, bemused.

"I feel like a pilgrim," she said.

Her feet were nettle-stung, bruised, and blue.

"—On the path to Gethsemane," she said. "Or Graceland."

She stood then with her back to the fire and pulled the night-gown over her head, struggled for a moment, caught in the finely woven wet fabric, a web, a noose, a net. Her skin was so pale that it made me sad and embarrassed for her. I looked away. She did not turn. She did not turn her back to me. She let the nightdress fall to the floor in a heap and sat down on the little wooden bench, naked and silent, rocking slightly tipped toward the fire, hugging her arms to her small bare breasts.

"Do you think," she asked, "she has forgiven me? Because, you know, I would have forgiven her."

I said that Owen would not forgive me if I let her catch a cold.

"Owen," she said. "He never forgives anyone. It's not in his nature."

"Don't move," I said.

"I won't move," she answered.

"I'm just going to get you a blanket."

"I'm cold," she said.

"I know, I know—"

"Do you," she said.

I do, I said.

"I'll wait here," she said. "I won't move."

The dog curled at her feet, damp before the fire. He turned his face up to her. He was waiting to see what would happen next. I brought her the tartan blanket, but she would not allow me to help her. She took it and with the grace of a deposed monarch, wrapped it around her shoulders, settled it over her bare legs to drape to the floor and graze the dog's ears. Brigid sneezed.

"One day even you will forgive us," she said. "But that won't be for a very long time."

"Do you want tea?" I asked her.

"Do we have cocoa?" she asked. "Is there anything left?"

She watched as I put a pot on the stove and turned on the gas flame. It took a moment to catch.

"One day," she continued, "you will wonder why you treated us so well, and why we let you do it."

No, no, I must have said.

I poured out milk and cream.

"Don't treat me like that," she said. "Like I'm crazy. I know what's going on. You have to believe me."

"I believe you," I said.

"Stop it," she said. "Stop agreeing with me. I'm not the god-damned ghost of Christmas future."

"Halloween," I said.

"Halloween?" she said.

"Today," I said. "It's the thirty-first. October thirty-first."

"You should go home," she said. "Do you have a return ticket? I can help you get home."

"I don't want to go back," I said.

"I know what's going to happen next," she said. "I've forgiven everyone, but I know that when it comes down to it, no one will do the same for me."

I spooned sugar and cocoa into the pot.

I stirred.

She sat wrapped in the blanket, facing the fire, her back to me.

"I feel better," she said.

"That's good."

"I shouldn't have gone out in the storm," she said. "But I couldn't stop myself. I felt *urgency,* do you know what I mean? Urgency. If not now, when? I was awake in bed. I thought, I must go to Franny's grave and ask forgiveness for reading her letters."

I stirred.

She continued, "But then when I was there, at the stone—I thought, oh, now I must go ask Owen's forgiveness. And I thought I could do this forever, yo-yoing back and forth between them. To betray one is to abide the other. To bear one is to betray the other. Do you see? So what do I do? What can I do?"

"I don't know," I said.

"Of course you don't," she said. "How could you?" She paused. "I'm sorry. I didn't mean to snap. I know that I am going to have to give him the letters, because they are his—more than they are mine. And yet I can't make myself quite accept this yet. I understand the future tense, I know that whatever he decides to do with them is their fate, and that this mirrors my own. That's what I think. Fate," she said.

"Fate," I said.

"We can't," she said. She turned slightly to face me. "Can we? Live indebted to ghosts, to the ghosts of people we never knew? That doesn't make sense. It's no way to live a life. I do what I can to appease them; I write their life stories. That's the best that I can do for them, for her. But to be forced to endure the same fate, to see it coming but to be unable to stop it—?"

"Maybe you should go home," I said.

"Oh," she said. "But I already am."

"To Iowa or—"

"Have I been that awful to you?" she said, smiling. "Have I really?"

No, no, of course not.

"Here is what I think," she said. "This is what I believe without subterfuge or, or, or dramatic exaggeration. I believe that Franny led me to those letters. We found them for a reason. But I don't know what that reason is. It is either to test my loyalty to Owen or to—"

"To what?"

"Do you have them?" she asked. "The letters. Are they in a safe place?"

"Yes," I said.

"Good," she said. "But don't tell me where. Because I have a mind to destroy them. Or give them to Owen."

"Will he burn them?" I asked. "What's the difference then?"

"The difference," she said, "is not in what will happen; what will happen is inevitable. The difference rests in *how* it happens."

"Do you want them back?"

"No," she said. "But if I did, would you give them up?"

"You once said that you felt as though you were living in a museum," I said.

"I did," she said. "Did I?"

"A museum," I said.

"Are you sure I didn't say a mausoleum?" she asked.

"You said that the future is a children's crusade—"

"Don't remind me," she said, "of all the idiotic things I say. My epitaph:" she said, *"Those who do not remember the past are condemned to complete it."*

"Please," I said, "don't."

"Here lies Brigid—"

"Stop—"

"What?"

"It's bad luck, that's all."

"Oh, you and Owen and your bad luck and your lucky stars."

"Just please, don't," I said.

"Fine," she said, "I won't. I won't get any older and I won't ever die. Because you have asked so nicely. Because I don't underestimate your concern."

The cocoa began to boil.

"Look," I said, "it's ready."

I turned off the flame.

"Just like that," she said.

"Just like that."

I handed her the cup.

"You know," she said, "that no matter what you have done, I would forgive you."

She looked at me.

"I wonder," she went on, "if we were reading the same letters, you and I."

"How do you mean?"

"We saw the same words on the page, but, you know, we couldn't possibly understand them in the same way."

I poured myself a cup of cocoa and sat beside her, no, at her feet really, beside John Paul Jones on the hearthstones.

"Have you heard of," she said, "heard about 'poison books'? That is, the ink is poisoned. Applying the eye to the word is a death sentence. This must be the perfect sentence, no? I suppose it's only a myth like any other. A parable about this or that, sight and vision. No different from Oedipus blinding himself? Or Adam and Eve cursed to see each other naked?"

"But they weren't," I said.

She shrugged.

"Some stories can kill you from the inside out. It's only a matter of how long it takes for the poison to work."

"I think it was Noah," I said.

"Really," she said. She blew to cool her cocoa. "I don't trust people," she said. "I am very distrustful, mistrustful of people who know too many Bible stories. But I'll make an exception for you."

"And for Owen?"

"Owen," she said, "knows absolutely everything. Owen knows so much that he makes it up as he goes along just to amuse himself."

She frowned, hands cupping her cup of cocoa.

"I wish we had whipped cream," she said. "The kind that comes in a can. There is absolutely nothing to it."

"I wish—"

"No more wishes," she said. "No more of anything. No more abstractions, let's deal only in the concrete. Let's bury ourselves up to the neck in concrete. Don't you have any stories, you know, to make me feel better by showing me how much worse things could be? Stories of suffering, broken hearts, abject woe?"

"A story?" I said.

"Tell me one," she said. She leaned forward, struggled to keep the blanket over her shoulders. "A good one. One with a ruined castle and an unhappy princess. One with a pirate and buried treasure. Tell me that the armies are advancing to save the day."

"Are you tired?" I said.

"Tell me your story," she said. "And then I'll go upstairs, then I'll go to sleep. Tell me?"

"I can't," I said.

"You won't," she answered.

"There's nothing there," I said.

"Like the whipped cream in the can?" she said. "Only it is very much there. One can taste it and feel it. One grows, even, fat on it."

"I don't want to go back," I said.

"Of course not, of course you don't," she said. "No one does. But why don't you?"

"I wanted," I began.

"Stop," she said. "The beginning is all I need. A subject and a verb. The rest is easy to figure out."

Rain fell.

"I'm tired," she said. "Your story has helped me to make up my mind."

"What story?"

"Did I really say a *museum?* Because I must have meant a morgue or mausoleum. I must have meant a catacomb full of bones. You didn't know," she said. "You couldn't have known."

"Known what?"

"That when you met us you stumbled onto a graveyard."

"I'll be okay," I said.

"Will you?" she said.

"You need, you just need to get some rest. The rain—"

She made a funny face, said it was always something. It was either the rain or the lack of rain. She said the cocoa was very good and hot, that it was vanilla and chocolate alike, sweet and bitter, innocent and experienced.

"There is one thing," I said. I hesitated.

"What's that," she said, her face propped wearily on her hand, the woolen blanket askew to reveal a pale shoulder.

"Where did they come from, the letters?"

"You mean how did they get here?"

"I mean that, yes, but who hid them?"

"I see," she said. "Because if Owen is looking for the letters, he certainly wasn't the one who hid them. And if it wasn't Owen—"

"Then who?"

She closed her eyes. Opened them. Said, "It is my turn to tell a story."

I didn't understand. That's my problem. I never do.

"It wasn't Owen," she said, "who hid the letters. Not that he doesn't have reason to. Not that he wasn't going to do it, to hide or to destroy. After all, he was the one who asked for the letters back from Elisabeth for the compilation. And it wasn't Franny. How could it have been Franny. She was already gone."

"Jonathan?"

"He was a child," she said.

"Please don't say that it was a ghost."

She rubbed at her eyes with outstretched fingertips. "I think we've brought all the ghosts with us. I think you should know that there was someone else. I knew—I should have told you before, but—"

"You were only being careful," I said.

"*Careful,*" she echoed. "What? No. We were protecting ourselves. We were thinking of ourselves."

"There's nothing wrong with that."

"There is everything in the world wrong with it," she said.

"So who was it then? Who else was there?"

"There is always someone else. People," she paused, "are lost every day. Not just buried under the rubble of earthquakes, but disappeared. Lost, gone, missing from parking lots, last seen in a shopping mall. Never heard from again. A car drives off the map. Who would look for you if you vanished? Never sent another postcard? What then? Who would imagine that you were gone forever? And anyway, wouldn't someone else just pop up in your place, replace you? Is it any wonder how one person here or there falls out of the world?"

"But there are things," I said. "Proof, birth certificates, credit card receipts, phone bills, I don't know, *artifacts*. Museums are full of artifacts. Everyone leaves a trail, if you think about it—it's hard to disappear."

"So what," she said. "So we have paper. And ink. And mummies. And the bones of the Elephant Man and the Shroud of Turin and a host of indignities bought and sold."

"What are you saying?"

"Owen wasn't going to put those seven letters into the book," she said. "He had them separated from the others. The others may have been, were, edited, changed. But they appeared in the collection. But he set aside, pulled the ones we read, that we found, and," she paused, "someone else found them. And she hid them. And that's what I'm trying to tell you."

"She?"

"She," said Brigid. "A girl, a girl, another girl. The one who came after Franny. The one who came before me. I suppose there were a lot of others, but that isn't, not specifically, our concern now, is it?"

"Who?"

"Said the wise old owl—"

"Do you really know?"

"Of course I know," she said. "I've known about it all along. Aren't you listening? Haven't you been paying attention? She doesn't exist. She's gone. She's disappeared. That's how it happens. You can write anyone or anything into or out of being. Just because she isn't in any of the books, the biographies, doesn't mean that she didn't exist. That's how he wanted it. Maybe Owen is right. It's no good to bury things. You have to burn them up."

"So this girl, this other girl, she hid Franny's letters, why?"

"Owen will tell you," she said. "All you have to do is ask him. Ask him," she said, "about Esther."

"In the red dress," I said. "At the party?"

"Yes," she said.

"And you knew about her—before?"

"Before," she paused. "Before what? I wasn't here. I was in Iowa for God's sake. I was playing kickball and selling Girl Scout cookies."

"—Before we read the letters."

"Does it matter? I will forgive him anything. Maybe one day you'll understand."

I hoped that I wouldn't. But I didn't tell her this.

"That's just how you are," I said.

"I am," she said, "something ridiculous. I knew about her, and yet it didn't occur to me until later. Not until we came here to this house—that no matter how difficult life was for Franny—how horrible it was for Esther to live in the shadow of that unhappiness.

Even when he told me about her, it was as an explanation. Does that make sense?"

"Of what?"

"Franny's death," she said.

She picked up her cup, stared down into it for a moment, empty.

"It was all so easily explained," she went on. "Franny died. You know, Franny was driven to suicide because Owen left her for Esther. That's how he likes to think it happened. And that she was crazy, of course. Which always helps. But there it is, there it was, *Esther*, an explanation. It was her fault and so it seemed fitting that her punishment was to be excised, written out of the world, as though she were never here at all. In this very house. Gone," she said, "just like that."

"Tell me how it happened," I said.

"It isn't my story," she said.

"Then tell me what you can."

"I think she saved those letters because they prove that she existed. Maybe she took them because of what they meant to Owen. Because of how he hated the way Franny pointed out his weakness. Maybe being young is an excuse, after all. I don't know. I don't know anything anymore."

"Why did you give them to me?" I asked her.

She opened her eyes, wide and bright and damp in the firelight.

"Isn't it obvious?" she said.

And she closed her eyes.

"I'll tell you one more thing," she said.

I waited.

"Owen left Franny for Esther," she said.

"And Franny was left at home with the baby, jealous—?"

"No, I'd say she was beyond that. But you've read the letters. It wasn't, it doesn't seem as simple as jealousy. Esther was a mystery for both of them, for Owen as well as Franny. The way he talks about Esther," Brigid broke off. "Like a secret—"

"Did he do it, solve her?"

"Oh, I don't think he wants to solve anything. That's the point. If there is a point. He wanted to keep her a secret because she was his excuse and his burden and his responsibility. Franny was Franny. Everyone knows her story. Everyone has read her book. But Esther belonged, belongs entirely to Owen."

"Where is she now?"

"Now?" said Brigid. "Now, she's dead, of course. I'm sorry," she said quickly. "That sounded coarse. It was rude of me. She's gone. Maybe she even hid Franny's manuscript. Maybe that will one day magically appear. Maybe her sketches are hidden in this very house. Or maybe not. And then she died. She killed herself."

"What?"

"That's how it happened, I think. This is how it happened. After Franny died, Owen brought Esther back here to take care of Jonathan. But he didn't count on how everyone, his friends, would turn against him for bringing Esther into Franny's house. Even people who had never liked Franny became her supporters after the fact. That's how people are. And they blamed Esther and she bore the guilt. I suppose that Owen let her. How does anything happen? She overdosed on sleeping pills and drowned in the bathtub. That's what happened."

I waited in silence.

"And then Owen sent Jonathan away to live in America with his sister. And then Owen went on with his life. And here I am. And I have forgiven him. I think that you should do the same. That is, when you think about him, about us, be a witness," she said, "not a judge."

"I'm neither," I said.

"I have a fever. I know it. I feel it."

She took my hand and lifted it to her forehead.

"Feel," she insisted. "Hot?"

Her forehead was warm and damp.

"I'll get some aspirin," I said.

She shook her head.

"Esther and Owen had a child," she said.

The fire crackled in the grate.

She drew the blanket more tightly around herself.

"Don't bother with aspirin," she said. "It won't help. Just let me end the story. Esther died," Brigid spoke slowly, "and when she died, she took the baby with her. The baby died," she said. "She drowned with her mother."

The fire continued to burn.

The dog slept.

And the rain fell.

"She died, the baby," said Brigid. "And I'm so sorry."

"You can't stay here," I said.

"But I don't want to go anywhere else," she said. "Don't you see? Don't you understand? I belong here."

"You have a fever," I said.

"I've forgiven him," she said.

She stood up from the bench.

"And you will too," she said. "Promise me?"

She wavered a moment before the fire.

"I have to sleep now," she said.

"I won't say a word—"

"That doesn't matter," she said. "Not anymore. He'll finish the story for you when he's ready. It all happened a long time ago. That's the only way to think about it. It isn't *now*. It isn't, of course, happening *now*."

"I'm sorry to have kept you up," I said.

"You're so like us," she said. "I said to O, I told him when we first met you, I said, what a funny girl she is—just like Snow White in her glass coffin. That's just what I said—" She leaned close and touched my cheek. She dropped her hand to my shoulder.

"Are you all right?" I asked.

"Don't mind me," she said.

"Do you want to go upstairs?"

"What about your secret?"

"What?"

"Your secret," she repeated. "You promised. When we began. When we began to begin, do you remember? You promised."

"It's nothing," I said. "It's, there's nothing to compare to any of this—just stupid things."

"Don't say that—nothing means anything at all if you go around comparing it to the most horrible things. And I like stupid things, I like stupid things the best—you know, whiskers on kittens and bright shiny mittens, those are the best things."

"Let's get you to bed."

"It was a boy," she said. "Wasn't it? It always is. Isn't it always?"

"You have a fever," I said.

"No, no," she said.

She placed a hand on the banister.

She stumbled on the stair.

"I forgive you," she said. "You are forgiven."

She rested her head on my shoulder.

"I'm so sleepy," she said.

She leaned on me.

We continued upward.

"I'm cold," she said.

"You'll feel better once you've slept."

"Owen is sleeping," she said. "Nothing wakes him. Not alarm clocks, not thunderstorms. Nothing can wake Owen."

"Then he won't know that you were gone," I said.

"Yes," she said. "I never left my bed."

"We're almost there," I said.

"I'm sorry," she said. "I am sorry."

"I know."

"I am fever," she said.

"Just one more step—"

"I am forgiveness," she said.

"Yes, yes," I said.

"My fever," she said, "is making me feverish."

"It never happened," I said. "It was all a dream."

"Yes," she said. "Or is it the other way around?"

"Look," I said, "here we are."

"You are forgiven," she said. "I am forgiveness."

At the top of the stair I let go of her. She walked waveringly, paused slightly to turn backward and blow me a kiss. Step by step she moved farther from me. The third wife walked on the morning of Halloween down the hallway to open the door of her bedroom where her husband slept. And I watched her then as I watch the now-tiny obscure four-letter version of the girl I used to be. She gets smaller as she moves further and further away. I went downstairs. I sat at the kitchen table and began paring carrots for a stew. I imagined it would make Brigid feel better when she awoke. I knifed the eyes of potatoes blindly. A white onion unwound before me awaiting its turn to be chopped. The sun did not seem to rise that day. And I did not know what else to do. She, Fern in her glass coffin, sitting, seated, sits before a mountain of diced vegetables, broken down before the halved red hearts of peppers. I clasped the knife. I put my face in her hands and cried.

Thebes

All day it continued to rain.

"A five-letter word," asked Owen, "for palliative?"

Brigid closed her book. She looked at him. She wore his flannel bathrobe unbelted over her white cotton nightdress. On her feet were woolen socks. She looked at her husband and at her feet, at the wind banging the windows, and the rain-darkened afternoon sky.

"I don't know," she answered, and turned back to her book.

"What do you think?" Owen asked me.

"I'm hungry," said Brigid.

"That means," he said, "you must be getting better. Spare, how does it go? Spare a cold, feed a fever?"

"Dear God," said Brigid. "Not in the least. Spare the rod, spoil the child. Feed a cold, starve a fever. Suffer the little children to come unto me."

"Do you want soup?" I asked her.

She nodded.

"Do I look awful?" Brigid asked. "Tell the truth."

"Truth," said Owen, "is one of those damned transcendent signifiers that not only means nothing, it continues to mean less than nothing. It's the monolith of absence—"

"I'm sick," pleaded Brigid. "Please don't start."

"Where did you learn to cook?" Owen asked me.

"What kind is it? The soup?" asked Brigid. "We had creamed turnip soup in London and it made me sick, didn't it O?"

He nodded.

"Yes," he said. "Perhaps you would have liked ice cream soup better?"

"Look at how he mocks me," she said.

"I'm not mocking you," he said. "It's only that if you like cream in every other form imaginable, why does it bother you in soup? Don't you drink a hot bowl of coffee soup for breakfast? What's the difference?"

"Now he's being funny," Brigid said. "And all I wanted to know was how you learned to cook—"

"Actually, Bee," he broke in, "I asked the question."

"No one really taught me," I said.

"Not in home economics class? Not even the Girl Scouts?" asked Owen.

"The Girl Scouts taught me to cook," said Brigid.

"You can't cook," said Owen. "And I don't mean to be rude, but it's a fact."

"I know, I know, I'm awful, a disaster, and I blame them entirely for it. Maybe I would have tried harder if they hadn't given me the badge after that first batch of burnt snickerdoodles. Were you a Girl Scout?" she asked. "Did you make taffy and sing Christmas songs at old folks' homes?"

"We made gingerbread," I said.

"That sounds complicated," said Brigid. "You must have been a very advanced group, I mean, troop."

"Not soup?" asked Owen.

"What kind is it?" asked Brigid. "I don't like shellfish."

"It's cabbage and aubergine," I said.

"I think you put aubergine in everything simply because you like saying 'aubergine.' And look, now we all have to say it all the time. If we want to eat we have to salute the stewpot and announce: I am ready for my oh-behr-zheen," said Owen. "It's a goddamn conspiracy."

"I feel better," said Brigid. "Or maybe worse."

"I'm going," I said. "I'm going to heat the soup."

"Come back," mimicked Owen. "Come back when you have heated the soup."

"I hate it when you do that," said Brigid, dropping her book to the floor.

"It's this incessant talk of illness," he said.

"I'm so sorry," said Brigid.

I could hear them through the open doorway.

"Do they have aubergine in Iowa?" Owen asked.

"You've been to Iowa," she said. "You know what they have there. They have poets. Growing in the fields like corn. Corn-fed, corn-ripe poets who are paid by the pop. If there is an aubergine to be found in Iowa they call it an eggplant and melt marshmallows on top. In Iowa it's Halloween."

Owen called to me in the kitchen, "—And bring her medicine."

"I'm so happy," said Brigid, "to have left Iowa."

"Iowa's loss," said Owen, "is Ireland's gain."

"We never leave the house," she said. "We could be anywhere. We could be in Iowa right now."

"And if a thousand bellboys in a thousand velvet jackets typed for a thousand years in the stairwells of a thousand Parisian hotels they might compose the complete works of William Shakespeare."

"And the sonnets too?" she asked.

"The Petrarchans," he said, "and the anti-Petrarchans."

"Let's go back to Paris," said Brigid.

"That's impossible now. You," he said. He paused. He rose from his chair. I stood in the doorway with the tray on which was placed a bowl of soup, the buttered heel of a loaf, spoon and napkin, the vial of pills, a cup of tea thick with honey. "You," he sat on the sofa at her stockinged feet. He tucked the blanket around her. He laid a hand on her forehead. "—have unfortunately begun to exhume a national hero with," he motioned for me to set down the tray, "a soupspoon." And for emphasis he lifted said silvery utensil from the dinner tray and pantomimed the digging of a grave. Brigid laughed.

"It looks like cabbage and potato," said Brigid.

"And aubergine," said Owen, dipping the spoon into the bowl and stirring.

"And Iowa," said Brigid.

"Everything that one longs for tastes of Iowa," said Owen.

Brigid took the spoon from him.

"Have you ever been there?" he asked me, "to Iowa?"

"No," I said, "never."

"How lucky you are," said Brigid. And with her mouth full of soup announced, "Hot, hot, hot—"

"Brigid is going to eat her soup," said Owen, "and take her medicine, and we, the survivors of this disaster of a holiday, will have to find other ways to amuse ourselves. Why don't you tell us—"

Brigid finished his sentence. "—Everything."

"Exactly," he said. "We are tired of ourselves. If we want to know about ourselves we'll read the latest review in the *Times.*"

Brigid laughed and upset her spoon.

"Jesus O, look what you and your sparkling wit have done now. I've spilled. I'm soupy. I'm p-p-paralyzed with soupiness."

"London Times," he continued undeterred as Brigid shrugged out of the wet bathrobe. *"New York Times, Times Picayune—"*

"Time for a new Timex," she interrupted.

I took the bathrobe from her.

"You're sweet," she said.

"At least wrap the damn blanket around yourself," said Owen. "We don't need you catching pneumonia along with everything else."

"But I'm hot," she said. "Cumin?"

"Cayenne," I said.

"It's good," Brigid said. "It tastes like burning. I feel the fever melting away."

She unloosed her hair from the clip into which it had been fastened.

"Did you have a happy childhood?" Owen asked me.

"Because all of them are alike in the same way," said Brigid.

"Unhappy is much better for stories," said Owen. "Why don't you tell us about your unhappy childhood."

"Tell a story," said Brigid.

"A ghost story," said Owen.

"All the best stories are ghost stories," said Brigid.

"So that's what they are calling biographies these days?" asked Owen.

"All the best people shave twice a day," said Brigid.

"And who could argue with that?" he said.

Brigid pushed back the tray, slipped down on her hip to rest her head against the cushions. Owen covered her with the blanket.

"All the best things in life belong to the past," she said.

He shook two pills out of the vial and held them out to her.

She shook her head.

"Marcel always takes *his* pills," he chided.

She opened her mouth, allowed her husband to place the tablets on her tongue, closed her mouth, closed her eyes, and swallowed. "If Marcel jumps off a cliff," she announced, taking a sip of tea, "I will too."

"Good girl," said Owen.

"Do I look awful?" asked Brigid, smoothing a hand over her hair.

"Fern is going to tell us a story," said Owen.

"Is it her turn already?"

John Paul Jones, who had been sprawled on the kitchen floor mournfully watching the stewpot, ambled into the living room, yawned, and proceeded to climb onto the sofa and lay his head on Brigid's hip.

"Look how sweet he is," said Brigid. "Why can't chocolate labs eat chocolate? I mean, people from Hungary get hungry, don't they? And if you lived in Bath, wouldn't you still bathe?"

"Because it is chock full of caffeine," said Owen. "Because their little doggy hearts would beat frantically—"

"But they would die happy," she interrupted.

"Caffeine killed Balzac," he said. "Was Balzac happy?"

"No," she said. "You must be wrong. Balzac was syphilis, no?"

"Flaubert was syphilis."

"Well then what about Keats?" she asked. "Didn't he drown? Or was it a duel? You never hear about Keats anymore."

"Drowned? No, I don't think so," said Owen. "You're thinking of Shelley. Shelley drowned. Byron caught Roman fever in Greece and died a patriot. Keats, God knows, expired, tuberculosis—"

Brigid nodded. "Consumption."

"The conqueror worm," he said.

"But what about Mary," Brigid asked, "Mrs. Shelley?"

"It's not a pretty story," said Owen. "Let's save it for another time."

"But it's raining," said Brigid. "It's thundering. It's all so very Frankensteiny—and you promised ghost stories."

"Fine," he said. "I'll go first but everyone takes a turn. Agreed?"

Brigid nodded. "Fern's got her fingers crossed. Owen, make her promise to tell one. I think she will tell the scariest of them all. I'm certain of it."

I held up my hands.

"Here lies Mary Wollstonecraft," he began his story. "In her grave only two days after having delivered a baby daughter—"

"I'm in tears," said Brigid. "Don't make it so sad—"

"Fine," he said. "Here we have sweet young Mary Godwin, the daughter of two infamous libertines, thinkers of deep thoughts, blue-stockinged Mary Wollstonecraft and a philosopher father. But when her mother dies two days after giving birth, little Mary is left to grow up unhappy and neglected. Her wicked stepmother barely allows the child to be educated, and she learned to read, it is rumored, by tracing the inscription on her mother's tombstone.

Coleridge came sometimes to tea. When pale young Mary met Percy Shelley she was fifteen and he was twenty-one—"

"It's so romantic," said Brigid. "Do they always avoid the sun? Do they speak in rhymed couplets? Do they subsist on dandelion tea, opiates, and flummery?"

"She was miserable," he continued. "And he, Shelley, was in the habit of using his great fortune to rescue young damsels in distress. When he met Mary, at the time they pledged their love at her mother's grave, he was already married to another miserable young lady. He and Mary ran off together, left the island for the continent. She was shunned, rejected by her family, imitated by her stepsister who had also captured Shelley's attention with her unhappiness—and so she went along with the young couple. Shelley's family cut off the cash. Poor Mary hated traveling. She found it dirty and oppressive; she lived in a constant miasma of seasickness and xenophobia. Their life, the three of them, was, in short, all those things that make the Romantic age so damned romantic to girls like you two. His wife," he paused, "died soon after Shelley abandoned her."

"How?" asked Brigid.

"What?" said Owen.

"How did she die, O?"

"Harriet Shelley drowned herself when she was seven months pregnant," he said.

"How awful," said Brigid. "But still, after the fact, a little romantic."

"And then Mary's older sister died, a suicide as well. Ophelia, as you may imagine," he went on, "was all the rage."

"What happened to the other sister? The stepsister?" asked Brigid.

"She was Byron's mistress," he said. "Briefly."

"*Byron,*" said Brigid. "Now there's a name. He would try anything twice. He was a try-sexual. That's what we used to say about him anyway. *Mad, glad, and dangerous to know.* Back when we used to, I don't know, talk about things like that."

"Who is *we?*" asked Owen.

"I can't quite recall. Us," she said. "Just girls."

"In the sorority house? Out in the fields watching the corn grow and reading Byron by the light of fireflies?"

"Having pillow fights," she said. "Wearing see-through nighties, poking pins in voodoo dolls, and longing for you."

"And then?" I said.

"You want to hear about the party, don't you?" he asked. "About their party?"

"As opposed to our party?" said Brigid. "Which isn't much of one at all. We don't have any candy or scary movies. What's Halloween without Butterfingers or Clark bars? No Smarties? Not even a caramel apple?"

"It's a wonder you have any teeth at all," he said. "Charlotte Brontë, did you know, lost every single pearly white by the time she was thirty-five."

"This is the part where Mary writes *Frankenstein,*" I said.

"Poor monster," said Brigid. "Why can't monsters get along with other monsters? Why did Frankenstein always fight the Wolfman?"

"It was June," he said. "And it was summer, not Halloween. And our frantic cast of characters, Byron and Shelley, Polidori the doctor, and stepsister Claire were staying in a picturesque chalet in Switzerland. Mary was there too, fresh from the two recent suicides of sister and rival, as well as her own miscarriage; she suffered nightmares—"

"Oh no," interrupted Brigid, "you're getting psychoanalytical, aren't you? You're going to ruin the story by over-explaining," she lamented. "You're going to say that it's a birth narrative or a creation metaphor or something not scary at all. Normally, I'd applaud it. But not today, O. Today let's blame the vengeful ghosts haunting the moors and not weigh out the five-pound universe, oh please, let's?"

"What's more scary?" he asked, "than psychoanalysis?"

"The phone call," she said, "is always coming from inside the house. It gets tiresome. I don't want to hear anymore about what things *mean*. I only want to hear the story. Is that too much to ask?"

"I'm telling the goddamn story," he said.

"Fine," she said. "Tell," she said, "the goddamn story."

"Mary and Shelley married and they all tripped off to Italy. They were happy or unhappy, drunk or likewise debauched until they all, one by one, except for Mary herself, succumbed to the heat, to fever, the Mediterranean—"

"And Keats?" asked Brigid, sitting up on the sofa.

Owen intoned, *"This grave contains all that was mortal of a Young English Poet who, on his Death Bed in the Bitterness of his heart, at the malicious Power of his enemies desired these words to be engraved on his Tombstone: Here lies One Whose Name was writ in the water February 24, 1821."* He coughed and added, "He died in Rome en route to meeting up with the rest of them in Pisa."

"That was very good," said Brigid, "but what about Mary?"

"Left in the graveyard again," said Owen. "Shelley drowned in a boating accident. She was twenty-four, penniless and alone in a foreign country with her two-year-old son. She went back to England, threw herself at the mercy of her family, eventually recanted all of her bold social theories, and lived unhappily ever after. She died thirty years later, if I recall correctly, of a brain tumor."

There was an uncomfortable silence.

The rain pattered the windowpanes.

"Syllogism," Brigid announced brightly, ridiculously. "I've got one O: Caffeine kills dogs; Balzac died of caffeine poisoning; therefore, Balzac is, no, was a dog."

"Are the pills working?" asked Owen. "Are they helping?"

Brigid slipped back against the cushions.

"Where's kitty," she asked. "Fern, is there going to be a kitty, Fern, in your unhappy childhood story?"

She closed her eyes.

"I had a kitty," she said. "In Iowa when I was a Girl Scout I had a kitty named Snowball."

"In Iowa," said Owen, "when you were a girl every kitty was named Snowball."

"Untrue, not true, transcendentally or otherwise untrue. Gray cats were called Smokey."

"She's going to sleep now," said Owen to me.

"No, I'm not," she said. "I'm so sad about Mary. I feel as though I've known, knew her my entire life. I'm, I'm, what do you call it?"

"Sleeping?" he said.

"And what about Mary Shelley, what did she call it?"

"Catnapping."

And what did Keats call it?"

"Forty winks," he said.

"And Byron?"

"Dozing."

"Shelley?"

"Slumbering."

"What about the doctor? Polidori?"

"The opiate of the masses," said Owen.

"And what did the Elizabethans call it?"

"Dying," he said.

"That's the best one yet," said Brigid.

"Don't be morbid," he said.

"The French still do," she said.

"Do what?" Owen asked distractedly looking toward the window.

"Call it dying."

"And if they do," he said. "*Le petit mort,* nothing to worry about, nothing to keep you from resting."

"Catnapping," she said. "Forty-winking."

Outside the bare limbs of trees scraped against the house. The wind banged the shutters.

"What's that noise, O?" she asked.

"Hail," he said. "It has begun to—"

He rose from the velvet chair and went to the window. He pulled back the sash of the curtain, disturbing the cat sleeping hidden on the sill. The afternoon had gone to black. Hail pelted the garden. Brigid pulled the blanket over her shoulders.

"I'm scared, O."

"You should sleep."

"I will," she said. "Owen?" she asked.

He left the window. The cat pawed the pane. He sat beside his wife on the edge of the sofa, smoothed her hair. She was asleep.

He looked at me then.

He rose from the sofa and returned to his chair, picked up the crossword puzzle and began filling in the blanks with his black inkpen. The hail was tinny and sharp. The fire burnt in the grate. The cat leapt from the ledge and Brigid with eyes closed buried her face in the brocade cushions of the sofa and slept.

And so she slept on through the afternoon into evening. And a romance writer prone to gently persuasive prose might poetically have penned that she slept like an angel with her flushed cheeks and disheveled halo, with the cream pale seductive innocence of one barely revealed bare and pink-tipped breast, sleeve having slipped a shoulder and blanket fallen away. A zookeeper might have philosophized that she slept like an animal oblivious to the bars of her cage. A moralist seeking meaning in this messy world might have seen her as a child awaiting instruction; while to a magician she was an assistant who desired nothing so much as the bliss of disappearance. But I thought she slept like an addict, her dreams poppy-rich and craveworthy. Owen fed to her spoons of ruby syrup for coughs, for sleep, for the sneezes, the shakes, for writer's block; thick, condensed, sweetened to taste like cherry soda. She said the bitterness came always as an almost pleasant afterthought. She had coughs and agues, fevers, rough dreams, inherited memories, déjà vu, swollen joints in the fingers of her right hand, allergies to pollen and peanuts, an iron deficiency, and a self-diagnosed ovulatory disorder that caused fits of abdominal cramping. She had a pale blue cast to her complexion that sometimes made it seem as though in bright light she were transparent. A witty drunken poet at a party had once touched a hand to Brigid's cheek and complimented her on the mathematical ratio of beauty to blood that allowed her capillaries to highlight precisely her cornflower blue eyes. She took violet pills for sleeping and green for pain. Sometimes she dissolved them in cocoa and rimmed the cup with chocolate syrup. She had not always been this way, Owen admitted. It was her gift. It was the biographer's transparency. She, of necessity, became less and less herself in order to become more fully her subject. She invented a world that had already happened. A new verb, intransitive: to proust. *I am prousting,* said Brigid when she had a headache. An adjective: *I feel prousty,* she announced over iced rum cakes. An imperative: with pointed finger and pronouncement, *Proust!* John Paul Jones immediately curled up on his doggy bed and pretended to sleep. An object: *Don't have a proust.* She split infinitives only for the sake of stretching out the pleasure of her pain. *Darling I lovelorn long to frantically proust you.* None of it made any sense and what did it matter? Owen admitted that most of the pills were harmless placebos. Brigid Lieb was no addict. She was merely impressionable. She was a tall sweet-tempered sweet-tongued see-through girl with a taste for sweet nothings. She liked ice cream, jam, baked apples, cakes, rice pudding, and sugar cookies scented of almond and decorated for holidays like the ones you could get in the bakeries back home in Iowa in October with orange and brown sprinkles, shaped like pumpkins, ravens, broomsticks, and witches' hats, frosted licorice black or with M&M's dotting the eyes, nose, and mouth of a vanilla-cream ghost.

Proust became a word that could transform into any part of speech, that could connote goodwill or ill-health based solely on the context and intent of the speaker, on Brigid herself who once, when taking her plum-colored pills with tea and cinnamon toast announced, *I proust therefore I am. Proust:* it was the tenth part of speech, the new and improved twenty-first-century signifier of celebrity that denoted nothing so much as the absence of everything that had been there before. We hold these prousts to be self-evident. I feel. I want. I desire. I covet. I creep. I sink. I slip. I sleep. I dream. I hunger. I haunt. I repeat. I replace. I lack. I cobble. I crave. I cringe. I mope. I miss. I pale. I pawn. I proust. And the rockets' red glare, the bombs bursting in air gave proust through the night that our flag was still there. Brigid slept on the sofa. Her blanket slipped and revealed the thin white fabric ghostly of her nightdress to have fallen away and in turn revealed the thin white fabric of her skin, ghostly. And the rain fell and diminished and turned to hail, and the hail fell and shattered and turned to snow. Afternoon subsided into evening. Day was no different than night. Night was no different than proust. Brigid slept. Owen sat working the blanks of the crossword puzzle. Letter by letter by letter until there were no more letters to be had or blanks to be filled and everything fell: his arm to his side, pen and folded newspaper, Brigid's stained bathrobe and blanket, the ice into snow, her woolen socks one by one, the overturned cups and spoons and saucers, the tattered novel by the most-forgotten of the Brontë sisters page by page collapsed spine-first to the floor. The rain fell into hail which fell into snow which lay in a blight of pestilence like a thousand locusts, a thousand lovelorn bellboys penning Petrarchan sonnets, a thousand busboys bringing the cream and lighting the candles, a thousand letters never reaching their destinations, a thousand young brides digging with soupspoons upward out of their premature graves, a thousand grooms in dove-gray top hats and tails tunneling ever downward to clasp once more those pale ring-bare fingers, one thousand times a hundred thousand snowflakes each one more pure and plagiarized than the next, fell and falling still upon the land and the gardens, freezing the apples and aubergine, falling and fell on the churchyards, the dime stores and bus stations, on Iowa and Ireland, the creaking beds in rented rooms, the wristwatches unticking the time it takes to unshoe and undo and unstocking the final catch to fall to the floor, on libraries and hospitals, kitchens where upon racks rest cooling sugar cookies in the shape of hearts and stars and wedding bells, on children on their birthdays, the trick candles on cakes unlighting, on the sick and the starving, the pigeons curling wing-weary beneath marble monuments to great men, the tundra and taiga, vodka-drunk passengers on the Trans-Siberian railway in the bleak violet hours before dawn, the hot and dry countries of this distracted globe, the displaced and denied and disappeared, the crippled who need only the hope of one more miracle and one more prayer and one more penny to throw away their crutches and walk, on travelers and tourists, priests and pilgrims, country wives and cross-dressers, jealous lovers, the dearly departed, the not-soon-forgotten, the wish-you-were-here postcard senders who offer neither regret nor remorse nor return address, on the one who was you once, twice with your hand on my hip, on ghosts and cream caramel goblins and the bare Halloween bejeweled breasts of licorice-whip witches, from bend of shore to swerve of bay, on Proust and Poe alike, on tubers, eggplant and the fat grinning faces of jack-knifed pumpkins, the vines, the weeds, the rot and ruin and wrack, on my inky hands, on Brigid's snowflake-speckled heart, on Owen's once black curls turned winter-white in the space of hours the snow falls and does not stop all around us while Brigid sleeps and Owen sleeps and John Paul Jones sleeps and kitty-cat sleeps and everything little by little and big by small and piece by piece falls to the floor to lie for a long time in the darkness before being forgotten, before disappearing from the real and retreating

into memory only to suffer the final insult of being replaced
snowflake for snowflake with words as the snow falls and does not
stop all around us and evening inks its way into night. And night
inks its way into proust. The lamps flicker. I know this: I want, I
wane, I wake, I recite, I refuse, I remember, I repeat, I snow, I storm,
I rage, I roam, I rain, I ruin, I riot, I rot, I recall. Brigid sleeps with
her face buried in her arm. Owen sleeps upright in his chair. The
gray cat paws the pane. Little by small it all falls to the floor and rests
for a while before disappearing.

Ulster

And then I woke up.

Owen lighted the candles in the sconces above the mantel.

The clock struck midnight. Snow fell, was falling. The fire burned in the grate. Brigid sat up on the sofa and cried out, her voice strange in the dark quiet room: *the witching hour!*

"I'm awake," said Brigid.

"We are aware of that," said Owen.

"No really," she said. "Let's do something. Anything. Let's play a game."

"Cards?" asked Owen.

She shook her head. "Something more spectacular. Something with tricks and treats."

"No cartwheels," he said. "Please, no displays of baton twirling prowess, no knife throwing, no spinning of plates on sticks."

She ignored him.

"Fern?" she said. "Fern?" she repeated.

I answered.

"Once I won a prize for best Halloween costume in my class," said Brigid. "You know how if Halloween falls on a weekday, you wear your costume to school? And if it's cold out you have to crush the skirt or the tutu with your horrible winter coat. And when you have to wear snow boots it's even worse. I was dressed as Wonder Woman. I wore an American flag leotard and a black wig. No one even recognized me. I had a little cord of rope, but no invisible plane. Not that anyone would have seen it. So tell me," she said. She paused. "What was your absolute best Halloween costume?"

"Pharaoh," I said.

"Of Egypt?" said Owen curiously.

"Is there any other kind?" said Brigid.

"Why a pharaoh?" asked Owen.

"I think it's darling," said Brigid. "Why not a pharaoh after all? Why so many hobos and windowsill pie-thieving mendicants?"

"Mendicants?" he questioned. "Pie-thieving?"

"You know, beggars," she said, "who steal pies left to cool—"

"I know what a—" he began.

"Well there you have it," she said. "There it is exactly. A grand pharaoh, and why not? You get to wear an exotic costume and eyeliner. Don't you think it would be much better the other way around—I mean everything is so backward these days—wouldn't it be better if children wore makeup, because they seem to so enjoy it? And adults didn't have to? Wouldn't that be nice?"

"Adults?" said Owen. "You mean women."

"That's funny," she said. "No really, did you wear a crown? Didn't you worry that the other children would make fun of you? I mean, a pharaoh, well, that's not a really popular, you know, a populist figure, is it?"

"Mostly they thought I was King Tut," I said.

"Oh," cooed Brigid. "The boy king! Yes, of course. Everybody likes him."

"Yes, of course," repeated Owen. "What's not to like?"

"There he was," she went on, "buried with all his treasures. You know I think the Mummy scares me more than any of the other monsters. I think it must be the bandages. It's quite horrifying, you know, to imagine what's beneath them. Plus there's the whole Mummy's curse, the desecration of the tomb—"

"The what?" said Owen.

"You know," she said, "his looted grave. The Mummy, he's absolutely a paradigm of postcolonial retribution. He's anti-British, isn't he?"

"And next," Owen agreed, "you are going to say that being called *the Mummy* is itself a state of his being a duly feminized 'other'?"

"It's no wonder, is it?" she laughed, "that I adore you. I wasn't going to say that at all, but it's very good."

"No," he said, "it isn't."

"What do you think, Miss Fern," asked Brigid, "our resident Egyptologist?"

"When you unwind the bandages from the Mummy," I said, "I always imagined that you'd end up with the Invisible Man."

"And all monsters simply become the next monster?" said Brigid. "So none of them is ever really defeated? They only change shape— like energy converted to new energy? How horrible. Must they always wander the earth? It's no wonder that they hate each other so, because each represents to the others his own transformation."

"Does anyone," said Owen, "would anyone like a drink?"

"Booze?" said Brigid brightly.

He rose and went to the sideboard cabinet.

"It's a holiday, O," Brigid said.

"I understand," he rejoined.

"You do?" she said. "How infinite you are. Not quite a pharaoh, or pharaohic, but still, infinite."

He searched through the bottles lining the cabinet's shelves.

"I want something funny," she said. "Do you know what my favorite drink used to be? *Original Cin.* That's C-I-N. It was, I think, cinnamon schnapps and hot apple cider. But at the moment that sounds far too sweet. Can you imagine, O, did you ever dream that I could find anything *too* sweet? I would like, dear bartender," she said, "something very strong and brutal without the least hint of sugar."

"Really?" he said.

"Entirely," she said.

"What would suit you?" he asked. "Gasoline?"

He set a bottle of vodka and three glasses on the table before Brigid.

"Ah," she sighed, "garnished with a lighted match?" And she turned then to me and patted the cushion of the couch. "Don't hide out over there in the dark. Come here and sit with us."

Owen poured out the glasses.

I sat with Brigid on the sofa.

She took her glass from him and expertly drained it. We watched her. She shrugged.

"Don't be so goddamned coy, you two," she said. "We're all from the Midwest, aren't we? Aren't we?"

"Whose turn is it?" asked Owen.

"To tell a story?" said Brigid.

I sipped at my vodka.

"It's my turn," announced Brigid.

Owen refilled her glass.

"Is it going to be about the Mummy?" he asked.

"And what if it is?" she said.

"Then go on," he said, "now that you've begun."

"I haven't even begun to begin."

"It's your turn," he said. "That's how the game goes."

"What game?" I said.

"You know," said Brigid. "Telling stories. Telling a story that follows in some manner the story that has come before."

"Shouldn't a game have rules?" I asked.

"Entirely," she said, "and we make them up as we go along."

"Are you always so literal?" Owen asked me.

"Wouldn't you rather be literal than figurative?" said Brigid.

"You are in danger," said Owen. He finished his glass. "Of forfeiting your turn."

"A rule arises from, of necessity," she said. "I am in jeopardy of losing my turn."

"Forfeiting," he said.

"My turn," she said.

"What is your story called?" I asked. "Does it have a title?"

"We've never used titles before," said Brigid. "They're so, so limiting, aren't they, O?"

"I like the idea," he said. "Let's have a title. Let's never not have a title."

"Fine," she said. "Fine, fine, fine. Then it is called, it is *entitled*," she paused. *"The Ugly Tattoo."*

"Really?" he said.

"Yes," she said. "Do you like it?"

He didn't answer her.

"One of us," she said, "has an ugly tattoo."

"Is this part of the story?" I asked.

"The story?" she said. "Oh, it's an interactive story. With audience participation. It's the latest thing, you know, very Parisian—"

"Well get on with it then," said Owen, "with your Parisian pie-thieving mendicant-ridden interactive tale of—"

"Mummies unbound," she said.

He poured vodka from the bottle into our three glasses.

"Get on with it," he said.

"There was once upon a time," Brigid began, "an old king and his queen who lived in a kingdom by the sea—"

"A fairy tale," said Owen. "How postfeminist."

"Don't interrupt," she said. "Please hold your questions until the end." She drank from her glass. She continued. "And when the queen died, the king was very sad. So he sent out all his armies to find a new queen. And they searched high and low for a suitable replacement. Some girls were too short and others too tall. Some were too skinny and some were too fat. It was not easy to find a new queen. And then one day, when the armies least expected it, they found a girl—"

"They always do," said Owen.

"But she didn't want to go with them. She didn't want to leave her home, and they seduced her with tales of the king until finally she left her home and went with the armies back to the kingdom by the sea. And the girl immediately upon first sight fell in love with the king, because of course, the armies were right. And the king was wonderful, as was the kingdom. And she found that after a while she forgot about home altogether because she was so happy. And as time passed there was only one problem—"

"There always is," he said.

"—That grew to haunt the girl, the new queen. She didn't know what mysterious fate had befallen the old queen. Now this girl, she was free to wander the palace and its grounds, to go wherever she liked, except for one locked room. So being by nature curious, being as curious as a girl in a fairy tale ought to be, should be, one day when the king was out, oh, pillaging or decreeing, she stole the key and opened the door to the locked chamber."

"And there she found," said Owen, "the gruesome skeletal remains—"

"Stop that," said Brigid. "It's my story."

"—the rotting mummified corpse—"

"Do you want to tell it?" she asked.

"I can't," he said, "I don't know who has the scar."

"Tattoo," she said.

He drank.

"What did she find in the locked room?" I asked.

"Shoes," said Brigid.

"Shoes?" repeated Owen.

"Heaps and heaps of them. Ruby slippers, riding boots, shoes, you know, *shoes.*"

"—that belonged to the old queen?" I asked.

"Yes," said Brigid. "It was very sad, very sad, you can imagine, for the girl to see all those shoes lined up, I mean heaped up like that—"

"Why, what in particular was sad about the shoes? Am I missing something?" he asked.

"How could you," she said, "ever be missing anything?"

"Fine," he said. "Shoes it is."

"It's symbolic," she said.

"Ah," he said.

"I mean, some people like them," she said. "I don't, not in particular." She slightly unwound, stared gravely at her feet which had been tucked beneath her, but now made themselves known bundled in wool socks. "I get blisters, don't I, O. You know," then she paused. "That's funny. *IOU*. My arches are collapsed," she said.

"Fallen," he said.

"Exactly," she agreed.

"The story?" I asked.

"Oh right," she said. "So anyway, blah, blah, blah, the girl was very sad to see all the shoes worn by the old queen locked away in the locked room. And it made her sad, of course, because the moral of the story is that princesses must realize that they will succumb to the same fate as those who wore the royal slippers before—"

"So it didn't," said Owen, "it doesn't have to be shoes. It could have been anything."

"Well, isn't that the point of symbolism?" she said.

"Did they wear the same size?" I asked. "The two queens?"

"She's drunk," said Brigid to Owen.

"You're the one who brought up shoes," he said.

"But you're the one who brought up vodka," she admonished.

"Have some more," he said.

And refilled our glasses.

"We need an ending to this story," she said. "The fact of the matter is that there were more than two queens. There were hundreds of them. And if the slippers didn't fit the queen in question, she was forced to lop off a toe. It was horrible, the things these poor girls had to do to be just like the girl who had come before—"

"Why did they do it?" I asked. "Was it for the king? Or the shoes?"

"No more shoes," said Owen. "Stop saying 'shoes.'"

"I said 'slippers,'" said Brigid. "Not 'shoes.'"

"I said 'shoes,'" I said. "But I won't say 'shoes' again."

"Anyway," said Brigid. "It was neither. They loved most of all the story that would be told about them when they each in turn found the locked room that contained the you-know-whats."

"The story that would be told," he said, "or the one that they would tell?"

"What do you think of my fairy tale," Brigid asked him. "From a clear-headed, from an absolutely rational male point of view, what did you think of the toeless queens hobbling around on the bloody crutches of extended metaphor?"

"I preferred," he said, "the pie-stealing hobos."

"I liked the mummies," I said.

"She's drunk," said Brigid. "Honestly O, she really is."

"Are we speaking only in symbols tonight?" he asked.

"Is there any other way to speak?" she asked. "I mean, I suppose we could carry around big burlap sacks full of objects, nouns, and whenever we needed, felt the need to express something, we could pull the real item out of the bag and so not use words at all—although I don't know how or if it would work beyond nouns. You know, you would pull the cat out of the bag when you found yourself, of course, in need of a cat."

"That's funny," I said.

"What is?" she asked.

"Letting the cat," I said, "out of the bag."

"The useful thing about symbols," she said, "is that they can replace anything or anyone. Right O? I mean, it didn't matter what the new queen found in the locked room, did it? It was the fact of finding something, anything at all. She could have found, I don't know, a skeleton, of course, or something more mundane, letters perhaps?"

"Who do you think," Owen asked me, "which one of us, do you guess, has the scar and which the tattoo?"

"She could have found letters," Brigid continued, "which in themselves meant nothing, so little, and were only interesting for the fact of having already become a symbol. She could have found letters that—"

"Let the cat out of the bag?" said Owen.

"Presuming there is a bag," she said, "or a cat."

"So," he said. He paused. "If we break down our symbols into more manageable and bite-sized portions, I am meant to infer from tonight's tale that you found the letters—"

"Letters?" she said. "Who said anything about *letters?* I was talking about royal slippers. The very thing the cobbler's child goes without. It would only be the writer's child who goes without letters, don't you think?"

"Yes," he said. "It's clever. It's all very clever. But you might as well come out and tell—"

"I am," she said with mock petulance.

"—the truth," he finished.

"Oh," she said, "I didn't expect you to say that at all. That changes things. Do you want the truth? Because I thought you wanted a story. But if you want the truth we can do it that way."

"Thank God," he said.

"God?" she rolled her eyes. "Has it come to that?"

"No more symbols," he said.

"No more," she agreed.

"And the letters," he asked.

"No more letters," said Brigid.

"Where did you find them?"

The bottle was half-empty. I was, as Brigid had suggested, drunk. The bottle, in the eyes of some bright-eyed optimist not in our present company, was also half-full. Sitting beside me Brigid was lucid. She was self-possessed. The liquor had an opposite effect on her. The more she drank the more sober she became.

"Hidden in a closet," she said.

He seemed neither angry nor surprised.

"And where are they now?" he asked.

"Gone," she said.

"Gone?" he said.

"I burned them," she said.

"I see," he said.

"You don't believe me?"

"I have reason, don't I, to be skeptical?"

"You *want,*" she laughed lightly. "You need proof?"

"I saw them too," I said.

"What?" he said.

"The letters," I went on, "I saw them."

"Well done, Bee," he said, ignoring my confession. "And here I thought your story would have no plot. You really pulled the rabbit out of the hat this time."

"Please," she said, bowing, "no applause," bending slightly from the waist. "Just throw money."

"And then you burned them," he said.

"Yes," she said. "The hand of a ghost led me to them. I'm not lying. You know that I'm not. I found them and I, we, we, read them. I know that we shouldn't have, but we couldn't stop ourselves. I knew it beforehand, I knew that we shouldn't—but, well, we did. And then I burned them. And that's what happened and how it happened."

"I see," he said.

"Yes," she agreed.

"Why?"

"Does it matter?" she asked.

"No," he said, "I don't suppose that it does."

"I know just what you are thinking," she said. "Because I always know what you are thinking. You are thinking that Moses, even Moses, especially Moses, was allowed to see the Promised Land that he wasn't fit to enter."

"I don't," he said, "I didn't need to see them again. I've seen them before."

"Then what," she asked, "is the problem? Did I deprive you of the thrill of burning them yourself? Is that it?"

"Don't be idiotic," he said.

"Is that what I am?" she asked.

"Why would you do that without telling me?"

"Don't you know?" she said. "Can't you guess?"

"No," he said. "Enlighten me."

"I have the tattoo," Brigid announced.

"Don't worry," said Owen, "we will get to that." And ignoring me sitting drunkenly in the candlelight he asked his wife, "Just tell me why in God's name did you let *her* read them?"

She said, she laughed, "You haven't gone dyslexic on me, have you?"

"Answer," said Owen, "the question."

"I would, honestly O, I would, but I don't remember what it was."

"Jesus—" he said.

"—was a carpenter," she finished.

The candles glimmered held aloft each by a perversely grinning Cupid.

"Show it to her," he said. "Go on. I'll provide the mood music." He drummed on the table and began to sing, *"There was a young lady from Munich, who was ravished one night by a eunuch—"*

"Oh stop," she laughed.

"—At the height of her passion—"

Brigid stood.

"He slipped her a ration—"

"You're awful," said Brigid. "You really are."

"—From a squirt gun concealed in his tunic."

"Oh stop," she said, unbuttoning her sweater.

"There was a lady named Wild, who kept herself undefiled—"

She removed her sweater.

"—By thinking of Jesus—"

Brigid turned her back to us.

"—Contagious diseases—"

She lowered her white nightdress.

"—And the bother of having a child."

And we could see in the flickering bright darkness of the room Brigid's tattoo.

"It's ridiculous," he said.

"Says the man who rhymes *Jesus* with *diseases,"* she said over her shoulder.

"Well, what do you make of it?" said Owen. "Go up close, get a better look."

"I know a verse to that song," she said. "Do you want to hear it? I don't care if you want to hear it. It's the tune of 'the Frito Bandito,' you know." And Brigid turned away from us, shoulders and back bare with the nightgown around her waist and sang—

> *On the breast of a lady named Gail*
> *Was tattooed the price of her tail,*
> *And on her behind,*
> *For the sake of the blind,*
> *Was the same information in Braille!*

"Charming," said Owen.

"You started it," she said.

"Put your clothes on before you get sick," he said.

"I'm already," she said. She slipped the nightgown up shoulder by shoulder. "Sick, aren't I?"

The tattoo on Brigid's hip was of a swastika inside a Star of David.

"Ask her why she did it," Owen said. "Ask her what this particular tattoo means to her."

"It's my family crest," said Brigid, shrugging into her sweater and sitting back down on the sofa. "I invented it. I think it suits me."

"Except," he said, "for how goddamned ugly it is."

"Oh well," she said, "except for that."

"I don't understand," I said. But I didn't really mean that I didn't understand the tattoo or its symbolism. I was somehow a moment behind them in the conversation. I was struggling to keep up. I didn't understand why Brigid said that she had burned the letters. I didn't know why she was lying. I didn't know how she continued to empty and refill her glass and how with each ounce of vodka she became more prescient while I fell further and further out of pace.

"Owen is so funny," she said, "isn't he? He likes to pretend, to imply, that I must have gotten my tattoo by mistake. He thinks it's, you know, *ironic*. I think everyone should know where they came from and of what just exactly, they are capable. I think," she finished her glass, "that you have to know what sort of monster you are before you can figure out what sort of monster you are going to become."

"There's more to the story," said Owen.

"You'll have to tell her that part," she said.

"That seems fair," he said. "Since you've so regaled us with your peep-show tribute to how well Iowa girls can hold their liquor—"

"Owen is from Minnesoh-duh," she said, "and he thinks this makes him awfully elite."

"No," he said, "just awful."

"Awfully awful," she agreed.

"Tell her what you told me after you got the ugly tattoo," he said.

"I said, I think I remember saying, *I am marked like Cain*. Do you think that's funny? Because he did."

"I did not," he said. "I found it disturbing."

"I can't say," she went on, "as Mr. O. G. Lieb here can and does, that all Germans are responsible for—for, oh you know—I can only say that I feel somehow as though someone must take responsibility into and upon their own skin, no matter how heavy-handed the metaphor. Is it quite a metaphor, O?"

Owen refilled my glass and handed it to me, but I missed, or I pulled back suddenly afraid to let his hand touch mine. The glass fell and tipped, spilled, hit the table, overturned without breaking and fell to the floor to land upturned, empty again on the faded Persian rug.

"She's lost," said Brigid. "She's absolutely smashed. And lost. You're going to have to explain it all very clearly."

My greatest fear is not of the dark or its intruders. I don't worry so much about falling into harm's way or violence. I don't care if my failings and secrets are exposed. I'm beyond caring about such trivial vanities as shame or embarrassment. I don't care if I'm called a liar. There are worse fates in the world than being disbelieved. I am not too terrified of being branded a pariah or a failure, of being called mad or stupid, egotistical, exploitative, or weak. I used to fear only the instance, the prospect, the possibility of getting lost in a strange city on an unfamiliar street and being unable to find my way. But from this original fear I found a more horrible situation—not that I will be unable to find my way home, but that I will have no home to find. And so I wander foreign streets in search of familiarity until the only familiarity that I know is the sensation of being lost. And in the end I will come to long for that sensation as much as any other.

"Help her to understand," Brigid said.

"Nothing," said Owen, "that any Jew says or does or thinks is free from history."

"Oh no," she said. "That was far too easy."

"You're right," he said.

"I know I am," Brigid announced. "I feel terribly right about everything tonight. O, I feel that everything we have done from the first moment we met has brought us here. Is that odd?"

In the movies a vampire must be invited into a house or else he can't pass through the doorway to enter. And in the tarot, the death card only symbolizes change. Biographers are in the habit of writing with great authority stories that already have endings. They do not pull endings out of their hats like rabbits. My card of the deck, Owen told me, is *The Magician.* There is a cereal commercial in which a rabbit pulls himself out of a hat. *Trix are for kids!* In romance novels young ladies swoon on fainting couches when missives of forbidden love fail to arrive. Brigid once asked me if I had seen a television commercial in which a talking roll of toilet paper exhorts his own softness and pliability. Is there anything, she asked, more vulgar than that?

"It's your story," Owen said to me.

"My turn?" I asked.

"No. He is telling you," she said, "he is trying to tell you your story."

Precautions like cloves of garlic and the wooden cross are useful once the vampire has already been allowed into the house. In the comic strip, *The Family Circus,* the children never grow up and therefore never cease speaking in the delightful baby patois of misinterpretation. Crème brûlée isn't French at all; it is, in fact, English. There is a funny poster that hangs on the wall in dentists' offices across America. It pictures a cat clutching the limb of a tree. The caption reads: *Hang in there!* The bodies of Adolf Hitler and Eva Braun were set afire with rags and gasoline. He shot himself in the head. She took poison. Saladin shamed the Christian Crusaders with humanity when the armies of Islam retook Jerusalem in 1187—without spilling, it is said, one drop of their enemies' blood. Arabic words introduced into English during the Crusades include: *orange, lemon, alfalfa, alchemy, algebra, soda,* and *checkmate.*

"I am telling you," Owen said, "why we brought you here. Nothing," he said, "none of this——" He broke off and with a sweeping gesture took in the room—the fire in the grate, dog at his feet, the vodka bottle nearly emptied, the windows outside of which snow fell on the frozen fields, the gold- and vermilion-flowered wallpaper, the cat who leapt up onto the mantel and sat perched studying the scene below. "None of it was an accident," he said.

"What?" I asked.

Brigid picked my glass up off the rug. She refilled it.

In the chapter after the last chapter in mystery novels the great detective always describes the deductive process that led him to the solution of the mystery. He points out the clues dropped along the garden path for good readers to collect. The standard definition of the difference between *story* and *plot* is this: Story is—*the King died and then the Queen died.* While plot is—*the King died and then the Queen died of grief.* In film a *travelogue* is a type of documentary which presents for entertainment purposes views of interesting places and events, often exotic locations abroad and colorful holiday celebrations in different parts of the world. In the tarot any card placed upside down is a reversal of fortune. The *camera obscura* is a device that established the basic principle of photographic reproduction: a small ray of light passes through a hole or lens in a dark box. An inverted and laterally reversed image of the outside scene appears on the opposite side of the dark chamber and is reflected by a mirror onto a wall.

"What do you mean?" I repeated.

"Just listen," said Brigid.

In *Oedipus,* the reader and the chorus wonder aloud why it takes the hero so long to realize that he need only look in the mirror to find the man who murdered his father. And metaphorically speaking, when he sees the truth for the first time, Oedipus blinds himself. In *Jane Eyre,* it seems that Charlotte Brontë enjoys too much the task of blinding Mr. Rochester. The author herself takes a hot andiron and pokes out his eyes. Count Dracula slept by day in a coffin filled with soil from his homeland. Percy Shelley rewrote the text of his wife's novel, *Frankenstein,* to reflect the lofty erudite prose style of the day. He found her writing coarse, uneducated, and simple. Marcel Proust was in the habit of eating one enormous meal a day after which his stomach was so distended that the waistband on his underwear would snap open. There is a television commercial in which Folgers dry crystals are secretly switched with brewed coffee and no one at the posh restaurant is the wiser. By the middle of the eighteenth century botanists had proved that plants owe something to each parent, a proof that helped cast doubt on the belief that human reproduction was a purely seminal miracle.

"Tell me," I said. "Will one of you tell me what's going on?"

Brigid took my hand in hers.

"Are you happy with us?" she asked.

I did not answer.

"Don't you ever feel," she said, "like you are looking into a mirror?"

Owen turned away.

Vampires can't see their own reflection in a mirror. Jacques Lacan hypothesized the mirror stage of development to be the moment when the individual sees and realizes that all of his parts and various limbs are connected to form a whole. Jews cover mirrors to mourn the dead. James Joyce wrote that the symbol of Irish art is *the cracked lookingglass of a servant.* There is a joke that asks: *What do Jewish girls*

make for dinner? And the answer is: *Reservations!* Chimpanzees griev-
ing for dead children feel such terrible despair that cases of suicide
by drowning have been documented. King Henry died in
Normandy on the first of December, 1135. His body was carried to
Rouen where his bowels, brain, and eyes were deposited. The body
was slashed by knives, sprinkled with salt, and sewn up in ox hides
to prevent the spread and taint of pestilence before being interred.
The man hired to chop off the head with an axe, though he wore a
linen veil, took ill and died soon after. There is a laboratory in which
a computer is writing the human genetic code like a mystery novel
from beginning to end. There is a joke that asks: *Why does the new
Polish navy have glass-bottomed boats?* The answer is: *So that they can
see the old Polish navy.*

"If no one else will say it," said Brigid, "I will."

"You belong here," said Owen to me. "You belong with us."

"Start at the beginning," said Brigid. "Start with Esther—"

He looked for a moment dazed.

"Esther?" he said. "Is that where it begins?"

"Tell her about the baby," she said.

"The baby," he said, "didn't die."

"You see," said Brigid, "she floated to the top like cream."

Owen said, "It was the only reasonable thing to do. She had to be
sent away. She couldn't have been expected to have a life, a normal life
under the circumstances, with that legacy, with a mother who—"

"But you were waiting," chided Brigid, "weren't you? The whole
time, all the while that she was growing up in an absolutely normal
family in the absolutely normal US of A, you were waiting for her,
weren't you?"

"Yes," he said, "I suppose I was."

"Don't say *suppose,*" she said. "You told me that you were waiting until she could understand—"

"How could anyone," he asked, "do that?"

"She floated down the Nile like Moses," said Brigid, "who was raised by an Egyptian princess."

"How very awake you are," said Owen.

"Yes," she said, "all along my skin."

"Do you need your pills?" he asked.

"Not just yet," she said.

"If I begin telling," he said, "there may be no stopping me."

"Sometimes it's like that," his wife said.

"We brought you here," Owen said. "You didn't stumble upon us. We found you."

It took a moment for me to realize that he was speaking to me.

"We brought you here," he repeated as though it might make me understand, comprehend, get the joke, see the light, "so that we could be together."

I was silent.

"Haven't you guessed yet?" said Brigid. "Haven't I been dropping clues like crazy?"

"I don't understand," I repeated.

"I think you don't *want* to understand. It's all very simple, if you think about it."

"Just listen," said Owen, "to the story."

There are signs and wonders. In Mexico City the face of the Virgin appeared carved in bite marks in a half-eaten apple. Baby Moses was floated down the Nile in a basket to save him from execution. Agamemnon sacrificed his daughter Iphigenia for the blessings of war, but the gods took pity and the girl did not die. And King Minos so loved gold that he gilded his own child with his touch. There is a television commercial in which a woman is transported from the unhappiness of daily life by sinking into a bubble bath. And there are precocious children who chant in unison the most beloved poetry of their age: *two whole-beef patties special sauce lettuce cheese pickles onions on a sesame-seed bun.* And the walls of Jericho came tumbling down at the sound of a trumpet. *Alpha, beta,* and *gamma* are not Greek words but come from Semitic terms for *ox, house,* and *camel.* There is a moment in suspense movies when through flashbacks all the pieces of a life lock together like a jigsaw puzzle. There is a magazine advertisement in which a menacing pirate doesn't mind walking the plank because he carries a flask of spiced rum to keep him company on his downward plunge. It is said that each and every crag in the ruins of the Western Wall is crammed full, stuffed with the rolled letters and pleas of passing pilgrims. It is said that if Jesus came back and saw all the deeds done in his name he would never stop throwing up. And that after surgery amputees feel the presence of a ghost limb, an arm or leg no longer there. And Freud in attempting to understand how Jews acquired their peculiar character wrote in a letter in 1937: . . . *the first so to speak embryonic experience of the race, the influence of the man Moses and the exodus from Egypt, conditioned the entire further development up to the present day—like a regular trauma in early childhood in the case history of a neurotic individual.* The stereopticon is a compound slide projector that can show overlapping images at once, or in quick succession so as to produce the sensation of one picture fading into another.

Have you ever awoken from a dream to realize that you had fallen into another dream?

I woke up.

And yet I did not awaken.

Or did I mention that already? I found myself in a dark room as night slowly gave way to the morning of All Saints' Day. Brigid's nightdress was slipped low on her shoulders. Her sweater was on the floor. And Owen poured himself a drink and told her she'd catch her death if she didn't cover up. She wrapped herself in a blanket. And he poured her a drink. And he took my glass and poured me a drink. I saw his face in the firelight. There is a cartoon character who after accidentally tumbling over the side of a cliff with an anvil strapped to his back hovers for a moment, legs spinning in midair before he begins to fall. And every time it begins to snow there is a chance, a slight chance, a remote possibility, that maybe just maybe this time the snow will never stop. It was November first and already the autumn had succumbed, been subsumed into winter by a pall of white.

Verdun

Owen spoke.

In the beginning there was nothingness. There was the absence of earth and sky and water. There was the lack of light and darkness. And God created from nothingness the darkness and the light. And he called the darkness Night. And there were then words for each shade of light and differentiation of shadow. There was Dawn and Morning and Evening and Night. And that was the first day. And the days of creation followed, one after the next; the oceans split from the heavens; the beasts of the field and the birds of the air. And on the sixth day, the Lord created Franny. And he saw that she was good. And he rested.

And God created Man of clay and dirt and ash. And Man did not understand the ways of the Lord. He did not understand the planets or the fishes. He did not understand the moon, and he feared the falling of the darkness from the sky. Man was ignorant. And Man created separation. For he took the creations of the Lord, light and darkness, as difference. And Man valued the light of the sun and feared the darkness of night. He owned and claimed dominion over all he saw. And what he could not see, he feared. And he could not see the presence of God. The presence of God was an absence to Man. And on the eighth day after resting, after placing Eden among the four rivers of the earth and placing the trees of life and knowledge in the garden's midst, the Lord created the Story. And he saw that it was good. And he rested.

And Man and Woman ate from the Tree of Knowledge. And they felt shame at their nakedness. Before they could eat from the second tree, the tree whose fruit held eternal life, the Lord cast Man and Woman out of Eden and banished them forever. For one must have the forbidden knowledge of the first tree to understand the bitter fruit of the second.

And they were cast out. And they went and dwelled in the Land of Nod, East of Eden. Man tilled the fields and was bitten and bruised on the heels by snakes. And all was not good for Man and Woman, who were haunted each in secret by the untasted fruit of the second tree.

Mornings followed and nights ensued. And it came to pass that Cain slew his brother Abel but the Lord protected Cain and made him to wander. And it happened that Man in general thrived and in specific was woeful. And he covered the earth and grew wicked. The Lord came then to Noah and commanded him to build an ark and take to the water with his children and animals each by each. The wickedness of Man would be washed away in the flood. For the way that we understand the Old World is to fashion a New World. For each disaster there is an explanation, and for each transgression there is expiation. And Man learned to make use of the creation of the Lord's eighth day. Man spoke and uttered. He confounded the real with the unreal. He told stories.

We are told that the Lord's time is not our time. He is a clockmaker who sets his dials winding and leaves us in the wilderness to remember and to rue and to live beyond the usefulness of our own memories. Shall we raise our glasses in congratulations and acknowledgment of a job well done? Seven days for all this majesty, all this useless beauty? For amber waves of grain? For the Lord was and is all things. But he was no thing more than a practical joker. He tested Abraham's faith through the sacrifice of Isaac. He asked questions to which he already knew the answer: Cain, where is your brother? Adam, did you eat from the Tree of Knowledge? And the Lord gave to Franny the gift of story. Franny could find no comfort in Nod. And she could find no happiness in the world. For Man had created divisions of light and dark, of man and woman. And Franny struggled. And she confounded the real with the unreal, because that was her gift. And that was her curse. Franny struggled and in struggling gave name to a happiness that was itself the fight against happiness. And she would not leave off struggling and fighting.

She died on the morning of the ninth day. As the Lord's time is not our time. And the storyteller's time is not our time. And the Lord's minutes are our lifetimes and his days are each a millennium.

At the gates of Eden there stands still, some say, the fiery blaze of banishment. Franny asked that in death her body be consumed by flame and cast upon the waters to return to ash and to scatter about the four rivers of the earth and so float back to Eden. And her husband obeyed her desire. Her body was destroyed. And her gifts from the Lord, her stories were paper and her words were stories and her words were set aflame. And her words returned to ash. And her body returned to clay and dirt and ash. And she was set free.

The Lord who is a practical joker and clockmaker alike had made for Franny a partner, who was a storyteller as well. And the two struggled against each other as they sought to create through stories a different version of the world. Each sought in the end to create the other. And the Lord saw that this was funny. And the Lord found this funny because he had created all the stories and the storytellers alike. Their gifts were his grace. Franny and Owen cleaved together and clawed apart. And the Lord created many humble creatures, those that slid on their bellies and those that flew on the wind. He created fire and water. He created all of the peoples of the earth who cried out in disparate languages. And they cried out: Why Lord? Why? And the Lord created the weak and the sick and the starving. He created the meek and the mild and the magnificent. The Lord created the leaves on the trees, the fruit as well as the vine. And the Lord created Esther. And he saw that Esther was good. And he rested.

Esther could not rest for she was a child of Cain. She suffered to wander the earth. She was cast out of homeland after homeland. And she could find no home. She was descended of Ham, the son of Noah. She was cursed with slavery. But she was not a slave. She could find no peace. She could take no rest. The Lord tests his creations. He tests the fish for swimming. And the birds for flying. He tested Job. And he tested Lot's wife. He tested Moses. And the Lord tested Franny with Owen. And the Lord tested Owen with Franny. And Esther could find no peace because she knew only wandering and slavery. And Owen saw Esther. And he saw that Esther was good. And Franny knew no happiness. And Esther knew no peace. And Franny gave to Owen a son. And Owen saw Esther who knew only wandering.

The Lord tested Franny. She answered him in defiance by writing the ending to her own story. So it was that Franny died by her own pen. And the Lord was unhappy and he saw that all was not good. And Owen took the belongings of Franny, the papers and books, and he set them aflame as all things must return to ashes. Franny did not fear the Lord. And Owen did not then fear the Lord. But Esther feared the Lord. As she had seen the worst of his creations. Owen and Franny had no fear. They were storytellers and fell under the sway of their creations. They had forgotten how to fear and they knew only jealousy and vanity and desire. But Esther feared the hand of the Lord. And she secreted out from the pyre Franny's papers for she knew it was the Lord's own agency to murder and to create. She hid the papers from Owen. As it is the Lord's providence to destroy and to rebuild. For the Lord created the match. And the hand that lights it. And Esther hid the story of Franny that Owen would not destroy it. And Esther kept hidden the story of Franny so that no future storyteller in vanity or desire or jealousy would finish her story or repeat her words. And the Lord pitied Esther as he pities the leaves on the Tree of Life which never die and never come to understand their own beauty.

The Lord created Franny who wrote the end of her life. And Franny wrote the deaths of all who would come after. When Esther died, it was the pen of Franny guiding her. And Esther died. And Esther bore Owen a child. The child was called Fern after weeds that tangle upon the earth and know nothing but wandering. The child was called Fern by her mother as a reminder of Franny who had come before her. And was the author of her own ending. And the child was a girl who would know only the unhappiness of her mother's slavery and the arrogance of her father's pen. And Esther succumbed to the ending that Franny wrote. Esther died as Franny had before her. Because God is a practical joker. And his time is not our time. Esther who loved her child and feared the Lord took the girl with her even unto death. But the Lord pitied Esther as he would a bird who flies so far from home that home becomes nothingness. And the bird knows only flight. And the Lord saved the child who floated in the waters. And the child did not die.

The Lord tested Franny, and she failed. The Lord tested Owen, and he failed. And the Lord tested Esther, but upon her he took pity for she was but a leaf, a moth, a bird. Owen in anger at the Lord for his trials and his jokes and his creations banished the girl. And the father swore never again to look upon the face of the past. And he wandered the earth. Even in his wanderings he knew that the child grew like a leaf or moth or bird. And would in the manner of such fallen creatures return to him. And even as our time is not God's time, our centuries barely a movement on the hand of the divine clock, our lives are but impractical jokes to wile away the endless hours of the Lord. Owen grew old. Franny succumbed to the ash of Adam. And Esther whose child was spared by the pity and humor and grace of the Lord was herself banished from the pages of history and story to dwell uninked between the words. And the Lord in his infinite jest created Brigid. And he saw that she was good. And he rested.

Brigid was a comfort to Owen. Brigid was a consolation. And they wandered together. And Brigid was a consolation to Owen who grew tired of his wanderings. They returned from their wandering to dwell in Nod and live among the creatures of the land, those who creep and those who crawl and those who slink low on their bellies in the dirt. To Brigid Owen told the stories of the beginning. And she took pity upon him and cried out for her husband's restoration. But the Lord was hard-hearted and obdurate. The Lord would not hear her pleas. For Owen knew that to be right with the Lord he must restore his house. And as Abel's blood seeped into the dry earth from his brother's blow, so fathers in their age long for their children. As blood cries out for blood. Owen sought out Esther's child. And Fern who was a wanderer like her mother and an outcast like her father found herself in the house of Owen and Brigid. And the Lord saw that this was good.

But the Lord is and was an impractical joker. He set in Brigid the ghost of Franny. He set in Esther the absence of Franny. He set in Franny the story. And he set in Fern the blood of her history. And he set in the child of Owen and Esther the longing for the knowledge of all the things that came before her. For Fern knew of nothing but the memory of slavery. And Brigid, who was a comfort to Owen, found the papers hidden by Esther. For Franny had died. And Esther fell off the page. And Brigid found seven letters after the manner of the Lord's creation of the world. Seven letters like the years of fat and the years of lean in the dreams of Egypt. And on the last day it is said that the Lord wound all the clocks in the celestial palace, and then he rested. And he is resting still.

Each letter betrayed the guilt of Adam and the wrath of Eve. And Brigid bowed her head and forgave Owen. And Brigid offered herself up to the will of the Lord for though she was neither leaf nor feather, neither bird nor bee, she was a creature of the earth shaped of God's providence. And so it was that Fern came to learn the story of her past. She neither believed nor disbelieved, for she was a wanderer by nature. She was a child born of water who knew no solid ground. And the Lord's time is not our time. But his jokes are our weaknesses, and his impracticalities are our arrogance and vanity and desire. And in Eden there is still now a gate of flame. So that none may enter. And in Nod there is land to be tilled, and none will have rest. Some are born to wandering and fall like the leaf on the wind. And Fern, who sits before me, created of dust and struggle and story, must choose from the Lord's creations, the earth or the ocean. She must find her home. Stay here, with us, this is what we are asking of you. Or leave and wander, as I have wandered, and suffer, as your mother suffered. And you will find yourself lost in the wilderness only to fall like a bird from the sky into the salt of an unfamiliar shore.

And this is the story of your genesis.

Stay with us or else repudiate the past and all to which I have this night confessed.

I am but a leaf, oh Lord. I am but a voice crying out in the desert for restoration. Consider me as you would a leaf, an ash, a spark of dying flame. For I have been tested and I have failed. I have been a fugitive in my own house. I have been weighed on the divine scales and found wanting. And still I cry out as the very earth that drank Abel's blood for vengeance and for renewal and for forgiveness. As blood cries out for blood.

And the rest is mystery.

The rest is the story of generations.

Brigid laughed. She tolled three peals of laughter like a church bell and then she fell silent with a dull clang.

The sun was rising in the east over the snowy fields.

"She's hysterical," said Owen.

"No," she said. "No, I'm not. I'm relieved. I'm only thinking how happy I am now that you have finally told her the truth."

"The truth?" I echoed.

"There is an inevitability to things now," she said.

"What happens next?" I asked.

Owen refilled his glass.

"Finally," said Brigid, "at last, now comes the ending."

Waterloo

Dear Fern:

   This is not an easy letter to write. I did not believe you were alive. Last month I received a letter from my stepmother informing me of your situation and the remorse she feels for her involvement. My father assures me that it is true. Or, in fact, that you are true. As I say, it is not easy to believe it, and yet knowing my father, it is impossible to disbelieve. His actions ceased to surprise me years ago.

   Still, I should have known he was up to something—that no ending is ever really an ending with him—no drama is too dramatic—there is always a trap door through which he steps to avert the latest disaster he has wrought. The best that I can do for you is to try to re-create those days of my childhood and offer you the few memories of your mother that I have, as I am certain that O.L. would relinquish not one scrap of sentiment from his stockpile. What can I tell you about your mother? I recall her face with no more specificity than the way a child remembers those who were kind to him, who buttered his toast and offered the spoon from the whipping cream. She was, of course, beautiful. But this is a condition difficult to quantify or explain. I can't begin to define or describe her physically, facially. It was (if I recall correctly—and everything, everyone in the past is vaguely suspect to fading and brightening) with Esther, a matter more of what she did not look like. I was only six years old when she died. She had black hair, and I seem to remember her wearing red and orange. And, of course, she had a little baby girl, who disappeared along with her mother. That's what they told me anyway. I spent so much time trying to piece together the fragments of my early years that now I have to question the strength of both memory and reconstruction.

335

I do know that after Esther was gone, the house was empty and solemn, and then I was sent to live with my aunt. Before I left though, a friend of father's from home, a lawyer, I think, came to visit. It seemed odd, no one visited us; we were in mourning. So, you see, I remember this lawyer and his cheerful young red-haired wife. And then they too were gone. Does this mean anything to you?

The most substantial things that I have learned about your mother come not from memory, unfortunately, but from an embarrassing black-mail attempt. Sometime after both our mothers were gone, and the American couple had departed (with you perhaps in tow?) and just before I was sent away—I was probably no more than seven—I happened to walk in on my father unceremoniously fucking Susan Rhys (one of my mother's many biographers, the first biographer) in my own bed-room. And while sadly it was not the most horrific sight in my young life—far less awful perhaps than the image of your mother scrubbing the staircase clean of dried blood—it was awful enough to carry a certain belated currency through the years. There are reasons for taboos, I suppose. Later, when I was eighteen or nineteen I began to try to force myself to remember how it was back in the old house, how it had been and how things happened before I went to live with Aunt Natalie who in turn sent me to boarding school (I am told that I look very much like my mother and that this is, or was, a face of which no one wanted to be reminded). So I was in college and I saw that Susan Rhys was coming to campus to give a lecture, something ridiculous, something like, "the obligations of the biographer." I went to hear her speech, and I couldn't stop myself from introducing myself afterward; I think I thought it would shame her, embarrass her—my very presence in her audience. It had been one of those high-minded pedantic talks about how the biog-rapher must keep "emotional distance" from the subject so as not to mar the story with partiality. I told her that I knew, that I saw; I told her what I saw that day when I was seven years old. I remembered how she had unceremoniously fucked my father, and I threatened in a very innocent

and genuine way to expose her as the fraud she was if she did not tell me
what she knew about my mother's death. I knew there were things that
my father had wanted to keep out of her biography.

I thought, as I say, that I was being smart. That I was forcing her
hand. She actually seemed flattered by both the attention and my recol-
lection of her with my father. She said that she would quite willingly tell
me whatever she could. She wanted, I realize now, what every biogra-
pher wants, to be part of the story. I was naïve. It wouldn't have harmed
her reputation to have her readers know that she had slept with Owen
Lieb. It probably would have helped her lagging book sales. For all I
know, she is hard at work penning her own tell-all memoir.

We arranged to meet the next day for breakfast. At ten A.M. she was
already slightly drunk. I remember that she rose to hug me in greeting as
though we were old friends. And she tried to order me a mimosa, but I
declined; she ordered herself another and settled into her story. Susan
Rhys began working on Bright Darkness *(referred to by the cognoscenti*
as BAD*) in 1966. She was only just out of college herself. I was three and*
you were not yet born. My mother had at that time a small but devoted
following for her novel, for her life, her death. And Susan came over
from London to interview my father for an article she was trying to
write. She was or at least she saw herself as an aspiring girl journalist.
Owen, I think, I imagine, knowing that biography was inevitable,
knew also that things would go much better from his point of view if he
had some control over the biographer. Poor Susan Rhys, she never had a
chance. He proposed the idea of the biography of Franny to her, and she
went along with it. She thought all the while that she was uncovering
clues, not following the trail he had set out for her. She was drawn into
their story until it became her cause, her cross—she took it upon herself
to prove that Owen Lieb had loved his wife, who was troubled, ambi-
tious, plagued with her own various demons, and largely unlovable.
That is, Susan made their life into a literary romance novel; the ulti-
mate message being that the distraught young widower must learn to

love again. Apparently and by all reports, he had and he did. If you haven't read BAD, *you might take a look at it for the sheer absurdity of its plot. You might find yourself laughing aloud now that you know some of the characters involved. Susan supposed in the end that it was the world at fault; the begrudging world, jealous of my parents' happiness that did them in. An amazingly romantic and short-sighted supposition, but there she was, Susan Rhys, years later, sipping mimosas and clinging to the myth, the dream, the ideal of the perfection of Franny and Owen Lieb.*

In 1966 your mother, Owen, and I were living in the old house. Susan had already begun the book, but Owen still didn't want her to come out to the house; he kept his own apartment in Dublin. He was also in the process of trying to collect my mother's letters for a compilation— which meant trying to charm Aunt Liz, to whom the bulk of the letters, especially the later ones, were sent. Susan wanted access to the letters for her bio, of course. So finally it was planned that Susan was going to come out to the house to study the letters, and Owen was careful to sort out a few that he didn't want her to read, as they might change the tenor of the book, or her opinion of him. I don't know if he intended to destroy them, or if he accomplished at least partially his intent. Though in truth, if Susan had read them he probably could have convinced her of some extenuating circumstance for the evidence that only seemed to incriminate him. The irony is perhaps that Susan ended up being the co-editor of the Collected Letters. *Still, he didn't want Susan to come to the house because of Esther. And even when Susan finally did come to the house, he never let her meet Esther. He wanted no mention of Esther in any book about Franny; he didn't want her used to either betray the truth of his infidelities or lay blame on Esther herself for his wife's suicide. But, of course, Susan knew about Esther. Susan Rhys laughed that morning at what she called my father's "romantic naïveté"; everyone in their little literary world knew about Owen and Esther. It was only that no one spoke of it in his presence. Susan did what Owen had asked her not to—show up at the house unannounced like the good reporter she had always wanted to be—but nothing ever came of it. She never met Esther, and she said that she always regretted that. And so the best that she could do was imagine Esther as a ghost trapped inside the house, peering down at her from behind closed curtains. After a while she gave up trying to meet Esther, she said, because she had constructed such a lovely version of her that no real person could live up to that fictional rival. And then you were born in 1969. The same year that you died; or didn't. But Esther died. And Susan finished her book and when it was published, in 1971, there was no mention of Esther. And thus the first myth of the marriage of Owen and Franny Lieb was born. There would be many more to follow.*

What Susan had found in her interviews of friends and acquaintances was that blame did fall on Esther, not Owen, for Franny's demise. And it was easy to blame Esther in those first years after Franny's death because Esther was invisible. No one ever saw her, saw them together, saw Owen and Esther as a couple. Do I talk about these people, Owen and Esther and Franny, like they are characters in a novel? If I do, I apologize. It is only that over the years they have come to seem less and less real to me. So, oddly enough, it turns out that Owen became the subject of a great deal of pity and that translated into more attention for his writing, more popularity in general; he had the good sense to keep Esther hidden, and people assumed that meant that he was ashamed of her, of her guilt. And at the same time, they thought he was protecting her, being very chivalrous, putting on a brave face and all that. It was a tremendously productive period for him—he wrote two novels and a volume of poetry. People were taken with his work—they thought through his fiction they might find the hidden truth to the sordid rumors of his life. Still, the books moved off the shelves, and I went to a very nice boarding school. And many profound and misguided theses were penned on the subject of subtext in the poetry and prose of Owen Lieb.

Maybe my memory is playing tricks—but it seems to me that from the moment Esther entered the house after Franny's death all she did was

*work. And Owen, Father, he was gone half the time with Susan work-
ing on the biography; so he left Esther alone to care for me in the house.
He could have hired help. He could have taken us both to the city with
him. But he left us alone out there. And when he was home he was
locked up working on his own writings. The same "friends" of my parents who reviled my mother when she was alive were her staunchest
defenders after her death—and therefore they found Esther to be a con-
venient scapegoat. Words that Susan politely said she had encountered in
reference to Franny were: self-centered, pretentious, snobbish, abrasive,
and humorless. Words that she said described Esther: mysterious, foreign,
and gloomy. It became a great parlor game, I've heard, for a while—to
list the qualities of the two women against each other and try to figure
out what had driven each of them to their unhappy fates. Both of them
suffered in the opinion of society for being less than cheerful. Again, I tell
you this because you have a right to know at least as much as I know,
even though I don't like to dredge up the recent past anymore. I concentrate on ancient history—and at times even that seems far too close.*

*Esther lived in Franny's house and slept in Franny's bed and took
care of me, Franny's child. She sat at night in the kitchen waiting for
Owen to return home. And I recall waking at night and hiding in the
doorway of the kitchen to watch her drawing, her hands blackened with
charcoal, the white paper covered with black lines, with faces, with
scenes from the past, I suppose. She drew pictures for me of dogs and
ducks. She drew the garden and the house. Bowls of apples, things like
that. She drew you, I remember, sleeping. I'm sure Owen must have
saved some of them. They can't all have been destroyed, can they? They
may be hidden. When I saw her sitting in the darkness of the kitchen, I
felt that she would not be with us for very long. Maybe I felt this way
about everyone after my mother died. But truly Esther was more of a
mother to me than my own was or had the chance to be. People, the
ghosts, and guilt did Esther in. There are a million theories. And in time
you will devise one of your own.*

I don't suppose that Susan told me too much that I didn't already know or suspect. But it was strange to hear how she spoke of it, of my parents, as though remembering the first time she saw her favorite movie. She confirmed what I suspected—that in keeping Esther out of the first biography (for the sake of the children, for the sake of the family, etc.), Owen had managed to keep her out of all subsequent biographies—each one built on the shoulders of the one that had come before. And Ms. Rhys was very happy to tell her side of the story to me as though she was getting the chance to speak to her own biographer.

The next part of what I have to tell you is far more odd than encountering Susan Rhys at a college lecture. About seven years ago, just before I moved here, in fact the very summer that I did move, I ran into Ben Wilcox on the street in New York. The name is probably unfamiliar to you. He was Esther's husband. Susan mentioned him, and although she had never met him (as he had refused all interviews), from what she gathered, from her own theories—she surmised that he had been so in love with Esther that when she left him for Owen he didn't consider divorcing her because he thought she might eventually return. He was willing to wait. I wouldn't have been able to picture or construct any physical image of him until I walked right into him coming out of the public library. He was leaving, and I was entering. We had one of those strange moments when strangers try to figure out how or why or where they could possibly have met before. Of course, when he said his name, I knew who he was. He couldn't have recognized me, still, when I introduced myself he showed no shock or surprise. He simply nodded. He said, of course, of course, that I looked like my mother. We ended up having coffee and we talked about everything but the very issue that had brought us together.

I asked him finally about his wife. He was surprised. He said he hoped that I didn't remember too much about that time. And I told him, for no apparent reason other than it seemed to fit the flow of conversation, that I had taken a teaching position in Alaska. It made a kind of sense. Then he told me about Esther. From his perspective: Owen and Franny used Esther as a pawn between them—but in the end her death had nothing to do with either of them. He didn't think that she had fallen or even gone willingly into their lives; they pulled her in. Owen had taunted Franny with his exotic Jewish mistress. And Franny, obsessed as she was with German guilt and the Holocaust, hated herself more than she hated Owen because she understood what he was up to, and she couldn't blame him for doing it. Esther to Franny came to represent everything, the world the Nazis tried to destroy—and yet Franny hated Esther too—not for being a Jew, of course, but for sleeping with her husband. And Ben said it seemed heavy-handed to say things like that, but he knew that's how Franny was, that if he had learned anything it was that sometimes one must make allowances for the heavy-handedness of reality. He said that he blamed himself for leaving Esther alone with them. But he was young then, he said. Ben and Esther had eloped in the winter of 1962 three days after they met. He was twenty-one and she was thirty. She had just arrived in London from Israel. He said they had gotten on so well because he never asked her about her past. Well, I suppose that is romantic and all that, but it doesn't help our story too much does it?

In the end all he could say was that Esther was everything Franny wanted to be. Esther didn't care about public opinion or fashion or society. She didn't care one way or the other whether she was liked or disliked. She didn't talk about her childhood or the concentration camps— she had been held in one, although she wouldn't say which. He could say with fair certainty that her family had been murdered, and somehow Esther lived and found herself at war's end on a ship of orphans and survivors sailing to Palestine in 1945 when she was about thirteen. Ben said he hoped I wouldn't be drawn into the conclusion that it is the fate of survivors of the camps to kill themselves in punishment for the very sin of surviving. He didn't want to say either that Esther's death had anything to do with Franny's. All he would say was that Esther was an unhappy person and that perhaps her nature superseded the events in her

life, although it certainly influenced how she dealt with them. She had,
he said flatly, bad luck.

It was a summer day. We drank our coffee and as I knew our meeting was drawing to a close and that I would most probably never see Ben
Wilcox again, I asked him what she was really like—Esther? He stirred
his coffee, watched a couple walk a Labrador retriever down the street.
He said that he had always liked my mother, that he thought she was
very witty. And he remembered most specifically that she had hung a
little sign on the kitchen door that read, "Genius at work." And they had
all laughed about it. Then we sat for a while and I said something about
the weather and how summer seemed more oppressive than usual this
year and I was happy to be getting out of the city. He said it looked like
rain or something like that. He never answered my question about
Esther. And after a while we parted ways.

I suppose it is all destined to remain a mystery. I'm sorry that I can
offer only suppositions and scraps, hypothetical scenarios of the lives of
our parents. I'm afraid that after my father and the biographers were
done with the looting of the papers, cutting, inking over, burning, bury-
ing and swapping, rewriting and editing, not much was left behind for
us—you know, the children Owen was so damned concerned about protecting. I don't believe he was thinking of us; he was thinking as always
about how his story would be told.

And at the end of our breakfast, Susan Rhys confessed somewhat
sheepishly to helping Owen one afternoon burn several cartons of papers
and photographs. When she told me this it reminded me of something I
had long forgotten—or maybe I created a new memory on the spot—I
recalled picking apples in the orchard on a day in September. It was
sunny and bright and Esther lifted me up into the branches, and she was
laughing. Father called to us and we turned, surprised—we didn't know
he was there—and he snapped a picture and we were still laughing. You
were sleeping in the shade on a blanket, and she picked you up and held
you out toward the camera, and he took a picture of the three of us. But

that photograph was probably in the box along with the others. They burned a lot of my mother's papers—maybe letters, maybe journals, the last manuscript? I'm certain that it happened—you were wrapped in a blanket, and then after the picture was taken Esther held you up into the branches of the apple tree just as I had been before—as though there were something magical up there to delight children.

I remember missing the house after I was sent away, and that since then no house in the world has compared to it. I remember as well forgetting everything and being glad that I could forget and remembering only that I could no longer remember.

What do you make of Owen Lieb? Do you think he lies? Or confabulates? Or simply can't tell anymore the real from the unreal? I think he lives as a monument to self-interest, but this alone does not mean that he was incapable of loving Franny and Esther. I'm not defending him. I'm not going to defend him. It is only that you will have to learn as I did that the things he facilitated—the deaths of two women who even if he did not kill them, he did not save—whatever quality or flaw that is in him is in us as well. He may have told you, he may have confessed that his only real crime is his susceptibility to beauty. I'd say something different. I'd say his real crime is being a bad writer.

Do you look like him? Has he shown you any photographs of Esther or is he still hoarding the few tokens he saved from the fire? Could everything really have been destroyed? I worry that I understand his motivations too well. He wouldn't have destroyed so much had he not thought that it was within his inestimable power to re-create any object, to resurrect the story, the characters, the pictures more perfectly and accurately through his own pen than the story left behind by the artifacts themselves. I suppose our legacy is this: if Owen Lieb had been a good writer, the world might have absolved him immediately of his sins, forgiven him anything for the sake of art—forgiven him for creating something of destruction. Have you read any of his books? Well, if you have, I think you may well understand his flaws; and if you have not yet, you soon will. But he has turned to you, to find you, to bring you back after all these years. The plot, as they say, seems to have thickened.

Here is how things are and will continue to be in the Lieb family: We do not speak to each other. We do not see each other. We burn artifacts. We hide what even in our most violent moments we cannot bear to destroy. We send birthday cards with preprinted poems signed beneath with our own increasingly indecipherable scrawls. And every once in a while one of us kills himself (no, no, herself, of course) and the rest of us close up ranks and start the burning again. And every once in a while someone writes a book. For a while it won't be easy. It may never be, technically, easy. For a while you will avoid mirrors. And then you will force yourself to read Owen Lieb's books, word by word. You will memorize them. And search for hidden meaning. And for traces of yourself. You may even decide to play detective and sleuth into your own past, digging and dredging and tracking down everyone still alive and willing to tell their side. Start with Susan, as I did, and work your way one by one through all of the biographers. They love to talk. I haven't met one yet who hasn't loved to talk. I have not met the third wife, Brigid. What are the odds of her survival? Is she more or less likely to suffer the fate of those who came before her? To be fair, this is the question that we must all ask ourselves. I've also heard that she is a biographer. Soon they will come looking for you, the biographers, to hear your remarkable story and rewrite a chapter or two for the new edition.

To see if your story holds up. To see if you look like your mother, though no one claims to know what she looked like; to see if you have the genius of your father, though no one will admit exactly what his genius is for.

So this is what I know about your mother. But wait, one last thing that Wilcox said—something that I almost forgot. That after Esther died, Ben asked Owen to send her things to him. He said that Owen agreed and packed up a trunk and shipped it to Ben who had gone home to Montreal. And that the trunk had traveled by boat—and that the boat hit rough waters and it sank and all the cargo was lost. Ben said that strangest part was that a year later a cache of waterlogged cargo washed ashore in a small town off Lake Ontario and that one of the items was identified as a badly damaged trunk addressed to B. Wilcox. He went to claim it. It was empty. Another riddle. He never knew what, if anything, Owen packed in the trunk.

If anything, any memories or stories occur to me, I'll send them along. Although it doesn't seem out of the question to imagine that only an empty envelope might arrive at your mailbox. I do know that the rumors about my mother's finished, lost manuscript say that it was the account of a love triangle gone bad, and that might have been something that Owen didn't want the world to read. And that he destroyed not only the manuscript but her notes because he didn't want anyone to copy the outline of the novel, didn't want any imitators getting the bright idea of rewriting Ten-Twenty-Seven. I believe that Franny never faulted Owen for falling in love with Esther because she believed that Esther was a character of her own creation. She was Franny's monster. Make of that what you will. I will continue to remember your mother as the woman with the long black hair who lifted me high into the branches of the trees so I could reach up to the apples. She was German, wasn't she? Or was it Russian? Even her accent is lost to me. She used to cut the crusts from my toast. And in the garden we lured crows away from the flowers and fed the blackbirds and squirrels with bits of bread. I'm glad you left them. The new girl, the new wife writes me that I should ask you to return, to go back to them. I'll pass along the message, but I will not endorse it. If they say that they love you, you can believe that they do—but it isn't the sort of love that is trustworthy. It changes by the hour.

Don't go back. That's the best that I can offer. Don't serve them for the sake of a history that Owen has spent your lifetime trying to destroy. We are alike, at least in some small way, not only because of our father, but because the history of our mothers is the history of the world. There are no first or last words. Everything is subject to revision.

Sincerely,

Jonathan W. Lieb

Xenia

Dear Newton:

Let's make a pact to remain absolutely absent. Vacant. Houses in which nobody is home. I'll be an abandoned mausoleum with gothic pillars. You can be a ghost ship scuttled at the bottom of the ocean. I'll be a shell shelling over nothing, an empty emptiness. You can be the Mummy unrolled of his bandages. You left on a day in October too cold for the season. It was wet and rainy. You can be a boggy lake. I'll be as remote as the moon. Your plane circled the runway endlessly in the crazy eights of infinity; no, no, it was only that the pilots were waiting for the fog to burn off, to clear. You mentally undressed the stewardesses. It got boring. You visualized world peace. It grew tiresome. The plane brilliantly soared through a rainshower. And then you were gone with a tip of your hat. There is so little space in the world for anything but disaster. And after you left, I finally rid myself of Alexander. Do you believe in great loops of heredity? If I were to believe in predetermination, I might say that something drove me, despite and in spite of my better judgment, to a petty tyrant like Alexander. Why do we love the might of our enemies? Why do we marvel at their majesty? And why, worst of all, do we seek their good opinion? Your plane alighted. Alexander brought his students over to our ramshackle house and allowed them to sit at his feet while he recited perverse parables. His world, his world. The ends justify the means. Some are born to lead while others are happy enough to serve. His axioms never bothered the girls who sat nodding over notebooks. But you don't want to hear about any of this do you? After all, Alexander was only an end to justify our means,

347

wasn't he? They used to play a study game in which questions were
phrased as answers. Or was it the other way around? Everything was
backward. I watched in reverse. Nothing made sense. History was a
game show and each inverted interrogative led Alexander and his
minions one step closer to the jackpot. Oh, oh, oh, what was it that
awaited them shrouded behind door #3? Consolation prizes for the
inconsolable? Oh, but Alexander's totalitarian charm had begun to
wear fine. In the end it wasn't even fun to fight his Fascism. There
was so little majesty left at which to marvel. The new mob had
already memorized the script before they arrived. They studied the
drill. They grabbed their pitchforks and hurricane lanterns. They
bore rakes, rope, shovel, stones, and the smashed necks of glass bottles. Someone I knew once used a term that sticks in my mind: *characterless passion*. That suits Alexander. It fits. Desire set to a
metronome's tock. Set to the marching of boots. The ticking of
time's bomb. Ancient history. The Romans built aqueducts. The
Christians were thrown to lions. The lepers were colonized. What
possible difference can this make to us? I'm so far removed that I
have to squint to see the details. It must have been a different girl
who lived in that time and place. She was the one who talked to
strangers. Who jumped without a parachute. Good-bye cruel world!
Not to belabor the point, he, Alexander, was growing plump and
piggish. There was a mean curl to his smile that was distinctly sneer-
like. And he was growing a knife-thin moustache. I've tried to spare
you the details. We don't need details any more. The chalk outlines
alone will do. I've done my best to leave Alexander unfinished, a
shape, a shade, a skeleton. A body strung together with words—but
even this raw form has begun to grow fat on adjectives: lumpy and
plump, perfumed, powdered, snide and sourish-sweet, composed of
meringue and jelly. Where is the sentence—where is the key that will
open the final door? Where is the line at the end of this confession
that will explain everything that has come before and lay to waste all

that will come after? I did not understand the story until Brigid lowered from her bare shoulders her nightdress to reveal her tattoo. I know that what drew me to Alexander was the immutable force of history that impels Jews toward Nazis, unable to turn back. Or moths toward flames. Or Alexander toward Jews. Or you toward airplanes. Or readers toward biographies. Tell me what you are going to do tomorrow and tomorrow and then the next day. Tell me about the dead oceans and dormant seas. About Manifest Destiny, acid rain, and the last novel that you read. Tell me how the story ends.

And so I set out to see the world, your world. Oh Newton, I went to all of your favorite places. I saw Paris and did Denmark. I searched for you among the ruins, in the cafés and cathedrals. I found you everywhere and nowhere all at once. In Chartres you clung like a gargoyle to a flying buttress. You walked the Bois de Boulogne after the style of Proust's fugitives in the half-light. In and around the boggy canals of Amsterdam girls swam like mermaids and called out your name. I saw Scotland and loafed London. The food was awful. I saw you spouting Marxist rhetoric from a soapbox in Hyde Park. It rained every day just as the tour books promised. In Dublin soccer hooligans overtook the city. The hotels and hostels were packed. I swear I saw you there as well. I know it was you. You were wearing a Doctor Seuss hat and cheering for the losing team. I went North and lost your trail. These are the facts of my case; these facts are indisputable. I have saved my canceled tickets, my receipts, the useless foreign coins. I have your letters. I have Franny Lieb's letters sealed safely in plastic and hidden from the light. I keep everything locked up. I am locked up. There is nothing to me. Snow White in her glass coffin. Oh, and can you imagine how it is for me to know that the outside world still exists? The way a shut-in dreams of foreign shores and the warmth of the sun but can't bear to speak the place-names aloud for fear of mispronunciation?

Here in my little room, I assure you, all the places, each grain of sand or leaf divested of tree; each umlaut, circumflex, and virgule belongs to me. I roll the syllables over my tongue. I chew them up and swallow them down.

I digest.

I colonize the world from my Smith-Corona.

There is so little territory left.

Everyone falls apart. Even the keys on my typewriter begin to imprint more and more lightly the certain letters I cannot live without. The J. The E. The W.

And there she goes—Fern, she is heading toward the train station. No one can stop her. Not now. Not ever. I watch in dumb reverence as she begins her journey toward the Liebs. But what of the others? You know, the long-suffering Jacobis. With the boys and the baseballs and bagged lunches? With school and supper. Saturday morning cartoons and shopping trips with mother whose candy-cane red hair smelled mysteriously of peppermint. With bathing suits and snow boots. And we sat, I remember, one evening before I left, planning my travel itinerary. They, this mother and that father, pushed a pencil across a map and forced a direction. A destination as likely as any other. And if I failed to mention earlier that there was a plan to my travels, I apologize. It was vanity. I wanted to seem hapless and carefree. It does not make me happy to see myself then as another pilgrim on the path home. With mop and bucket. With scars and tattoos. I wonder about the smallness of connections. The fine thread that kept me moving toward the Liebs. What if I had missed a train? Gone south? Joined a cult? Could the story have been subverted by a rainy afternoon? A bus running off-schedule? And then I met Marie in the train station. But I don't think it was part of the plan. It was dusk. She had a baby boy. And a daughter who asked me in that empirical tone that only children can evince—if I enjoyed green eggs and ham half as much as she did? Or did I prefer kitty-cats? I stayed with Marie and her children and her silent but good-natured young husband for two weeks. I cleaned cottages and washed windows before I left one morning to exorcise a haunted house. With bleach and baking soda. The Lieb house, a monument to madness. A museum of malcontents. A document of dislocation. You would have liked it. In fact, you may be interested in renting a room there if your travels ever take you that far up the coast. Prices are reasonable. Tragedies are Grecian. Accommodations and availability never vary. I hear that the girl who cooked breakfast has long since packed up and disappeared. But you've navigated rougher waters than those that boil in a teapot, and after all, how hard can it be to crack a green egg? I am summing up the summary for you. I am telling you that I was an unhappy, ill-fit child. I was a word out of context. A girl lost in a department store who goes to luggage sales and waits patiently for the next train to arrive. The next train never arrives. The next train dropped me off right at the winding walkway up to the Lieb mansion. And absolutely everything was green and gold and apple-bright. I cleaned and scrubbed and earned my keep. But that girl is gone. So don't ask her how to remove catsup from linen. I'm not doling out recipes for carrot muffins. I shoveled ash from the grate, emptied garbage pails. I'm through with being useful. I'm letting the old stains set. And my hosts? Those illustrious two whose favor I so sought to curry through my toil and grime-destroying tenacity? What more can I tell or betray about them? Brigid was tall and prone to trembles. Her husband, marked by a letter O, took her arm and walked her down the aisle. The third time is a charm. But this is not a nuptial note, no anniversary announcement. It is a letter of forgiveness and vengeance; repetition and refusal. Forgiveness and vengeance, impossible to separate. They are like an old married couple. Where one begins, the other ends. One dies and the other dies of grief. Brigid Lieb was tall. I am prone to finding her type pretty, but not everyone will agree with me. Some may find her too sweet, as though her very face was copied

from an advertisement for angel food cake mix. Her cheeks were
stained with the hypochondriac's sympathetic strawberry soda. Her
husband was a brooding malcontent who raged at the world as
though history were an upstairs neighbor who refused to turn down
the stereo. You know, the type who is always promising that he is on
great terms with the landlord? And Brigid, she was the illegitimate (is
there any other kind?) granddaughter of Marcel Proust and a plump
German girl named Greta.

Owen brought Brigid back to the old house.

The sun did not shine. It was too wet to play.

So we sat in the house all those cold cold wet days.

And then things took a turn. We spent Halloween together.

Owen said I had a mother.

Brigid said I had a father.

I say this story is all I have.

Follow me, keep close, hold onto the word that came before the
last word. Don't be distracted by the clicking shutter, the explosion
of flashbulbs. Don't trip over the tangle of cords or lose footing in
the darkness. Stop mentally undressing the castaway huddled beside
you in the lifeboat. Stop wondering if that last vaccination booster
will keep you safe one more day, one more hour. No one can survive
the new strains of bacteria that creep into the heart and nestle there
longing for love. So give up. Get out. Give over. Imagine Brigid and
Owen the way I first spied them, loverlike among the damage,
caught up in the deluge. They were perfect and unblemished. They
were not bruised. Why didn't the nails on the floor cut or scrape
their skin? Why weren't they sliced with splinters? Diced with desire?
Why was there no blood at the crime scene? I think I know the
answer. Because they weren't like us. They weren't created of flesh
and blood. They were flammable—composed entirely of paper and
ink. The right degree of sun and a reflecting glass could set them
aflame. And I was witness to it all.

And I ran from the scene.

Isn't that just what you would have expected from me?

And if everything led up to that moment, everything since has been a falling away from it. Now I am shut in, locked up reading an atlas as though it were a mystery novel, running my fingers over the blue lines of highways glowing like veins beneath skin; red stars and rest stops and reservations, monuments and mountains, the slope of hills, the grand looping loops of incoherence, destinations that neither begin nor end, the mythic majesty of place-names without place, the amber waves of grime. Each mile marked. Every inch accounted for. See, some mysteries have been solved. You can make the world disappear by an act as simple as folding up the map. I have my little window on the winter world. All along Swann's Way there are roses in torrential bloom. No country suits me. I have not yet learned to say Esther's name aloud. It is difficult enough to spell it. I leave out letters. They fall to the floor in a flurry of snow. They cause delays like bodies on train tracks. Esther? Where should I begin to look to find traces of her? In photographs? I haven't seen any. In a book? I can't find her story. On a map? The boundaries keep shifting. The names are forever changing. Lost in a crowd of pale refugees stunned with sun among groves of oranges on a foreign shore? Which one is she? Pick a face, any face. She has become for me every cause and its inevitable effect. The ruins of the Austro-Hungarian empire. The foot of every pilgrim on the path to the Holy Land. The flashbulb of every tourist on the bus to Hollywood. She was the second wife of Owen Lieb once removed by the fact of nonmarriage. As futile as the scars of erasure on a forged document. After Franny and before Brigid there was Esther. Is it true, have you heard? That the French government is exhuming the body of Marcel Proust to study the remnants of bones and brittle candies that were once his teeth? They are secretly substituting his ashes with rich Folgers crystals to see if geneticists can tell the difference. I don't know how many legions of pretty blonde girls from Iowa have stepped forward to claim their legacy. I only know my own story, no less ridiculous than Brigid's, is true. Why should I any longer bother to disbelieve anything? Every glass is full. Every grave is empty.

I believe, I believe, it's crazy, but I believe.

Dear you: what are you going to do with me?

I am a dictionary of disaster. An alphabet of aberration. An encyclopedia of ecstasy. Isn't that what you wanted from me? A little bit of blasphemy to salt your stew? A moment on the lips, an eternity on the hips? Someone whom you could shut out with the shutting of a book? You have me for one last hour, unrequited. You unpeeled me as an onion until even my absence was absent. You were a vast ugly lake seething with lichen, bean-green and true-blue with algae, bacterial, with moss for skin and the eyes of a million fishes staring upward through the mire, unblinking. And I was the moon, so distant and cold, so much craggy cheese smuggled in from Denmark by American tourists and pared down to bite-size chunks skewered on plastic swords and served up on crackers to feed your fans. They were always so hungry. Nothing could sate them. Nothing would slake them. They gobbled up your sentences and left you for dead in a heap on the dais. But I bought a kit at the corner store and put you back together myself with bolts and brackets, threepenny nails, soldering gun, clay, blowtorch, spirit gum, shellac, and macaroni shells. Don't tell a soul about the secret ingredient; I borrowed a brain from an unmarked jar in the laboratory of a local mad scientist. It took some time. Some planning and prophecy. Some dice-throwing and divination. Oh, but it was worth the trouble when at last I found you on the steps of the library where in the basement there were and are still row after row of untranslated tomes, stacks of water-damaged books on the floor, books heaped up against the collapsing walls, plaster and pipe corroding around the shelves lined and sagging with the works of Iranian poets. Nothing seemed more beautiful than a language that I could not read. I created you as such to find something redeeming in my incoherence. And the moment you were complete, when the last pin was popped into place, when the flame of your match struck your cigarette in the combustion of God's fingertip to Adam's on the ceiling of the Sistine Chapel and you drew in, inhaled, you became whole, miraculous, as unlike yourself as any two snowflakes; at that moment you set about, you proceeded to piece by piece dismantle me. This was not a flaw in your design. This was no reason to revise or revisit the drawing board. It was part and parcel of your program.

I began to fall apart. An arm. A vowel. A curl. A kaleidoscope. Nothing but skin to the onion.

And neither of us could speak a word of Persian.

Let alone having been to that forgotten place. But we saw it marked on ancient maps. We knew the names of the places that have long since replaced it. And after all, how different are love poems from one language to the next?

There is so little of the past with which to contend.

You were a lake grown boggy with rainstorms.

And I was the moon. I looked better from a distance.

Owen and Brigid and I sat in the great room among and amidst the faded grandeur of the past, the worn brocade sofa and velvet armchairs sagging with flophouse ennui, the candy dishes and compotes of wax fruit, the beau-pots and pillows, curtains like ghost sheets with a sash of braided cord, rickety end tables, the comfort, the calamity, the grinning cupidity of the candle sconces, the woolen blanket that covered Brigid when she came in from the rain or fell asleep before the fire, and the fireplace itself, marvelous, ludicrous, a transforming mirror which promised that for the price of a peek we could but for a moment see ourselves as others see us. Step right up. See the murderer! See his golden-haired assistant sawed in half. Witness the magician who knows no tricks.

Each destruction of the past causes a new destruction to spring up in its place.

We are great mythmakers, are we not, Newton?

Such visionaries, prognosticators, seers of the future and sellers of the past, hawkers of the here and now, collectors of rags, bearers of bottles, unburiers of bones? I believe, in spite of everything, despite disbelief and the strangeness of circumstance, that this story should not be passed off as aberration. Things like it happen every day. In small and large ways. A hurricane destroys a city on the other side of the globe. The name tags are switched on two sleeping infants in a maternity ward. Another box of papers is heaved into the incinerator. Another virus resists antibiotic cure. Every day sources are obliterated and antidotes run dry.

Such a long story and such a short time to tell it. Crammed into a Frankenberry lunchbucket.

Owen Lieb's version of the past began in Eden and ended in babble. The Lord created void from substance. He came. He saw. I was conquered. Oh well, someone always has to be. And those who are conquered either forgive or swear vengeance. What shall I do? Please pass your ballot up to the front of the room. I won't hold your vote against you. I am the moon, cold and impervious. You are the lake, weed-weary, basking in bacteria, sucking in everything and everyone. Each tipped rowboat brings you a new best friend, an old shoe divested of its foot, a fishing line, wedding rings, lures shining beer-can bright, fallen coins and floating bobbers. I am the moon, empty, the doormat to infinity, nothing more than a sheet of tracing paper in the sky. You heave and sob, drawing in, casting out both refuse and redemption, solace to the suffering, suffocation to the sinful in your remote depths.

You've come to bury the ending, not to praise it.

Have you had enough of original sin and cinnamon and synecdoche?

You've come to hear how the ending ends.

Let me know how it turns out.

I'm hiding out here. I'm in all of your favorite places. The salvage heap. The swamp. The slaughterhouse. You were a slave to syntax, but those chains never suited me. You were passionate for the plots that can be culled from everyday horrors. Maybe I should have heeded your hierophancy?

Owen Lieb is my father. And Brigid Pearce is my stepmother. I beg my birthright, the bloodline removed by marriage, a connection to the bleak house of Usher. I tell you, dammit, I write today, I hold proverbial pen to paper, I place finger to key as the step-great-granddaughter of Marcel Proust. I think you will find in me something of a family resemblance. As they say, everything skips a generation or two.

I'm the moon. I'm so tiny you need a microscope to see me. You can be Loch Ness offering anonymity to the monsters hidden fast asleep in the depths of your briny bed.

Don't lose your way on unfamiliar streets. Guard your papers. Keep them dry. Seal them in plastic. Write your name just below the author's in every paperback novel that you own. One so needs proof of everything these days. These days identities are bought and borrowed and sold.

I am the word that replaces me, makes me tiny, makes me small, inks me into extinction. But cheer up. It's not quite the ending. It is only the evening of the third day. There is no more sun. It is gray and blue and violet. I will finish before midnight. I will finish before morning, before the mail trucks begin their slow grinding haul through the snow delivering sad salvaged packages, spreading the news, offering magazines with glossy pictures, *National Geographic* and *Country Living*, bringing catalogs, chain letters and disconnect notices, postcards, invitations and returned holiday greetings without forwarding address, doling out as medicine sale circulars and scenes of sodomy wrapped in brown paper; still the mailboxes overflow. Every day there is more of it. More samples of shampoo and dish-soap. More money and souls and children to save with the buying of raffle tickets to the Boy Scouts' pancake breakfast, by join-ing a new Church or athletic club, by purchasing tinned meat two-for-one at the drugstore. More and more of everything and less of you every day until, I know that it is inevitable: one day there will be no more of you at all. The last morsel devoured. The prescription bottle emptied. No more Puritans. No more pop culture. Your face becoming little by little a replacement of all the other faces that have come to replace you. It's better this way. After all, wasn't it the same for you? There were a million of me. One in every city and town, one in every room for the night or paid out by the hour. Girls with knapsacks and others with suitcases, girls who were glass-half-empty visionaries and others who were hopeful harlots, some with histories too shabby and sad to recount and others who found solace in the beauty of their own young faces. And each with a story. Too many addresses and all the streets so similar: Ash, Oak, Elm. Too many girls with names like flowers, saints, gems, or princesses of long-defunct dynasties. Too many names to recall ending in *a, y,* or *e.* Names that never stop ending up on the floor in a heap among the sordid syntax of strings and straps undone. I said this would be a tale of surrender, and I have given up a hundred thousand times in my dreams. But you have failed to sign the document, thus leaving it null and void. Empty. A house that stands vacant with no *For Sale* sign. Just weeds, all rot and the slight encroachment of nature, year by year, at first gentle, even welcome, a sprig of ivy here and flower of lilac blue there, until bit by bit the leaves become more brash. The vines thicken. The tendrils take hold. The windows are a sea of green. We never lived there. How could anyone live there? Nature overwhelms the walls, the bricks and mortar, the lime and loam. Stone becomes sediment. The plots of dirt that we dug are now looming hills, snow-capped mountains clustered with mint and juniper, with lily, mandrake and moss, roamed by sheep and ravaged by birds. Nothing of us remains. It's best this way. Pin on me any face and know that I don't, that I didn't, that I won't, that I couldn't have ever minded being replaced. I was the moon and always too far away to pick up my mail. And you were an ocean. The ink on the postcards that I sent to you ran into smudges before you had time to read the words. Don't worry. Cheer up. They all said the same thing. Having fun. Wish you were here.

Yalta

At the end of his story, Owen rose from his chair and said good-night to us.

Certain cruelties in my nature have become apparent to me. Excuse the unintentional pun. Or rather, don't excuse it. Pardon nothing about me. Refuse to sanction the world I was born out of and into and finally, to mix my last metaphor and allusion both, tossed like Jonah over the side of the boat. The sea quieted briefly, for say twenty years, only to begin anew its impossible blue, bluer, bluest rolling demand for vengeance. Before I began writing this memoir I could not spell *vengeance*. I had to consult repeatedly the dictionary for the correct order of the letters until at some point I realized I knew it, the word, phonetically, intimately, grammatically by heart. I type it now. V-e-n-g-e-a-n-c-e. No more red pens. No more fathers. No more mothers. All of my fathers killed all of my mothers. It was only that they could not stop themselves. And my mothers, for their part, went willingly to the chopping block.

Owen left the room. Brigid in her thin white nightdress sat on the sofa and noticed that the fire had gone dead.

You may have begun to guess what I have tried to keep hidden. I do not know much about the order of letters that form the word *history*. Oh yes, yes, there have been books read and essays consumed. But I remain ignorant. There have been romances and betrayals, great battles and minor skirmishes, inevitabilities and star-crossed disasters. I have been told more than once under the benefit of darkness that I am pretty. I ask you—how could I not be? Have you seen my father? Noted his blue eyes and black hair? Read his exquisitely painful prose? The striking way his tone hints at intimacy

361

long past the time his words have fallen away? I will never be free from the force of his will. It is inscribed in my skin like a great alphabet. You believe me now, don't you? When I say that I tried to be good? And when I say that I could not stop myself, do you understand my legacy? It is in my nature. I used to call myself weak. I used to believe that cruelty, dispassion, selfishness, and infidelity were my faults. But I was wrong. They are all I have to call my own.

Brigid said that she hoped we could be happy together. She said that when Owen told her he was going to find a way to bring home his long-lost daughter, she had at first balked at the madness of it. But then she came around to the Gothic possibilities of reanimating a corpse. And she agreed to reserve her judgment until she met the girl, who was me, and by the time that happened she was hip-deep in the intrigue. There was something torturously pleasurable about her situation—as though she knew how the movie ended and was dying to let me in on it. Only I was always tripping obliviously over the clues. From her point of view, it was all quite maddening. *All you had to do,* she said, *was to look in the mirror. I kept waiting for you to ask me. I would have told you everything.* But keeping secrets had taken its toll upon her. She was a nervous wreck, and although she was slightly uncertain whether the adage was correct in her case— she felt like she was stealing from Peter to pay Paul. *What does that mean really?* she asked. I heard her asking it as I got up and left the room. I left her alone with the fire gone cold.

So you see, all along I was *that* sort of person, *that* sort of girl exactly. I never saw her until I looked in the mirror at my father's face. I was a girl who could lie and steal and somehow live through it all, and worse, justify my actions as plot development in an outline of a life. It occurs to me that had things been reversed, had I been happily ensconced with Newton when I met a character named Alexander, I would have done exactly as I did, but in opposite. *Because.* I would have betrayed Newton for Alexander. Why?

Because that's the sort of person I am. No, no, I don't know a thing about history beyond the spelling of the word. I don't have a clue as to the mysterious reasons why Brigid would stay with Owen as the third wife following the second and the second following the first. I can only speculate and say: they were each *that* sort of person.

Despite the way the events unfolded, despite the fact that I wandered haplessly into a domestic melodrama and did not know until the final credits were rolling that I was the ingenue, that all the scenes had been scripted and anticipated, there was one thing still that my father could not prophesy: himself in the mirror that was me. And this beyond suicides and burnt offerings to angry gods, beyond lost photographs, hidden letters, magnificent conspiracies of consanguinity, beyond manuscripts and manna, this fact my father would too late come to understand. Having erased my mother, he had left me to be his child alone. I am no angel of forgiveness. I am the embodiment of his wrath. I am thankless, unlovable, indelicate, sullen, ill-tempered, and defensive. I do not say clever things. I am useful only for work. Labor was the only way that I knew to set myself free. I have relinquished even that honest pastime. I am not good company. I struggle as one who is forever drowning in air and longing to return to water. I am what he feared most. The empty set. The reflection without referent. The child without parents who is stripped of history and responsibility. The face of the girl gone through the mirror. With ragged claws. With blue hair and black eyes. With a mother who had once, if only briefly, lifted me high into the branches of apple trees. But I'm bound to the earth and I fell to the ground with a thud. And up I climbed. And down I fell. And she is gone. Even the memory of her is gone.

I am a liar.

I tell only the truth.

When I left the house that day I took Franny's letters with me.

I am a thief.

I trace the images drawn and left behind by someone else. My only excuse is that I make my stolen pictures so tiny that no eye can comprehend my intricate thievery. The snow was beginning to melt. The gray of dawn gave way to a shockingly bright morning. It was the first day in weeks with no sign of impending rain. I came down the stairs from the attic with my bags packed. Brigid was waiting for me in the kitchen. She looked out the window at the still-white gardens and orchard. She wore her sweater over her nightdress, hugged herself slightly for warmth. Her hair was undone. She would not stop me from leaving. She would not ask for the return of the letters. And I knew as well that this was the last time that I would see her. I wanted to remember her standing in her kitchen on that cold but sunny morning like Marcel Proust trapped in a French textbook being chased for the eternity of lost time by the first-person conjugation of the irregular verb, *être*. She sat then at the table and without speaking offered me my familiar chair across from her. And *they*, whoever this unreasonable force of history is and was, *they* would get to her, to Brigid, as surely as *they* had gotten to Franny years before. *They* had schemed to bury Esther in the pages of a story that was not even her own.

So this is what they call seeing the world?

I think Brigid Lieb was the child of the twentieth century; a self-created miscegenation of evil, good, beauty and ugliness. Or maybe she was only a girl from Iowa.

I stole the letters. They are their own story. It is a story that shifts with the understanding each new reader brings to it. I stole the words and the paper they were printed upon. It was as though Brigid and I were reading two different sets of letters. Encoded between each word for her there lurked another character who would come to embody the secret that separated her from her husband. And me? I was reading only to find out what would happen. For a liar and an infidel, I seem sometimes too innocent to be true. I should have taken the bundle of letters and hidden them back in the closet where

Brigid first discovered them. But I did not. I have them here beside me today. Ask the judge what to do. Poll the jury. Demand the truth. Ask in the future that all of your storytellers forswear fiction. Read the final chapter. Close the book. Do me in. Do me the favor. The sun shined that morning on the snow. Blackbirds bathed in clear pools of melting ice. I claw at the past. I did not sit at the table with Brigid. I took my bag and my stolen letters and I left. I walked out the door from the kitchen that led, that leads still, out to the orchard, the door from which Owen Lieb had entered that first morning that Brigid and I had sat together at Franny's table. I left Brigid to her fate. I cannot help but see my father's face in the mirror. I have no choice but to call it my own. Do you know what I said to Brigid before I left? The last thing I asked her? The morning unfroze, little by little, to reveal the bare blackened limbs of trees and tangles of dying, no, dead flowers. Brigid wrapped her sweater more tightly around herself. The dog lapped at water in his dish. The cat slept on the cold hearthstones before the fire, which Brigid had only just lighted. *Will you leave him?* I asked. I wanted to know if there was anything, any act or action beyond the mad grace of her forgiveness. She was twenty-nine years old; it is now my own age as I finish this remembrance. She had not slept. Just as I have not slept. Just as I have forced myself to play every character in turn to understand all that I did not, could not, at the time when these events transpired. I feel like a schizophrenic circus clown. At some point I will have to stop jumping out of the tiny car and run head-on into traffic. I have to stop pulling myself out of the hat. Brigid's illness and her weakness fell away in the night. Drunkenness had burnt her clean. *No,* she said. *I can't. I won't. Don't you understand yet? It's not in my nature. I'm not that kind of person. I can't give up on him because of his past. I made that choice a long time ago.*

Or maybe she didn't say that exactly, but that's how I remember it. She said she loved him.

I did not turn. I did not look back. Maybe from her window she watched me cross the snowy fields until I vanished from her sight. Maybe she was lonely after I left.

Maybe she didn't watch me but instead she left the kitchen, paused to pet the dog, coo to the cat, walked up the staircase to her bedroom where her husband lay sleeping and, lifting the thin night-dress over her head, naked in the cold bright morning, bare breasts, white arms, bruises, bones, tattoos and scars, scrapes, skin, long-lost Brigid Pearce, now Lieb, of Indianola, Iowa who had once won a clock radio for selling the most Thin Mints in Girl Scout Troop 813, who had been given a long-haired cat named Snowball for her eighth birthday, who had been a cheerleader, who had loved horses, who had worked summers in high school bagging groceries, who was fond of the sad girlish conceit (she had read it in *Seventeen* and found it clever) of admitting she had *misplaced* rather than *lost* her virginity one night at a fraternity party, who for her own amusement and to the delight of others could sing television theme songs in per-fectly melodic French, who was growing to prefer vodka to gin and salt to sugar, Brigid, who would never bear Owen his third child, Brigid, who would never raise a hand or use a word against him, this last Mrs. Lieb so pale that she vanished against the sheets crawled back into the warmth of her inherited wedding bed and fucked her husband.

Love conquers all.

That was what you wanted to hear, wasn't it?

Love obliterates obligation.

And history never repeats itself.

And isn't this, after all, nothing more than a love story?

I returned home, my passport stamped on November 3, 1990. And while I will not say where exactly I am writing this, I admit that I did not return to either the city or state where I grew up, or to the college town from which I had departed. I find myself now

in an anonymous Midwestern city, landlocked as by divine punishment, no salt, no sea, no blood sausage for breakfast, no girls queu-
ing for buses along the Liffey, no Owen, no ghost of Franny, no
Admiral John Paul Jones, no gray cat to whom Brigid fed clotted
cream with a pewter baby spoon engraved *JWL* that she found in
the bureau, no Brigid, no fog-thick green mornings or nights without streetlamps when I remember running through the fields and
orchards down to the sea by the ever-dimming lights of houses
presently and suddenly until all was darkness. No place-names. No
places. No place like home.

The only thing left that seems remotely real is the most unreal of all:
Julia's room. And even that secret place bears the taint of observation. A painting on the wall of a schooner sailing a sunny sea; the
frame hides a camera. Ah well, my elaborate but off-kilter timepiece
is winding down. The hummingbirds are tolling the hour. Little by
little the grand coach is coming to resemble a pumpkin in the moonlight. Now comes the ugly part. Now our roads must diverge. By the
time you read this, the names will have been changed. New names
will replace the people whom I once knew. Perhaps you would have
cared more for a less self-conscious story. I'm sorry that I couldn't
give you what you wanted. Maybe the next girl can or the next book
or the one that follows that. This is where my story splits from yours.
Yours becomes of necessity a replacement of mine with the names
changed to protect the guilty and innocent alike, to cover what was
once real with something equally unreal. A spoonful of sugar hidden
in a jar of salt. The camera peeking out from the picture frame. Did
you see it just now? There, right above the mizzenmast? By the time
you read this, you will not be able to find the books written by these
characters as you would their real-life counterparts. But be certain
the Liebs exist, by whatever name you choose to call them, they
exist. They once existed. But for the sake of these pages and in the

case of this story alone, under the aegis of infinity and the black inky
eternity of typeface, we all, all of us, will continue to exist.

Now it is the time to be brave, dear reader, you who are my
judge, my jury, my executioner, hypocrite, twin, my doctor, cartographer and collaborator, my ticket puncher, my stenographer and
soul mate; be stalwart. Be like the lamb in the den of the lion. Be
like the baker who knows that even his most beautiful lemon chiffon
cake is subject to the fork. Be the one who brings me back to life
with the miraculous vinegar of your disbelief. If these characters
seem familiar, I assure you, they were once as real as you or I. If you
have an instinct, if you've found a clue, if you think you know just
exactly which library shelf to plunder, you are probably on the right
track. Any book will do. Read them all, one by one. You will find
that each tells the same story. A history of dust.

I hand over willingly my memoir to you. Take the characters as
your own. Close your eyes and invest them with the faces of your
dream lovers, of movie stars, bathing beauties, five-star generals and
lantern-jawed captains of industry. Bump your face up close against
the mirror and perhaps you will see the seams of illusion. The toupee
fallen askew on the nightstand. The hand cupped beneath the rubber breast. The fifty-foot-wide face with eyes of Prussian blue staring
out from a billboard advertising a new brand of cigarettes. The tran-
scripts of your desires spelled out in the icing on someone else's cake.
Spoon up the story like warm chocolate pudding. I've changed the
names and obliterated the places. The only thing left standing is the
endless echoing connotation of an empty phoneme. The husk, the
shell, the hermit crab scuttling across a sea of kitchen floors.

If it is any consolation to those readers who long for moral sustenance from memoirs and biographies, I did learn a lesson. And if
I never learned how to become a better person, I understand at least
the source of my dislocation. It is easy now in hindsight to fit every
piece of my life together like a jigsaw puzzle. There is an explanation

for every moment. Nothing is wasted. Nothing need go to waste. I went through the mirror to discover that even people who lie and steal, who have no depth of compassion to match the breadth of their wants, no hope or urgent claim toward either expiation or absolution, even those of us who cannot begin to ask forgiveness for our inherited sins, even we had mothers who once lifted us high into the boughs of apple trees on sunny autumn afternoons. The world in which I used to live is terrifying to me now. It is an obstacle course. It is composed of corrosives and solvents and acids; they burn and they blister and they bleach the bones clean. I don't know anything about history, but I've learned a lesson from it. I have no one to blame but myself.

I am only beginning to learn how to become more perfect.

Wherever you are now, Franny, hidden away in your palazzo in Tuscany; ashes in the belly of a seabird; cataloged by the Library of Congress and placed in your place on the bookshelf; wherever you are tonight or were last night, you don't need my defense. You don't need me borrowing your best lines and then returning them to you worn, wrinkled and in disrepair. You need me even less than you needed my mother to push you on to finish your last chapter. I'll be the one to apologize. I'm sorry. For everything. And everyone. I have borne the guilt of my parents on my back: read it. It is a dictionary of digression. A pornography of purpose. A deposition of desire. A how-not-to guide etched in disappearing ink. An anthology of what-ifs in which each supposition is stacked on the shoulders of all those that have come before to form a grand wobbling ziggurat. I am a conjunction, the most ignoble part of speech. An irritation. A connector. Something that gets you from *here* to *there* without too much fuss. But Franny was born at the end of October on a day of rain when the planets fortuitously aligned to place Jupiter in the realm of Cancer, promising fame and success.

They got to her.

She floated to the top like the witch she was.

She rose to the top like cream.

Have you ever told yourself a bedtime story to help you fall asleep? It's nice, isn't it? It's nice to be in your own bed with the snow falling outside and sometimes you can sleep and sometimes you forget. If you are with someone you hate yourself for it and if you are alone you imagine there is someone out there dreaming of you. And that's the one you want. The one who is never there. The one whose name means everything and whose presence means nothing. That's how it was for Franny, do you see? And when she was certain that they, her husband, her readers, her suitors, when they gave up and left off dreaming of her, when no one called her name in fitful sleep, that was, that is the exact moment when Frances Warren Lieb fell out of the world.

I told you that I lied.

It can happen as easily as that.

You can fall out of the world.

And, oh, by the way, there is no *they*.

Only us.

One of us will. Be made a better person for it. I am drowning in him. It is an impossible ugly death.

And she fell.

Out of.

I saw it for myself.

The world.

And so I have written this because I want desperately to become a better person, if only for the sake of unbecoming myself. I cannot write the obituary or the biography of my mother. Maybe someday I will. She was born on a day I do not know, in a country which no longer exists, into a world in which history is an endless practical joke—time pulling the chair out from under reason to land pratfall face-first into an overflowing bathtub. The audience howls with laughter. There is no other way to react to the past. I have no image of her beyond the glimpses left behind in Franny's letters, and this, as much as any other reason, is why I keep them safe. I see Esther in her red dress on the sofa. A profile drawn in soot and charcoal, eyes fingered in ash. A door shutting. I do not know from whom she thought she was saving me, but I have an idea. Remember Esther. I ask you to do this because no one else will. Because even if you remember only a reflection of what was once real, it means that she existed. That's the only reason I can offer. They say that she was my mother, and after all, she might be yours as well.

So you see, I have had to offer you Franny's death in place of Esther's. Remember Frances Warren Lieb, because no detail of her life was left unscrutinized. She was born on October 27, 1933 at 4:48 in the morning and died February 28, 1964. Her life was a romance and her death a mystery. Her confessional second novel disappeared. Her successor became her avenging angel. Her husband never stopped loving her even when he was in the arms of other women. Her biographers dissected her life, her death, and one of them in an article entitled, "Inventing Franny: If She Hadn't Existed Would We Have Created Her?" called her "a sort of schizophrenic Charlotte Corday . . . who in killing Marat in the bath served ultimately only to murder herself, as he was her author . . ." And the biographers analyzed what Frances Lieb ate for breakfast: toast with butter and sour cherry marmalade, halved grapefruit, scrambled eggs, pork sausage, bananas, tinned peaches, coffee, broiled tomatoes, oat porridge, blackened bacon, waffles, hollandaise sauce, brioche, bread pudding, American fried potatoes with gravy, grapes, cold chicken, cornbread, Western omelets, crepes with clotted cream, smoked salmon, rosemary biscuits, custard cups, buckwheat flapjacks with maple syrup, and in particular for the midnight supper before the morning of her death, lemon seedcake. And they speculated on the

color of her blood: pink, currant, copper, berry, red, burgundy, gar-
net, eggplant, bitterroot, pomegranate, scarlet, vermilion, plum,
blush, candy apple, hellebores, aubergine, mauve, rose, nightshade,
magenta, claret, poppy. And the temperature of her bathwater:
approximately 108 when drawn to 88 degrees at the time of her death
to 53 degrees Fahrenheit when the body was found. And they pronounced her death a tragedy, a loss, an act of violence, criminal, fem-
inist, suspicious, vengeful, destructive, selfish, self-destructive, self-
loathing, self-preserving, escapist, insane, shameful, delusional, accidental, childish, a murder, a creation of a new self from the flames
of the past, and finally, a rich textual mystery.

Frances called Franny lived, wrote, documented, died, desired,
hated, loved, betrayed, believed, and married in no particular order,
Owen Lieb. He is as guilty of her murder as you or I. And me? If my
father has written one book, then I will write five. And if he has written five, I will write five hundred. Everything undoes itself. Everything
undoes the next thing. Every sentence makes impossible and useless
those that have come before. I will spell vengeance rewriting each
word he inked until I get to the first word and there is nothing left to
undo, nothing left but to finish this story. I am my father's daughter,
a ghost, a ghoul, a graverobber. Don't think for a moment that I don't
know this. Don't think for a moment that I don't hate myself for it.
That, unfortunately, is the sort of person that I am.

Zion

On the night of November 6, 1998, while driving on a rain-darkened country road winding westward from Tipperary to Limerick, the black Peugeot carrying home Brigid and Owen Lieb drifted dreamily over the center line to crash into the headlights of an oncoming produce truck. Brigid was pronounced dead on the scene. Bananas littered the road prompting rescue workers to morbidly speculate that the cars had not so much crashed as slipped on the peels. Both the driver of the truck and his passenger sustained fatal injuries. But Owen Lieb, that basilisk of fate, climbed from the wreckage to survive with only a bruised collarbone and broken arm. He lived and I could briefly come to hate him again. But as I say, it was only briefly. I thought Owen Lieb would live forever. But he didn't. He couldn't. Two weeks after the accident while in the waiting room of St. Nessan's Orthopedic Hospital, he passed away quietly; his heart ceased beating and he went gently without a sound of suffering. He sat for a long while in silence slumped with a copy of *The Paris Review* fallen to his side before anyone came to realize he was not sleeping.

So really there is no one left with whom to be angry. This is, this has become a story about people in history. There is no one left to sue me, no one to reveal where Franny's manuscript or Esther's sketches may still be stashed. We'll have to rely on secondary sources, on biographers, archivists and librarians, on our own discriminating judgment and the absence of everything that has come before us. In case you are wondering, Brigid's book, *The Fugitive Years: An Intimate Biography of the Secret Life and Loves of Marcel Proust,* was published two months before her death. She was dismayed, no doubt, that the book was being analyzed not in terms of her alleged biological association with

Proust, but her status as the girl who followed after Franny Lieb in the
bed of the infamous Owen. How can I best say this? Her memoir was
read as a bold act of fictive transference. But the Brigid Lieb I knew
had long-since given up on fiction. History contained all the stories,
the peaks, plateaus, and thrilling denouements that novelists crave to
create. She didn't like practical jokes or plot twists that were nothing
more than a disservice, an injustice done to those not here to tell their
own tales. She was, all in all, a biographer. They were on their way
home from a book signing when the accident occurred. That's what I
read in the newspaper. I still read obituaries. I scan them for the names
of people I once knew. And I thought that this story was finished too,
dead, laid out in a shroud of white typing paper. But how can it end
when it seems to have never begun? I'll tell you what has befallen my
sad cast of characters in the ensuing years and then we can both agree
to close the book once and for all.

Alexander Piltdown went on to marry a zoologist named Leda
who has twin sons from a previous marriage. I think he's probably a
good father, teaching them binary thought and Boolean logic,
wrestling holds and lessons from the old wars, the straight line
between black and white; good and evil; day and night. I think, and
I may be mixing my myths with my metaphors again, but I swear to
God the boys' names are Romulus and Remus. Newton, that bulldog
journalist, always on the job, I admit, I miss him. You would have
expected as much from me. He went on to marry fact with fiction
and find the kind of solace in the arms of the nonfiction novel that
he could never have found with me. I received a check from a lawyer
settling between Jonathan and myself our father's estate. I guess we'll
be okay. I've got a room and a window and a typewriter and I think
if I go at it long enough I can evince from the lovelorn faces of the
past the complete works of William Shakespeare.

Some stories will not be told. Some people have been disappeared. Some stories will be swallowed down like spoons of cough

syrup by history. I have given up cleaning. Not out of desire or disgust or despair, but principle. Can you imagine? Me? *Principled?* The
Nazis were fierce with cleanliness. They called it showering, what we
call murder. They called it a solution, the business of sewing skin
into lampshades. I stand before you foul and filthy wishing I were a
clever girl who could construct a way-back machine and with the
flick of the jackpot's lever travel back in time and not have met
Owen Lieb. Or go back beyond that September day and not have
been rescued by him from sinking under into the waves. Imagine
that, to have been the baby thrown out with the bathwater. Some
stories will not survive. I don't know if this one will, but I've daubed
a dot or two of Zyclon B behind each ear. I've unslipped a strap from
my shoulder and am biting my lip in anticipation. I am ready for my
close-up, Herr Himmler. I am ready to burn, burn, burn like some
fabulous flesh-tallowed candle. I'm waiting. I'm waiting for the
world to change. I'm waiting for the nerve to burn his letters. I'm
losing a fighting battle. I lose one more ounce with each page I pen.
There is less and less of me daily. I am a genuine theory of diminishing returns. Soon I will fall off the page and disappear. I've been
pacing the room and pawing a new stack of pages. What I wouldn't
give for a biography right about now, before dawn, something to
keep me going, something to push me on to the end of this story,
something warm and moist and milk-chocolatey, the kind you could
buy in a train station from some doe-eyed newsstand dealer. He
keeps the good stuff, the unauthorized versions, the tell-alls and
tabloid tattletales under the counter. He'll hook you up with a hefty
Hemingway. He's got Nijinsky and Kant. He's got Madame Curie in
a shiny cellophane wrapper. You're dying to crack the spine. To get
your damp fingers between the pages. Just for a slice of Albert Speer,
a morsel of Doctor Mengele. I'm willing and I can pay. I'm craving
and I can cough up the cash. These books have my skin go sallow
and heart clock off-time. I'm snowed in like a blizzard. I'm smacked

like an open hand across a cheek. I'm sad and sick and sour. But you love me anyway, don't you? Because the only thing that matters to us is not truth or fiction, not past or present, but desire: the desire to change, the will to be different. Look at me, I'm a different girl every day. I'm more innocent than I was yesterday because I'm ploughing ahead; I'm putting all those other girls that I was behind me. I'm making a genuine concerted effort. I'm laying off the books and the booze and the boys. Love me or leave me, that's what I say. And in the meantime could you just go to your stash on the shelf and read a line or two? Something with place-names, a biscuit to out-madeleine Proust himself. A story with jam and bread. A story in which all unhappy families are alike. I want to change, really I do. Tell me, what has bothered you most about my ramshackle ramblings? Was it the infidelities? The one-night stands worked into epic odysseys of the heart? The lies, alliterations and assonance, the suicides and psychobabble? No, go on, don't be shy, it's good for me. It helps. How else will I learn? I'm making a list. What have you liked, if anything, thus far? How pretty Owen and Brigid were, how white and creamy and impossible like two movie stars waving to the disconsolate crowd on Oscar night? Do you like stories that offer you escape from your humdrum world? That present compelling landscapes to be traveled in dune buggies? With cats though you are allergic? Drafty haunted houses while your own thermostat is set perpetually to cozy? With unfaithful spouses while the last time you checked, yours was safely at home professing love in tattoos and tollhouse cookies? Did you like the letters we exchanged? My youthful romp and circumstance? The endless rounds of vodka and tonic? Or do small things satisfy you? The turning of the page? The promise of a new day? The neat black words like ants marching one by one, hurrah! Hurrah! They all go marching over and under and upside down. As Newton said: *Words, words, words all over everything.* As Owen said: *By the time Jesus was born the world had already conceived of every possible idea and philosophy and sexual perversion. Christianity has been nothing more than an embarrassing exercise in self-gratification.* As Brigid sang: *Sometimes you feel like a nut; sometimes you don't. Peter Paul Almond Joy's got nuts; Mounds don't.* As Alexander said: *Biology isn't destiny; well, except for women.* Oh Alexander, when you saw the breadth of your domain, is it true that you wept for there were no more worlds to conquer? You know, you knew, you must have known all along that I was awaiting you like a city to be sacked. Did you visit the oracle at Delphi to have our future read in the Magic Eight Ball: *Unlikely!* You owned every empire. You saved me from myself. Alex, I've been colonized and am none the more pretty or popular for it. Alex, in your camouflage fatigues you fit right in, but I'm fraught with failure. You massed the militia and battered the border towns. You garrisoned and conscripted. You stripped and sold me for parts. It seems I've fought my entire life to get away from you waging to win and willing to fish me out of the whirlpool at the last moment, just when things start to get good, when there is less air and the colors are bright and green and dizzying, when I eddy on toward oblivion. Oh, no, oh look, here comes Newton creeping into the room like Mr. Hyde searching for Doctor Jekyll; I see you with your mournful dark eyes and drunken travelogues. You say we'll run away together. You know all the hidden stops and stations; we'll take the Empire Builder; book passage on the Orient Express; double down the tracks bruised and box-carred like Jews waxed into soap and burnt as candles all along the lonely Dachau line. We'll round the Cape of Good Hope and follow the slave ships which trade tires, saccharine, and petrol for hoarded heaps of human heart; past the Spice Islands and we'll be singing traveling songs as we go: *Hey Christopher Columbus, whaddya know? The Nina's too fast and the Pinta's too slow!* I'm world-weary and bedraggled. Even my signature begins to look less and less familiar. I'm sad and sick and soggy. I'm jettisoning. I'm sandbagging. I'm throwing out the baby with the bathwater. Everything must go! A fire sale. Prices slashed. Forget the girl I used to be. She jumped ship. I'm done with all the old stories. I'm writing a new one about Frankenstein, a monstrous biography, the inside dope, the boy I knew *and how!* He was creepy but committed. He was post-ironic and passionate. He was Isaac Newton and Alexander the Grape. He wore black and always picked up the check. He smoked crack and slept in. He was outta work, underpaid, and went unloved. We were dirty and despairing. I read our future painted on the Grecian urn: *All signs point to yes!* What happens in the alternate version of my life, the one on the cutting room floor, the one that didn't test well with the audiences, the one on the other side of the mirror in which events and outcomes are snow-dome shaken? I grow up as the daughter of Owen and Esther. We madcap-shamble across Europe fleeing from guilt to graveyard in search of lost time. And do you know what? In every version—on a battlefield, in a boardroom, in Versailles among the gilded lilies of the summer palace, in Sebastopol, Appomattox, and the mineral springs of Yalta where hot promises were penned on the dash-dot-dash of the Maginot Line, in the ravages of Verdun and swimming the typhus-tainted canals of Venice, in Petrograd or her snowy snubbed sister, St. Petersburg, Newton always finds me. Even in the headlock of history I cannot escape him. Even in the arms of other men I find traces of his investigations, a camera tripod, an eye to a keyhole, a trail of peanut shells, his voice echoing down the stairs long after he is gone: *J'accuse!* This is not complicated. This is the ending of a story that never stops beginning. This is the chapter after the last chapter. You may have gotten the joke on page one and not needed four hundred successive pages to pack the punch. Alexander taught me to appreciate the classics and I studied and I learned. Who could have guessed I would be quick with cross-references but so faulty with footnotes? I bided my time. I kept crib sheets and confessions to myself. I went on to find some dim candle of respite with Newton, that jalopy of a journalist, that I'd-rather-be-smashing-hierarchies hedonist who had no faith in the church of our future because it was built on the rock of my rebellion. And while in the dark he professed to believe in nothing, when push came to shove, and oh, it does, it did—he believed in the straight and narrow tulip-stemmed capital T of Truth as much as the next guy. And really, who can blame him? So I sinned and served and was, in fact, a little slutty. I'm paying my dues on the installment plan. A quarter for every consonant; a dime for each vowel. I am waiting, did I mention? For a knock on my door. Who would have anticipated this turn of events at such a late hour? Who among us could have anticipated Bachelor #3? The new and improved Prometheus! I know that the moment I stop writing this he will appear. There is only one realistic course of action: I must never stop typing. I am going to need your help. Please, before you sign and stamp your next fan letter take a moment to ask Newton about me. Don't be too obvious. You know, be subtle. Say something like: *Dear Mr. Graves, I greatly enjoyed* November Nocturne, *your new nonfiction account of the wreck of the Edmund Fitzgerald. The Great Lakes have never been so great as when you describe them! I could taste the salt brine and literally palpate the heaving bosom of Molly, hale and hearty, the ship's whore. By the by, I happened upon a certain minor character, nothing to write home about—just a scullery maid with a greenish complexion who reminded me of a girl you might have known one night a million years ago. I know, I know, she was disagreeable and dim-witted, but can you find it in your heart to forgive her for not choosing you? Are the stories she tells as fact-based as your own fables? I think the nonfiction novel is like a Reese's Peanut Butter Cup: two great tastes that taste great together! Is it true that you are somewhat hip-happy? Did you know that smoking in bed is the #1 killer of American men aged 17-62? Also, that girl I mentioned, did she have to meet such an unfortunate and ugly death? Chopped to bits and salted for seasoning in the stew? Mostly I agree with your plots as they are wrenched from the pages of history with the crowbar of authority. They rise and fall like the sheets shrouding Handsome Molly and Cappy Bly in chappy six. It is only that sometimes I wish there was a little more cuddling and less full frontal nudity, but this is not a criticism per se, only a comment. All in all, I wish you only the best! Warm regards, a fan! A reader! Your semblable!*

I don't want any of them. I've got a bed and a bottle and a box of typewriter ribbons. I can hold out. I can hole up here for a while. I know a guy who knows a guy who knows a guy who lives in Montana who knows the exact day and hour the world will end. I think I can get a date with him as I am easy and not much for small talk. I'll meet him halfway, but I won't wash my hair for it. I have a room. And a window. And look! It's snowing. Each widdle fwake is mwore pwerfect than the next. Somewhere Alexander and Leda are sleeping among the swans. And Romulus is pinning Remus to the palace floor. Somewhere Casey is at bat. Somewhere someone is opening a book for the very first time and sinking in rich chocolatey goodness. Somewhere on one of those darkened roads that winds and twists like the gentle caress of Cappy Bly's wooden leg resting tapping thump thump thump against Moll's whalebone corset, Owen and Brigid are heading homeward. Somehow on one of those deep-green misty nights when one feels that the air has miraculously transformed into water and we are free from our past sins to swim among the fishes, Brigid rests her head on Owen's shoulder as he falls asleep at the wheel. And time stops, but only briefly. And Brigid goes through the windshield like Alice through the looking glass. Somewhere in a room not unlike this one, my poor Newton toils to tell the true story. He has a bed and a bottle and the blinds are pulled. The sheets smell of cigarettes and the clock ticks thirteen. Somewhere after the adulterous scarlet *A* and the purloined *P,* the frantic *F,* judgmental *G* and Gnostic *N,* the trademarked *T,* essential

S, complacency of *K* and *Q* alike, the seawracked *C,* elusive *L* of *Elohim,* duplicitous *W,* the letter *I* infected with deceit, desire and double meaning; between the spread thighs of that sometime-vowel *Y,* borne on the bared breasts of *B,* excised, decussated, excited by a triple *X,* wrapped in the archetypal arms of *R,* embraced by *M,* accepted, loved, denied, spoken, taken down deep against the uvular *U* pushing unrequited, undone, untoward, toward the epiglottal *E* until, oh, disseminated, oh, decimated, obliterated in the onomatopoetic *O* of an open mouth, oh; spun on the spinning zodiac wheel, pick a letter any letter, a time, any place, the Czarist empire, xylophonic, xenophobic, the zoom lens, the Zorro slash, the zygote begotten of the dozing dreamer's first and final *Zzzz,* somewhere lost amongst the ruined fragments of the alphabet and the graveyard where the Liebs lay buried, there will be a knock on my door. A good way for a story to end is with someone dying and someone else valiantly carrying on. I don't think this is how my story will end.

Good books are brewing at coffeehousepress.org